FEB 5/2019

12-28-76

11

A LADY BOUGHT WITH RIFLES

A Lady Bought With Rifles

Jeanne Williams

Coward, McCann & Geoghegan, Inc. New York

Copyright © 1976 by Jeanne Williams

All rights reserved. This book, or parts thereof, may not be
reproduced in any form without permission in writing from the
publisher. Published on the same day in Canada by Longman Canada
Limited, Toronto.

SBN: 698-10745-4

Library of Congress Cataloging in Publication Data

Williams, Dorothy Jeanne, 1930–
    A lady bought with rifles.

    I. Title.
PZ4.W7233Lad   [PS3573.I4485]   813'.5'4   76-9842

For Foster
"In our dreams, at least, we are fabulous and free."

ACKNOWLEDGMENTS

It would be difficult to list all published and unpublished sources that provided background for this novel, but I wish to credit some that were especially helpful and that might interest readers who'd like to know more about the period.

Articles: Evelyn Hu-Dehart, "Development and Rural Rebellion: Pacification of the Yaquis in the Late Porfiriato," *Hispanic American Historical Review* (February, 1974); Edward H. Spicer, "Yaqui Villages, Past and Present," *The Kiva* (Arizona Archaeological and Historical Society, November, 1947); Ronald L. Ives, "Kino's Exploration of the Pinacate Region," *Arizona History* (Summer, 1966).

Books: G. M. Trevelyan, *English Social History* (London: Reprint Society, 1948); Asa Briggs, *They Saw It Happen: 1897–1940* (Oxford: Basil Blackwell, 1960); Ronald Pearsall, *The Victorian Scene* (London: Weidenfeld & Nicolson, 1968), Nicolas Bentley, *The Worm in the Bud* (London: Weidenfeld & Nicolson, 1969); William T. Hornaday, *Campfires on Desert and Lava* (New York: Scribners, 1908); Carl Lumholtz, *New Trails in Mexico* (New York: Scribners, 1912); Rosalio Moisés, Jane Holden Kelley, and William Curry Holden, *The Tall Candle* (Lincoln, Nebraska: University of Nebraska Press, 1971); Charles C. Cumberland, *Mexican Revolution, Genesis Under Madero* (Austin, Texas: University of Texas Press: 1952); Anita Brenner, *The Wind that Swept Mexico* (Austin, Texas: University of Texas Press, 1971); Edward H. Spicer, *Cycles of Conquest* (Tucson, Arizona: University of Arizona Press, 1962); John Kenneth Turner, *Barbarous Mexico* (Austin, Texas: University of Texas Press, 1969); C. L. Sonnichsen, *Colonel Greene and the Copper Skyrocket* (Tucson, Arizona: University of Arizona: University of Arizona Press, 1974).

Very special thanks go to Betty and Dana Smith and to Bill Broyles, who introduced me to the Sea of Cortez and shared so generously their love and knowledge of the region. Bill showed me the awesome Pinacates, lent me maps, suggested sources, and supplied much material from his private collection.

Dr. Don Worcester, expert on horses and Latin America, offered constant help and read and criticized the manuscript, as did my daughter, Kristin. Leila Madeheim, as always, did more than a typist should, pointing out snags in credibility.

The patience and faith of Claire Smith, agent and friend, are very much a part of this book.

Patricia Brehaut Soliman, my editor, has sensitively managed to excise detail that obscured the narrative and has developed a much better book than the one I sent her.

JEANNE WILLIAMS

A LADY BOUGHT WITH RIFLES

One

Miranda

1

The small turquoise crucifix called me home, or rather, to my mother, for the distant place of my birth, a hacienda in northwestern Mexico, was alien and strange as the deserts of the *Arabian Nights*. Miss Mattison, our headmistress, had shown me that corner of Mexico on a globe, south of Arizona Territory, bordered on the west by a sea stretching to Baja California. So far away. Across the ocean and most of North America.

At least I was not the only pupil at Miss Mattison's whose parents were abroad. Probably a third of the girls had fathers scattered about the empire in commerce, government service, or the military, and mail from Australia, Canada, Africa, and India was as common as that from Sussex.

In spite of our prayers for men fighting the Boers, several girls were orphaned when their fathers died in South Africa. I felt like an orphan my last few years at the school, for though I had a living mother, she could not write in English. Father was killed in a mine accident when I was fifteen. After that I had no letters from Sonora, only packets.

Jewelry I could not wear at school, fans, beautifully

embroidered hand-sewn chemises, nightdresses, drawers, petticoats, and camisoles, these so daintily worked that our needlecraft teacher handled them with awe and asked leave to show a nightdress to the class. Once, from a box of linen handkerchiefs embroidered with flowers, I found one with an eagle driving curved talons into a hare. A crumpled paper slipped from the folds. "*De Reina*," it said. This only gift my half-sister had ever sent both fascinated and repelled me. I put it at the bottom of my drawer where I kept my mother's notes on top, though they all said the same thing.

"*Te quiero, Miranda. Te quiero, hijita.*" I love you, Miranda. I love you, little daughter. How I cherished those small perfumed bits of paper! And how I wondered why, if they loved me, my mother and father had sent me so far away.

It was because Father insisted I have an English upbringing, of course. The youngest son of a Wessex squire, he had refused to go into the Army as his parents wished. After a bitter family quarrel, he had gone to Mexico to work for British rail interests, saved his money, become partner, then full owner of a gold mine, and married the lovely young widow of a wealthy rancher. Doña Luisa Dubois de Anza had defied her relatives to marry the tall Englishman, but she would not leave her country, so my father stayed on in Mexico, though he brought me to Miss Mattison's when I was five.

He visited me every few years, but when I begged to come home, he would say I must have an education that would fit me for life in England if I married there. If I asked to come for just a visit, my father would say perhaps next year. That year never came.

Still, apart from missing my parents, I was content at Miss Mattison's. Father wanted me to have an English background, but of a special, almost eccentric kind. In the school library hung the motto: "The truth shall make you free." With all Miss Mattison's heart and soul, she clung valiantly to that, though she now and again lost pupils because we studied Darwin's *Origin of Species* and Mill's *On Liberty* and *The Subjection of Women*.

While most English schoolgirls were learning to read, write, do simple arithmetic, speak some French, embroider their petticoats, and paint timid watercolors, we were reading Tolstoy, Zola, Hardy, Lecky's *History of European Morals,* Carlyle's *French Revolution,* and Sir James Frazer's *Golden Bough.*

Miss Mattison's girls also had the advantage of her brother's outspoken views. A prominent though controversial London physician, Dr. Mattison, when visiting his sister in Sussex, gave her pupils lectures, meant to inform and encourage though they were also frightening since his fierce blue eyes, ruddy moustache, and gruff voice intimidated girls who seldom saw men other than tradesmen, gardeners, and the rector. On one occasion he propped a bolster up in front of the class and labeled its midparts LUNGS, HEART, LIVER, STOMACH.

Around these he placed a whalebone corset, laced it with vicious jerks, and then glowered at the class as the maltreated bolster, squeezed almost in half, sagged against the brass-inlaid teapoy where his sister kept the makings of her one indulgence.

"Torture and insanity!" he proclaimed. "All for a wasp waist! Young women, if you value your health, never let vanity or sheeplike conformity imprison your vital organs. We condemn the Chinese custom of bound feet; how much more crippling to constrict lungs and heart!" His cheeks puffed out as his voice boomed louder. "Observe the corset forces upward what it does not squeeze. This, with the fact that to breathe at all, the victim must literally pant, causes a continuous heaving of the upthrust bosom, which—"

"Brother!" Miss Mattison rose quickly, pink to the roots of her faded blond hair. "Thank you for a most instructive lecture. Now, girls, those of you who have your compositions done may bicycle or play tennis till tea."

Though she felt certain subjects were too delicate for young ears, Miss Mattison believed in developing body as well as mind and had rejoiced when the first modern Olympic Games were held in Athens in 1896. Unless there was a downpour, we bicycled or took long walks every day, led by Miss Mattison in her cherished old Bloomer suit. Besides tennis and archery, we had weekly riding lessons from a local stable.

As well as being warned of the dangers of tight lacing, we knew more about our physical functions than most women. Dr. Mattison left the *Lancet* and other medical publications in the library, and though a few older girls insisted that a woman's flow stopped when she was pregnant because the blood went to nourish her baby, most of us knew that the curse or "the flowers" accompanied the casting off of the unfertilized ovum.

And we knew that Queen Victoria's accepting chloroform to ease the birth of Prince Leopold back in 1853 had popularized its use as an anesthetic and that Joseph Lister had used antiseptics as early as 1867 though his rules of hygiene were still not always followed by careless doctors, even after Florence Nightingale proved during the Crimean War that simple cleanliness could save countless lives.

"Be sure, young women, this concerns you more than romantic dreams or Latin verbs!" thundered the doctor. "If you aren't careful of your physician, one with dirty hands could leave you with childbed fever that can kill you or permanently disease your female organs."

I couldn't imagine doing whatever it was that got babies in the first place. Certainly I would have been terrified to share a bed with a man like the doctor. I was glad to escape his urgent warnings and lose myself in the books of Dickens, Victor Hugo, Rider Haggard, Oscar Wilde, H. G. Wells, and Arthur Conan Doyle. I was proud that my father had contributed several important volumes to the well-stocked library: John James Audubon's *Birds of North America*, with its beautiful color plates, and Prescott's *History of the Conquest of Mexico*. He had also donated a stereoscope with hundreds of cards showing animals, birds, and other countries.

For Sunday reading, after services in the old gray Saxon church, there was Bunyan's *A Pilgrim's Progress*, John Donne's sermons and meditations, Milton's *Paradise Lost*, and other edifying books. Sunday was a day we yawned through once we had acquired the ability to sit through services without squirming. It was not a time for "worldly" pleasures, though it was hard to think of anything at Miss Mattison's school that fitted that description.

Oh, but when Father came, I knew delight! We would go by train to London and be borne by elegant hansom to the Savoy, where we had a suite of two bedrooms, sitting room, bathroom, and W.C. After the austerity of school and my narrow lumpy mattress, pile carpets, Japanese wallpaper, gold frieze, carved mantels, and walnut furniture seemed overpoweringly grand. I would just be getting able to sleep in the big smooth postered bed when Father's visit would be over and he would leave me at Miss Mattison's to remember the fairy-tale time we had shared. Luncheon on the terrace overlooking the Embankment, the famous Savoy Dinner or Opera Supper after a play, ballet, or opera. I loved Gilbert and Sullivan, and as I grew older, Father took me to Wilde, Ibsen, and Shaw. And there was the National Gallery, the British Museum, the Natural History Museum, the Victoria and Albert Museum, and the Royal Botanical Gardens at Kew as well as the aquarium in Regent's Park.

But better than the opulent food, the luxurious suite, plays, pantomimes, ballet, and opera was being with my father, reveling in his undivided attention. I thought he was the most handsome man in the world with his chestnut hair and moustache, deep blue eyes, and erect figure.

When I was too weary to go to the public rooms, Father had tea brought to our suite—scones, pâté, dainty egg and cucumber sandwiches, lobster salad, walnut cake, and chocolate cake. We would feast sumptuously while playing chess or while Father talked of Las Coronas, the hacienda, or the mine, which had so much pyrite gleaming from the slope that it actually looked like a golden mountain though the real ore was hidden deep inside.

Some of his miners were Yaqui Indians and he spoke of them with increasing concern because the Mexican government was killing or deporting them by hundreds and turning their ancestral lands over to Mexican and United States' colonizers. So far, Father had managed to protect his workers, but he was terribly worried about what was happening in Mexico.

"Don Porfirio Díaz and his *científicos* cannot rule forever," he told me. "Yaquis are not the only oppressed ones. A few Mexicans are incredibly wealthy, but in spite of the reforms attempted by Juárez after he drove the French from the country, most Mexicans are debt slaves, peons, completely at the mercy of their masters. Unrest is growing all over Mexico. A revolution is coming. It will be terrible." He took a deep breath. "I'm glad you will not be there."

Revolution was, to me, aristocrats riding in tumbrils to the guillotine. I could not link it to Mexico and would restively change the subject, ask about my mother and the half-sister of whom I was jealous because she lived with my parents, and saw them every day.

"Do you love her best?" I had blurted once when I was about seven and in tears at Father's impending departure.

"Of course not!" He had swept me up, held my face against his broad shoulder, where I felt so safe, so loved. "But she is wholly Mexican. You are not."

"Is she p-p-prettier than I?"

"No, little goose!"

"Cleverer?" I persisted, snuffling, trying to find some reason for the hurtful separation.

"Her Spanish is better," he teased, putting me down. "And I must say that she does not ask questions!" But I sensed that he was uneasy about Reina, that she had something strange about her.

He never visited his relations in Wessex, though he told me once that his brother was dead and the present squire, Father's nephew, had a host of daughters to marry off and was an automobile fanatic. He had bought one of the first Royce's back in 1884. This by itself was enough to violently prejudice Father against him, for Father abhorred the internal-combustion engine and all its attendant works.

Father belonged to the Victorian empire, to the time of men like Livingstone, General Gordon, Gladstone, and Shaftesbury, when one-third of the globe's ships had British registry, when Europe was the Englishman's playground, though he made his fortunes in Australia, Canada, the United States, Africa, India, or Mexico. It was fitting that Father died in the same year as Victoria and that he was in England when she died late in January of 1901.

He took me to London for her funeral procession. The whole nation had gone into mourning. Public buildings were swathed in black crape and rather ugly black wreaths hung from doors and windows. Many women were entirely in black and men wore black armbands. Even our hansom driver's whip was tipped with the dolorous color.

Father had rented a hotel room overlooking the procession's route and we watched silently as the famous eight cream horses, the gold and crimson trappings a shout of color, pulled the gun carriage topped by the coffin with its white pall and imperial crown. There were ranks of slow-marching military, arms reversed, and behind the gun carriage followed the new king, Edward, and the royal family, including the Kaiser, who had come from Germany to honor his aunt.

Crowds were half a mile deep where there was space. "She's the only queen most of us remember," Father said quickly. "She ruled for sixty-four years and seemed the only sure point in a changing world. It will be strange without her."

He talked a long time that night, as if I were another adult. "A time has passed with the queen," he said. "Motorcars and lorries are just the beginning. Heavier than air machines, much faster than zeppelins are being developed. You'll see them flying above, you may even ride in one."

"So may you," I teased.

He smiled and shook his head as he brushed back my hair. "No, Miranda. I'll live out my time by the rules I know."

That was his last visit. He was killed shortly after his return to Mexico and his body was never found in the mine. With his death my ties to Mexico grew more dreamlike than ever. His solicitor said my mother wished to obey father's wish that I finish my English schooling. So I stayed at Miss Mattison's and caught occasional rumblings from the world outside: the first submarine, the laying of the trans-Pacific cable, the Wright brothers at Kitty Hawk. The Boer War finally ended, and in America Henry Ford built a cheap automobile.

We heard of these things tucked away in our peaceful gray flint building in the cathedral close, where one day followed another much like it except for the boredom of Sundays. Then the letter came, the letter with the crucifix that at last called me home.

"Your mother is dying," wrote a strange scrawling bold hand. "She wants to see you. Come as quickly as you can." It went on to say that my father's solicitor was being instructed to arrange my passage and pay my final account with Miss Mattison.

Stunned, I gazed at the writing as if my father might have written it from the grave to reunite my mother and me, but the heavy slashing script was not his. The letter was signed Trace Winslade. I was sure my father had mentioned him, but I couldn't remember how.

Miss Mattison and I wept at parting and I promised to write, but as I stepped aboard the Cunard liner, I had a fated certainty that my English life was ending, that I would never return. I had never really belonged there, but would I belong in a place I only dimly remembered, a land of deserts and mountains open to the blazing sun? My mother was a soft voice and perfume, but my memories of Reina were of violent pinches beneath the table, shoves in a dark corridor, being called La Inglesa. Father always had spoken English to me. I had known Spanish as a young child, of course, but had forgotten most of it. Truly, I belonged nowhere, but as I journeyed by ship and train, I longed to have a home, be part of a family.

I was met in Hermosillo by Señor Otero, the family's lawyer, who drove me to Las Coronas, a full day's hard travel. He spoke very little English, but when I asked him why we had an armed escort, he made me understand that Yaquis had been raiding in the area. A slight, nervous little man with a pointed beard, he obviously did not wish to have any more to do with me than necessary, an attitude I found echoed in the servants when we finally reached the hacienda.

Did they distrust me because I had grown up in England?

That seemed absurd and determinedly I put it out of my mind as I sat in my mother's darkened room, holding her frail hands while candles flickered on all four sides of the bed and the priest droned.

I had stayed like this for most of three days, leaving only to eat or for a few hours' exhausted sleep. My mother was restless when I was not with her, and though I was overwhelmed with grief and long-stored anger that she had allowed us to be separated, I clung hungrily to these hours— all that I would have of her, all that I could give.

Reina came in and out, pausing by the bed, her lovely face unreadable. She must have had her green eyes and red hair from our mother's French father, an officer in Maximilien's army who, even after his emperor was shot, stayed in Mexico for love either of a woman named Torres or of her domain, an expanse of desert bounded by mountains and sea. Reina was three years older than I. If I could remember how she used to pinch me, surely she must, too, but she made no reference to our shared childhood. She treated me politely, like a stranger.

My Spanish was coming back as long-buried memories unlocked experiences. Reina spoke some English so we could communicate, but when I tried to know her, she turned my efforts away.

"Did you have the letter sent to Miss Mattison's?" I asked on the second day when we chanced to be having breakfast at the same time. I was not only trying to reach my sister, but I was curious about the strong slanting script that had called me out of exile from the sheltered distant world that itself now seemed the illusion.

"Trace Winslade took it upon himself to write. He is a *pistolero* your father sheltered."

"A *pistolero*?"

"One who uses pistols. A man who lives by his gun. But Winslade, when he is not exceeding his authority, has charge of the Las Coronas horses." Pride entered her voice. "Our herds are divided by color in the old fashion. They are famous."

"Winslade is English?" I persisted.

She curled her lip, yet something burned deep in her black-lashed green eyes. "He is *yanqui, tejano.*"

From what I knew of the War Between the States, neither Texan nor Yankee would appreciate Reina's careless equating of the terms, but in spite of Miss Mattison's rigorous instruction, I didn't take issue with my half-sister. I wanted desperately to be friends with her. We would soon be each other's only living near relation, and in this country I was a stranger, isolated by training and language. But Reina ignored me and I rose from the long carved table to go to the dark room filled with incense and prayers I did not understand, servants who bowed their necks to Reina but not to me.

Once I was seated by Mother's bed, it seemed I had never done anything else but lean close to her, clasping the frail hands.

My head throbbed from the oppressive thickness of stale scented air, guttering candles that seemed to gasp for life. Holding the same position made my shoulders cramp. In weary bitterness that welled up before I could check it, I wondered why my mother had wanted me after all these years.

It was too late for us to know each other, too late to laugh, to share. She had called me only to mourn, watch her dying. Why hadn't she let me learn of her death through the same muffled distance that had separated us in life?

Then her eyes opened, saw me, shone with a joy that spread over her tired face. "Miranda," she whispered, lifting her hand to my hair with obvious effort.

And then I was glad of the long journey, the vigil in this room, welcomed the pain, for at least it gave me my mother. She loved me, whyever I had not been with her. She loved me, I knew it, and now I could never be without that certainty.

"I love you," I said, and wet her hand with my tears.

Two days later Reina and I stood on either side of the bed as the priest murmured and signed and anointed our mother. When he stepped back, she took Reina's hand and mine, tried to bring them together, but lost all strength. She arched her head and there was a sound in her throat, her fingers spasmed, then relaxed, and her life was over.

My knees would not support me. I leaned on the bed, pressing the thin hand to my face, craving some word, some glance—any of the slight gestures of life that had seemed so weak and futile to me before but now seemed miracles. Beside this utter quiet, this loss of spirit and breath, all of life seemed a wonder.

"Leave her!" Gripping my shoulder, Reina shook me hard. As I stared in confusion, she stormed on. "You wait till Mother is dying and then come to perch by her bed like a vulture!"

The vicious injustice struck me dumb for a moment.

"I wanted to come home!" I managed at last. "Do you think I enjoyed feeling like an orphan?"

Reina's eyes blazed. "You call this home? Not for you, Inglesa! The sooner you go back to England the better for all."

"I've nothing to go back to," I said, stunned at the violence of her onslaught. And then before she could attack further, there by our mother's still-warm body, I raised a silencing hand. "Let's not talk about it now, Reina."

"Good sense." We both whirled toward the voice from the door.

2

A lean tall man with eyes like the turquoise in my crucifix and skin the color of his leather vest and trousers moved into the room with a surprisingly light tread for a man of his size. He dropped his dusty gray hat on a chest and went to stand by the bed, dark head lowered. The muscles in his gaunt cheeks ridged like cords.

"Madonna," he said under his breath and bent to her hand, pressing it to his face.

He stayed like that a long time while the priest hovered over him like a bat, all but squeaking, as if protesting the decorum of this man's grief. Reina watched him with an eager, hungry look and I realized it was the first time I had seen her beautiful face reveal anything besides anger or pride.

"Trace," she said.

He turned slowly, face impassive as a mask, those curious eyes startling as a glimpse of sea beyond the desert. They brushed me swiftly—but even that cursory glance brought blood to my face—and fastened on Reina, who wore a dark-green dress that accentuated her waist, slender without corsets, her high full breast, and the creamy richness of her

24

skin. Her lips were parted, and even though she had called this man—for he must be the Trace Winslade who had written to me—a *pistolero*, there was no hauteur in the way she looked at him—a beseeching, rather.

"So," he said to her in Spanish, which I followed fairly well. "You and your sister are fighting before Doña Luisa is even buried. She deserved better."

Reina flushed, hitched a shoulder toward me. "This one has no right here."

"She has the right that her mother wanted her to have." His tone cut like a thin blade.

"Mother is dead." Reina's voice didn't waver.

"But she left a will," Trace said.

"I am the eldest! I have lived here, always, taken over much of the running of Las Coronas. You know that, Trace, better than anyone."

"There is a will," he said again.

Without another word he left the room. The priest closed Mother's eyes. Reina cast her what I could have sworn was a glance of fury, then flung from the room, her heels clicking on the tiles, as she hurried after the man she had scornfully called a Texas gunman. The priest gave me a distracted frown and followed her.

I moved back to my mother. We were alone. Now I could weep.

Doña Luisa lay in state that day while servants came to pray and mourn. I caught snatches of what they murmured about her—how she had nursed the sick, been godmother to babies, eased the last hours of the dying, been generous with food and drink at *fiestas*. Along with their sorrow, I heard undertones of fear.

"It will be different with La Peliroja," said Catalina, the majestically fat head cook.

"La Inglesa seems kind, like her mother," whispered her companion, a golden-skinned middle-aged woman named María whom I often saw patting out endless tortillas.

The older woman shook her head. "Too young," she said dolefully. "Too gentle. La Peliroja will wither her."

Would she? For the first time I really wondered what would happen to me now.

As I entered, the women fell silent, crossed themselves, and went out, hard bare feet scuffing. I knelt to pray by my mother's bed, but in spite of perfumes, a sickening odor permeated the room. In this hot climate a body needed, swift burial. Nausea compelled me to retreat to the courtyard, around which all the rooms were ranged. Trees cast welcome shade and blossoming vines trailed along the adobe walls and arches. The earth was covered with pebble mosaics leading to a great octagonal fountain, tiled in bright blue and yellow, where goldfish swam.

Flowers were everywhere, in beds and pottery jars and big stone troughs. The far end of the court was shaded by giant grapevines twining over a trellis that now seemed more supported by them than the opposite. There were benches under this shade, and in niches of the adjoining arches were statues of the Virgin and some starved-looking saint.

There had been no time to loiter here before. Now I watched the gleaming fish, the tumbling splash of the fountain from a curious bronze tangle of cherubs and dolphins.

One of my earliest memories was being pushed into it by Reina. I still remembered flailing about till I realized I could touch the bottom and had been found by one of the gardeners as I tried to scramble out. Reina had run off after shoving me and I hadn't told on her. Even then I'd been ashamed that my big sister, whom I worshiped, had found me so unsatisfactory that she'd tried to drown me. And even now I felt as if there was something wrong with me that provoked her fierce rejection. Just as I had secretly believed my parents sent me to England because of some secret shortcoming of mine, something that kept me from belonging at Las Coronas.

And now with my mother dead and my schooldays finished, where did I belong? The plain, terrible truth was . . . nowhere. I knew I should be grateful that at least there should be no money problems, but I had not one real friend in all the world. The only people who had loved me were dead. Devastating loneliness weighted my heart, seemed to crush air from my lungs.

"When are you going back to England?"

I turned guiltily to meet Trace Winslade's eyes. Where had he got that scar? It ran like a knitted seam from his cheekbone to his jaw. He was leaning against an arch and now came forward with a gliding muscularity that reminded me of a large cat. I didn't want him too close. He had an aura that was physically overwhelming; those strange blue-green eyes exerted power that made me unable to move. Foreign, he seemed—and dangerous.

"I'm not going back," I said defiantly. Did I look so milksoppish and timid that everyone assumed I couldn't live in my parents' country, the place of my birth if not of my rearing?

Though the pupils of his eyes didn't move, he was seeing me from toe to crown. He gave a slight, regretful shake of his head. "You don't fit, Miss Greenleaf. It was always a hard country and times are getting worse. If you don't want to live in England, you should try the United States. Won't take you long to get a husband, especially if you stay in the West."

"Mr. Winslade!" I said in a voice that shook with anger—fortunately, anger that warmed my numb senses, brought me more alive than I had been since my mother's death. "You think me incapable of living without a husband? Just as you say that I can't manage in Sonora? You must hold me in contempt."

"Contempt?" he asked roughly.

His eyes traveled from my face to my throat, lingered on my breasts in a way that sent a tingling all through me, a sweet dizzying sensation that was far from being all shame. My blood felt charged, powerful, ready for something. Something Trace knew. I stepped back, involuntarily making a shield of my hands against him though that could not defend me from the tumult in my body.

Somehow he knew what I was feeling. "You see?" His tone was soft. "I didn't even touch you."

"No gentleman would stare like that."

The hard edge of a smile curved his long mouth. "But men will. If you don't have one to protect you, others will do a hell of a lot more than look. You're too sweet and soft and tempting not to be picked, Miss Miranda."

I felt my throat and face grow hot. "I won't marry just to keep men from watching me. That's ridiculous."

"You're in Mexico. A manless woman is fair prey. You must understand that here a woman's men guard her jealously."

"For their own honor."

He shrugged. "I'm saying what is, not what should be. If you stay here, you need a man."

"Who'll regard me as property, a chattel? I may never marry at all."

"Did I scare you that much?" He cocked his head, amused.

How dare he act so superior? He wasn't *that* old. If he'd spent most of his recent life with horses and vaqueros, how could he know much about women?

"Let's not fall out about it, Miss Miranda. I reckon you won't be single long."

I scowled at him. "However long it takes, I mean to stay single till I know where I belong and who I am."

"And how about what you are?" He didn't put out his hands, yet I felt as if he touched me, reached to hidden secret parts where rapture might be stored but fear certainly was. "You're a woman. Will you learn about that before you marry?"

I retreated from the blue fire in his eyes.

"Why go to the grief of establishing all this independence?" His laughter was rich with masculine indulgence. "When you marry, you'll be your husband's."

"Then I won't marry."

His dark brows shot up. "I thought marriage was the dearest aim of all young ladies."

"It seems to me more like a—a death, an end of what I could be."

He gave a shocked whistle, then crossed his arms and chuckled, the moment during which he had seen me as a person, taken me seriously shoved away. "That English girls' school couldn't have given you much idea of life and men. Let's hope your mother had something planned for you. Her lawyer's coming tomorrow to read her will."

I asked something I'd wondered about ever since I knew he had written the letter telling me to come home. "Why did you write to me instead of the lawyer?"

"She asked it," he said, face setting in those lines that made him seem truly a *pistolero*, a man of desperate habits.

"My father hired you, I believe?"

He laughed briefly. "You might say so. He broke up a little party some bandits were having with me and brought me to his house. I would have died except for your mother. When I was healed up, your dad gave me charge of the horses. Sometimes I couldn't figger his accent, but he was a real man."

I listened hungrily. It was good to hear about my father. But how ironic it was that this employee knew him far better than I—had seen him oftener, talked with him more.

"A man, yes," said Reina, appearing in the door behind Trace. "But Señor Greenleaf never became a Mexican. Which leaves us with problems now. Trace, please come with me. I need to consult with you."

He nodded to me and followed her readily through the arch, the worn leather of his garments contrasting with her silky gabardine. She took his arm, swaying against him as they moved off. She wanted him, that was certain, though her pride of place and name might prevent marriage.

How did he feel about her? That question depressed me. Could there be a doubt? Reina was an uncommonly beautiful woman and an heiress. She was plagued by none of the doubts that gnawed me. She was Reina Anza y Dubois.

I feared she was also a spiteful bitch, which did not promise much for our future. I drew some comfort from Trace's suggestion that Mother might have arranged something for me, though with one part of my being I wanted to stay at Las Coronas, at least till I regained the sense of home I had lacked for so long.

Mother was buried that night beside my father's memorial

in the old chapel set among orange, fig, and pomegranate trees. There was no reality in the priest's words for me. I was glad that the wasted body was under the stones instead of where I would vainly try to get from it vanished love and sweetness.

That night I slept a deep, heavy slumber that held no dreams and woke unrefreshed. The will would be read before the noon meal. That seemed some kind of goal, some important thing to reach through my numb misery. I had coffee and a crisp roll and went out into the patio. My silent room was unendurable just then and I feared to seek out Reina, dreading a rebuff.

Wandering near the grape arbor, I saw something hunched behind the stone bench at the end just as the cook, Catalina, burst out of the kitchen, scolding viciously. The small figure by the bench pressed even flatter to the pebbles.

"Ah, señorita," breathed the cook gustily as she stopped short. "A thousand pardons. That little hell-imp ran out here—"

"Imp?" I echoed the Spanish, which was returning, though with many gaps and distortions.

"The little Yaqui slut."

From my childhood, memories stirred—tales of the fierce unbelievably brave Indians who had stopped the Christian faith from the white man but never his rule or his ways. The Spanish, who really never subjugated them, gave them the name of the "brown race that knows how to die" and the Mexican government had intermittently waged war against them, wars that never ended because the Yaquis believed God had given them their lands.

"An Indian child?" I asked.

"Indian devil!" rasped the fat woman. She held out a wrist that showed small bloody toothmarks. "Bit me like rabid coyote. When I find her, I'll beat some respect into her."

"Hatred, more likely," I said.

Just then the cook's gaze flicked past me to the arbor. She lunged toward the skulking figure, dragged the girl to her feet, and gave her a savage slap that sent the child reeling into the bench.

The girl did not cry, did not make a sound. There was absolutely no expression in her black eyes as she watched the cook advancing, heavy arm lifted.

"Stop!" I said, grasping the woman's shoulder.

"But, señorita, she must learn. She is wild, a savage."

"It is savage to beat children."

The woman stared at me as if I were mad. "It is Yaqui," she protested. "The soldiers left her here a week ago. A week. And she will not obey."

"Where is her family?"

The cook moved her shoulders sullenly. "Dead. The soldiers killed the adults and babies. This brat was too young for the soldiers to keep with them."

"Dead?" I felt sick, unbelieving. "You mean there is war?"

"There is always war with wild beasts," came a voice behind me. Both the cook and I whirled to face Reina, who watched us with equal contempt. "Catalina, take the girl and put her to work. She is not going to eat her bellyful and do nothing."

"She will stay with me," I said. "You asked if I wanted a maid. I will have her."

Reina stared. Then her long throat arched back and she burst into laughter. "That creature? As well expect the serpent to brush your hair or the lion cub to mend your dresses."

"Then why try to make her into a kitchen servant?"

Reina shrugged. "One always tries. It is a duty to care for orphans and at least attempt to civilize these wretches."

"If that is accomplished by beatings, mules should be wonderfully civilized, Reina."

She turned her back on me and gestured to the cook, who reached for the girl. I put the child behind me.

"She must learn," Reina said in exasperation. "And so must you, sister mine. You do not comprehend this country."

Foreboding ran through me. I felt alone, abandoned, almost as vulnerable as this little slave, this small captive of war who watched us with proud stoicism though her parents were slaughtered and she was in the power of enemies. If she could be that brave, surely I could find some courage within myself.

"I will keep the child," I said. Taking her limp hand, I

started for where my room opened into the court.

"You are a fool," mocked Reina. "She will kill you for your trouble if she gets a chance. Better fondle a scorpion."

I got her to my room, closed the barred door on Reina, the cook, and public opinion, and didn't know what to do with her. It didn't help to imagine that she was a younger girl fresh come to Miss Mattison's school. I couldn't even visualize how one of them would react to what this child had endured. She stood in the center of the room, silently waiting for whatever came.

Her long thick hair was tied back with a bit of leather. She wore a coarse once-white sort of tunic. Bruises and weals, some fading, some newer, showed on every visible part of her honey-brown skin. She was barefooted and an ugly sore on one instep oozed pus.

I stepped to the door and rang the bell hung outside it. When one of the maids came, I asked for plenty of hot water and, pointing to the girl's foot, explained that I wanted some medicine for it. Though she stared at the child as if I had adopted a panther, the maid nodded and disappeared.

"Can you speak Spanish?" I asked.

The girl only watched me with those impassive eyes. I patted a chair invitingly, and the first glimmer of understanding shot across her face. She had large, almost Oriental eyes set above strong cheekbones, features that were out of proportion now but that promised exotic beauty later. She sank down on the thick Saltillo rug, propping her injured foot on top of the other.

I touched my breast and said, "Miranda." Then I pointed to her and looked inquiringly.

For a moment it seemed she wouldn't answer. Then she responded slowly. "Mi-ran-da." She touched her flat chest. "Sewa."

Thank heaven it was easy. Our conversations were sure to be limited for a long time. Was there anyone about Las Coronas who spoke Yaqui? I wanted to know if Sewa had any relations or people she would like to go to, and it would help to have her told in her own language that I would not hurt her.

Casting around for some way of expressing goodwill, I took

a large juicy peach from the basket of fruit by my bed. It was replenished daily, along with the flowers on the carved chest by the window. If I had to choose one or the other, I would have kept the fruit, with its mellow hues and delicious textures of plums, guavas, and peaches.

I offered Sewa the peach, took another, peeled away the fuzzy skin, and bit into the rich sweet flesh. Sewa nibbled, then took larger bites. As if each morsel whetted her hunger, she gulped the last mouthfuls, but she did not look at the fruit basket.

If she had been starving herself, too much food at once might be bad for her, but when the maid came from across the courtyard with two large copper buckets of hot water, I told her to dump them in the rose- and cherub-encrusted tub in my dressing room and to fetch some cheese and a bit of brown sugar.

As soon as she had brought these and a vile-smelling salve dispensed by the housekeeper for everything from broken legs to rheumatism, I gave Sewa the hunk of hard brown sugar and tried to coax her into the tub.

She balked. I washed my hands, trying to make the lathering soap seem delightful, but Sewa clamped her small jaws tight and would not be induced. Physical force was the last thing I wanted to use with her, so at last we worked out a compromise. She soaked her sore foot in a small basin and let me scrub her with a towel wrung out in the tub. I longed to see the long oily hair clean and fragrant, but that would have to wait. She made no fuss about exchanging her torn and dirty garment for one of my chemises, which was just long enough for modesty's minimal needs.

Though her foot was so swollen and angry that the slightest touch must have hurt, she never winced while I applied green salve and bandaged the instep with some clean rags I'd found in the chest.

Where could she sleep? An ornate chaise lougue at the foot of my bed was broad enough. I lay down on it, closed my eyes, rose, and pointed to her.

She went to the window and stared away at the mountains. Was that where she'd been captured? I might save her from beatings and feed her, but what could heal the inner wounds that must fester more deadly than the ugly secretions from her foot? Before I could decide what to do about her, I needed to find someone who spoke Yaqui.

Sighing, I came back to my own problems. It was time for the reading of the will.

"Sewa." With signs and expressions I tried to tell her I must go but would return, pointed again at the chaise. I hated to leave her so soon but had to hope she sensed my friendliness and wouldn't run away. The priest might know Yaqui, or perhaps the lawyer. . . .

Neither did—in fact, Señor Otero, fiddling with his pointed gray beard and gold watch chain, behaved as if I'd asked him if he could speak coyote. Trace Winslade, standing at the back of the library, came toward me.

"I speak some," he said, those turquoise eyes touching me so that I felt seared with quick flame. "And an old Yaqui healer lives in the canyon above my place. Why do you need Yaqui?"

I started to explain when Reina cut in sharply. "Let us hear the will. Señor Otero wishes to start back to Guaymas tonight." She gave him a frosty smile. "Please read slowly, señor. My half-sister has forgotten most of her Spanish."

I thought I was doing extremely well, considering my age when I left and the short time I'd been back. However, I was determined not to quibble with Reina over small matters; I suspected I'd need all my strength and resolution for vital questions.

The will was simple enough. Reina, whose father had added his holdings to the estate, was first heir to Las Coronas, though she was enjoined to offer me a home there. Mother's jewelry was divided between us. I inherited the mine, Mina Rara. Reina was to serve as my guardian till I was eighteen, six months from now. Trace was given a hundred acres of his own choosing, an Arab stallion, and five mares—"so that he may build his own herd while tending ours," ran the will. There were bequests to the servants, provisions for their old age, gifts to several religious orders.

I scarcely heard the lawyer drone on. My stomach was knotting and I fought back tears, forced to admit how I'd hoped Mother might have left some miraculous instructions for me, the name of some friend or relative who could give me some guidance. Waves of the sense of desertion that had so often engulfed me as a child overwhelmed me now, intensified by my knowing Reina scorned me.

Why did she have to be the way she was? Why couldn't we comfort each other? But if she felt any of the same need, she didn't show it. When Señor Otero finished, she asked a few peremptory questions and dismissed him, saying that the housekeeper had a meal ready at his convenience.

The bearded little man bowed and expressed his hope that all would go according to Doña Luisa's wish. When he was gone, Trace glanced from Reina, who stood by the bookshelves, over to me.

"Will you be staying here, Miss Miranda, as your mother obviously intended?"

Involuntarily I looked at Reina, whose eyes evaded mine. "I would like to stay," I said. "But not if I'm unwelcome."

"The house is big enough," she said tersely. "Mother wished it. As your elder, I have a duty toward you. I hope that you will stay at Las Coronas, Miranda, at least for a time, though I don't feel it's a suitable permanent home for one of your upbringing and character."

It was as ungracious an invitation as could be imagined. "I wonder what you can know of my character," I said slowly. "And perhaps I should remind you that I have never had another home."

"Was it my fault your father insisted you be schooled in England?" she demanded. "You *are* a foreigner, and if you live in my house, you must respect my knowledge and experience."

"Of what?" I asked, blood heating. "Ways to abuse orphan children?"

Her eyes shot green flame. "You are warned about that creature. If she slips a knife into anyone, I hope it is you. Would you please excuse yourself? I have things to discuss with Winslade."

He came lazily forward. "You interrupted my talk with Miss Miranda. I'll come to you when we've finished." She stared at his audacity. So did I.

"Oh," I began, "you can see me later, Mr. Winslade."

"Now," he said. He held open the heavy carved door for Reina, regarding her with calm eyes as if there were no question of her obeying.

She swallowed, glared at him, and at last shrugged, crossed to the door, and paused.

"Winslade, don't return to your horses till we have discussed our business. I will be in the office." She swept out.

He shut the door, came to me, pulled up a rawhide stool, and took my hands. "All right, Miranda. Tell me."

To my utter confusion and shame, I began to cry.

3

At first I tried to fight back the tears but I'd held them in too long. Suppressed grief, anger, and fear kept welling up, shaking me with tumultuous sobs. I beat on the leather chair with my fists, past caring what this perplexing man thought. I'd already disgraced myself. I might as well try to get rid of this savage despair.

"Why?" I gasped. "Why is it this way? Why didn't Mother send for me when I could have known her, grown to feel at home here?"

"She wanted you," he said slowly, and I knew he was trying to be fair to both my parents. "But she'd promised your father to let you finish school, and then she fell ill. Your father hoped you'd marry in England and stay there."

I had to laugh bitterly. "Yes, one meets so many eligible bachelors in a Church of England girls' school."

"If he had lived, he'd have seen to that, but your mother had no contacts there. Besides, though she deferred to your father, she always hoped you'd come back to Mexico." He sighed, took out a large snowy handkerchief, and daubed clumsily at my face. "Whatever you think, she loved you. They both did."

I considered that and, for all my resentment, could not deny it. "All right. But they kept me from having a home."

"Hell!" he exploded. "You had a safe place to stay, food, and good care. That's more than most of this world gets."

His wrath at my self-pity stung, mostly because he had said what I'd so often told myself. I repudiated his handkerchief and got to my feet, trying to hold my chin up. "I'm not asking you to sympathize. But I—I'll never feel I belong anywhere—"

In spite of my attempt at hauteur, my voice frayed. He came to stand so close that I felt physically overcome and those sky-water eyes seemed to probe the depths of my soul.

"Does anyone?" he asked. "Does anyone belong?"

I gave a doleful sniff. "Everyone seems to except me."

"Few people belong to themselves. But that's the only way to have balance, to be heavy enough not to be blown away by changes. There are going to be big changes in Mexico."

"I don't know what you mean," I argued, though I did, a little. "Miss Mattison belonged in England. I can't picture her here at all. Mother fitted Las Coronas. So does Reina, in a different way. Father—" I pondered, was forced to admit rather shamefacedly, "He was rooted in himself. He must have lived successfully here, but when he was in England, that seemed to be his place."

"Jonathan Greenleaf could rope with vaqueros, swear with miners, dance at a *fiesta*, or kill when he had to. Yet he was the gentlest man I ever knew."

"I'm not like that."

"Of course you're not," he said with pitying amusement. "Lord's sake, girl, you have to *do* things to become."

Knowing he was right but angry at him for detecting my self-pity, I stared wordlessly. His face changed, softened; his long lean hand came up to brush my cheek, lightly touch my mouth. "A woman has to love, Miranda, to be a full person. Understand what she needs, how to enjoy it, and how to give." He stepped back, the scar showing livid. "Hell, why are you so young?"

Trembling, desolate because he'd taken his hand from me, I said with all the dignity I could muster, "I'm older every day."

He laughed at that. Some of the tension went out of his tall spare frame. "So am I, Miss Miranda. Don't fret your mind about all this right now. Life sort of sneaks up on you and makes things natural that seem hard from a distance." His eyes swept over me, sent that hot rush of awareness through my veins. "When you learn what you've got, Miranda, God help us poor men!"

I suspected he was trying to give me self-confidence but I liked the caressing way he said my name. It was the first time I'd heard it used as an endearment. Talking to him had helped. His matter-of-fact attitude had steadied me; so, in a different way, had the knowledge that he found me attractive. I managed a wavery smile and got to my feet.

"You said you speak a little Yaqui. Will you come with me?"

He frowned, shoving at the thick black hair angling across his forehead. "Don't tell me you've got a Sierra Yaqui camped out in your room!"

"Come see," I teased, glad to bewilder him for a change.

He moved with little sound in spite of his boots. I was intensely conscious of him as we passed along the corridor to my room. As we reached the door, his fingers closed hard on my wrist, turning me to him.

"I wonder if I shouldn't teach you about being a woman."

I could only watch him, captive to those strange storm-fire eyes. He let me go, but his breathing was jagged. "Forget that. I can't be your man. But I know what you mean about a home place, Miranda. You'll make yourself one. Sometime, somewhere."

"Easy to say."

"It'll happen." He tilted my chin up. "Till then, you just remember this. People who get their identity from living on a certain piece of ground might as well be dead and under it. We've got feet to move on. If God had meant us to stick in one place, he'd have rooted us like trees."

The absurd picture of earth's millions growing out of their soil like so many cabbages made me giggle. Trace laughed, too, and I knew he was trying to help me.

Before I could answer, he opened the door. My dressing gown had dropped to the bedside rug that morning, and in my haste, I had left it. Sewa lay curled up next to it, hugging it as if it were somebody. She jerked up as we entered, shaken from sleep, stared from me to Trace with eyes that widened but betrayed no fear—or hope, either.

Trace stopped a distance from her, dropped to one knee. He spoke softly in what I supposed was Yaqui. She didn't answer at first, but his third or fourth question evoked a hesitant word. He sat cross-legged, she relaxed slightly, and within a few minutes she was talking. He asked a question now and then, and though his voice stayed kind, I could sense growing anger in him.

He turned at last to where I had taken a seat by the grilled deep window. "Some Sierra Yaquis—those are ones who've taken to the mountains to fight the Mexicans—have been raiding Mexican settlers, so the soldiers retaliated at this child's village. The men and older boys were sent off to be slaves in Yucatán, the married women were killed with their babies, older girls were kept by the soldiers. Young children like this one—I would guess her at eleven—were given away to be servants."

I could scarcely believe such a thing. Sick to my bones, I heard two of the maids laughing outside and wondered how ordinary life flowed on when such horrors were so close.

"Her family?" I asked when I could speak.

"Her father and brother were taken away to be sold and sent to the plantations. Her mother was hanged and her baby sister brained against a tree."

"There's . . . no one?"

He asked the child a question, shrugged as he turned to me. "Her mother's brothers went off to the sierra some months ago."

"So they would be fugitives?"

"Rebels against the Mexicans, yes." He answered my unspoken question. "The girl is best with you for a while. Even if she found a home with Yaquis, it might be torn apart and next time she might not be so lucky."

"Lucky!"

"She's alive. That's where you start, Miss Miranda. And her name—it means flower in Yaqui."

Flower. I bit my lip. If he could call this bruised and battered child lucky, what would he consider me? Yet he hadn't been unkind or scornful in the library, only unyielding and tough in a way that had given me a foundation.

"You said a Yaqui curer lives near you?" I remembered.

Trace nodded. "Cruz was suspected of witchcraft while he was still a young man in Torim, one of the old pueblos farther south. Yaquis tie up their witches and toss them in a fire. Cruz had power but used it only to heal and couldn't see being fried like that, so he traveled fast and far."

"And he's lived alone all his life?"

"He seems to like it that way. Besides, people come a long way to be cured by him and often stay till they get well or die." Trace touched the scar on his face. "Cruz saved my life a couple of years ago when some horse thieves left me for dead." He touched the scar connecting high cheekbone to lean jaw. "I owe him for it still. We visit quite a lot. He's not what you'd call a hermit."

"Would he do something for Sewa's foot?"

"He'd have to."

"Why?"

"He told me he can't refuse to help anyone. If he should, his power will turn and kill him."

I shivered. "Then I wouldn't want it."

"I don't know that Cruz does. But he was born with it and accepts it as he does his pulse or breathing. Let me have a look under that bandage."

Speaking in a gentling tone to Sewa, he took the foot she reluctantly extended and undid the wrapping with a swift deftness surprising in such a large man. The wound, puffy and blackened at the edges, was still draining. I couldn't tell whether my ministrations had made it better or worse.

"She gashed it with a stick," he explained after asking her another question. "She hoped the soldiers would either kill or leave her, but they made her walk anyway and it's got maggots in it. I could cauterize it, but she'd have more faith in what Cruz would do."

"Faith?"

"That has more to do with healing—and sickness—than

anyone thinks. Anyway, let me take her to Cruz. That'll save at least a day and I'm afraid of blood poisoning."

He redid the bandage, talking to the child. She didn't protest but seemed to shrink within herself even more and her large dark eyes clung to me. I knelt beside her.

"Sewa," I began and stopped in frustration. She couldn't understand my poor Spanish and I had no word of hers but her name. I glanced appealingly at Trace. "Did you tell her Cruz is Yaqui, that he'll help her?"

"Yes, but she can hardly be expected to trust anyone right now. She may think I intend to get her away from you under that pretext, then give her to someone who knows how Yaquis should be treated."

That went straight to my own tormented heart. Alone I surely was, but I could help this child. "Supposing I went with her to Cruz?"

The turquoise eyes narrowed. "You'd do that? For this little scrap?"

"Of course, if it will make her well. Could we get there tonight?"

He considered. "There's a full moon. We should do it by midnight and then I'll fetch Cruz to my place. Eat and change into riding things. I'll get horses. Can you ride?"

Miss Mattison believed every English lady should be a reasonable horsewoman so every week we had fared out for a decorous circuit of some country road. "Yes," I said, never doubting I spoke the truth. A sudden thought struck me. "We—we'll have to stay the night."

"You bet you will. In fact, you'd better plan to stay several days."

"But— Is there a woman at your place?"

"I doubt it." He grinned. "At least there wasn't when I left."

The careless tone suggested that there could be and I didn't think he meant a cook. "Mr. Winslade," I blurted, "I know this is Mexico but—"

"Good Lord!" he said, astonished. "Your reputation!" He threw back his head, laughing till I flushed and spoke in the iciest tone I could summon.

"It may be a humorous matter to you, sir, but I have no wish to be thought a—a harlot!"

"You know the word!" he cried and went off in another peal of delight. Sobering, he drew his dark brows together. "I can sleep outside. You and Sewa could probably stay in Cruz's hut. Or we can take along a *dueña*."

A chaperone? Even Miss Mattison would have approved of that solution, considering the circumstances. "I'll see what my sister thinks," I decided, already dreading *that* interview, though I could scarcely go off without any explanation.

Trace frowned. "She won't like it. But I reckon you two have to come to an understanding and this should supply a damn good battlefield." He spoke briefly to Sewa, nodded to me. "I'll have the horses outside in an hour. If a chaperone's coming, send word to the stable so I'll have a mount for her."

The prospect of what I was sure would be a battle with Reina took away my appetite, but I rang for a maid and asked for cheese and fruit and bread. While waiting for the food, I got out my riding habit, the most becoming outfit I owned and the only one that required a corset. To lace occasionally surely wouldn't kill me, but it *was* uncomfortable. It was velvet, a rich brown so dark it was almost black, exactly the shade of my eyes and hair. There was a matching hat with a pheasant quill slanting rakishly from soft gathers. The boots were suede, almost as soft as the velvet, and there was a creamy scarf to tuck in at the throat. Apart from the gray school uniform, I had only a few dresses and there had been no time to have anything made before leaving England. This riding habit was the only truly elegant thing I'd ever owned, except for those hand-embroidered undergarments Mother had sent.

When the food came, I motioned to Sewa to help herself, straightened my hair, stiffened my spine, swallowed hard, and marched out in search of my intimidating half-sister.

Trace Winslade must have just left the office, for Reina flung open the door at my knock. Her eyes were swollen as if with recent tears, but they flamed at sight of me.

"So!" she hissed and erupted into such a torrent of Spanish that I caught only the rhythm and general intent. That was enough.

I was a *sinvergüenza*, totally without shame—a disgrace to the family, though what could you expect from mongrels. My mother barely in the ground and I go chasing off with a *yanqui tejano pistolero* of no breeding and less morals—and all on a flimsy excuse of treating a trifling hurt self-inflicted by a sullen Indian brat who ought to be whipped till she earned her bread—

By then I was trembling with rage. "I came to ask your advice," I interrupted, clenching my hands till the knuckles ached. How I longed to grab her shoulders, shake her till the ugly venomous words clogged her throat. "But I don't want it, you—you bloody-minded bitch!"

I swung about.

"Stop, *puta!*" she screamed at me.

I wrenched free of her clutching fingers, pushed the door shut in her livid face. As I walked down the hall, she shrieked things I'm sure it was better I didn't understand. Bolting the iron lock of my door, I hurled myself down by the beautiful habit and burst into stormy tears.

The beastly, wicked, hateful . . . I'd stay as many nights as were needed and to the devil with her opinion! But the awful things she'd said, the fact that my own sister could frame such accusations cut deeply and cruelly. In spite of her childhood enmity, I had longed to be friends; even when she behaved coldly at my homecoming, I'd hoped against hope that she would soften, treat me like a sister. But our mother's death had ended all restraint.

I had to face it. Reina hated me. *Hated.* It was no passing grudge or fitful jealousy. If it were possible, she detested me more because of our shared blood.

I couldn't stay under this roof, where she was bound to dominate. Anything would be better, though I was still resolved not to go back to England. When we returned from the curer, I would contact the lawyer, get funds, perhaps some advice, and leave Las Coronas forever.

There was a tug at my sleeve as if a bird had tweaked it. I peered up between my fingers. Sewa was offering me a peeled peach. The gesture from this child, who had suffered so terribly, cut through my self-pity.

Sitting up with a shaky laugh, I took the fruit, thanked her, gave her a bite, and let the sweet, slightly tart lusciousness of the fruit trickle down my throat, found I was hungry, and devoured it.

Time to dress! Washing peach juice from my face and hands, I put my overnight needs into a small valise, located a shawl for Sewa to wrap in once the desert night cooled, and dressed in a hurry, fixing the hat firmly in place with several pins.

Bundling cheese and bread in a napkin, I tucked them into the valise. Would the curer want money? I had only a few pesos. Trace could pay, though, and I'd return it.

Taking Sewa by the hand, refusing to let her struggle with the valise, I bundled through the hall to the front veranda. Trace was there, standing at the head of a handsome steel-gray gelding. A boy held two mares, a burnished chestnut and a small yellowish one with dark mane and tail and a dark streak tracing the spine.

But what stopped my breath sharp in my chest was Reina. She sat erectly confident and graceful on a black horse that kept tossing its head. Her garments made me feel overdressed and foreign. She wore a divided skirt of soft creamy suede, a cropped matching jacket over a plain white shirt, and a low-crowned black hat secured under the chin with a thong. There was a sheathed knife at her belt and a carbine thrust in the saddle holster. Her long-roweled silver spurs gleamed like the mountings of her bridle, with its cruel-looking bit, and the ornate saddle. A bedroll was fastened behind her saddle as well as on mine and Sewa's.

"I'm going with you," she informed the air above my head. "No one shall say I neglected my duty to my sister or failed to do my utmost to keep her from folly."

"Your sacrifice passes belief," I said smoothly. "Now people can gossip about both of us."

She gave me a furious stare and sent the black horse stepping forward. Trace tied my valise behind his saddle, then gave me a strong hand up before lifting Sewa on the little yellow horse, showing her how to hold reins and standing by her till she seemed reassured.

"So you have a *dueña*," he said to me with a droll droop of one eyelid. "Don't worry about trying to ride at her pace. In fact, I'd be obliged if you stayed close to Sewa. We can't go faster than our slowest rider. If your sister wants to ride circles around us, let her have her amusement, but don't tire yourself. It's a long way."

He swung up himself and kept his magnificent gray tuned with the mares, though enough in advance to point the way. My chestnut had a harder mouth than the gentle mounts I was used to, and though it seemed unmalicious, I had to concentrate on handling it. At first Sewa had held on for dear life but gradually loosened and began to timidly stroke her horse's dark coarse mane, crooning softly.

Our saddles were very different from those I'd used in England. They had deeply embossed skirts, and the stirrups had leather-covered fronts to protect the feet. I worried about the cruel-looking bits. Trace explained they were Spanish spade bits, which must be used with care or the horse's mouth could be butchered. He used a plain bit and had found these for Sewa and for me.

"Why does your saddle have two girths?" I wondered.

He looked puzzled. "Oh, you mean cinches. I was raised in Texas where we use double-rigging. What the rest of you have are Spanish single-rig with one cinch. Does it sit funny for you?"

"No. I think once I get used to having so much cantle and horn, I'll feel more secure."

He nodded approvingly. "And you will be. Those little English pads are fine for jumping and fairly short rides but for hours in the saddle, stock saddles are a damn sight better."

Reina kept well ahead of us for the first miles, but when she apparently decided Trace was not going to match her pace, she fell back and summoned him to her, saying she wanted an account of the horses.

They rode a little ahead and to the side, Trace obviously determined to keep an eye on Sewa and me, but our horses' hooves and the creaking saddles blanked out most of their words. Left to mull the situation over, I was more than ever convinced that Reina was infatuated with Winslade, no matter what scornful names she called him. She had been enraged at the prospect of my being with him for a few days and had seized the role of chaperone to prevent that—and to give herself time with him?

What his feelings were for her, I couldn't guess from his behavior. They were a striking pair on their spirited horses. I thought with a pang that Reina was a fitting woman for him, beautiful, fiery, exciting. Beside her, I felt prim, plain, and foreign. He was kind to me as he was to Sewa for much the same reasons.

I drew such comfort as I could from a certainty that Reina would want to marry a man of wealth and family. If Trace stormed her, passion might overcome her pride, but I felt he would never stand for being thought a fortune-hunter and any advances would have to come from her.

She seemed to have decided to ignore my existence. Her throaty laughter floated back now and then, and though Trace kept a watchful eye on Sewa and me, he seemed content enough to stay near Reina.

We had left in the heat of the June day. I was soon miserably hot in the snug velvet and knee-high boots. My hat might be fetching, but one with a wide brim would make more sense. I envied Sewa the loose chemise and bare legs. There was no shade and I thought with longing of oak forests and lanes where trees made a thick cooling arch on the warmest days—not that anyone in England could even imagine heat like this.

I marveled at the many kinds of cactus; cardons, rearing tall as small trees; nopal, spreading in thick mounds of prickly oval pads; cholla, drooping strangely jointed clusters that looked like grapes or forked like antlers. The occasional grass was yellow and sparse, except where it outlined stream beds that presumably ran water sometimes, if only after a rain, and along these washes, mesquite grew thick and luxuriant along with ironwood and fragrant cat's-claw.

My lips, chapping from wind and heat, stung when I wet them with my tongue. I longed for a drink but hated to demonstrate weakness to my sister. I was getting tired, too, my knee cramped from being hooked over the horn. The corset had become a torment, biting into my flesh, trapping perspiration.

Like a steamed clam, I thought inelegantly. Reina must be hot, too, in all that leather, yet she showed no sign of discomfort or weariness though I calculated we had been riding at least two hours. Which felt like ten. Sewa was used to heat and the thin cotton chemise let the air reach her. If I lived, I vowed grimly to get some clothes I could tolerate even if they verged on indecency. When Trace finally stopped by a dry watercourse where vanished rains had produced a scattering of *acacia* and *palo verde,* I almost tumbled into his arms. He steadied me for a moment while my head spun dizzily.

"All right?" he demanded. "Here, get in the shade. Damn it, girl, if you needed to stop why didn't you say so?"

"I—I'm fine," I answered with a tongue that felt huge and puffy dry.

He gave me a disgusted stare, lifted my bed roll and forced me into the haven of the largest tree, settling Sewa next to me. He didn't let her walk on the sore foot, but simply carried her. Reina had dismounted and strode over to raise arched eyebrows as she inspected us.

"Strange how those who cannot do a thing will always try it," she said with a thin smile that gave her rather narrow face a fox look. "You're red as fresh-butchered meat, Miranda. I fear your complexion is no more adapted to this region than your dress."

Trace took the scarf from his neck and wet it from the leather water bag he then offered me. I passed it to Sewa who drank slowly, only a few sips, before handing it to me. Following her example, I wet my throat, savored the tepid water and let it trickle down my dry throat. It was the first time in my life that I had truly appreciated water, the body's imperative need for it. Reina sipped from her own hide-covered silver flask, but before Trace drank, he wiped my face with the scarf, pressed the wet part against my temples.

"You're sun-burned," he said and I knew how frightful and bedraggled I must look. "I should have told you to change hats. Wear mine till the sun gets low."

"But—"

"Wear it," he said, tossing the battered broad-brimmed gray felt down beside me.

We rested perhaps ten minutes. It galled me that it was on my account, but I consoled myself with the knowledge that the horses were also glad of the break. Humbled to realize I had less endurance and strength than anyone in the party, even a starved child with an infected wound, I resolved to toughen myself to match this new country for though I had not altered my decision to leave *Las Coronas*, I still intended to try to live somewhere in Mexico—and not the existence of a sheltered house plant, either.

I rose without the aid of Trace Winslade's extended hand and heaved or dragged myself into the saddle while he swung Sewa into hers. This time I noticed she returned his smile with a tentative surprisingly sweet one. Once again, Reina led. I settled Trace's hat, which smelled strongly but not unpleasantly of tobacco, campfires and sweat salt, snugly over my head, grateful for its protection from the glare of desert and sky. My velvet cap with its feather was tied ingloriously to the leathers at the front of my saddle like some bedraggled trophy.

At sundown we came to where cane grew thick and high along a shallow river. Trace loosened the saddle girths and we watered our horses, then rested while he made coffee in a tin pot and shared out strips of thin exceedingly tough meat. I got the cheese and bread from my valise.

"Beats jerky," said Trace and for the first time that journey I felt I'd done something that wasn't inept or ridiculous.

As day waned, the moon shone brighter and brighter so that when we started on, it was not much darker than at twilight. We could see the purple bulk of the mountains, the silvered stretch of the desert with *cordones* upthrusting arms like giant candelabra. They were much like the *saguaros* that grew further north, only bigger and more squared at the tips. A faint shrill yipping broke out, to be answered by similar choruses from other points, a song I remembered from childhood.

"Coyotes," Trace said. And I saw Sewa smile to herself as if it were good to hear wild things.

The air cooled fast once the sun was gone. Sewa wrapped my shawl about her and I was glad of my heavy velvet dress, though I swore that once I got the corset off I would throw it away. Why should I squeeze my ribs into my lungs to look a few inches slimmer? Dr. Mattison was right. One might survive on half-breaths in moist English air, but not in this merciless land where man, if he came, must adapt, even though he couldn't grow a waxy thorny shield like the cactus and store water as it did, or develop tiny leaves like the trees, exposing less vulnerable surface. When one considered what plants had to do in order to live here, it was a wonder man succeeded at all.

We'd entered a long wide valley between mountains, watered by a stream. Coarse high grass reached our horses' hocks. A whinny sounded from a distant herd, dark phantoms in a side valley, and Trace's horse threw back his head and answered.

We passed a big round corral of latticed mesquite limbs. Sheds and the unwalled roofed structures known as ramadas were scattered at one end. Beyond these were several small adobe houses. Trace stopped by one of these.

"So here we are," he said. "I'll help you unsaddle and ride after Cruz. The sooner he sees that little girl's foot, the easier I'll be in my mind."

Men came out of the other two adobes, welcoming Trace, falling hushed as they recognized Reina. Trace told them Doña Luisa was dead. They crossed themselves and murmured. A man with lean hips, massive chest, and a curious moustache, white on one side, black on the other, approached Reina and spoke in a stilled rumble.

"We have much sorrow, señorita. Your mother was a great

lady. May the saints receive her and comfort you."

She thanked him quite graciously, but when Trace explained that I was also Doña Luisa's daughter, Reina ignored his proffered hand and swung down by herself. The broad-chested vaquero waited till Trace had helped me from the saddle and then bowed.

"I am Lázaro Pérez, at your orders, señorita. I regret you have had such a sad homecoming." His gaze moved to Sewa.

The child kept her outward calm, but I knew she must be shrinking inwardly. Lázaro said sharply to Trace, "Yaqui?"

Trace nodded. Lázaro swung from the girl without a word and took Reina's horse and mine while a second man led away Sewa's after Trace lifted her down. He carried her into his house, kicking the door ajar, put her down, and lit a candle.

The dim yellow glow showed a square room plastered with clay, benches of adobe built out from the wall, and a fireplace at one end. There was a rough table, a chair, and a bed spread with a serape in tones of brown and gray. A shelf by the fireplace held a few dishes and cooking staples. Clothes hung on pegs. The floor was hard dirt and there was only one window.

One of the vaqueros brought in the bedrolls, my valise, crumpled hat, and Reina's saddlebag. "Can't you send him after this witch doctor?" Reina inquired acridly.

"No." Trace shook out the pallets, put one on his bed. I helped spread the others on the floor.

"Why not?" she persisted.

"The men won't ride up his canyon at night."

The green of her eyes was almost hidden by swelling black pupils. "Then he *is* a witch!" she breathed.

"Wise," Trace corrected. "Though to be wise or even sensible in this world comes close to magic."

"Surely it can wait till morning," she urged.

Trace went to Sewa, who still huddled on the bench where he'd placed her. He undid the bandage. The stench made my stomach turn. Reina gagged and flung away in disgust. Trace's nostrils twitched. He rewound the bandage and said briefly, "I'd better take Sewa with me. Now."

"It—it's that bad?" I asked, heart constricting. Blood poison, gangrene—terrible names I didn't fully understand thrummed in my head.

"I'm afraid so."

"Then I'll come, too."

"Stay here, Miranda. You're done in. There won't be any way for you to help." But when he spoke to Sewa, her dark eyes sprang to me.

She didn't ask; she never would. But I dragged my body up and said, "I'm going."

He started to argue, glanced at Sewa, and gave in. He shouted out the door for fresh horses and coffee, if any was left. In a few minutes Lázaro brought coffee that was at least lukewarm. Reina declined the bitter brew.

"You are mad," she told me. "Trailing about in the dark to find a Yaqui witch."

"Cruz?" demanded Lázaro. He stared at Trace. "That one is an *onza!* If you have business with him, leave it till morning."

"We are friends," said Trace.

"Perhaps by day," retorted Lázaro. "But once in his cat shape, an *onza* has no friends."

"Crazy talk," snapped Trace. "Didn't Cruz set that broken ankle for you? Didn't he cure Roque when he was dying of snakebite?"

"He is still an *onza,*" Lázaro maintained stubbornly. "I beg you. Wait."

"We cannot."

Lázaro cast a hate-filled look at Sewa. "All for this vermin!"

"Enough!" said Trace. He rose at the sound of horses.

"Am I expected to stay the night alone in this hovel?" demanded Reina.

"You may sleep outside," suggested Trace. "Or ride with us."

She stared at him, touched her full lower lip with the tip of her tongue. "And if I command you, as your employer, to stay here?"

He said softly, "I would tell you, señorita, to go to hell."

As her green eyes dilated in shock, he picked Sewa up. We

went out, Lázaro closing the door with flowery assurances to Reina that she would be as safe as if she were bolted in her chamber in Las Coronas. She shrieked something that might have made him revise his opinion of her, but I was too frightened for Sewa to care about Reina's moods.

Lázaro helped me mount. My every bone and muscle ached, and this new horse, possibly vexed at being caught up after dark when all decent beasts can rest, moved in a jarring, jolting trot that was torture. Trace had decided to carry Sewa in front of him, which I took as an ominous sign—perhaps he thought she wouldn't be coming back or, if she did, would be unable to sit a horse.

A short distance from the adobes, we seemed heading into sheer mountain walls, but Trace led through a narrow defile that presently widened into another canyon, so deep that the moon reached only the center, casting a luminous trail with darkness on either side.

The valley of the shadow of death. Ice closed on my heart. Death hovered over Sewa, I was sure, or Trace would have brought the curer to her. "*I will fear no evil*," I prayed desperately. "*Fear no evil. . . .*"

Our horses' hooves echoed the words, mockingly pounding them into my mind. For I did fear evil. I feared the infection in Sewa's body, but even more the chilling hate in Lázaro's eyes, the venom in Reina's. I feared the cruelty that could do this to a child more than all those bogies of the litany: battle, murder, and sudden death.

"*Good Lord, deliver us*," I pleaded. "*Let the child get well.*" *Onza* or witch, I didn't care what this Cruz was, so long as he healed the small figure cradled in Trace's arms. I envied her that place of comfort as we rode on in the night of black and silver.

Evil, evil, evil. I . . . will . . . fear. Fear no evil. For thou art with me. My eyes kept closing from sheer fatigue. Then my raw-gaited horse stopped so abruptly that I would have gone on over his neck if strong hands hadn't caught and lifted me down.

Shaking my head to clear it, I looked into a dark face that might have been carved from mahogany.

"Do not be afraid," the stranger said. "The child will not die.

But we must hurry." He turned and I followed to the hut Trace was already entering with Sewa.

4

Cruz did not explain how he knew we were coming, but there could be no doubt he was prepared for visitors. A candle burned on a ledge. Water was boiling on a sort of brazier improvised from a Standard Oil can with a grate on top.

Cruz poured this water into a jug. An aromatic smell quickly filled the room. Trace had placed Sewa on a woven straw mat. Cruz, humming to himself, got something from a chest and gave it to her. It was a flute made of cane. I was astounded when he sat down next to the child and began to show her how to coax notes from it. When she got her first birdlike trill, she gave the first laugh I'd heard from her.

Cruz went to pour his steaming brew into three earthenware bowls that he handed to Trace, Sewa, and me. I noticed he added something to her drink.

Why didn't he look at her foot? Ask how she'd been hurt and when? He'd guessed we were coming, but I didn't want him to guess about Sewa. Urgencies sprang to my lips, but I felt Trace's eyes on me, bit back my questions. He would speak when it was time. I knew that more surely than I knew my name. It was a strange sensation. Following his example, I sipped the brew. Pungent, spicy, slightly acrid, it was amazingly refreshing.

Cruz unwound the bandage. Putrescent ooze showed in the dim light. The smell was sickening. Cruz spoke gently to Sewa. Her eyes seemed to grow even more huge. She drank her tea to the end, set down the bowl, and picked up the flute. Trace asked something. Cruz nodded.

Muscles stood out like steel cords in Trace's jaw.

He spoke again, almost pleadingly. Cruz's answer was terse. To me, in English, Trace said, "He says the foot is gangrenous. It must come off or the girl will die."

"Off? Her foot? You mean—cut it *off*?"

"Yes."

"No!" My voice started to rise. I choked it down, swallowed, looked from Cruz to Sewa to Trace again. It couldn't be. A child that young to lose her foot, hobble all her life? She was watching me, big eyes grave but not fearful. "Does—does she know?" I asked.

Trace nodded.

"It really *is* gangrene?"

"Yes, Miranda. The infection has cut off the blood supply. What it amounts to is that the foot is dead, rotting. And if it isn't removed, the gangrene will spread and kill her."

I wet my lips, sicker by the minute. "How will Cruz do it?"

"He has a little saw." Cruz was putting it in the kettle of boiling water.

"Is there anything to dull the pain?"

"Cruz put a narcotic in her tea. Jimsonweed. It can kill, but used with Cruz's knowledge it will help. And he has a sort of hypnotic power." Trace smiled thinly at my anxious scrutiny of the hut. "She'll fare better than in most hospitals, I promise you that. Will you go outside or can you help?"

How I cravenly wanted to stay out of sight and sound. But Sewa couldn't leave. And she must live with the results for the rest of her life.

"What shall I do?" I asked in Spanish.

Cruz told me to sit by the girl and talk to her, hold her if necessary. I sat on the mat beside her, trying not to wince as Cruz put a poker in the fire. A saw—red-hot iron. Instru-

ments of torture. And this *would* be torture, though done with
merciful intent. Trace knelt beside us, took the flute, and after
a little testing made bird sounds from it. Sewa laughed and
reached for it, trying to imitate his notes. He showed her
which holes to finger.

Soon she was making sounds like some of the birds we'd
heard that evening, soft and plaintive or brisk and chatty.
Cruz had been making another potion and handed it to me.
"She should drink it slowly," he cautioned.

So Sewa drank and played and sipped and fingered the
flute, but her motions grew uncoordinated. Her eyes were
brilliant, widely dilated. Cruz washed her leg with an
astringent-smelling liquid, then placed it on a scrubbed board.

She did not seem aware of what he was doing. He talked
quietly to her. Her body relaxed even more. I moved closer
and she settled into my arms, still clutching the flute, though
she no longer seemed able to hold it to her lips.

Trace stepped to where he could hold her leg and also block
our view, for which I was grateful. He spoke to Sewa, who
opened her mouth and let him slip a piece of wood between
her teeth. He wrapped his doubled scarf a few inches above
Sewa's ankle, knotted it, put a stick through it, and twisted it
tight as Cruz came over with the little saw.

The tourniquet stick between his teeth, Trace gripped the
child's leg so she couldn't move, clamping down the other leg
with one of his. She twitched. I knew the blade had started; I
cradled her against me and spoke in her ear, English, Spanish,
anything I could think of, just kept talking while clammy
sweat rose on both of us, her teeth clamped on the wood with a
grinding sound, and her heart pounded against mine, wavered, faltered, seemed to stop for those hideous moments
while the saw gritted through bone, then beat faintly, distant-
ly.

She went limp. I saw through my tears that her eyes had
closed. If she could stay unconscious— For Cruz was bringing
over the glowing poker.

I drove my teeth into my lip to keep from screaming but
could not check convulsive sobs as there was a sizzling sound, a
smell of searing flesh. The small body in my arms contracted

and a moan came from her. I fought back the hotness that
rose in my throat. Couldn't get sick now—not yet. Pray God
she'd stay in merciful blackness awhile.

Trace loosened the tourniquet, wiped his face with the
scarf. Some blood had spattered on it and left marks on his
face. It didn't seem to matter. I felt drenched with blood,
though it was only sweat, mine and the child's.

Cruz was busy with salves and a coarse white cloth he got
from a chest. "I think we are in time," he said in slow Spanish
as he bandaged the stump. "We will keep the leg raised for a
day to keep the pressure off the healing part."

"Will she wake up soon?" I asked, pressing my ear to the
scrawny chest and receiving the slow dulled sound of her
heart.

"Not for some hours. And for a few days I will ease her pain
as much as possible with my brews."

The body pain would go. But never to walk free and light
again, to be maimed, reminded of it every time she tried to
take a step—what a thing to happen to a girl named Flower.

"She can use a crutch," Trace said roughly.

I cried out at that, a wail that made the drugged child flinch.
"You must all sleep," Cruz said. "Señorita, you and the girl
rest here. Trace and I can spread mats in the ramada."

"We have bedrolls," Trace said.

We put Sewa on hers, injured leg propped on a folded
poncho, the flute beside her. Trace put my pallet touching
hers. I didn't expect to sleep, but either weariness or Cruz's tea
sent me into quick heavy slumber with only a passing thought
of what Reina would say about the necessity of staying here for
several days. Compared with Sewa's ordeal, Reina's opinions
seemed of very little consequence.

I woke with my sister's voice in my ears, blinked, sat up,
glanced around the dim room, knowing that for some reason
I didn't want to wake up. Then my gaze fell on Sewa huddled
next to me and I remembered it all and broke out in
shuddering cold sweat.

Reina shrilled on. She'd wake Sewa at this rate, a thing I hoped to postpone as long as possible. I had slept in my chemise and petticoat. Slipping into my thoroughly draggled riding habit, I fumbled shut the most strategic buttons, shoved my hair back, and hurried out to the ramada.

Cruz was nowhere to be seen, but Trace had apparently been repairing a saddle when Reina appeared. Lázaro, a good hundred yards from the ramada, stood between Reina's handsome black and a jugheaded sorrel. Even in daylight he wasn't getting closer than necessary to the witch's house.

Reina's green eyes swept over me. "You!" she exploded. "Dirty, crumpled, in company with outcasts, men even Texans and savage Indians reject—"

"Don't shout," I told her, too astonished at the grounds for her attack to be immediately angry, though I could feel blood heating my temples. "That child is sleeping. You can thank heaven *you* don't have to wake and get used to having only one foot!"

"If it weren't impossible, I'd think she was yours, got in a bush someplace. What a fuss, all for a Yaqui whelp!"

"Be quiet," I said. The words broke in my throat. I heard the saw again, hacking bone, glimpsed the poker, smelled seared flesh. "Go away, damn you."

"And leave you with *him?*" she demanded, pointing at Trace.

I walked some distance from the house. She hesitated, then with a toss of her fiery head, she came after me. "You must come back to Las Coronas at once," she decreed. "The witch will see to the girl. But no one can mend your reputation if this gets about."

It was a good time to make it clear that my behavior would shortly cease to be any of her concern. "Sewa cannot travel for several days," I said. "I want to bring her back to Las Coronas till her leg is fully healed. But then, my sister, I will take her and go away."

Surprised relief showed in her face before her eyes narrowed, swung to Trace, who was out of earshot, then back to me. "Where? Where can you go?"

"Hermosillo is the capital of the state, is it not? I might live there. Do not concern yourself. It's plain you don't want me at Las Coronas."

Reina's jaw dropped. "But our mother asked—"

My eyes stung and my throat ached. Why did it have to be this way with my only kin in all the world? "Mother didn't know you hated me," I said. "I can't help it. Maybe you can't, either. But it's plain we could never live at peace. So ride home. Put your mind at rest about my good name. It's none of your concern."

"That *pistolero,*" she said between her small perfect teeth. "Has he made you brave? Offered protection?"

There was no use talking to her. I turned to go. She caught my wrist, snapping me around. That did it.

"Take your hands off me," I said.

Her fingers dug into my skin. I raised my free arm, meaning to hit her as hard as I could. Trace Winslade who had come up soundlessly, stepped between us, moving Reina forcibly away.

"That's it," he said. "Miranda, the child is waking. Better go to her." As I started for the house, he said to Reina, "Señorita, shall I tell Lázaro to escort you to Las Coronas?"

"Suppose I order you to take me?"

My ears strained for his answer, given in a politely expressionless tone. "I should tell you, señorita, to, as we *yanqui-tejanos* say, go chase yourself."

What she said to that I couldn't hear, but as I stepped inside the hut, I heard voices, including Lázaro's rumble, then hoofbeats. As my eyes grew accustomed to the dim light, I saw the girl's eyes were open, though she didn't seem to be aware of anything.

"Sewa?" Dropping beside her, I took her small brown hand in mine. It was limp, gave a chilling impression of lifelessness. "Sewa!"

Cruz spoke from the door. "I have some soup for her, also a little honey. Can you hold her while I feed her?"

I raised her against me. She took wooden spoonfuls of a tasty-smelling broth, opening her lips when Cruz touched them like some sort of spring-wound toy. But after the honey had dissolved in her mouth, she chewed the comb as if to obtain more sweetness. So she could still taste, still desire, and when I moved a bit to ease my cramped legs, her fingers tightened on mine.

"She should drink a lot," Cruz said. "And I will steep manzanilla, a plant that brings sleep, into her tea for this day and tomorrow. Sleep heals. But it cannot last too long."

"What if you hadn't been here?" I asked. "Or if Mr. Winslade hadn't known you?"

"To ponder ifs is trying to find the first sand of a desert." His face creased into deeper lines that I took for a smile. "If I were asking questions, I would wonder what brought you from a far country in time to save a life. For saving life is a heavy obligation."

"I don't understand."

Cruz brought a bowl of tea and together we got Sewa to drink it. "Her life would have ended without your intervention. In a way, you gave her life. So you are responsible for what she does."

I didn't like his idea at all. "That's frightening," I said. "Anyway, I don't believe it. It's natural to help other people but quite something else to be held to account for whatever they do."

Cruz's smile only grooved deeper. I had been too disturbed to notice him much last night, but now I saw that he moved with the lithe wiriness of a young man. He wasted no motion. His plentiful coarse black hair was clubbed in back with a piece of rawhide and his eyes were a strange pale gray like the flake left on charred wood.

"Tell your heart not to pound so fast, señorita. Lives are so bound together that at the last we are both responsible and blameless, the bow that bends and the string that draws the arrow that is our will."

While we were speaking, Sewa had drowsed. Cruz helped me to ease her to the pallet. He adjusted the poncho beneath her stump so that it was lowered slightly, studied her for a moment, and nodded. "She will recover. She is strong. And if it daunts you to be responsible for her, señorita, remember that Trace and I share that with you. In a way we have become her godparents." Those light eyes twinkled. "Among Yaquis that is a serious relationship. And I'm sure that makes us *compadres*. Could you have dreamed, in England, that you would be related, even ceremonially, to an ancient Yaqui and a Texas horse tamer?"

Following out the door, I said dryly, "I'm not sure that I am. I suppose Mr. Winslade told you I am from England. But how did you know we were coming last night?"

He shrugged. "It is something that happens. I was asleep and suddenly I was with you in the canyon. I could see the child's wound. So I got up and made ready."

"Can you see like that anytime you want to?"

"No. It is like a veil that moves back and forth. Sometimes I can draw it at will. Other times it hangs there, so thin I can almost pierce it, so fragile it seems my breath should move it, but utterly impenetrable."

"Then it's no use asking where Mr. Winslade is?"

"Use your ears," Cruz advised.

When I listened, I heard the crunch of footsteps, and in a few minutes more Trace came in sight. "I watered the horses," he explained. "There's enough grass that I think they'll stay in this end of the canyon without being hobbled unless your goats run them off."

"My goats are peaceable," said Cruz. "But they're protective of their young."

"I noticed," said Trace, laughing and rubbing an elbow. "I went over a pile of rocks like a jackrabbit when that biggest one took after me. But I guess I'll forgive her if that's her cheese you've got there."

Cruz had been putting tortillas and cheese on a wooden slab by the bowls we had used for tea last night. He now filled these with steaming coffee from the pot sitting on the can stove in the ramada.

"After breakfast I must go count the kids," he said. "They are young and foolish and sometimes get caught in thickets or wedged between rocks."

"And they never get very smart," said Trace, wrapping a tortilla around the pale soft cheese.

"There you are mistaken." Cruz wagged a reproving finger

at Trace. They seemed excellent friends who respected each other but did not have to weigh words. "Goats are like people. Some are stupid, some are crazy, most ordinary, and a few highly intelligent. My goats are intelligent."

"Of course." Trace grinned.

"Not of course," said Cruz austerely. "Because I began with a clever pair and have always slaughtered off dullards. The goats in my canyon are some of them eight generations of the fittest."

That sounded rather like Mr. Darwin, but I felt sorry for those dullard goats. Surely they felt the knife as much as their intelligent brethren?

"What are you thinking, Miss Greenleaf?" Trace's voice made me jump. I noticed somewhat wistfully that "Miranda" was gone. He must have called me that last night to give me courage.

I almost choked on a swallow of coffee. "I—I was thinking stupid goats enjoy life, too."

Trace's blue-green eyes widened. His long mouth twisted in a way that held back laughter. "I'm sure you're right," he granted. "But it's sadly true that any stupid creature is more likely to fall in traps and be less able to defend itself than brighter individuals."

"But mightn't there be some valuable traits that don't necessarily go along with ability to survive? Would you call Socrates less valuable to mankind than Attila?"

Trace gave me a long, considering look. "I never heard of either man—if they were men," he said. "But of course there's more to life than being strongest or richest or smartest—or even most beautiful. There are things we all can do. Breathe good air, enjoy the food we get, look at what's happening in the world and how lovely and cruel and great it is."

As if he read my thoughts, Cruz added, "Sewa can do these things and many more. If being lame makes her slower, she may see and savor what many run past."

"I must look over the horses and pick a few for Court Sanders, who runs Mina Rara," Trace said. "The ride might interest Miss Greenleaf if you can look after the child till evening."

"I must watch her closely today in any case," Cruz said. "Perhaps you could count my goats on your way. There should be six kids." His ash-colored eyes scanned me. "Señorita, the sun has burned you. Before you ride today, let me give you an ointment."

"Good idea," said Trace. "And wear my hat. I've got another I can pick up."

My face did feel well-boiled and I hadn't done my hair that morning. Just as well there was no mirror, especially after Cruz carefully smeared a greenish stuff on my face and neck, explaining that it was aloes. I sighed ruefully at my stained riding habit, which was by now snagged in numerous places. It was past repair, though my skin should right itself in time. Again I told myself it was lucky I needn't be at pains to spare my clothes; I could follow Trace through any brush without worrying.

"You're sure Sewa won't need me?" I asked.

"You would only tire yourself watching by her today," said Cruz. "Tomorrow it will be important that you are close, and that will not be easy. Any good hours you can have today will help you and Sewa, so enjoy them with a free heart."

I went in to see her while Trace was getting the horses. She slept, face tucked against her arm, the flute under her hand. Merciful that Cruz could give her sleep, but soon she would have to face the loss of her foot. I'd do whatever I could. Perhaps an artificial foot could be made. But nothing could restore the bend of her ankle, the use of a living part of her body. Nothing could bring back her family.

Brushing hair from her face, I bent suddenly to kiss her, a deep fierce tenderness rooting itself in me. She would be my sister and my child. I would take care of her. For the first time since my mother died, I felt less alone.

The horses of Las Coronas were loosely separated according to color. There was a predominance of blacks because the primal stallion of these horses, brought over by the Spaniards, had been a magnificent black. But now there were duns, bays, roans, and grays. Each band of thirty to eighty had its own range and was kept in line by a lead mare and the stallion who protected and utterly dominated his harem.

"Court wants a gray gelding about sixteen hands high," mused Trace as we turned up a box canyon where a gray herd found such graze as it could. "I think Roque has a good three-year-old that'll do, providing it's free of blemishes."

"Mr. Sanders dislikes imperfections?"

"That's not the word for it. He's near crazy when it comes to things he owns or uses. They have to be the best. He paid a sight of money once for a fancy gun. When it jammed on him, he just tossed it down a gorge."

"His wife must have a perilous time of it!"

"She would, if he had one." Trace's lip curled. "He's from some high-powered Yankee family—reckon he thinks nobody south of Boston is good enough for him to marry."

Gazing out at the horses, he dismissed Court and spoke with the drawl I found so delightful. "Would you believe that all the horses in Mexico and South America came from those brought by the Spaniards, along with most of those in the western United States?"

"The English brought horses," I argued.

He shrugged. "Sure. So did the Dutch and French, but precious few of them got west of the Mississippi till after the War Between the States. The very first horse to run wild in this country is supposed to have been a colt foaled on one of Cortez's ships a few days before they landed. When its mother died on the march into the mountains, the colt was lost, and when seen again, it was living with a herd of deer."

"So it found a family," I exclaimed, charmed.

Trace glanced at me, his eyes serious though he was smiling. "It's surprising how often animal orphans do. I knew a hen that mothered a kitten and a fawn that grew up with dogs."

"Really? What happened to the fawn?"

Trace's smile faded. "Some strange dogs killed it."

"Oh!"

He shrugged, reining his horse about. "Don't be too sorry for the fawn. He had a few good years of frolic. Guess he never lived with the fear his wild kin had, always ready to run."

A short fearless life or a long one bought by constant vigilance? I thought of Sewa and wondered if she would rather have died than live a cripple. Saddened, I rode after Trace.

We rode down a box canyon toward a band of horses ranging in color from cream to buff. "The ones with black streaks along their spines are coyote duns," Trace said. "Some people think they're throwbacks to the first horses in all the world and that they can stand more than other colors."

"Do you?"

He grinned. "I've had good horses of every shade. This *manada* has the top stallion, though. He has about fifty mares, double what most can handle."

I gazed at the magnificent silver-gold creature grazing on a rise behind and to one side of the herd. "You mean he's their husband?" I fumbled, felt blood wash up to the roots of my hair at Trace's startled hoot of laughter.

"You might say that," he managed. "He's a protector-tyrant who keeps the herd together, breeds the mares, and fights off dangers. Only the best stallions can do this, so the heritage from a range sire is usually strong. Trouble is, any mare looks good to a stallion, he's as unparticular as a drunken cowboy at the end of a trail drive."

"That must not be a mare he's after, then. Look! He's driving that horse away."

To the far side, a horse had tried to slip in among the stragglers, but the stallion drove at him fiercely, biting the haunch, ramming the stray's ribs with the crest of his neck. The intruder fled. The stallion chased him from the canyon, punishing his would-be follower so cruelly that it flattened almost to its belly in its hurry to escape.

"Yearling looking for a home," Trace said. "Stallion cuts them out of the herd, even the fillies, when they get to be that age." He shook his head in rough sympathy as we watched the vanishing youngster. "Reminds me of when I was a kid."

"You didn't have a family?"

"Just an aunt and uncle who didn't want me."

His short answer warned me not to question further. "What'll happen to the colt?"

"He'll hang around with other colts or old stallions past their prime or other lonesome bachelors. In another year he'll probably be sold or gelded for use on the ranch. Only the best are kept for breeding."

The stallion, pacing back triumphantly, snuffed the air as if scenting some totally irresistible odor. He trotted up, arching his neck proudly, to a creamy mare. She tried to evade him in the herd, but he kept after her, nipping her flank and shoulder, driving her to the periphery.

Isolated at last, she sidled nervously, dodging his attempts to mount. Finally she lashed out with her heels. He still pursued. Rearing around, she bit at him, and not coquettishly.

The stallion checked. One could amost sense his bewilderment and thwarted lust. After a moment he went after the mare again—differently, brutally, much as he acted toward the rejected yearling, driving her back into the herd.

"She's like some women," Trace said. "Likes to keep a male stirred up but won't deliver. It's not safe for a woman to try that game in Mexico."

With an almost laughable air of self-righteousness, the stallion trotted back, snuffed where I had seen a mare urinate while the stallion was punishing the recalcitrant mare, and pranced up to a small buckskin.

He snorted and sniffed her, nostrils swelling, made eager whinnying grunts as he lipped her flanks and rump. Then he reared, neck arching, fitting his forelegs over her shoulders to hold her in place. She quivered, bracing. His long thick rod drove into her. She squealed, but his weight held her fixed except for her head, which moved back and forth. Again and again he hunched himself, and at each wretching lunge, she shuddered.

That wild energy—that surging, driving power.

My mouth was dry. Something hot, sweet, melting licked through me, centering low in my belly; I was painfully conscious of my nipples prickling, standing out hard and erect against the soft linen of my chemise. I could not look away as the stallion pumped his force into the mare, his tail flaring high, mane tossing as he sought to exhaust his lust.

His haunches contracted; he gripped the mare with a convulsive spasm, his head fell weakly by her side before he withdrew so suddenly that he almost touched the ground with his rump before he walked off, swinging his head dazedly from side to side. His organ, hard and gorged minutes before, now swung limp, emptied, dripping.

The mare had squealed again as he fell off her, and now she stood shivering. She looked after the stallion, who was still running in that peculiar choppy way. He did not glance back at her, I noticed with wry amusement. Then she dropped her head and began to forage.

For the stallion and his mare it was over. I swallowed, trying to quell the hungry excitement in my loins, and turned to find Trace Winslade watching me.

Fearing that my eyes would reveal what I felt, I dropped my gaze to his hands. Long and brown, they held the reins with a light certainty that could harden to steel in an instant. I could not check a vision of them gripping my thighs, readying me for his pleasure as the stallion held the mare.

If he had touched me then, pulled me from my saddle, I could not have resisted him, would not, in the depths of my body, have wanted to. The mating had filled me with awe—and envy. Raw, primeval abandon, the imperative urge that constantly created power and life. When would I feel it? With whom?

Trace, eyes smoldering as if he guessed my almost uncontrollable longing, swung his horse about. "Sorry." His tone was muffled. "Didn't know that was going to happen. But I guess you'd see it eventually, living on Las Coronas."

"Has—has Reina?"

His broad shoulders stiffened. He didn't answer for a few seconds. When he did, his voice was dry. "Yes."

We rode on in silence, but my thoughts ran riot and my body felt imprisoned, tormented, ready to explode. If the coupling had affected me like this, what would it do to Reina? Sensuous, confident, she wouldn't let Trace turn his back to her, ride off like that.

"Trace!" I called.

"Yes, Miranda?" He reined back slightly but didn't turn.

Plea, protest, accusation, whatever it had been, stuck in my throat. Instead, I blurted, "Trace! Why did the stallion chase the first mare off?"

Without expression, he answered, "She wouldn't let him mount."

I mulled that, part of the mightily intriguing but baffling play that went on between all sexed creatures. If I could understand the stallion's behavior, I believed I'd know more, too, about Trace.

"Does the stallion expect his mares to let him do that anytime he chooses?"

Trace cast me a severely chiding look before his mouth twitched. His head went back and he shook with laughter.

"I don't see what's funny!"

Swallowing his mirth, he scowled again, shoved his dark hair under his hat. "Dammit! I beg your pardon, but— dammit! I don't know what I should tell you, what's fit for ladies."

"Why not the truth?"

I glowed at his approving look. "Maybe that's the best notion." He frowned, carefully thinking out each word. "A stallion won't pester a mare unless it *is* the right time. When he smells her, and he can from a long way off, it drives him wild. All he has on his mind is mounting her. If she won't take him, he drives her back and finds another." He added grimly, "Might be better for people if it was that clear and simple for them."

Dr. Mattison had been explicit about corsets and childbed fever, but he'd never gone into explanations of what happened inside all those tender parts he didn't want steel and whalebone to compress. We girls had speculated and tried piecing together bits and pieces of information, but nothing had foreshadowed the way I felt now.

"Are people like that?" My cheeks flamed, but I had to ask, try to comprehend what was happening to me. "Do they have a—a right time?"

I shrank from his astonished laughter. He saw that and sobered contritely, though a spark of indulgent humor lingered in his eyes. "Men are generally ready—too ready, I guess. Some women never are, though I'd reckon that comes from what they're taught and trained to, crazy ideas about what's ladylike."

He spoke with such disgust that I said defensively, "You don't seem to have much use for ladies."

"I prefer women."

"And how do you define a woman?"

"She enjoys her body, being with a man."

"A lady can't?"

"Not and admit it." He grinned, white teeth shocking in his dark face. "If she admits it, she's no lady."

"You mean you wouldn't respect her?"

"Now who said that?" he growled. "It's *women* I respect. They know who and what they are. Ladies! Crippled with clothes and rules, all cramped and caged! I'm sorry for the lot of them."

Was it his scorn or the memory of the stallion thrusting hugely into the trembling mare that drove me to demand in a queer breaking voice that I scarcely recognized, "Am I a woman, Trace?"

"By God!" A vein pounded in his temple. He was out of the saddle, trailing the reins, brought me from my mount. "Let's find out! You've been driving me crazy, but I figured that raised in that fancy school, not much more than a kid . . . "

His voice muffled in my hair as he caught me up, carried me to down the wash where the sand was clean and bare. My bones melted in spite of vague warnings in my head. I didn't want to resist his hard warm hands, which found their way inside my clothes to stroke my breasts, my tightening loins, smooth my legs and thighs as his tongue teased my nipples. His tongue and teeth nibbled my breasts and belly, nipping lightly in a way that made me moan and lift myself toward him, craving deeper, sharper sensations, the force he was holding back. His hand caressed the soft swollen place between my legs, explored and played till I arched my back, filled with urgent cresting need.

And then he swore.

He straightened, yanking down my skirt, turning away.

"Trace?"

"Goddammit!" He groaned, hit the sand with his fist. "You're a virgin!"

"I don't care. It doesn't matter!" I caught his shoulder, trying to bring him down to me again. "I don't want to be a lady."

He smiled briefly. "Don't worry, Miranda Greenleaf. You won't be."

"Then—"

He shook his head, smoothed my hair. "I can't take your maidenhead."

"Why?"

"The man who has you first should marry you."

"I don't care about that."

He stared at the distant mountains. "You will, Miranda. You'll care one hell of a lot when a man you want to marry won't stand up in church with you because you're not a virgin."

"He won't be one either!"

Trace laughed wearily. "Poor baby, if you think that'll cut any ice!"

It was all so many words, hard and pitiless as hailstones. "Please!" Sitting up, I leaned against him, shameless with ungratified desire and the frustrated rage of a child promised a tabooed delight that's been snatched away. "Please, Trace. Show me."

Sucking in his breath, the muscles in his face so taut he looked cadaverous, he jerked me to my feet, roughly fumbled my bodice shut, brushed sand from my skirts.

"Come on!" He dragged me toward the horses, almost hurled me to the saddle.

His hand brushed my knee, pressed convulsively against it. Sweet dizzying warmth radiated through me. He was breathing hard. He took his hand from me, knuckles showing white.

"Damn you, Miranda! For damn sure you better save what I didn't take for the man who'll marry you."

"Damn yourself." To my chagrin, I was sobbing. "Why did you start what you won't finish? Why?"

He swung away, caught up the reins. "Because of your

folks," he said, once he had vaulted into the saddle. "Because you're a child."

"I—I'm not!"

Heeling my mare, I shot past him. Not looking back, I hoped fiercely that the ache thrumming deep in my loins was matched by a similar pain in him.

Women, ladies, virgins!

What did names have to do with the sweetness of his hands and tongue tuning me like an instrument he then refused to play?

5

It was late afternoon when Trace had given Roque and Juan, the two remaining vaqueros, instructions about which horses to catch for delivery to the ranch when Sewa and I were ready to go back. He got his old hat from his adobe and some coffee and beans, treating me with the elaborate casualness he had practiced since those incredible moments in the wash.

"Don't like to eat up Cruz's provender," he explained. "I pretty well keep him in coffee anyhow in return for his help when a horse gets sick or hurt."

"And because he saved your life?"

"Oh, that'll take a lot of paying back. And the way his people are being treated, I imagine Cruz may ask me to do something for Yaquis rather than just him."

"What?" I demanded.

He shrugged. "They need guns."

"But wouldn't that make you a rebel?" In spite of my bewildered anger at Trace, a thrill of fear ran through me.

He grinned briefly. "Dear lady, I sure don't mean to get caught."

"I hope he won't ask you to run guns."

Trace seemed to lose interest in the subject. "Don't worry about it," he advised.

As we rode back into the canyon where the Yaqui lived, we circled to where a small flock of goats was rambling. Kids frolicked and seemed to skip along the small hills.

"Six of the little boogers," Trace said. "We can tell Cruz he hasn't lost any."

"What's that beneath that tree?" I asked, leaning forward. Something black moved jerkily in the grass.

We rode closer. "It's a raven," said Trace. "A young one. He looks big enough to fly. Must be hurt—"

Dismounting, he went swiftly to where the bird frantically tried to escape, fluttering its wings, tumbling sideways. As Trace bent to pick it up, it jabbed him with a beak that was out of proportion to the rest of its body. Trace picked it up anyway, looked up in the tree, then examined the bird with deft fingers.

"He has a broken leg and the wing's damaged," he said. "Even if the parents would take him back in the nest, he'd get shoved out again, and he can't get away from anything that fancies it as a mouthful. Guess it'd be kinder to wring his neck."

"Oh, no! Let's give him to Sewa. Maybe she could feed him while she's getting well. It might be good for her to have a pet."

"We can try." Trace handed the raven to me, taking great care, I thought, not to brush my fingers. "Hold him so he can't peck your hand in case he gets rambunctious again. He's got a sharp bill."

Cruz splinted the raven's wing and leg, though he didn't think either could be used much except for balance. He put the bird in an old basket cushioned with grass and fed it meal softened with water. "He'll give the child something to think about," Cruz said. "But I think he'll never fly."

And she will never run, I thought, watching the little brown girl. But she can do other things. She still had sight, hearing, hands, everything but a foot. She could be happy someday in spite of the wretched things that had happened. She *would* be.

Cruz had saved some corn gruel for us. We ate that and some of Trace's invincible jerky, then went to bed early, for tomorrow would be a hard one for Sewa and Trace needed to go back to his work till she was able to travel. I told myself I'd be well rid of this baffling, disturbing man, yet all night long I dreamed of him.

I woke to hoarse croaking, frightened till I saw the raven floundering about. Sewa was watching him with interest, though her face was drawn and her skin had an ashen cast. Cruz came in as I sat up.

He gave Sewa some meal pellets and talked to her, evidently explaining about the bird, for she made a sound under her breath and peered at him, then presented him with a bit of the damp meal. The beak closed hungrily on it and the scrawny raven lifted its head, gulping, then looked for more.

Though she must have been in pain, Sewa laughed delightedly and fed the bird till all the pellets were gone, timidly touching the black feathers. I hoped he wouldn't peck her. He didn't, perhaps already understanding that he would be fed, not hurt, by these strange creatures.

Cruz refilled his water shell and fetched a bowl of tea, which he told me to give Sewa. While I propped her against me, she stared at her bandaged stump, eyes very wide, her soft mouth pressed tight.

Did she remember? She turned her cheek against me as if hiding from the sight. "Oh, my sweet," I said brokenly, though she could not understand. "It's terrible. Horrid! But perhaps we can get you an artificial foot, and anyway you can do lots of things. You must get well and then—"

I couldn't go on and turned my face so my tears wouldn't fall on her. "Give her the tea," Cruz ordered. And while I blinked and controlled my nervous fingers, guiding the bowl to her lips, he talked to her at length, calmly, matter-of-factly, even with an occasional laugh. Then he picked up the flute and played, a gay trilling melody like the dance of sun on rippling water and changed into birdcalls at dusk.

"Awk! Awwwk!" went the raven. He lurched toward Cruz, perhaps deciding this was some kind of superbird. Sewa gave a small cry of pleasure, looked at Cruz pleadingly.

He smiled and gave her the flute, demonstrating which holes to close. After a few strange discords, she coaxed out a very creditable note, and then another and another. The raven scrambled over to her, splinted wing and lame leg dragging, settled against her side.

It was a long, long day. I bathed Sewa from water Cruz brought in a gourd; brushed her hair, though it was no time to work out the dusty tangles; held tea to her lips when her fever rose. But she played the flute often, even when her face twisted with pain and sweat dewed her forehead and upper lip, and the raven responded with his raucous notes. When I tried to imagine what the hours would have been without the bird and the music, I could not bear it.

I stayed by Sewa all that day, and Cruz sat with us often. He talked in Yaqui to her and I guessed that he was telling stories even before she laughed and repeated, "Ku!" Then she touched the raven's black head and said again, "Ku."

"So he's named," Cruz explained. "She has called him after the Ku bird."

"The what?"

Cruz laughed. "A very handsome creature in Yaqui legend. He had no feathers at all, but the birds pitied his nakedness and each gave him a feather so that he had a thousand colors. In a year, when he would have grown new plumage, he promised to return the borrowed feathers. But he vanished, that most beautiful of birds, and no one has seen him since. Some say he is enchanted and lives in a pool near the sea." Lightly, Cruz touched the alert black head of the young raven. "It is said truly that love is blind. What else could give this sooty fellow the shades of a jewel rainbow?"

Ku, to me, resembled a raffish bandit of callow years, in black swagger too big for him. But he diverted Sewa all that harrowing day. She never cried, but sometimes her small form grew so tense that I rubbed her arms and shoulders and the back of her thin neck till my own fingers ached.

"I'll give her the sleeping herb now," Cruz decided when the late sun shone in through the door and dyed the walls ember red. "Her body is healing itself now. The poison has not spread."

"She would have died without you," I said.

"Or you," he added. "Or who knows? Perhaps it was the flute and the Ku bird that made her want to live."

Cruz brought more meal and a few bugs for Sewa to feed her pet before she had her soup and soporific tea. Trace got back in time to sit by her and hear how her wonderful bird had been named and watch a demonstration of how Ku croaked along with the flute. Trace held the child's hand while her eyelids drooped. When she was breathing deeply, he gently freed himself and motioned to me. I put Ku in his nest and followed Trace to the ramada.

"Lázaro rode back this morning," he said. "Your sister would like to discharge me, but she can't under the terms of her mother's will." He managed to sigh, shrug, and grin all at once. "We may be in for interesting times at Las Coronas. I think I'm going to find plenty to do at the different sections."

I had caused the trouble. As we sat down to share a pot of beans, tortillas, and strong coffee, I told Trace that Reina would doubtless be easier to deal with once I was gone.

"Gone?" Even in the twilight, his eyes shone. "Where can you go?"

"There's money for me," I answered, fighting the trembling of my lips. "I can go to Hermosillo, perhaps. Mexico City. Somewhere."

"Alone?" He sounded horrified, which was strangely gratifying, though it didn't say much for his estimation of my survival powers. I knew young women were normally not supposed to be able to endure without a male guardian or formidable maiden aunt, but it was clearly an ability I would have to assume, like a virtue, if I had it not.

"I shall take Sewa," I explained.

"And the Ku, no doubt!" Trace sounded angry, switching into English. "Miranda, you little fool, women, especially toothsome pretty ones, don't go traipsing around Mexico alone!"

"I can't stay at Las Coronas."

"Your mother wished you to."

I swallowed hard, eyes stinging as bitter hurt and regret welled up over my crushed hopes of finding family warmth with Reina. "She didn't know how—how it would be. Las Coronas is my sister's home. I must find another."

My voice broke. Trace poured my bowl full of the pungent

coffee. "Drink up," he commanded. "Then we're going for a walk and talk this over. For a properly brought-up English lady you don't seem to have any sense at all."

I tried to fire up at that remark but was too grateful for his concern. Also, there was something in the mood between us that echoed the madness that had sent us into the wash. To be alone in the night . . .

Now, though tingling with awareness, I was also frightened, half afraid he might decide to take what he had refused. In the sanity following my frustrated desire, I'd realized well enough what it would mean to be "ruined." But even as I told myself that Trace would observe the conventions and I must hold him to them if he showed signs of wavering, deep in the center of my being, I knew he could take me if he went about it properly, roused those tempestuous feelings that had utterly vanquished my fears and modesty.

I was throbbingly conscious of him as we cleared up after the simple meal. His voice was strained and husky when he told Cruz we were going for a walk and not to wait up for us.

Was it a trick of light from the dying cook fire or did Cruz smile? "I'll sleep in the door so I can hear the child if she rouses. Walk in moonlight."

Trace took my arm. I had to fight to keep from swaying weakly against him. Trace mercifully appeared not to notice. After a moment, the heavy faintness left me and we started down the canyon. It was a silver-blue night, the grass and flat land luminous—*cardones,* arroyos, and mountains limned dark. Nesting birds, alarmed at our passage, winged from their homes in cholla and paloverdes.

"It's too bad they can't know we won't hurt them," I said, and then blushed at such a childish remark.

Trace sat on a rock ledge, drawing me down beside him. "If we were hungry, we would," he said, an edge of roughness to his voice. "It's one thing to be benevolent on a full belly and another when you're starving."

"If you're going to extremes," I began, surprised and somewhat hurt by his manner, "no usual rules hold."

"They told you that in school, but you don't really know it," he said. "You're in Mexico, Miranda, in the desert. Extremes are the rule."

"You mean I have to change? Grow thorns or a poison sting?"

"God forbid." His tone was fervent. "It's just that you don't—can't—have any idea of what goes on here, what can happen to a woman traveling or living alone."

"I've watched Sewa," I reminded him. "And if you've heard of Jack the Ripper, Trace, you know nothing worse could happen to me here."

"Nothing bad should ever happen to a girl with a name like yours." He laughed, soft and deep in his throat, as if with pure pleasure. "It's a nice name, Miranda. Fresh and springlike—English, the way you look. It hums in my mind like that other old song, you'd be surprised how often. 'Greenleaf was all my joy, Greenleaf was my delight. . . .' "

"Trace!" I protested, though my heart sang. Did he think of me, even if it was only because I had a strange name? "That sounds ridiculous!"

"So does 'Greensleeves' unless you're used to it," he argued. "A leaf's a damn sight prettier than any sleeves I ever saw!" I didn't know how to answer. He turned and stared at the mountains. "May I call you Miranda, Miranda?"

"I wish someone would," I said. "Greenleaf does belong to England, just as in a way my father always did. But Miranda's me."

"That's a very proper name for what must be an explosive mixture," he teased, shifting back toward me a little. "French and Spanish on your mother's side, English from your father."

"The English is jumbled up, too," I admitted. "There's Saxon crossed with Norman and Celt and some shipwrecked officer from the Spanish Armada memorialized himself in my grandmother from Cornwall."

Trace chuckled. "Funny how purebred the English seem to Americans. Actually, I'm Scotch-Irish and Welsh, and that's it."

"Those bad rebel bloods," I joked.

"Reckon so. The men in my family always seemed to be jumping out of frying pans into the fire. They'd have all been hanged or shot long ago if they hadn't generally married peaceable women."

It struck me with a pang that he was old enough to have married, that he might still be. "Have you?" I asked, trying to sound playful.

"Have I what?"

"Married a peaceable woman?"

Pale light washed the stone of his face. "No. I married one who loved to dance."

My heart lunged. To hide how I felt, I bantered with him. "Surely a woman can dance and be peaceable."

"It's the *way* she danced." I could almost picture her, smiling, luring, glancing up at men from under lashes as she moved from one to the other.

Silence grew between us, heavy, full of questions I both needed and feared to ask. At last he said, "I don't know where she is. I killed a man who danced with her too often, and she must have thought I'd do the same to her. She ran away."

"Was that why you left Texas?"

"No one blamed me for killing the man. But he was the sheriff's brother."

"But that wouldn't make you a *pistolero*," I said, then clapped my hand to my mouth.

Trace laughed bitterly. "Is that what Reina called me? She was right enough. I worked on a ranch in the Big Bend, where rustlers were busy, and sometimes I did more gunwork than cow." He shrugged. "I've made my mistakes. But what we've got to talk about, Miss Miranda Greenleaf, is how to keep you from making very serious ones."

"There's no use telling me to live at Las Coronas."

He rubbed his chin. "Reckon not. But don't you have some relations?"

"Distant ones in England. Father quarreled with them years ago and the present squire has hosts of marriageable daughters. They won't want me—and I don't want them!"

The thought of going back to green, peaceful, shady, *dull* England was so impossible that I knew I never would.

Turning to Trace, I said urgently, "There really isn't *anyone*. I just have to make my own home."

"We can do a little better than send you out blindfold. I have some friends in Hermosillo. I'll take you and Sewa up there and get you settled, introduce you to folks who could look out for you. Chances are someone would have room enough for you to stay with them till you decide what to do."

"You're very kind, but since I must rely on myself, perhaps the sooner I start the better."

"Miranda."

Something in his voice stabbed to my depths. Why, oh, why did he have to have a wife? I wondered if Reina knew and if there was anything between them. He had been kind. I could scarcely help loving him. But he mustn't guess that or he'd pity me, find me pathetic.

"Miranda," he said again.

I slid down from the ledge, but he was suddenly before me, and though he kept his arms rigidly at his sides, I feared to move past him. I knew instinctively that a motion of mine could send him out of that tight control. Though I thrilled to the thought, whatever went on between men and women was to me a fascinating, somewhat terrifying matter of conjecture. The depth of my ignorance had me believing it was blood, not semen, that men discharged. In spite of what had happened after we watched the stallion, I still didn't know exactly what went on between men and women, both wanted and feared it. I waited by the rock, pinioned by eyes that had taken on the cool glow of the moon.

"I never worried much about my crossed trails," he said, keeping his hands at his sides. "But they've got me where I can't say or do what I'd like to. I can't—won't—hurt you, Miranda."

I *was* hurting, and I knew he was. A yearning that was more than desire was almost palpable between us. As if to break his silent intensity, he spoke in a louder tone. "I owe your parents my life. If you let me help you, it's the only way I can ever pay them back."

It would be ungracious and foolish to refuse an offer made like that. Even though the future could not be guessed at, knowing this enigmatic man would be my friend made me feel much safer. I managed a shaky smile.

"Thank you, Trace."

He gave a quick nod of satisfaction. "Good. When Sewa can travel, I'll take you to Hermosillo." He slipped his hand beneath my elbow, turning back down the canyon. "Don't forget, Miranda. As long as I live, you have a friend."

Friend?

I should have been glad of that, but I felt a surge of anger at his marriage, the woman in his past who barred him from me, everything that forbade my loving him. Overwhelmed, I looked up at him. "Oh, Trace!" I said forlornly. Then, in this strange world of moon and shadow, I could say what I never would have by day. "Trace, kiss me."

A tremor went through him. I felt a surge of power, of confidence, almost as if I were the older, experienced one. Taking his hands, I kissed them, carried them to my breasts, excited by his hesitation. His breath escaped in a shuddering sigh. He brought me into his arms, bent his head, and kissed me, parting my lips, finding my tongue with his.

"All right," he said in a funny, ragged tone. "All right, my sweetheart. I can do something for you. Make you feel good without hurting you for marriage."

"But that doesn't sound fair for you, Trace."

He shrugged. "Don't worry. I'll love it—just seeing you, holding you, doing what I can." He had brought me down on a flat rock ledge, his hands opening my bodice, freeing my breasts, molding them with his fingers, which lightly brushed the tips till I arched against him, avid for his caresses, his mouth, the long hard length of his body.

He nuzzled my nipples with lips and tongue. One hand pushed aside my skirts, stroked up to the eagerness between my legs, toyed in a way that brought parts of me alive that had slept till now. Then, as the friction of his hand, though pleasurable, became a bit painful, his tongue left my breast, and in a second I felt a slow deep stroking, an incredibly sensitive yet virile exploration varied with light, swift flicks that sent liquid fire through me, centered it beneath that sure expert tongue that stroked faster, faster, coaxing till that secret part of me seemed to burst into lovely pulsating explosions.

My own voice, moaning, called me back to reality. "Trace! Oh, that was heavenly!"

He laughed softly, held me with my head on his shoulder. I could hear the heavy pound of his heart.

"Am I a woman now?" I ventured.

He laughed, held me closer, stroking my back. "Almost. Almost, Miranda."

"Is that what happens?"

"What you felt should happen, but it can be caused in different ways. What you had was the pleasure without the problems."

I thought about that.

"Is there a way for you? A way you can feel good without whatever it is we mustn't do?"

He didn't answer. I sat upright and tugged at his shoulder. "Is there, Trace?"

"Yes," he admitted slowly. "But—Oh, hell, Miranda! You shouldn't know such things! What are you getting me into?"

"Please?" The completion, the delight I had experienced, made me feel rich and generous, eager to make him happy, too. "Trace, show me what to do."

"I don't need paying back."

"Show me."

He took my hand, did something with his clothes. My fingers encountered something hard and warm, vulnerable and eager. The sharp intake of his breath, the way he lay surrendered with that strangely independent part absolutely rigid, filled me with wonder. I stroked and fondled, keying the pace to his response, my own excitement mounting as he thrust against my hand, pushed and delved and gasped, crying out my name. He spent it all in a convulsive arching that reminded me of the golden stallion's final effort, lay back exhausted as a warm thick fluid filled my palm.

We lay under the moon on the stone slab. Whatever he said about virginity, I felt as much his as if we had been joined in front of an altar. I was only sad that the energy, the beautiful force he had vented in my hand had not entered into me.

The next day was much like the one before, except that Sewa appeared a bit stronger, ate with more relish. Cruz taught her more tunes on the flute and she would practice to Ku's glee. When she was absorbed with her music and the raven, Cruz told me more about the Yaquis.

They had lived since remembered times along the mouth of the Río Yaqui, which twice yearly overflowed the rich land along its banks so that corn, beans, and squash could be raised in abundance. According to tradition, after a great flood, a group of angels joined Yaqui prophets and traveled from south to north, "singing the boundary," and ordaining the sacred limits of Yaqui territory. After that, the Yaqui prophets had visions at eight different places, locations for "the Eight Sacred Pueblos." Though the Yaquis bloodily repulsed Spanish military might, they had accepted the Jesuit priests who came to live among them in 1617 and the Indians wove the Catholic faith into their own myths and traditions. Spanish religious policy clashed with political, however, and the Jesuits were expelled in 1767. From 1825 till his execution in 1833 Juan Banderas, the great Yaqui general, fought the Mexican government's attempts to tax the Yaquis, divide their lands, and assimilate them. After his death, Cajeme and Juan Maldonado Tetabiate took up the struggle against the Mexicans.

Blending old patterns with the Jesuit mission system, the Yaquis had evolved a way of government that suited them very well. All matters of importance to a pueblo were discussed at a junta, or village council, attended by the five governors, church officials, members of military and ceremonial societies, and the elders. These leaders decided how problems should be settled; they could punish offenders by lashes of a rawhide whip, a time in the stocks, or even execution. Cruz had been sentenced to death by such a junta, but he still spoke of the system with respect. When more than two pueblos were concerned, a joint junta was held.

By 1900, the Mexican authorities had decided to settle the Yaqui rebellions once and for all. Yaquis would be watched closely and any resisters would be deported to work far away. The Bacatete Mountains, where rebellious Yaquis hid out and from which they conducted their raids, were surrounded so that Yaquis from the north who wanted to return home to fight could not get through. Since most supplies came from the north, especially Tucson in Arizona, this seriously hampered Yaqui patriots.

"Now Rafael Yzábal, who became governor of Sonora last year in 1903, thinks he has the answer," Cruz said. "Since soldiers, settlers, and extermination have not worked, he's got the federal and state governments to cooperate in a slave trade. Yaquis are sold and transported, men and women, for sixty pesos apiece, to henequen plantations in Yucatán or sugarcane fields in Oaxaca."

"Like Sewa's father," I said, looking at the child, who had drowsed off with the raven crouched against her arm.

Cruz nodded. "Yzábal is killing babies, prostituting girls, and enslaving men and women. He thinks he will grind the Yaquis into the earth, but we are *of* the earth and we will be here after he's dead—he and his friend Ramón Corral, who devised this. Corral is rotting even now of a disease he caught from a whore. I wonder if he thinks his blood gold will comfort him in hell?"

Cruz also told me that he wasn't a witch but a *sabio*, "one who knows." He hadn't worked for the power or wanted it, and even now it wasn't completely under his control. Sometimes he "saw" what was happening, or what would happen, or where a lost thing was, or what sickness a person had and what would cure it. It was when he hadn't been able to heal the brother of one of the governors of his pueblo that he was accused of being a witch.

"And Yaqui law is that a condemned prisoner shall spend three days in the jail, arms tied, without food or water. Three *madrinas* and three *padrinos*, his godparents, make him a brown burial robe and each puts a Yaqui rosary about his neck. The *maestros* chant the funeral liturgy for three days and then most prisoners are shot. But a witch is tossed, bound, into the fire. And so, in my second night in the jail, I worked my bonds loose and escaped by the help of one of my *madrinas* who didn't know whether or not I was innocent but didn't want me to die in either case."

"Was that long ago?"

"One forgets. It was before Cajeme drove out the Mexicans in 1876. Call it thirty years."

"And you've never gone back?"

He gave me a wry look with those ash-colored eyes. "No. I am a bigger witch than ever since I got away. But some of the villagers come to me now and then and have all gone away cured." He laughed. "A few very love-afflicted ones have come for ways to make their sweethearts love them, but in that witchcraft I do not meddle."

I thought of Trace, that marvelous yet separated way we had made love, and asked before I could stop myself, "Can you see my future, Cruz? Any of it?"

"I have seen you high in the Sierra after great danger."

"Do you know what will happen to Sewa?"

"I have seen her wedding with *pascolas* and a feast and you there watching."

"Are you ever wrong?"

"Not that I know of."

I wanted to ask about Trace, if there would come a time when we could marry but I felt I had no right. Sewa woke then and we played a game we had begun that morning wherein she named things in Yaqui and I in Spanish. When Trace came with twilight, she played one of the tunes she had learned. Ku fluttered excitedly and joined in with cries that made Sewa stop playing and burst into giggles that flushed her cheeks, showed her dimples, and made her look like a happy child for the first time since I had met her.

Trace sang for us that night, cowboy songs that I under-stood little better than Sewa and Cruz because of the peculiar phrases. What, for instance, were "firies and snuffies"? Or little dogies? Surely one didn't "ride round 'em slow" if they were actually dogs. But he sang one I understood, which was lovely and sad as the old English ballads I loved so well, and his eyes were on me so I could scarcely breathe. I longed for his mouth and hands till I burned as if with fever.

> Eyes like a morning star, cheeks like a rose,
> Laura was a pretty girl God Almighty knows;
> Weep all you little rains, wail, winds, wail—
> Up along, all along the Colorado trail.

When Sewa had her sleeping draft, we went to our beds, but I was restless, anxious about the return to Las Coronas and how to find a home later for myself and Sewa. Most of all, I couldn't put the refrain of Trace's song out of my mind or forget the way his black head tilted back as he sang—how gentle he was with Sewa when he had carried her out to see the moon and smell the night scents for a while. What I would have given to have been in his arms like that again and not have him stop because of concern for me or his debt to my parents.

When I fell at last into shallow, dream-filled sleep, I seemed to be with a witch, a *bruja*, who was like Cruz but not him. And I asked for a philter, asked for a charm, the way to make Trace love me.

Then the witch's eyes were turquoise, and he spoke to me in a voice I knew, in Trace's voice, and he said, "I can give you a charm, but it would cost you more than you can pay." And then he faded into the shadows, except for those blue-green eyes and the echo of his words.

Two days later Trace took Sewa and me back to Las Coronas. Cruz walked beside our horses to the end of his canyon and then gave me a bag of herbs I was to brew for Sewa till her leg was completely healed.

I didn't realize how fond I'd become of the old Yaqui, how I'd come to depend on him, till that time of farewell.

"Oh, Cruz," I said, breath catching hard. "Oh, Cruz, thank you—"

"It was my joy to help the child." His eyes twinkled like pale bright stars. "And to hear the song at last of that miraculous Ku of a thousand colors!" He touched my hand to his heart, then spoke softly, strongly to Sewa, who watched him with beautiful grave eyes. He put a staff into her hand, set with turquoise in the top. Then he crossed himself and kissed her forehead before he shook hands with Trace.

The men had rigged a kind of sling on Sewa's saddle so that her stump thrust forward in a cushioned split of bamboo. Ku nested in a basket molded against her saddle horn, cawing hoarsely at the excitement.

We traveled slowly, so that the late moon had set when we rode at last through the gates of Las Coronas. Dogs raised a bloodcurdling din and a man loomed out of the cottonwoods, his rifle barrel reflecting the little light there was. When Trace called out who we were, the guard bowed, escorted us to the house, and held the horses while Trace carried Sewa through the patio to my room and placed her on the couch. She was so tired that I didn't make the tea, but told her good night and moved Ku's basket close to her.

"You need to get to bed yourself," Trace told me when I would have walked back to the horses with him.

"Will I see you before you go back to the horses?"

His teeth flashed in faint light from the bedside candle. "Unless you sleep till noon. Good night, Miranda. Have sweet dreams." Before I could move, he dropped a swift light kiss on my cheek and strode across the patio.

My head and shoulders were being shaken violently. Wrenching away as I opened my eyes, I stared into my half-sister's constricted face.

"Why did he leave without seeing me?" she demanded. "Why?"

I realized with shock that she'd been crying. Her eyes were swollen and her ivory skin had that mottled look that follows heavy weeping. At the same time I felt a stab of hurt disappointment.

"Trace?" I asked, sitting up. "Are you sure he's gone?"

"Of course I am! The guard says he left a few hours after bringing you and this little scarecrow back." Reina watched me narrowly. "He didn't tell you he was going?"

I swallowed, forcing my head high. "No. In fact, he spoke as if he'd be here till noon."

"Ah, *you* feel like crying!" she exclaimed with brutal satisfaction. "So you must be speaking the truth." She glanced at Sewa, who watched with wide dark eyes, cradling her raven. Reina's gaze snagged on the bandaged stump. Her lips curled in disgust. "My God, your contribution to Las Coronas is a

crippled savage. All this fuss for a girl who won't even be able
to work."

For a moment I was too outraged to speak. Flashes of the
last days, that first horrible night with the saw grating bone
came back with dizzying force. Springing out of bed, I pointed
to the door.

"Get out!"

"This is my home."

"And mine, too, if you have any respect for our mother's
wish." Checking, I brought my voice under control and tried
to speak reasonably. "As I have told you, Reina, I intend to stay
here no longer than is necessary." Did Trace's leaving so
abruptly mean he had decided not to be concerned with my
problems, where I went from Las Coronas? That he regretted
making love to me? I writhed inwardly at that thought. "When
Sewa is well, I shall take her and go."

"Where?"

"That is none of your worry."

She stared at me as if her probing eyes could pry out my
thoughts. "Has that *pistolero* promised you help? The help you
will get from that sort is a bastard."

"I can't imagine why you're so interested in Mr. Winslade if
you have such a low opinion of him," I said. "This is a large
house. If you'll stay out of my room, you needn't even know
I'm here. Also, since you grudge it, I'll leave money for our
food when I go."

"Is this how you speak to your guardian?"

"Guardian?" It was my turn to stare. My heart felt as if cold
steel had closed around it.

"You will not be eighteen for another six months." Reina
smiled coldly. "Oh, yes, *hermana mía* I remember very well
when you were born. A useless ugly scrap, but everyone
making such a fuss! Until then, as the oldest of your family,
I'm responsible for you and also in charge."

"But you don't want me at Las Coronas."

"True, but at least I can watch you here, take care you don't
disgrace our name."

It had the horrid ring of fact—a woman seemed always

under the command of men, fathers, brothers, or husbands, and a woman under legal age might as well be feebleminded. Desperately thinking back to the reading of the will, I challenged Reina.

"You may be my guardian, but I recall that any important decisions had to be agreed upon by Mr. Sanders, the lawyer, and Mr. Winslade."

"Important matters, yes." Reina smoothed together her beautifully kept hands. "The sale or buying of land, a change in livestock, acquisition of a fine stallion or bull. But who will question a sister's loving concern for a headstrong girl who does not understand the country or its ways?"

Before he broke his promise and left during the night, I would have counted on Trace to defend me if he knew Reina was abusing her position. But his abrupt departure seemed to say louder than words that he'd decided not to be bothered with me. I felt abandoned, utterly friendless except for the child, crippled, almost as helpless as her skinny raven. Cruz was our friend, but he was far away.

Struggling to maintain outer calm, I strolled over to the grilled window to look out on the patio and for the first time experienced the bars as those of a prison. Careful. I knew with instinctive wisdom that unless and until Reina took the plunge into being wholly oppressive, she had only the power I accorded her. And she was answerable to the men appointed by our mother to help manage our affairs.

"I don't understand you," I said slowly. "We would both be happier if I left Las Coronas."

"You will leave in time," she assured me with a patronizing smile. "Unless I decide it best for an unbalanced sister to remain in the secluded peace of my home."

My blood chilled. Remote as we were, Las Coronas was a private kingdom. It was horribly possible that I could live out my years there as a captive. Only I didn't think Reina could bear my presence, constant reminders that I existed. My history lessons, full of unhappy heirs and hostages spending their entire span in more or less close captivity, sprang into mind: the Pearl of Brittany, pacing the battlements of Corfe Castle so as not to imperil the crown of her wicked uncle John;

the princes in the Tower, once again killed at uncle's behest; Elizabeth Tudor kept close by Bloody Mary, her half-sister, and in her turn imprisoning her tragic kinswoman, Mary Stuart—there was no end to the parade of wasted youth, of walled-in lives. And most had been confined by close relations, those who should have nurtured them.

I didn't know how far Reina would go. She might simply be exercising her power. My continued presence at the ranch could be only a problem and irritation for her, and I didn't really believe her capable of murder. If I seemed to accept her authority, to apparently resign myself to the fate of a young woman still under the tutelage of her kin, she might weary of the game, even exert herself to help me find an alternative dwelling.

If she didn't—well, my acquiescence would throw her off guard. When I had a chance, I'd get away even if it meant Sewa and I had to hide out in the mountains like Sierra Yaqui. If we could get to Cruz, I was sure he'd help us. I thought of Trace and clamped my jaw tight. If I turned up begging on his doorstep, he'd doubtless do *something*, but I'd rather take my chance with strangers. Why had he made such a business about settling me in Hermosillo and then left without a word? He'd seemed genuinely fond of Sewa—one would think he'd care what happened to her if not to me.

Could there have been some reason for his sudden departure? There might have been hundreds, but surely he could have left a message, some kind of explanation with the watchman. No, he must have thought the problem over and decided to keep clear. I shouldn't blame him too much. After all, his best interests lay in getting along with Reina. It was possible that her feeling for him might conquer her pride of name and blood so that he would by marriage acquire wealth no man could scoff at.

Now, turning from the window, I summoned an indifferent shrug and met my sister's inquisitorial look with what I hoped seemed boredom.

"I'd no idea you took your responsibility so much to heart," I told her. "It was only dislike at staying where I seemed unwelcome that ever made me think of going elsewhere. Since

I was mistaken, let me thank you for your concern and go have some breakfast. I find I'm very hungry."

Her eyes widened suspiciously but found nothing to cast doubt on my bland rejoinder. "We must discuss your future in detail at another time," she said.

Turning on her heel, she went down the hall in a swing of divided leather skirts. Air rushed into my lungs and I realized I had been holding my breath. For the moment, at least, my deception was working.

Kneeling by Sewa, I told her with a mixture of gestures, Spanish, and Yaqui that I would bring her some food and cut across the patio to the kitchen.

Consuelo, the youngest maid, wanted to bring me a nicely prepared tray, but I pleaded imminent starvation and collected fresh *sopapillas,* honey, preserves, and two mugs of hot chocolate, added a hunk of brown sugar and a few plums. Consuelo carried the copper tray to my room and set it down on a table before turning to regard Sewa and facing me with a rueful movement of her slim shoulders.

"The poor little one lacks a foot. What can become of her now? She was only let live to be a servant."

The young woman wasn't cruel, merely brought up to consider Indians as wild animals. This struck me as peculiar, for the Yaquis had been devout Christians now for almost three hundred years. Hadn't it always been on grounds of heathenism that Christian conquerors felt justified in subjugating natives? Of course, when I thought about it, I had to admit that Christian nations had butchered each other ferociously even before the Reformation gave them the excuse of checking heresy.

What was it then? Consuelo's skin was dark as Sewa's; there might be a tincture of Spanish blood in her, but she must be predominantly Indian herself, though she would call herself Mexican. This contempt or hatred for a people was the ugliest, most dangerous attitude I could imagine, but it wasn't skin color. I remembered a schoolmate whose father was a wealthy landlord in Ireland; she had spoken of their tenants as one might of a subspecies, despised because they were "brutal," feared because they had human intelligence. It was not only Turks who had slaves; right here in Sonora the federal and state governments were splitting up Yaqui families and sending the survivors to sweat out their lives on plantations, terribly shortened lives.

So, restraining an impulse to belabor Consuelo for the sins of the country, I told her that I was keeping Sewa with me.

"Why?" she burst out in jealousy. Evidently she was counting on being my maid and companion. "What can she do?"

"She can play the flute," I said. I wouldn't have explained even if I could that the child gave me someone to care about, someone to whom I could be important.

I hastily placated Consuelo by giving her the ruins of my brown velvet and showing her how it could be reconstructed into a skirt. When she left, hugging the rich cloth to her breast, I put the tray on a table by Sewa.

After we ate, I managed through mixed language and gestures to get Sewa's timid assent to going out in the patio for a while. First I carried out Ku in his basket and put him in a large stone planter of cerise bougainvillea while his basket aired. Then I got Consuelo to fetch several straw mats and help me carry Sewa out to them, to lie in the shade of the huge cottonwood that cooled my side of the patio.

Settling her in reaching distance of Ku, with her flute and brown sugar, I told Consuelo to brew Cruz's herbs for the child and keep an eye on her.

I wasn't clear on exactly how to set about getting away from Las Coronas, but Sewa needed time to get well anyway and there was the chance that, if I seemed content to stay, Reina would herself smooth my departure. And if I could, all innocence, annoy her sufficiently—

Telling Sewa I'd soon be back, I went in search of my sister.

6

"Who is it?" called Reina's imperious voice as I rapped for the second time on the thick library door.

"Miranda," I fairly shouted.

The door opened so quickly that I almost stumbled into a tall man whose attire was absolutely startling, a suit of finest gray worsted, pale-gray silk shirt and a dark-gray silk tie swept into an Ascot puff as elegant as any one could see on Pall Mall.

"So the English lady has a voice." His golden eyes played over me in a way that made me feel naked. He made a deep bow, kissed my hand before I could prevent it, and laughed at my confusion.

His tawny coloring and powerful neck and shoulders reminded me of a magnificent lion. In spite of his carefully matched garments, there was a primitive force about him, a formidable strength that I somehow feared could be released with lightning speed. Wrenching my gaze from his, I came past him to the huge desk, remembering how Father used to work there and how he'd kept sweets for me in one of the drawers. Now Reina sat there, brows arched.

"Well?" she demanded. I had the feeling I'd interrupted an

extremely personal moment, yet how could that be? Surely I hadn't misjudged her feeling for Trace? "This is Court Sanders from Mina Rara. Court, this is Miranda Greenleaf."

After acknowledging the introduction, I turned to Reina and said, "My clothing isn't suitable for ranch life. And I had little anyway, except for school uniforms. Would it be possible to send for some material?"

"So you ruined that expensive brown velvet," my sister accused.

I held my ground, refusing to look apologetic. My clothing was not out of her pocket, and if our mother had inherited Las Coronas, my father's mine had supplied the means to maintain and increase it. At last, Reina shrugged. Probably she didn't wish to seem grudging in front of Court. "Well, in spite of your foolishness, you must have suitable clothes, but it's not so easy here, we haven't shops on every corner."

"I don't need anything grand. In fact, what I could use best is a divided skirt like yours for riding."

"There may be enough tanned leather for Emilio to stitch one for you this week," Reina decided more graciously. "When the weather cools, I plan to go to Hermosillo and do some shopping. We can outfit you then. And you might ask Catalina what cloth we have in the storeroom. It will be cheap stuff but would make you a change."

I thanked her and started for the door, congratulating myself on this first step in making her believe I was resigned to staying. Court Sanders moved forward, both to open the door and to block my way.

"Perhaps when you ladies visit Hermosillo, you will stop at Mina Rara. I could make you comfortable and it isn't much out of your way."

"Thank you," said Reina, grimacing, "but I have seen the mine."

He smiled at me, tawny eyes roving to my mouth, lingering on the trapped pulse in my throat. "Miss Greenleaf hasn't. Since she is the owner, it should be of interest."

I didn't like or trust this man, but he might be useful in breaking free from Reina when the time came. Also, as a matter of self-preservation it seemed to me that the more people of influence who knew me, the less likely Reina was to abuse her authority. So I bowed slightly to the big blond man, said I hoped to accept his offer, and left the room.

Taking meals with Reina would give her another dose of company I was sure she didn't want, so I had a cup of tea while Sewa lunched; then I took her to my room to have a nap and went to the big dining room.

Court Sanders, in a black Prince Albert coat and white silk shirt, rose to seat me. Reina looked a trifle sour and again I had an uncomfortable sense of intruding, though Court at once began to ply me with questions about London—what plays and concerts I'd attended, where I preferred to dine, whether the Savoy was as luxurious as reported.

I answered as best I could, miserably aware that Reina was seething in her place at one end of the great trestle table opposite Court, while I sat between, facing a carved panel depicting the martyrdom of various saints. I shared their anguish, skewered between Court's probing and Reina's sulks. The straight-backed heavy chairs were a fitting legacy of the Inquisition, torturing the body to edify the soul.

Confessing that I'd never been to the races at Ascot, I said rather pleadingly to Court, "You must remember that I was at school deep in Sussex, Mr. Sanders. I got to London only when Papa was visiting."

" 'Only,' " mimicked Reina. "He spoiled you shamefully! And much good your English education will do you here. You should never have come."

I had to clench my hands to keep from shrinking. Tears sprang to my eyes, tears of hurt and anger. How could my sister humiliate me so in front of this stranger? In spite of my discomfort at his questions, I blessed him as he smiled lazily.

"There's a reason for all things. I'm delighted that you could bring yourself to leave the culture and pleasures of England for life in this raw country."

"Raw?" echoed Reina. Her green eyes smoldered. "The Anza family settled here over three hundred years ago on a grant from the king of Spain!"

"Indeed," murmured Court. "A pity there hasn't been more to show for such a length of tenure."

It was a brutal remark, and though it was ironic for me to try to protect Reina, I interposed hastily, "Are you pleased, Mr. Sanders, with the horses Mr. Winslade chose for you?"

"They'll do." Court shrugged. "Careless of him to leave in the middle of the night, though, before he'd made sure I was satisfied." Strong white teeth showed in sudden amusement. "Perhaps that's why. I've sometimes kept him busy for a week till he found what I wanted."

"It is doubtful, Court, that you *know* what you want," thrust Reina. Her creamy breasts swelled from her bodice, almost revealing the nipples. Court's eyes lingered on them in the way of a man admiring what he has had and can have again.

"I know what I want," he said cheerfully. "Finding it, as with horses, is the problem. I don't mind temperamental, difficult creatures, but I won't for long ride anything that bears the marks of another man."

Reina's exposed flesh crimsoned. I took no gratification from her embarrassment. Court, as if sensing it was time to lighten the charged atmosphere, set himself to be entertaining. This was fortunate, since I could think of nothing to say and Reina was brooding.

"Will you eat with your Yaqui pet tonight?" she asked as I folded my napkin and rose, excusing myself.

"Why, no," I said pleasantly. "Since I'm to be at Las Coronas, I should try to become part of the household, surely." Her green eyes bored into me, but I kept my smile.

"I have spoken to Emilio," she said at last. "His wife will come this afternoon to fit you for the riding clothes."

Could Reina, too, be trying to make the best of things in spite of her antipathy? I thanked her warmly and went down the hall to my room, hoping there might be enough leather to make an outfit for Sewa. It would be fun to have matching ones and all girls, even my sadly maimed little one, must get a thrill from new clothes.

Emilio's wife, María, was Catalina's sister, but as thin as

Catalina was fat. Her black hair hung down her back in a thick braid and her golden earrings gleamed as she measured me for a skirt and vest.

"Is there enough leather for her?" I asked, indicating Sewa, who was watching with those wide dark eyes.

María's lips tucked down. "I think not, señorita."

"Then use what would go in my vest and make her a skirt like mine."

"There may not be enough—"

"I'm sure there would be if she were not Yaqui," I cut in firmly. "Please tell your husband to do the best he can but to get *two* skirts." I took the measuring thong and twined it around Sewa's skinny waist, measured below the knee, and gave the thong, knotted, back to María.

Back stiff, she marched out, bare feet slapping the tile. I sighed. This was not increasing my popularity at Las Coronas, but people were going to have to accept the child. If they would see her as a girl, an orphan, instead of as a Yaqui!

I spent the afternoon with her, admiring her music, helping feed Ku, and laughing at his lopsided tricks. He seemed to be trying to talk. Sewa was picking up Spanish much faster than I was learning Yaqui and I wondered if later on I might teach her English. When we had our home.

Throughout the day Sewa had the tea that Cruz had said would promote healing. He'd also told me to change the dressings in about three days and so on thereafter until the stump was scabless. I'd hoped to find someone on the ranch to make an artificial foot but was not too encouraged by the hostile attitudes. That might have to wait for Hermosillo.

At an interminable dinner that evening Court Sanders tried to draw me out about my life in England and Reina kept bringing the conversation back to Las Coronas and Mexico. I welcomed this, for it gave me a chance to learn more about the situation of my homeland, of which I was woefully ignorant.

"Díaz will keep down all these fanatics who want to take over the country and divide the land," said Reina positively.

Court shook his head. "Díaz can't live forever and forces

are swelling that even Dan Porfirio can't stifle. Robbed by authentic bandits on one hand and Díaz's *rurales* on the other, the peons have little to lose. It's said that Mexico is the mother of foreigners and the stepmother of Mexicans. One percent of the population controls nearly all the country's wealth, and much of that one percent is foreign. There's Weetman Pearson, the Englishman who built the Tehuantepec Railway connecting east and west and who discovered vast oil deposits. The Guggenheims own mines and smelters, controlling at least ninety percent of Mexico's most important industry. The value of American holdings in 1902 was guessed at about five hundred million dollars." Court paused and savored his wine. "The city of Monterrey and the state of Nuevo León charge the Guggenheims no taxes on capital invested in Monterrey. William Randolph Hearst owns hundreds of thousands of Mexican acres. Díaz stripped the Indians of their ancient communal lands so that most are virtually serfs. The Terrazas' estate in Chihuahua is about the size of Belgium, Switzerland, Denmark, and Holland put together. The landless masses have *nothing* to lose. Times are going to change violently—it will be like a whirlwind, and when it has finished tearing up and hurling down, we will not recognize what's left."

My scalp prickled. "Are—are you talking of war? Revolution?"

"The bloodiest, Miss Greenleaf." For once there was no mockery in Court's ombré eyes. "There are rumbles everywhere, but I hear a lot of such discontent at the mine. Why do American workers earn double the Mexican wage? I've gradually replaced them with Mexicans and Yaquis, but the memory lingers. Why do Mexico's minerals enrich other countries?"

"Where would the Yaquis fit in a revolution?" I wondered. "They certainly don't love the central government, but would any other treat them better?"

"The mine's work force is mostly Yaqui," Court said. "Your father set a policy of treating them fairly and they haven't been bothered by the slave raids Yzábal began last year. The ranchers, landowners, and industrialists of Sonora are going to put an end to that traffic one day, not out of humanitarianism, but because Yaquis are the hardest workers, whatever they turn their hands to."

Court was an analytical man, detached from the passions he described so coolly. No doubt he was an excellent superintendent, one of those nationless professional men whose abilities made them indispensable to whatever forces ruled a country.

Revolution?

I hoped he was wrong. Change was necessary, but I shrank at the thought of slaughter, pillage, and useless death.

"Rebellion will not affect Las Coronas," Reina said, tossing back her red hair so that the emeralds in it gleamed like serpents' eyes. "I'll arm the men if war comes and hire enough *pistoleros* to train them and help defend our boundaries."

Court shrugged. "A private army could have its uses—*if* you can control it."

She smiled. "Trace Winslade can."

Something flashed across Court's face. Jealousy? It was gone before I could be sure. "Ah, Winslade. But will he?"

"He'll do as he's told," Reina said almost shrilly.

Court smiled. "Maybe. I never figured him as a run-of-the-mill hired gun, even though that was how your father, Miss Greenleaf, originally employed him."

"I thought he was in charge of the horses," I said.

"Yes. That happened after he took care of a few other matters."

"He can wear his guns if it's required," declared Reina. "Or perhaps, Court," she added with some malice, "you think you'd make a better defender?"

His eyelids drooped, and though his teeth showed, I would not have called his expression a smile. "My dear Reina, it would all depend on what was in it for me. That's my single law, unalterable as those of the Medes and Persians." He laughed at my involuntary frown, raising sun-bleached eyebrows. "That troubles you, Miss Greenleaf? You think I have no honor? I do. The largest part is honesty with myself."

"And under that self-righteous stance you do what you will," gibed Reina.

With a mocking inclination of his head, Court said, "I think there are no complaints about my running of Mina Rara."

Some devil made me say, "I believe you must let me inspect it before you're so sure of that, Mr. Sanders."

Reina shot me a surprised glance and I could almost hear her doing a hasty reevaluation of my fiber. Court's startled look changed to one of amusement and he watched me with male speculation. "I shall be delighted," he said with an extravagant bow. "At any time."

Reina sounded the silver bells for coffee. I decided I wanted none, excused myself, and yielded to an urge to stop by the chapel before going to my room. The talk of revolution had frightened me. I wanted to be close to the mortal remains of my mother, shelter in the timeless peace of the little church.

The houses of the people of Las Coronas were built in an oblong of which the church and storerooms formed one side. Most were dark, but I heard one mother singing a lullaby and children playing here and there.

Entering the church, I moved to the front, where a candle burned by the blue, white, and gold crowned image of the Virgin. She looked distressed, almost horrified, as if she knew she couldn't answer most of the entreaties she received. Though I did not believe in prayers for the dead, I did send my spirit reaching toward my mother's and father's, imagined that I was talking to them, telling my perplexities. I knelt for a long time and rose, feeling comforted, strengthened by the one thought I have held to ever since.

Heroic it is not. Sustaining it is. I didn't aspire to do what another person had not been able to, but I believed that I could do what other people had—live through struggle and death and war, find my own place, care for a child. Whatever was the day's task, I would do the best I could.

Crossing the patio, I heard soft male laughter above quick sobbing breaths and protests, the sound of scuffling.

"Who is it?" I called sharply.

Court Sanders faced around, still holding the wrist of Consuelo, the prettiest girl in the household. Her blouse was torn, exposing ripely firm breasts, and in the dim light from the kitchen I could see tears running down her cheeks.

"Good evening, Miss Greenleaf," he said with a bow, just as if he hadn't been engaged in manhandling one of our maids.

"It's not a good evening, Mr. Sanders, when a girl is molested."

"Molested?" His eyebrows climbed. "Oh, come now, Miss Greenleaf. Even if you *were* reared in England, you must know girls of this class don't mind a little rough wooing."

"It looks more like rape," I said flatly and spoke in halting Spanish to the girl. "Consuelo, have you encouraged this man?"

"No, no!" Vigorously shaking her head, she used her free hand to straighten her blouse and skirt. "I am a virgin, señorita. If this gentleman has his will, my sweetheart would never marry me."

"That seems a good practical reason," I told Sanders. "So unless you are prepared to stand at the altar with Consuelo, I must tell you to leave her alone."

He still held her and his tone was patronizingly amused. "My dear young lady—"

"I'm a woman," I cut in. "I believe the poorest of us has a right to decide what man, if any, shall have her."

He let go of the girl as if losing all interest, folded his arms, and gave me a cool raking survey that would ordinarily have been humiliating but now only made me fiercely indignant so that I stood my ground as Consuelo murmured thanks and sped away.

"I thought you were skim milk and toast," he said, an echo of that conquering laughter back in his throat. "But now you sound—and look—like wine and meat, as if you could intoxicate a man but feed him, too."

"Why, you insulting—"

He waved his hand carelessly. "It's no insult, Miss Greenleaf. Most proper women are skim milk or sour milk or water, though the nicest are good sweet milk. Boring at best, nags at worst. So I've usually taken the ones who were whiskey or wine or tequila—and most have been rotgut."

"Your escapades, Mr. Sanders, are no concern of mine, as long as you conduct them with willing partners." A sudden thought occurred troublingly and I said gingerly, "I hope you don't use your position as mine superintendent to take whatever workers' women tickle your fancy."

He chuckled. "Why don't you come on that tour of inspection?"

"You may be sure I will," I said coldly. "The mine, after all, is where I get my income from, so I should interest myself in its condition and your methods."

His jaw hung for a moment, but he recovered quickly. "I should be happy to arrange for such a visitation," he said mockingly. "And to simplify at least part of your inspection, women I haven't favored with my attentions could wear blue rosettes." With a lift of his massive shoulders, he went on, "I'm not that much of a fool, Miss Greenleaf, to toy with the wives or daughters of my men. Accidents in mines are too easy to contrive."

"So you save your lust for our household women?"

"My dear," he said with elaborate patience, "I have an outlet that need not concern you."

"Is she whiskey?" I couldn't help asking.

"She looks like the best Scotch," he said, smiling slowly after shooting me a surprised glance. "But she tastes like raw tequila. And leaves the same headache." He moved to where my face was in the window light and his lion's eyes reached into me. I felt as if he were physically invading my mind and body, and I fought a heaviness, a compliant languor robbing me of strength while paradoxically those depths of me which Trace had revealed stirred. I didn't want to respond to this ruthless man, yet I did. Feeling naked and abased, I stared at the wall.

Court's voice rasped in my ears. "Has someone had you?"

"No!" Retreating, I shielded myself from those devouring eyes, crossing my arms across my breasts. "No!"

"You'd swear it?" His nostrils dilated and the muscles corded in his neck as he kept his hands clenched at his sides.

Who was he to ask such questions? Commanding slow calming breaths, I drew myself up as tall as I could, forced myself to meet his hungry eyes. "Mr. Sanders, I don't have to tell you anything, much less swear. You are *my* employee." Turning to avoid him, I finished coldly. "I bid you good night."

Swift as a panther, he barred my way. "Discharge me if you

please, Miss Greenleaf. You'll have a hell of a time getting a dependable man at Mina Rara these days." He dismissed our roles with a wave of his large, well-formed, yet somehow brutal hand. "Unless you swear no man has had you, I'm going to."

"How dare you say that?" I choked, completely astounded. "Here, in my mother's house?"

"Because it's where we are." He dropped his hand to the wall so that I was imprisoned. "I want you. You want me, too, I can tell." He laughed, a sound far back in his throat. "I can play the correct games if you're innocent. Woo you, kiss your forehead, wait, and ache. I want to wed a lady. She might as well be you. But I'm not going through that nonsense if you're fledged—and something in the way you look makes me think you are."

"That's my business."

"I can find out," he warned softly. "Your danger there, Miss Greenleaf, is that even if you prove a virgin, I might not be able to stop by the time I know."

Glancing desperately about, I saw that the courtyard was deserted. "If you scream," Court said lightly, reading my mind, "people will simply conclude someone's entertaining himself with a girl—and that will be the truth."

He moved forward.

I stepped back, met the wall. He had me. And those hands were reaching . . .

"No man has taken me," I blurted.

He paused reluctantly. "You swear?"

"I swear." His approach made me ready to cry, try to dodge past, but I knew that, if I broke, it would snap his last restraints. A sigh came from him.

"That had better be the truth, my gently reared English lady. Because someday I'll know. And promise you this. If you don't come virgin to my bed, I'll train you to tricks the vilest whore shrinks from."

Turning on his heel, he swung away into the darkness.

I stared after him a moment, heart pounding, senses tingling, then ran to my room as if pursued.

Flinging myself across the bed, I trembled and longed for

Trace, who had ridden away without a word, left me to cope with a ruthless and experienced man like Court. My deepest being feared and hated him. For Court Sanders a woman would be a possession, protected simply out of his own egotism. I was almost certain he had been Reina's lover.

In spite of all this, I was strongly aware of him. In resisting him, I had also to battle my flesh, the hungers he roused. How could I feel that way when I loved Trace? There must be something fatally wrong with me. My body throbbed and burned. I hated and cursed it. After a long time I slept.

Court left next morning immediately after breakfast, accompanied by two vaqueros to help with the horses. He told Reina and me good-bye at the same time and didn't make even oblique reference to what he'd said to me last night.

"I'll be expecting your visit, ladies," he said as he took the reins of a mettlesome, unblemished gray, the one Trace must have selected. "After all, Miss Greenleaf, you should inspect your property."

"We will inform you," said Reina stiffly. There were dark circles beneath her eyes and faint bruises on her arm. I was convinced she was his raw tequila, that he had gone to her after our encounter in the patio.

Court bowed ostentatiously. It was clear he liked to annoy her, burlesque the employee role. Springing into the saddle, he was off with a wave of his gauntleted hand.

"*Fanfarrón!*" Reina spat. "He fills the eye and well he knows it! Arrogant, like all *yanquis*." She turned to scan me narrowly. "You and your inspections! Now he will plague me till I take you to the mine." She gave a disagreeable laugh. "Court is so obvious. He dreams of marrying a lady, well-brought-up, virginal. Oh, he has told me his views on this subject boringly often. But what he would do with such a finespun doll I cannot imagine. His passions are those of a bull—so I have heard."

When I didn't answer, she swept up her skirts and vanished into the house. Slowly, I followed. Had Court told Reina he planned to marry me? Could and would she help me evade him?

I had no intention, certainly, of being his wife, but if he used his strength, overpowered my resistance, could I keep from responding, becoming his thing, his possession? I clung desperately to the memory of Trace, the clean fierce passion that had flowed between us. But that was gone. He had abandoned me.

Next morning, fighting waves of nausea, I changed the dressing on Sewa's foot. It wasn't that the stump looked so terrible. Scabbed, puckering at the edges, it was not inflamed. What was dreadful was what was not there—a small, brown, high-arched foot, the marvelous articulation of an ankle and flexing toes.

"It's healing splendidly," I told her, supplementing mixed Yaqui and Spanish with smiles and gestures. "Cruz would be proud."

She nodded, though she couldn't have understood very much. I bandaged the stump with clean white rags and then, with Consuelo's help, got Sewa out in the patio and settled Ku near her.

The raven was stronger and seemed every day to be a bit more fully and blackly feathered, but the splinted leg looked dead and the drooping claw did not respond to touch. I couldn't tell anything about the wing, but I suspected that when the splints came off in two more weeks, according to Cruz's advice, Sewa would never have to worry about a pet that could fly away.

Consuelo lingered. "Señorita, thank you for—for last night. My family is very grateful."

"It should never have happened," I said. "It is my place to be sorry, and I am."

She raised one cinnamon-honey shoulder and it was easy to see why Court had been tempted. "Men try. I know I must keep out of their way, but we thought Señor Sanders—" She broke off in confusion. "Anyway, señorita, a thousand thanks."

She hurried off, leaving me to wonder what she had almost

said about Court. That he was thought to have a woman at Las Coronas? Why would she have choked off that supposition? If his mistress were one of the people, it would surely be definite common knowledge.

I thought of Reina and wondered. She loved Trace, I was sure, but so did I. And if Court Sanders would still stir my senses, wasn't Reina as vulnerable for all her pride of family?

Reina and I sat at opposite ends of the long age-mellowed table through a practically silent lunch. "Perhaps you would like to go riding with me tomorrow," she said as I rose to leave. "I wish to look over our south boundary near the mountains. It would acquaint you with that area."

"I'd like to," I said, hoping in spite of myself that she might be developing a certain grudging fondness for me. That I seized on such a slight opening made me conscious of how much I'd desired her love, how much I'd wanted a sister.

"Be ready and we'll leave after an early breakfast," she ordered. "If your riding skirt isn't ready, you may borrow one of mine." She tossed down her napkin and strode out ahead of me.

I didn't understand her, but the prospect of a ride and a warming relationship lightened my heart. I'd have to get Consuelo to look after Sewa tomorrow and keep her company some of the time, so I cut through the patio toward the kitchen but was still on the gallery when a small procession entered through the gate.

First came a wiry, shriveled man whose skin resembled the leather he carried. Behind him was María, also holding leather, and behind her walked Consuelo with a peculiar object that resembled a boot.

"I am Emilio Sánchez," said the gnarled man, halting a few steps away. "Consuelo is the child of my dead brother and sister-in-law. My wife and I are in your debt, señorita, for your acting to save Consuelo from shame."

He shook out a gracefully cut suede riding skirt, a bone-toggle-closed vest and matching jacket, all stitched painstakingly. "These are for the child," said María, smiling with some effort as she approached Sewa and displayed a smaller version of my skirt and vest.

Sewa stared, unable to comprehend, till María, who on closer confrontation evidently found the girl more like the children of the ranch than not, bent to her, and held the vest. Sewa's face glowed like a flower candle as the soft leather fitted around her shoulders. She touched the fringes with amazed delight and produced one of her few Spanish words.

"*Gracias—gracias.*"

"*De nada, muchachita,*" said María. Impulsively, she gave the child a hug, fell back as Emilio cleared his throat authoritatively. "I have made a sort of raised boot for the child like one I made for a friend who lost his foot from a rattlesnake bite. Let us see how it fits—yes, señorita, I know the girl cannot stand on it yet, but I can get an idea of the length and whether I need to add another sole or trim this one down."

Kneeling, he slipped the boot, opening widened, over the stump, gently straightened out the good leg, and compared. "I must add another half-inch to the sole," he decided. "Otherwise it seems perfect. Look, señorita. The foot part is filled with shaped wood. On top of that is a cushion of goose feathers. Then the boot closes up to the knee with these broad straps. It will take time to learn to use it, but it is much more natural than a crutch."

"Wonderful!" I said, dumbfounded at this outpouring of goodwill. "I had meant to look today for someone who might make Sewa an artificial foot. This is much better than I'd dreamed."

Emilio beamed. "You will try your riding clothes, señorita?" he asked. "I wish them to fit exactly."

Gathering them up, I went to my room, changed, and emerged feeling very much the *ranchera*. The soft belt of the skirt fitted snug at the waist, the vest had a jaunty cut, and the jacket gave ease around shoulders and arms without being bulky.

"It feels altogether right, Emilio," I told him. "And I'm glad to have it, for tomorrow I ride with my sister."

He looked stunned. A glance passed between him and María. "Ah," he said with a heartiness I found strained. "It is good that you become at home here. But be careful while riding, señorita. Our horses must be different from those of England."

"I've learned that," I said with a laughing grimace. The Sánchezes departed, leaving Sewa and me to admire our new clothes.

"And you'll be able to walk," I told her in mixed language and signs.

She nodded with such joy in her eyes that my heart ached for her. To have to be glad that one had a contrivance instead of a real foot!

She took a scrap of leather that had dropped from the clothes and wrapped it around Ku, who blinked at this robing while Sewa laughed merrily and said, mostly in gestures, that till he could get his coat of a thousand colors, this one would have to do.

Consuelo promised to bring Sewa her meals and tea and stay with her awhile each time so the child wouldn't get too lonesome. Now that the Sánchezes were kindly disposed toward Sewa, I felt easier about leaving her for the day. I kissed her good-bye next morning after breakfast, explaining that I'd be back by night and that she must ask Consuelo for anything she needed, then hurried to the front of the house.

Four vaqueros were waiting. They wore bandoliers and rifles were thrust in their saddle scabbards. Two were holding saddled horses, Reina's black and the little chestnut mare I'd ridden before. Reina came out, smiled graciously, and mounted smoothly while the vaquero holding my mare gave me the cradle of his hands to boost me up.

"So your outfit was ready," noted Reina. "Let us hope your riding soon becomes as appropriate as your clothes."

We rode out the gate beneath the heavy arch carved with the three crowns that gave the hacienda its name, two men ahead, two behind. "Is there trouble?" I called to Reina.

"No more than usual." She shrugged. "But there have been clashes between soldiers and Yaquis near the boundary and one never knows what a gang of Sierra Yaqui may do."

I felt like saying there seemed no point in taking chances, but was sure that would bring down her scorn, so I patted my mare's neck and took in the country.

Mesquite and giant cardones, prickly pear, cholla, ironwood, palo verde—I closed my eyes to imagine English oak, yew, wych elm, and chestnut, but I could no longer evoke a sense of reality about them. I opened my eyes again to the glaring sky, the reflecting desert, and wondered if it would ever seem familiar. I doubted it. One might as foolhardily hope to be comfortable with God.

Cattle were scattered about, and as the day heated, those that could find shade got under it, lying under the cottonwoods and giant mesquites shading watering tanks of earth. These few bright green spots showed where water was and a swath of green followed a dry stream bed. Reina explained that Las Coronas could ship cattle by driving them thirty miles to the railroad at a place called the Switch.

By noon the Bacatete Mountains rose jaggedly before us. I wondered how many Yaquis were hiding there and what was happening on the other side of the range down on the Yaqui and Mayo Rivers in Cruz's Eight Sacred Pueblos.

The mountains were the boundary of the estate and we stopped in the foothills to rest. The vaqueros loosened the horses' girths and made a fire for coffee, which we drank black and steaming from tin cups, washing down bread and cheese.

"There are jaguar in the mountains," Reina said. "Also the bighorned wild sheep. It is a place fit only for wild beasts and wild Indians."

I was too tired to make any comment, though I suspected she was trying to intimidate me.

I hadn't been on a horse since riding back from Cruz's five days ago. My muscles screamed and I had to keep myself from hobbling by an effort of will. Reina looked as fresh as when we started and her back was arrow-straight as she bantered with the men. So long as she was clearly *la patrona*, she could be friendly, and the vaqueros watched her with admiration that made me despair of getting help from them should I ever clash with her.

After our short break, the girths were tightened and we continued, riding along the mountains. Suddenly one of the advance riders reined in, lifting his hand. He rode forward, around a hill, to return and call to Reina.

"Some dead Yaquis are ahead, señorita! The soldiers must have caught them only today, for they are not yet stinking. Let us swing to the plain and avoid them. It's not a sight for ladies."

Reina flashed me a hard smile. "Oh, but it is!" she said. "My sister needs to understand the country, get rid of her English softness. Come!" She urged her black on.

"Señorita!" protested the man, but she rode ahead and he had to follow.

So did I, partly because someone might be alive and needing help, mostly to prove my nerve to Reina. But I hadn't counted on what we saw as we rounded the hill.

Men lay with cut throats swarmed over by flies. Vultures lurched heavily away from the corpses, flapped awkwardly into the air. But what made me turn my head and gag was three women hanging naked from a large mesquite, feet nearly touching the ground. Their purple tongues protruded from hideously contorted faces. Milk had curdled and crusted on their breasts, where it had oozed from their nipples. At the base of the tree three tiny bodies had been carelessly tossed, apparently after being swung against the tree to crush in the soft little skulls.

"Oh, no!" I heard myself wailing, and could not stop. "Oh, no, no, no. . . ."

"I told you this was not good, señorita," said the lead vaquero reprovingly.

Sweat dewed Reina's face, but she said, "Six men. They must not all have been married, or perhaps their women had not cubbed and could be sent to plantations."

I wiped my mouth and rose to where I couldn't see the women and babies. "Bury them, at least," I begged of the men. They glanced at Reina. She shrugged.

"Do what you will," she told them.

The lead vaquero spat. "Your pardon, señorita, but Yaquis cut off the soles of my father's feet, made him run barefoot through the desert till he fell and died of sunstroke."

"They impaled my sister on a cactus," said another man.

"They have had their chance to be Mexican," said the third horseman. "But all they have done for over a hundred years is rebel and raid. Let these carcasses stay here to teach the rest a lesson."

I turned to the youngest and last man, slender and lithe, not long out of boyhood. "*Por favor,*" I pleaded. "I will pay you well."

He hesitated only a moment. "Ride on," he told his friends.

"You will bury these dogs for money?" demanded the chief.

"I will bury them."

"Hard work for offal," said the leader, shrugging. The others started on. I paused by the young vaquero.

"Thank you," I whispered. "Truly, I will pay you."

"You already have," he said, loosening the machete at the back of his saddle. "Consuelo and I are betrothed."

So I rode on, sickened, weak with horror. I couldn't doubt that the vaqueros had suffered in the ways they had mentioned. I was beginning to understand how the very name Yaqui brought fear to Mexicans. But those women, those babies . . .

Perhaps Court Sanders was right. A whirlwind must be rising to sweep away such terrors.

7

Except for meals, I saw little of Reina for the rest of the week. I was haunted by the bodies of the women dangling like ripe bloated fruit, and there was no one I could talk to about it, not even Court with his cynically detached intelligence. When I cuddled Sewa, I knew she had seen her family and neighbors die a similar death, and I marveled that she hadn't gone mad or into complete and utter hatred of strangers.

She was getting stronger every day. It wouldn't be too long before she could try Emilio's boot foot. She was becoming something of a pet with those of Las Coronas who had occasion to pass often through the patio, and Ku was growing plump from tidbits he received for croaking accompaniment to the flute. Enrique, the young vaquero who had buried the Yaquis, sent word through Consuelo that he was gentling an exceptionally sweet-tempered *burra* for Sewa to ride.

"For me?" she repeated when Consuelo told her, for she had rudimentary Spanish by now.

"For you, little flower-bird," promised Consuelo, laughing at the child's delight. "And my Uncle Emilio is making a leather nest with high sides in which your Ku may ride."

But after Consuelo had gone about her work, Sewa's joyful excitement faded. "La señorita will permit?" She was speaking of Reina, who, though she ignored Sewa, managed to exude a withering hostility on the rare occasions she came in sight.

"Reina probably won't even know," I told Sewa, and diverted her into a chess game Emilio had improvised from scraps of wood and leather. Our board was of toughened hide with the squares marked by a hot iron. The queens wore suede skirts and the knights were vaqueros with tiny horsehair lariats. I wished Miss Mattison, with whom I had spent many vacation hours playing chess, could see this array.

There had been no word or news of Trace. My persistent hope that he'd had to leave unexpectedly and would send an explanation had to be forgotten. Reina began to plan our trip to Hermosillo, and though it would have been simpler for me to get away from her there, I knew she wouldn't let Sewa come along. I didn't want to leave the child for several weeks, so the answer seemed to be to get to the railroad thirty miles away. There, at the Switch, Sewa and I could take the train to Hermosillo and—

And what? The money I had wouldn't keep us long, and my hunting employment, if indeed there was anything I could do worth money, would surely come to Reina's ears if she decided to track me down. I thought longingly of the help Trace had offered, then tightened my lips and put back my shoulders. A little thought must have convinced him that he'd better not offend Reina. I wouldn't ask him to make good his word.

No, the only possible solution I could think of was leaving the train at Mina Rara, for I knew it stopped near there, and hoping Court Sanders would shelter us till it was safe to go to Hermosillo. He could send my income there and Reina need never know what had happened.

Would he help?

I thought he might. He wasn't intimidated by my sister.

And that wild way he'd behaved that night in the courtyard? Was he truly set on having me or had his threat-promises been a passing impulse sprung by my thwarting his rape of

Consuelo? Remembering her bared breasts, her terror, and his indifference to it, I thought with a wave of panic that I must be mad to even dream of seeking refuge with such a man. Even though I was his employer, isolated as the mine must be, I would be very much at his mercy, a quality I doubted he possessed.

But what was the alternative? Trace had vanished, and Reina was bound to look for me at Cruz's. I had no money to live on and must soon or late arrange with Court to receive my income from the mine.

Perhaps going to him would put him on his honor. I might be able to keep him on best behavior—and he'd said he could play the conventional courting game—by not dashing his hopes outright while I was at the mine. Sparring with such a formidable opponent frightened me, though. I suspected he'd known and enjoyed many women, most with more wordly wisdom and poise than I would ever have. But he evidently placed great store in innocence. If I could keep my nerve, my very lack of sophistication might be my best safeguard.

Besides, Court was a practical man. He valued money and power. Apart from vague hints of future favors I didn't intend to give, I could make honest promises I *would* fulfill. If he would help Sewa and me, I would gladly give him the principal interest in the mine.

With that for a reward, surely he'd befriend us!

But if he wouldn't? What if he persisted in making love to me? I shrugged that threat aside. It was the only feasible way to get money and evade Reina till I came of age. Though she had done no more overt menacing, I could never feel safe under the same roof with her, and I suspected that an unfortunate accident might leave her sole heir to Mina Rara as well as the ranch.

So Enrique or Emilio would bring the little *burra*, called Ratoncita because of her soft mouse color, leave her outside the patio, and carry Sewa out to place her in the saddle while I put Ku in his leather nest before mounting my own horse. We rode near the corrals and orchards while Sewa learned to use the reins. She used her soft voice also, talking constantly to this wonderful new friend who had, I learned, "such elegant long lovely ears."

We were coming back from such an excursion late one afternoon when Reina strolled out of the shade by the stables. "I must apologize for letting you become so desperate for a ride that you jog along beside a *burra* and Yaqui brat," she said. "I had thought you needed time to forget the unpleasantness we found at the mountain boundary. But if you are bold again, please join me in the morning and we'll have a more interesting excursion."

I didn't want to arouse her enmity. I was sure she would strike in time, but docility on my part should lull her into feeling there was no hurry. I agreed to meet her after breakfast, left our mounts to Enrique, and helped Sewa hop across the patio to the shade of the big tree.

After a cooling drink, I changed her bandage and was glad to see that the stump was nearly healed. "I think you could try your boot," I told her. "Would you like to?"

"Yes," she said with a kind of sighing and I knew that using the boot sealed the reality of her maiming. A person may be sick, unable to walk, for many reasons, but there is only one reason to use an artificial foot. I brought out the contrivance and slipped it on, settling it gently in place, crossing and recrossing the broad rawhide straps till they reached the knee. Sewa gazed at it with an unreadable expression, finally gave it a tentative small shake.

"Look!" she cried when the boot moved. "It works!"

Scrambling off the bench, she swung herself erect, unsupported for the first time since the amputation. The boot was turned to one side and she moved her hands to maintain balance, but she *was* standing.

She threw herself into my arms and I learned that Yaquis can cry, for she did. So did I.

We moved about the patio for ten minutes or so, Sewa using my arm to steady herself. Her stump was long enough to direct and control the boot fairly well once she grew used to this new way of walking, but Emilio's device was infinitely better than a crutch. In fact, with a matching boot on the other foot and long skirts, Sewa wouldn't look crippled. She'd have to move deliberately and might need a stick on uneven ground or for steps, but this was far more than I could have dreamed the night Cruz took off the gangrened foot.

"Let's stop now," I said. "It wouldn't be good to make your foot sore.

Sewa let me guide her to the bench, but her eyes glistened. "I can walk!" she breathed. Leaning toward Ku, she whispered, "Oh, Ku, I can walk!" She made a sound of contrition, glanced woefully up at me. "But Ku—cannot walk or fly! He is too little for a boot?"

"I'm afraid so. But you can carry him. Perhaps we can make a perch to fit on your shoulder. And he already has his own saddle nest." I laughed, trying to cheer her. "Not many birds have that. I bet he has the only one in all Mexico, maybe even the world."

"The world?" Sewa wrinkled her brow, but after I'd explained the best I could, she gathered her pet to her and told him that he was a peerless fowl who would ride on her shoulder as the holy saints were borne on litters. Any common old bird had wings and legs; but how many had a leather nest swung at a saddle horn? Or someone to play the flute?

For the first time I felt really hopeful that Sewa, after all, could grow up to lead a busy, happy life. I must see that she rode and walked every day now so she would be ready soon for our attempt at freedom.

We rode far to the east next morning, along cattle trails through thick mesquite growth, through dense canebrakes along the river courses. Since this was a comparatively safe area, only two vaqueros rode with us.

Reina, as usual, had her rifle along and kept shooting at birds, rabbits, javelina, and in one case, a mule deer. "Your luck's not so good today," I couldn't help saying when she missed the deer, for I would have hated to see the graceful creature dead.

"It *is* luck," she retorted. "I usually kill what I aim at." As if chagrined, she stopped her almost wild firing. I slowly began to relax and enjoy the ride. There were rare clouds today and a cooling breeze.

Glancing ahead at Reina's shining hair, I thought wistfully of how different everything could have been if she had liked me, sternly checked such useless imaginings. The sooner I was away from Las Coronas, the home to which I could not belong, and Reina, who would not be a sister, the better for us both.

We stopped for lunch under a giant ironwood gripping the eroding sides of a dry wash. The horses, enjoying their loosened girths, moved about lipping the high grass that grew along this low stretch. This was the rainy season, but so far I hadn't experienced the violent thunderstorms everyone kept predicting.

Reina called for the horses. As I was halfway up, the saddle turned, dashing me downward. My foot hung in the stirrup. The reins slipped from my fingers. The horse, frightened, began to run. Trying to kick my foot free, I caught at a sapling and held with all my might, though my ankle felt as if it would break off. Then my foot slipped free. I snapped back against the arching tree, thoroughly scuffed and scratched, breathless from the pain of the wrenched ankle—but alive.

One vaquero rushed to help me up while the other rode after the mare streaking through the scrub, utterly panicked by the jouncing boot. If my foot were still inside it—if I were being hauled over cactus, thorn and rock . . .

I shook uncontrollably. "It is all right, señorita," the vaquero said kindly. "Your foot—can you stand on it?"

Gingerly, I put down enough weight to make me wince. The pain was bearable, though, and when I tried again, I began to hope it was only strained and would not be a nuisance very long.

"Clumsy," remarked Reina, circling to gaze down at me.

"The saddle twisted." For the first time I realized it might not have been an accident, and before I could debate the wisdom of voicing my suspicion, I added, "The girth had to be loose or faulty."

"Are you sure?" demanded Reina. Frowning at the vaquero

who still supported me by the elbow, she asked if he had tightened the cinch.

"Not I, señorita," he said defensively. "I saw to your mount. Felipe looked after your sister's."

Felipe had roped the mare, slowed her, freed the boot, and was now trotting back. "Did you tighten my sister's cinch?" Reina asked Felipe as he dismounted and handed me my scarred and dusty boot.

"Yes, señorita," he said, nearly cowering. "But this mare, she puffs herself up. She must have deceived me."

"I don't permit such mistakes," blazed Reina. "The foreman will pay you what is owing. Leave the ranch tonight."

"But, señorita! I was born here. My father and his father . . ."

"Must have tended their duties better than you or they'd have been lashed to death. You will go, Felipe. This very night."

"But . . ."

"Enough! If you are here in the morning, I will turn you over to the *rurales* for the attempted murder of my sister." She rode ahead.

The two men looked at each other. Ramón retested the girth, helped me into my boot and on the mare. "I'm sorry," I told Felipe. "I'll write a letter to Mr. Sanders, asking him to give you work at the mine."

Felipe's face worked. "You are very kind, señorita," he said huskily. "But I have always been a vaquero. Of Las Coronas."

There was no answer to that. My intercession would only make Reina more adamant. It was not a pleasant afternoon ride. I was distressed for Felipe and my ankle throbbed while my scratched hands burned from sweat and the reins. As we neared Las Coronas, circling to the corrals, I saw a *burra* outlined on a slope. Reina slipped her rifle from the scabbard. Before I could guess her intent, she aimed and fired. The *burra* gave a near-mortal scream, jackknifed, ran a few jolting springs, and collapsed.

I rode forward. Oh, horrid anyway! But let it not be Ratoncita.

As I neared the still-shuddering animal, I knew it was Sewa's pet even before I recognized the bit of red wool she'd plaited into the *burra*'s sparse mane. I slid down from my horse, ran to the little gray beast, whose neat hooves had furrowed the earth in her agony. She went motionless as I reached her.

So useless, wanton! I turned to face Reina, who had followed and now watched with a faint smile playing at the edges of her mouth.

"Why did you do it?" I blurted, unable to control my outrage, though I knew it fed some appetite of hers.

"It made a good target. And it was mine. Every living creature on Las Coronas is mine, or subject to my will."

"You have no right to kill like that—for no reason at all!"

She shrugged, expertly reining her black around. "Oh, there was a reason."

"What? Why on earth . . ."

"To show you that I could," she said, and spurred her horse away.

Trembling with anger and pity, I touched the *burra*, slaughtered because of a conflict it could know nothing of. Animals, compared with humans, were so unmalicious that it seemed whoever or whatever had put us both on earth should look after them better. I looked up to find the two vaqueros waiting, Ramón holding my mare.

Coming to lightning decision, I told him to take the horse on to the stable and asked Felipe to walk with me. His dark face showed his bafflement.

"But your ankle, señorita!"

"It is all right," I said, though it pained. He dismounted and started for the corrals.

"Felipe, you are leaving tonight?"

"What else? The *rurales* would shoot me, even though . . ." He checked himself.

I took the plunge. "I want to leave tonight too."

"You, señorita?"

"Yes. With the Yaqui child. I'll pay you well to help us get to the railroad, and if you want to go with us to the mine, I'll make sure you are employed."

"You go to Mina Rara? Señor Sanders knows?"

"No. But the mine is my property. And I cannot stay here. My sister hates me."

"More than you guess," grunted Felipe. He stared at the ground a moment, then threw back his head. "Señorita, *she* made me leave your cinch loose! If you had died, I wouldn't have been ordered off Las Coronas."

It made me sick, though I'd half-suspected something of the sort. "I didn't want to do it, señorita," Felipe protested miserably, his words tumbling out. "But your sister told me that otherwise she would accuse me of stealing valuables and send me to prison for life. It was wrong, I know that. And I tell you this because you should know before you trust me."

"Well, you have told me," I said briskly, and wondered that I could sound matter-of-fact about the certainty that my sister had tried to have me killed.

To fear a possibility was one thing—I'd kept hoping that it wouldn't happen, that Reina didn't detest me that much. Now that desperate hope was gone. She hated me, hated unto death, and I had better not give her time to arrange another accident. We had stopped by the corral. I turned to Felipe, searching his eyes.

After what he'd admitted, did I dare put my faith in him? What else could I do? I didn't want to involve anyone who was staying at Las Coronas and it would be difficult, if not impossible, to get mounts saddled for myself and Sewa without attracting attention. Further, I much preferred a guide to the railroad.

"I believe that your telling me what you tried to do means you wouldn't try it again," I said. "I know you might get back in my sister's good graces by telling her my plan, but I hope you know you cannot rely on her."

"Yes. She would probably see that I died to make sure she was never exposed," she said. "If you believe me now, señorita, I swear by my head that I will hold your life above my own."

"And the child?"

"She is yours." He shrugged after brief hesitation. "I will protect her."

"Then let us go. When is the best time for you to bring mounts?"

"About an hour after darkness. My friends will be sorry and give me what food they can."

"I can get food. Will we need to sleep on the way?"

Felipe gave an expressive shrug. "Not unless we are ready to sleep permanently, my lady. We can rest, of course. The horses will travel well in the cool night—and there is another *burra* that children have ridden."

"I hate to tell Sewa about Ratoncita, but I don't want to lie, either."

Felipe smiled at this foible. "No need, señorita. I will tell her that her *burra* is where we cannot catch her easily. God knows that is true."

Sticking to principle seemed less important than sparing Sewa more heartbreak. Feeling relieved about that at least, entered the patio and crossed to my room.

Sewa took the news that we were leaving that night with little emotion, except for cuddling Ku to her heart. "Can we take it?" she asked. The big brown eyes were hopeful, though she had stilled her face to stoically receive whatever had to be.

"Of course we'll take it," I said, trying to sound gay.

I wished that I could convince myself that this was a thrilling adventure like those I had read about in romances where, if danger threatened, a strong handsome man appeared to set everything right. The trouble was that I had seen a child lose her foot, I had seen the massacred Yaquis, felt the venom of my own sister's hate. Court Sanders was a dubious protector and Trace, who had seemed so earnest and caring, had gone off without a word. Still, I tried to act confident for Sewa as I packed our things into two canvas bags that could be tied behind our saddles.

I left my coat and heaviest garments in the armoire, touched my books and alabaster dresser set lingeringly. It was impossible, horseback, to take even the few possessions I had and it made me sad to think I might never see them again. Later, when I was of age and Reina was over her worst temper, perhaps I could get them back. I touched the books one by one, their faded covers.

Shakespeare, Bacon, John Donne, Dickens, Dumas, the Brontës, Balzac, and George Eliot. Father had given me Mark Twain and Longfellow, Emerson and Thoreau, Louisa May Alcott, and even Walt Whitman, of whom Miss Mattison had vigorously disapproved.

"So many books," murmured Sewa. "You must have all the books in the world. . . ."

"No, darling." I laughed, turning from the shelf. "There are thousands and thousands of books in our world, in many languages, some very, very old."

"Older than Jesucristo?"

"Much, much older."

She looked at me in that grave way that revealed a struggle between her faith in me and her common sense. "We had a book in my family," she said at last. "There were written the names, far, far back, with the society a person had been in, or their office. One of my uncles was a general and my grandfather was one of the five governors of the pueblo. The soldiers burned it."

I didn't sentimentalize longer over my books, but went to the kitchen to see what I could scavenge without being noticed.

I dined with Reina, scarcely able to look at her after her senseless killing of the little *burra*. "How is your ankle?" she inquired.

"Only a bit tender." Which was both true and lucky.

"I should have held that careless Felipe for the *rurales*," she said, studying an emerald ring that glowed no more coldly bright than her eyes. I was sickened by her duplicity till I decided she doubtless felt like punishing the vaquero because I hadn't been dragged to death.

Shrugging, I took a sip of wine and said, "I wish you hadn't dimissed him. After all, he was born here."

"He must go." Her tone was harsh as she ripped the flesh from a fowl bone. "He knows he's fortunate to get away with his life. We don't tolerate careless servants in Mexico."

I wondered what she would think when Sewa and I were

missing next day. Of course, the tracks of three mounts would tell the story, but long before pursuit could start we should be on the train.

I refused to consider the possibility of Court's handing me over to Reina. Surely I could bribe or persuade him into hiding me if she came snooping about the mine, and in six months she would no longer be my guardian.

Excusing myself after a dessert of cool melon, I left Reina brooding over her wine. Once in my room, I bolted the door and helped Sewa dress in her leather outfit before I changed into mine. Darkness settled gradually in the patio.

In another hour . . .

I fought to keep from pacing, betraying my tenseness to Sewa. "Tell me Ku's story in Yaqui," I suggested. "As you would to a little child who didn't know many words."

"I will like that." Sewa smoothed her pet's feathers and trilled the flute. "I will make music, too, for the speech of the birds. This is the owl. Here is the dove. This is the woodpecker and this the quail." She contrived a droll sound like a rusty chain rattling. "That's *paisano!*" She turned solemn and began in Yaqui: "Long before the coming of the Spaniards, there was a bird, all alone. He had no feather, no, not one—"

The latch of my door lifted, but the bolt, of course, held. My heart turned in my throat. There came a pounding, Reina's angry voice.

"Why do you lock the doors in my house? What wickedness are you concealing? Open at once!"

She would have men break the door down. Our only chance lay in pretending everything was as usual. I stowed the saddle packs under the bed and hurried to the door, realizing that both Sewa and I had on our riding clothes.

No time to change. Mind shuffling frantically for an explanation, I opened the door. Reina swept through, checked, and her eyes glinted from me to the child and back.

"In leather? The two of you! Where did that brat get such an outfit?"

"There was enough leather."

Reina's lips tightened. "If Emilio has so much time, I'll see what I can do to keep him busy! Why are you dressed like this at such an hour?"

"You must remember Sewa has lost a foot. I—I was entertaining her by showing how her outfit is like mine."

"Well, God knows you are fool enough to waste your time in such foolishness," Reina snapped. "I tell you now that neither brat nor crow is going to Hermosillo with us. And I have decided not to wait on the weather. We will leave in the morning by carriage."

"In the morning! Why, that's not time—"

"If I can be ready, so can you."

I thought that acceding too quickly might stir her suspicions. "But I thought Mr. Sanders wanted us to visit the mine," I protested.

"So we will, on the way back. What a rabbit you are, Miranda! He must suit our convenience, not the other way around."

"You must remember that I was educated where we were taught respect and consideration for other people, even if they were employees."

She drew herself up, radiating scorn. "I can't believe you're my sister! All that pious, prim shopkeeper talk! Leave Court to me—but be ready by nine."

She went out, swinging the door after her so that it jarred with a crash. I went quickly to Sewa, hugged her close. "It's all right, little flower. We'll soon be where she can't bother us. Go on with your story. See, Ku's ready to sing with you!"

Time, measured by the ornate gilt clock, seemed to crawl. Fears and awful imaginings filled my head. Supposing Reina hadn't been fooled? Supposing she'd surprised Felipe and he wouldn't be at the gate? Supposing she followed to the mine?

Grimly, I pushed these fantasies aside, helped Sewa on with her boot, and fished the packs out from the bed. Sewa held Ku to her breast and steadied herself with the sotol staff Cruz had given her. Our steps, quiet as we tried to make them, seemed to resound in the patio and my heart battered against my lungs so I could scarcely breathe, but at last we reached the gate. Felipe stepped instantly from the shadows. We all knew the importance of quiet. Sewa leaned against the wall near a *burra* that, to me, looked exactly like Ratoncita, but the child gasped.

"Your *burra* was where I could not catch her," Felipe said softly. "This one is her sister."

"She is nice," Sewa murmured in Spanish, her voice heavy with stifled tears. "But her ears are not so splendid as Ratoncita's."

"No, they are not," Felipe agreed.

His confirmation of her *burra*'s superior beauty helped Sewa accept the substitute. She reached out to stroke the new beast and I went back for the other saddle pack.

When I returned, Sewa was mounted, Ku in his leather nest at her saddle horn. Felipe finished strapping the first pack behind her saddle and tied the one I had just fetched behind mine, then gave me a hand up. In a moment we were riding.

We circled the corrals and house at a distance, rejoining the road some distance from the gates and guard. A sickle moon pinned together the last night from the western horizon and the deep blue of the higher sky. The white dust of the road seemed almost luminescent as it cut through mesquite and cholla, the giant cardones. Heat still rose from the ground, but the breeze came cool from the western sea and I thought it wouldn't be long before Sewa and I needed our jackets.

Thinking of Emilio's handiwork made me remember Reina's displeasure at his kindness to Sewa, and troubled me in case she thought he or Consuelo had helped us escape. A moment's reflection persuaded me that Felipe's disappearance and the three tracks would exonerate other Las Coronas people. Reina would doubtless question them, but their genuine puzzlement should convince her, and though I had been sorry not to tell our friends good-bye, I was glad now I hadn't, for their sakes.

We rode in silence except for the rubbing of leather and sound of hooves. I'd been too anxious to feel tired before, but now weariness spread through me so that I felt heavy and ponderous, as if a strong wind could tilt me out of the saddle.

When Felipe called a halt, my descent, even with his help, was more fall than dismounting. We drank from the water bags, the water tepid and smelly, and I walked Sewa about. She said the foot boot helped her balance so she wore it while riding. Even Ku exercised in his hopping lurch and our mounts enjoyed twenty minutes of loose girths and the bits of forage Sewa and I found for them.

"Let's go on now," said Felipe, beginning to tighten the girths. "At the next stop we can sleep an hour, and when we reach the railroad, we can rest till the train comes."

"When is it due?"

"Due?" Felipe chuckled. "Señorita, it is supposed to reach the Switch about seven, but it could be noon."

"Noon?" I groaned. "My God, my sister could have men here by then if they rode fast."

"*If* they rode fast, señorita."

I couldn't see his smile on the dim blur of his face, but I heard it in his voice. "You mean the vaqueros wouldn't try to catch us?"

"Most of the men are my comrades. Some admire *la patrona* for her beauty and boldness, but they say you are kind like your mother and just as your father was. When I told them what *la patrona* made me do, they were angry. No, señorita, they will not hurry."

"But my sister might ride with them."

I caught the bulking of his shrug. "There are always accidents. Perhaps I turned the horses out of the corral and it will take hours to catch some up. Perhaps her mounts have gone lame or cast their shoes. My friends could not delay her forever, of course, but a few hours?" He chuckled. "They will manage that, señorita."

Thinking of Reina's driving force, I wasn't so sure. Hadn't she pressured Felipe into leaving my girth loose? But there was no use worrying any more than could be helped. If the train was reasonably on time, we were safe. If not . . .

Leave it to heaven, I decided, between Shakespeare and Mexican fatalism. I put Ku in his nest and we started on.

It was eternity till the next stop, a haze of creaking saddles, clopping of hooves, the occasional sound of one of the mounts blowing through its nostrils. I felt like a bag of sand that had started out evenly distributed but had now been shaken till all the weight loaded my thighs and legs and there was nothing left above my waist but a giddy, drowsing head.

In this half-stupor, dreams, fears, and wishes drifted through my mind: my mother amid the chanting with candles at head and feet; the Yaqui women with milk dried on their wasted nipples; Sewa, stiffening in my arms while the iron seared; Trace, watching me with those strange eyes, promising his help, leaving without a word.

Oh yes, even the horrors didn't startle me more awake than the fleeting bittersweet memory of his touch, of his eyes, his voice. . . . Court Sanders? He roused me, too, but in a confusion of attraction and dislike that was close to fear. He was like a lynx or wild cat—handsome, amoral, yet at this time my only chance of refuge.

Too exhausted to be uncomfortable, I held the reins mechanically, kept jerking awake. I hoped Sewa wasn't too tired. She'd napped that day and hadn't done anything very active, but I was afraid her stump might be sore from prolonged contact with the boot.

After what seemed a century, Felipe stopped again. We let the horses drink at an earthen tank and this time we tossed the saddles down and hobbled our mounts. I helped Sewa off with her boot and cuddled up with her against the saddles, mumbled thanks to Felipe, who spread a serape over us. Ku, in his nest by Sewa, gave a sleepy croak, ruffled his feathers, and composed himself.

Face touching Sewa's hair, which smelled cleanly of orris-root, I identified the pungent odor of Felipe's corn-shuck cigarette and fell into heavy sleep with only a flicker of wonder that Miranda Greenleaf, late of Miss Mattison's school for young ladies, in flight from the sister who should have been my haven, huddled with a Yaqui orphan, a crippled raven, and renegade vaquero under the stars of Sonora.

8

The night and ride would never end. We were snared in a pattern of darkness, muted hooves, weariness where time had stopped and our destination moved farther away the closer we came. My spine ached; I ached all over. Yesterday's perilous ride with Reina seemed to have taken place a century ago. I'd been in the saddle most of the last twenty hours, and the hours between the time Reina had shot the *burra* and Sewa and I left with Felipe had not exactly been restful.

The east began to lighten. Streaks of coral and red appeared, glowed more intensely as the horizon behind us, broken by distant mountains, exploded with the sun.

"We're almost there," Felipe assured me. "The Switch is just beyond these little hills."

It was, marked by a shed and some corrals. We watered the horses and *burra,* turned them loose so they could make their way back to familiar grazing. Felipe put my saddle, bridle, and Sewa's in the shed where Las Coronas people should find them, but he kept his own riding gear. It was all he possessed after thirty years at the ranch.

We ate, drank water while we wished for coffee, and Sewa

and I tidied ourselves as much as possible. Thoroughly awake but feeling hollow and shaky, I turned to Felipe in sudden dread.

"Could the train have come already?"

"Early?" His dark brows shot up. "Señorita, what a compliment!"

"Well, it would seem possible," I said defensively, ruffled at his mirth, though it was reassuring.

Felipe convulsed with laughter, straightened, gasping. "May I tell you a joke, señorita? I would not give offense, but it will tell you about trains in Mexico."

"Please do," I said.

"A lady was on the train and at last she sought out the conductor. 'Señor,' she told him, 'the train must stop. I am going to have a baby.' 'But, señora,' protested the conductor, 'you should not have got on the train if you were in that condition.' 'Señor,' the lady answered, 'when I got on the train, I was not in this condition!' "

I had to laugh in spite of the impropriety, and that eased my fears enough to make me suspect Felipe was deliberately trying to amuse me. For which I blessed him. But I certainly hoped the train would come before the pursuers I was sure Reina would send after us.

If Sewa was nervous, she didn't show it. I envied her calm as she leaned against a paloverde's scarred trunk and played her flute to Ku. Felipe smoked and braided rawhide into a rope. He must have been worried, too, because if Reina caught him helping me, she would find some terrible way to punish him. But he whistled and sang and soon he and Sewa were harmonizing appealingly.

They fell silent as I raised my hand. "Was that a train whistle?"

It came distinctly. Felipe nodded, getting to his feet. Ten minutes later we were safely on board and heading north. As the train pulled away from the Switch and the road to Las Coronas stretched blankly away, I breathed deeply for the first time in hours.

We had made it. At least for now.

If Court would only help . . . I set my jaw. He would, one

way or another. He *had* to. The train chugged on and I leaned back in my seat next to Sewa's. The sun was hot on my face, so I tipped my hat over my face. In a few minutes I was asleep.

I woke to jarring, wheels grinding slower and slower as the train shuddered like a stricken monster. For a moment I didn't remember where we were—who we were, for that matter—till Sewa's fingers tightened on mine and Ku gave a croak of annoyance. Felipe, sitting across from us, peered out the window.

He sat down at once as if his knees had buckled.

"What is it?" I asked.

His lips moved several times before he could speak. "Yaquis. Sierra Yaquis." He reached inside his shirt, pulled a knife from the sheath dangling around his neck.

I could scarcely understand. My brain moved sluggishly, as if by refusing the situation a normal one could be substituted. "What do they want?"

Felipe stared as if I were an idiot. "Money, jewelry, clothes—whatever we have. And blood."

"Sewa is Yaqui. She can tell them—"

"Maybe, if she has a chance." Felipe concealed the knife up his sleeve. "Do what they say, señorita. I will try to protect you, but there are a score of them and they have guns."

I had enough wit to unclasp the little crucifix my mother had sent me. It wasn't worth much in money, but it was my most prized treasure. I slipped it into my mouth, the safest place I could think of.

The conductor appeared in the door, shouted into the rising commotion as passengers, most of them prosperous Americans or Mexicans, realized why the train had stopped.

"Ladies and gentlemen! Please step outside quietly. Do as you are told. Otherwise you may be killed."

"But—but you must protect us!" spluttered a plump American woman who was traveling with her scrawny husband. She wore a dress of peacock blue, pinned with an amethyst and sapphire brooch. Peacock feathers trailed from her elaborate velvet hat. Her husband was in black, but a heavy gold chain draped across his waistcoat and his tie stud sparkled like a real diamond. I suspected it was.

"Madam," pleaded the conductor, "they have cut the throats of our two armed guards. If you wish to preserve your own neck—"

"Come, my love," said the small man briskly, extending his arm, managing to propel her bulk along the aisle.

"But, Harry—"

"Goddammit, Ruby, keep still for the next ten minutes or you may not have a tongue!"

His profanity shocked her into obedience. They were first off the train. Urged by the conductor, the others followed. We came last because of Sewa's foot. She held fiercely to Ku and I thought how bitter it was that a child should be afraid of her own people. Would she know any of the robbers? Would they recognize her as Yaqui and spare her, at least?

Yaquis. I had known Sewa, and Cruz, and had witnessed the slaughtered group in the foothills. Now I saw the aspect that made Yaquis feared, turned them into bogies to frighten children. It wasn't a large band, perhaps twenty souls, but each was a shout of ferocity, ruthless determination, from the apparent leader, a squat man with coarse black hair splayed about his face, to a boy not much older than Sewa.

There was one woman. Lean in flank and face, her breasts swelled under a khaki shirt, defined by crossed bandoliers. She had long black hair tied with a red ribbon and her face had the harsh beauty of carved stone.

"Your jewelry and watches, your money," she said in slow good Spanish.

Some of the passengers must have known only English. They looked puzzled for a moment till other passengers, with more or less speed, began to follow the order. The youngster walked along, collecting watches, earrings, necklaces, rings, wallets, and money. Another man followed, inspecting pockets and handbags, confiscating objects some had hoped to secrete. Several robbers were tossing suitcases and trunks off the train, rifling them for valuables.

"But that's my mother's wedding ring," objected one man

whose wife had just been stripped of a plain gold band. "It's not worth much to you, but to us—"

"Please, sir, don't argue," cautioned the conductor. "If we don't anger them, we may get off with our lives."

"Outrageous!" bawled the woman in the peacock dress. "My husband has invested heavily in this dreadful country. If we can't be protected—"

"Ruby, shut your mouth," advised her husband, yielding his gold chain. He removed her brooch and handed it to the boy. The second Yaqui flipped off her hat, stuck it rakishly on his head to the mirth of his comrades. The woman gave a wail of impotent rage.

As they neared us, Sewa spoke to the boy in Yaqui. I got the gist of it. She was telling him about her murdered family and that Felipe and I had helped her.

The boy gave her an astonished look, but the man behind him had heard. He held up Sewa's face, asked her a few questions. Then he called out to the woman and leader. The woman dismounted, came to examine the girl with intent dark eyes, frowning at me.

Her rough but melodious voice drilled out questions. She touched Sewa's boot, listened to how she had lost the foot, crossed herself at the mention of Cruz's name. Then she took Sewa's hand. "You must come with us," she said in Spanish. "We live hard and fight the Mexicans, but it is a better way for you than to be the house pet of this gringa."

Sewa didn't struggle but neither did she follow. "I want to be with Miranda," she said in Yaqui so slowly that I understood most of it. "She is my sister-mother."

"Nonsense! She is your enemy!"

"I am lame," Sewa reminded them. "I would be a hindrance."

"That is true!" called the leader. "We have enough mouths to feed, Tula. Let us get on with our business."

For a moment I thought the panther woman would argue with him, but then she shrugged and let Sewa go, stepping back.

"Now, señores and señoras, we will have your clothes," she

commanded. "We need them more than you. It is cold in the Sierra."

A gasp went up from the women. "Harry!" shrieked the fat one, clutching her debrooched bosom. The young man who had pleaded for his mother's ring stepped in front of his wife.

"Such dishonor—" He choked. "I—I'd rather die!"

"Nonsense," said Tula. "No one is raping your wife." She spoke, not unkindly, to the terrified young woman. "If you want your brave husband to live, give us your things quickly. You may each keep an undergarment."

"Please," the wife whispered to her husband. "This only lasts a few minutes. You would be dead forever."

"She is more intelligent than she looks, señor," observed Tula, and strolled toward me. "I can use those skirt-trousers," she told me. "No, little one," she said to Sewa, who was struggling out of her things, "we do not rob our own."

I took off my jacket and vest, fumbled at my skirt. Why did training make it so hard, even under threat of death, to cast off our coverings? The fat matron amply corseted, buried her face in her hands while the peacock dress lay on the earth. Her husband looked like a plucked chicken in his long-legged drawers. If it hadn't been for the shame and fear, we were a laughable sight. Tula discarded her ragged skirt and pulled on my divided one, surveying it with delight. It was easy for me to imagine her at Sewa's age, orphaned and hounded. I couldn't hate, though I certainly did fear her.

The young wife stood in her camisole and petticoat. One of the men shouted something that Tula translated. "Your underthings are so pretty that he wants them for his girl friend. Here, you can hide yourself with my skirt."

She thrust the rag at the flinching girl, whose husband seemed to go mad. Springing on the Yaqui who was just picking up the peacock dress, the young man wrestled him to the ground, stumbled up with the rifle, fired without aiming into the robbers.

Tula cut him down from the side, but a husky American had charged the horsemen. He died from a machete swing that opened his body under the ribs, almost severing it in half. The leader shouted in Yaqui.

"Now there has been death, we must kill them all so it can seem the work of any robbers."

The Yaquis raised their guns and machetes. Tula snatched Sewa out of range, though the child screamed and tried to get back to me. So this was the end of it, on a clear fine morning under a bright sky?

So unreal I couldn't believe it. The leader's gaze fell on me. He spoke to Tula, who scowled but pulled me away from the edge of the group.

"You can't do this," I pleaded, speech stumbling because of the crucifix concealed in my cheek. "These people haven't hurt you."

A crash of bullets drowned my words. There were a few who had to be finished with knives or machetes, including the fat woman who flopped about in her own blood till the leader severed her jugular.

The young woman's camisole and skirt was so blood-soaked that the man who had wanted it turned away in disgust. I ran to Felipe. Bloody froth pumped from his mouth and nostrils.

"Señorita," he panted. "Señor Winslade—the night he brought back you and the child, he—he—" Felipe convulsed, tried to form another word, died as blood gushed from his mouth.

Tula grasped my arm. "Come! Lío says we must not kill you because you helped this small one, but God only knows what we can do with you." She handed me my shirt. "Put it on. If that fair skin cooks, you will be even more trouble. You can have my skirt."

The youngest Yaqui, whom they called Domingo, offered me his horse, a scrubby dun. Tula had Sewa, clutching her flute, lifted up behind her, and Domingo, at Sewa's begging, brought Ku in his leather nest. We rode away from the stranded train and the half-naked dead. Though my body wouldn't be found along with Felipe's, Reina would scarcely bother to search for me. It would be convenient to blame robbers for my death, and in time she would doubtless inherit the mine, since I had no other close relative.

What had Felipe tried to say about Trace? Would Trace care a little when he heard what had happened to me?

Glancing around at the desperate little band, I wondered what *would* happen. They had spared me because I had helped Sewa, but if food ran short, if I became a danger— We rode for the mountains, grim and desolate in the distance.

As the shock of the massacre was dulled by growing weariness, thoughts trailed wispily through my mind. Perhaps we could persuade this band to leave us with Cruz? But if he had a sworn enemy in the group, that would imperil him. Or what if Court Sanders would pay a ransom? The Yaquis needed money for buying weapons in Arizona. Court might prefer to play Reina's game, of course; she'd probably pay him well to leave me in Yaqui hands. But he *might* help. There were no certainties left, only mights and maybes and ifs. I put the crucifix around my neck. It was not valuable and no one seemed to care.

We paused once and I was given a swallow of water from a skin. In halting Yaqui I asked Domingo if he didn't want to ride now.

"I can walk." He shrugged. "I am strong. It is not far."

We rode through a narrow defile. It opened into a valley that twisted between fierce, gaunt little hills that looked as if the sun had baked them, like unglazed pottery, into their present shape without giving them time to grow. We came to what seemed to be sheer rock wall. I hoped we would stop here, but Lío rode to the end of the barrier, where, hidden by an overlapping cliff, there was a passage just broad enough for a horseman.

Above us was a fissure of sky, dazzling with just the edge of the sun. Numbed, inert, I longed to rest, but also dreaded the time when we would, for then life would start again, the need to think, decide, act. While we journeyed everything else was suspended. Already I could scarcely remember where we had begun—the fat woman and her skinny man, the young married couple, the half-split-open American. It was a flash of nightmare, not experienced enough to believe. And what lay ahead I could not even guess. It was as if I'd been born to ride with these silent people through the narrow canyons of their hidden fastnesses, never looking back, never arriving.

"Here." A voice jarred me from the haze. Domingo gave me a hand down. My legs buckled and I stumbled against him. He braced himself and let me lean against him till blood tingled in my feet and my mind cleared from the hypnosis of shock and exhaustion.

We were in a high basin ringed by palisades and shallow caves. Six ramadas extended from cliffside depressions and what seemed about a hundred children, women, and men hurried out to greet the raiders and exclaim over their booty.

"Food!" cried one seam-faced old woman. "We need flour and beans more than clothes and jewelry."

"True, *mama grande*," placated Lío. "We brought the food on the train, but there was not much of use that could be carried. We can exchange the jewels for food, though, and for guns and ammunition."

The horses and mules were unloaded and left to graze at the far side of the basin. Clothing was piled up and a feast prepared from what had been salvaged from the train kitchen: ham, loaves of bread, preserves, cheese. But remembering Felipe and the others who would eat no more, I only drank water and forced down a little bread.

Sewa sat by me near a rock outside a ramada and Domingo joined us. He was fascinated by Ku or Sewa or both, and I was glad someone near her age was being friendly. Several of the older people came to speak with the child about her slaughtered family.

The old woman, Camilda, embraced Sewa and told her she was ceremonial kin to one of Sewa's dead uncles. She offered to let Sewa live with her and an astonishing collection of relations by blood, marriage, and ceremony, but when Sewa asked if there was room for me, Camilda's wrinkled face tightened.

"We are too many now for one ramada," she said, and went back to the feast.

"You would think her thatch was a bishop's palace," scoffed Domingo. "Stay in my cave, lady." He pointed to a grotto some distance from the others. "There is room for all three of us and your Ku bird, little Sewa."

She laughed. The sound and the sparkle of her eyes was a marvel and wound to me after what had happened that day, but I had to remember she was back with her people after what had amounted to captivity, no matter how I cherished her.

"We will be a family," she said, grasping my hand and hugging Ku. She hesitated. "But, Domingo, your parents—"

"They are dead." Pain convulsed his young mouth for a second before he stilled his face. "Tula is my sister, but I do not live with her. I was better alone. Till now."

A fire was lit as twilight settled. From the discussion of the men I gathered that three of them would take the money and jewelry. One would buy as much food as possible in a village a day's ride away and the other two would travel to Arizona for guns and ammunition.

Summoning my courage, for my impulse was to remain unnoticed as long as it was allowed, I straightened my clothing and ventured into the shifting glow of light. Tula sat near Lío and I spoke to her in Spanish, for though I was understanding more Yaqui, I couldn't say anything very complex in it.

"I think I can only be a problem for you. You know the Mina Rara?"

She nodded, ruddy light defining the angles of her face, accentuating her smoldering gaze. "We know it. Some of us have relatives there."

"The superintendent, Court Sanders, knows me. I think he would pay if you would let me go."

Tula threw back her head. Laughter pulsed from her throat. "And then you could tell the soldiers and *rurales* where we are and that we killed the train passengers."

"I would not tell."

Tula rolled a corn shuck around black tobacco, lit it at the fire, and deliberately blew smoke at me. "I do not believe you."

"But you can't keep me here forever!" I cried desperately.

"*I* would have left you at the train," she said, and there was no mistaking what she meant.

"Please." I loathed begging but feared what might happen

if I didn't force a decision now. "I swear I will not betray you. I am sorry for what is happening to your people. The money Sanders would pay for me could buy many guns."

Lío stirred himself, staring at me through eyes that were narrowed slits. "Sanders' woman?" he asked in halting Spanish.

I shook my head, flushing with embarrassment. "My father owned the mine."

Lío really sat up. "Don Jonathan?" he asked slowly. "Your father Jonathan Greenleaf?"

"Yes."

"And you helped the child Sewa."

"I could not do much."

Lío pondered a moment, shoulders hunched in a bull-like posture that made him seem solid and lasting as the boulders around us. "You shall go to Mina Rara and not for money," he said at last.

"Lío!" blazed Tula, catching his arm. "She will tell where we are! If it's known we did the killing today, we will be hunted more than ever and already we live in fear of our lives, stealing enough grain to survive!"

"She is Don Jonathan's daughter. I accept her word."

"And what was this Don Jonathan, this Englishman, to you?" the woman sneered.

Lío spoke heavily, a bull trying to elude a stinging fly. "My father worked at the mine and was hurt in a fall. Don Jonathan had a doctor for him, gave him his house and enough to keep our family till I was old enough to work."

"A man preserves his beasts of burden," said Tula.

"No. Don Jonathan kept us alive, in decency, for five years when there was no man working and six children to be fed. We were not beasts to him. We were people."

"You are a great fool, Lío!"

He shrugged. "Nevertheless."

"At least get money for her."

"My father had the money many years ago."

She got up and walked away with an angry swing of her rounded hips outlined by my divided skirt. "In a few days," Lío told me. "In a few days I will send you to the mine."

"Sewa? May I keep her with me?"

He scowled, leaning his chin on his knee, and sighed. "Let me think. She may need you now and she would be safer with you, but can we let her forget her people?" I would have spoken but he waved me off. "Let me think," he repeated. "And let me set your mind at rest on one point. My men might kill you but they won't rape."

Back at the grotto, Domingo had made a large communal nest for us, two straw mats beneath, a horse-and-smoke-pungent serape, several shawls from the train pillage, and a ragged tarpaulin. It was cool now in this higher region, and we soon arranged ourselves, Sewa in the middle, Ku at her head under a protecting ledge. Stars winked above the palisades and talk went on in the other ramadas and around the fire, but we were soon asleep, sharing our warmth, joined by the rising and falling of our breath.

Three men left next morning with jewels, watches, and money. The pair bound for Tucson wouldn't be back for weeks, but the one sent to buy food in the village might return next day. He was also carrying such clothing as was not needed by the people in the basin to give a Yaqui group hiding out in another canyon. Lío had told me to select a dress and I'd found one of my own in the pile, so I no longer needed Tula's rags.

There was coffee from the train for breakfast, and old Camilda gave us some tortillas. Domingo went off hunting with some of the men. Most of the women were busy altering and devising garments from those looted from the train, though they did carry water from a spring to the squash, corn, bean, and melon patches in the center of the basin. They watched me curiously and a few talked with Sewa, but we were mainly left to ourselves.

"I want to stay with you," she told me. "Will Señor Sanders permit it?"

"The question is, will Lío?"

"I am lame," she said matter-of-factly. "And this band has enough children. He will let me go."

"I hope so," I said and turned to greet Camilda, who had come to ask for the third time all the details of the destruction of Sewa's family.

I diverted the old woman's attention by asking how long the band had been in this basin. "Since spring," she said and went on to tell how they were remnants of several *rancherías* that had been raided and the strong adults sent off to Yucatán as slaves.

"I had a good house," she lamented. "My two sons and their families lived with me. They were farmers and hunters. We always had enough to eat and could even hold *fiestas*. Where are they now, my daughters, my strong sons-in-law?" Weaving her gnarled hands together, she swayed and intoned her answer. "Antonio they shot, and my daughter, too, when she clung to his body. Chepa and Pablo were marched away with their oldest son. The two small children were given away like pups or cats, I suppose, to be brought up as Mexicans or slaves. May God damn these devils for what they do to us."

As the day wore on and I met other women, I heard variations, over and over, of the same story. There was not a person in camp who hadn't lost family in the government raids, not a person who didn't burn for vengeance. But they were facing the fact that they'd have to live indefinitely in the wilderness and were beginning to build homes for the winter—adobes, not the traditional mud and wattle or airy cane houses sufficient in the frost-free valley. Soldiers had come near them many times, but the solid-appearing rock wall had so far deceived their enemies.

Lío, Tula, and the men had struck at different Mexican ranches, stealing all the food they could get, terrorizing these intruders on Yaqui land. Any time they saw a military force that wasn't vastly superior in numbers, Lío devised a way to ambush it. In the past four months, the band must have killed five times their number of soldiers. If only they had enough guns. That was the refrain.

Though Lío was the acknowledged leader, he was not despotic. Camilda scolded him for snoring the night before, and he spent the afternoon consulting with Tula and the men about a proposed expedition against Mexicans who had taken up land of deported Yaquis along the river of the Eight Sacred Pueblos. Even so, he found time to admire Ku and teach Sewa a new tune on the flute. Tula didn't like this, scowled from a distance, and finally called him.

That night one of the men played a yucca fiddle and Tula sang with a wild sadness that stirred the blood, watching Lío, making it an intimate plaint. When Domingo, Sewa, Ku, and I settled to rest, it seemed we had been together a long time.

Lookouts were posted at various points, both for defense and to spot possible sources of booty and any groups of soldiers or *rurales* the band could hope to vanquish. "We nibble like ants at a carcass," Lío had said the day before. "Yet I have seen many a bull or stallion stripped to the bone by the little warriors."

Several days passed uneventfully. I hoped Lío would send me to the mine soon but feared to press. Then one morning we woke to a flurry in camp, saddling up, horses whinnying. "Do you want to go with us, young one?" Lío called to Domingo. "There are a dozen well-equipped Mexicans riding past the canyon, and most have good rifles, Paco says. We can keep their best horses and slaughter and eat our worst ones."

Domingo looked at Sewa, who had waked and was watching him with fatalistic knowledge that was terrible to see in so young a face. What lay ahead for these two who had already endured horrors that most people seldom even hear of? I hoped to protect Sewa, but what could become of Domingo, hiding and fighting till the inevitable final crushing of his people?

As Domingo hesitated, Tula strode over. "Up!" she told him. "Have you become a girl child?" She thrust a tortilla into his hand. "Eat and get your horse."

Domingo sighed. His hand brushed Sewa's cheek. Yesterday's leisure with Sewa and Ku must have been like an echo of his lost childhood, sweeter for being irrevocably lost.

"See if you can teach that ugly raven how to sing," he told the girl.

Sewa clung to his hand. "Come back," she said. "Please be careful."

He laughed. For a moment I caught a glimpse of how he

would look in ten years, if he lived. "I shall grow very old, *mama grande* says. She dreamed she saw me with long yellow teeth like a mule's." He croaked in Ku's offended face, tweaked Sewa's braid, and ran for his horse, cramming the tortilla into his mouth.

The group, led by Lío and Tula, rode out of the basin. I was torn by sympathy for them, affection for Domingo, and distress over the probable fate of the Mexicans they planned to swoop on, probably men like Felipe or Emilio or Enrique.

Sewa was morose that day, in spite of Camilda's telling jokes and stories. Later that afternoon, I found her sobbing, Ku hopping about in frustrated curiosity as it tried vainly to nestle under her arm.

I sat down and took her in my arms. "What is it, darling?"

She wept in real earnest, rubbing her face against my shoulder. "I—I don't want Domingo to die. But I don't want him to kill anyone either. Oh, Miranda, can he stay with us at the mine? Would Señor Sanders let him?"

The same thought must have been working deep in my mind, for I felt a sense of relief when she asked it. "It's not so much a question of Sanders," I explained, stroking her hair. "If he accepts us at all, he'll do what I ask. But Lío needs men and Tula— Well, you saw what she did today."

Sewa's hand crept into mine, so trustingly that it wrenched my heart. "Lío reveres your father. It is possible he will do this thing for you."

"I'll ask," I promised. "Now why don't you pay some attention to Ku? He's about to turn somersaults!"

She laughed and I gave her a bit of tortilla to feed him. Just before sunset, when the palisades glowed crimson and the sky was a shout of glory, Lío's troop rode into the basin.

In their midst was a woman, hands lashed to the saddle horn, blindfolded, garments ripped, but head held high. As they halted, she swore at her captors and the last sun gilded her hair.

It was Reina.

9

I ran forward, forgetful of everything except that my sister was a captive and might be hurt. A man hauled her from the saddle and removed the blindfold. She stumbled, bound hands hampering her, and I kept her from falling.

"Reina!" I caught her arms, steadying her. "Are you all right?"

Her head snapped back, her green eyes flashed. "You!" her raw voice grated between cracked lips, but after an impotent reaching of her hands, she screwed up her mouth and spat.

Too astonished to dodge, I felt spittle strike my cheek.

"So this is where you went!" she hissed. "Hiding out with these devils. No doubt you've had the lot between your legs, you with your prissy English rearing."

"Didn't you find the train?" I asked. "Felipe?"

"We found it, decided bandits had taken you away, and good riddance, too!" Disgust hoarsened her tone. "I never dreamed that even you would become a woman of these Yaquis. I was doing my duty, hunting for you, when this band attacked us."

"Your men?"

"All dead."

Dread squeezed my heart. "Enrique?" I asked. "Ramón?"

"Were they your lovers, too?" she sneered. "Ramón is dead. Enrique didn't come."

Lío, with his bowlegged stride, had come over, observing us. "You know this redheaded one?"

"She is my sister."

He stared at her, shocked, then gave a shake of his massive head. "You mean she is the child of the Mexican woman. She is not Jonathan Greenleaf's daughter."

"No, but we have the same mother."

"She spat on you."

"She is still of my blood."

"It is a difficulty then. I learned today that three of our men are captives in Torim. The commandant might barter their lives for that of this *hidalga*. I have sent a messenger with the offer. If the commandant refuses, I have sworn to send him the broken body of a woman."

"Won't that only cause more reprisals?"

Lío shrugged. "My people are being killed and deported for no reason. And just as this woman is your sister, the three men in the Torim *guardia* are my comrades, valiant fighters."

"You could have bargained with me."

His grizzled head moved slowly. "No, I could not."

"But I must ask you to. Let her go and use me to win your friends' liberty."

He spread his thick callous hands. "They may not go free. And I keep my oaths. If they die, so must a highborn woman of the Mexicans."

Slowly I said, "I wouldn't expect you to break your word."

His lips broke against his teeth in a rueful grin and he rubbed the back of his head with a big hand. "It would be hard for me to keep it—but I would. You believe that?"

"I believe it."

"Why will you not go to safety tomorrow? It is clear this one hates you, sister or no."

"Our mother loved us both."

"You are not your mother."

"No, but she is in me. I don't love my sister, but our mother in me cannot leave her, maybe to die."

"Well, I cannot argue." Lío shrugged. "If you understand that you stand in this woman's place and accept her fate, she can go."

"I would rather stay!" Reina blazed, standing very straight, gazing around as if to imprint the basin and every person there in her memory. "I don't want to owe my life to this whore."

Lío struck her face with the flat of his hand. She staggered against Domingo, who had come to listen, pushed away from him, and smiled on Lío with bloodied lips.

"You are a man of oaths, and for that blow, if I live *I* swear that I'll see the birds peck the eyes in your severed head."

He bowed slightly. "You are brave, lady, but I do not like you. Perhaps I cannot, in justice to my band who depend on me, let you go. I can risk my own head and eyes, but I have no right to risk the others."

"Your head will do," Reina said slightly. "God knows it's ugly enough."

He eyed her, considering. "You promise not to hurt my people if they fell into your hands."

She shrugged in her turn. "I can't help what my vaqueros do if they meet your men in open fight. But you know I'll try to find you."

"And if you do?"

"Your head. Yours only."

He laughed hugely in a great bull bellowing. "Yours if you can get it, lady! But if you come into my hands again, I will rape you till you do not talk so merrily of lopping off heads. Come now and eat. When you have rested, I will send you away."

Tula sent Reina a glance of pure hatred and I wondered if Reina would have died, had Lío kept her. "That is a she-dog," Domingo muttered as we went to Sewa, who was waiting with her heart in her eyes. "It is a crazy bargain, lady. Lío will do as he says."

"Let's hope the commandant lets the men go," I said, but I felt sick and couldn't eat.

If I had kept still, we would be on our way to the Mina Rara in a few days. And Reina had as good a chance as I to live, I wouldn't have been abandoning her to certain death. Now it would mean more watching, fearing, wondering. . . .

But there was nothing else I could have done.

Lío permitted Reina to rest for an hour after supper. Then she was tied in the saddle, blindfolded in spite of the darkness, and sent between two men out of the basin. Lío had placed her in the saddle, his hands had lingered, and I wondered what would happen if they ever met again. I didn't tell her good-bye. If she had hated me before, she would abominate me now and I doubted that she would have consented to the switch if it hadn't been for the vision of Lío's head to kick in the dust. The canyon swallowed her up, and I lay down with the children.

Domingo took Sewa walking around the basin next day. He hadn't spoken of the clash with the Las Coronas vaqueros. Had he killed yet? I couldn't ask. Through the day, as I worked on the shelters, I watched, glimpsing the children now resting on a ledge, now strolling along the canyon, Sewa using the sotol staff Cruz had given her.

"They are fond of each other," Lío said, startling me since I hadn't heard him coming. "Domingo will miss the little flower—if she goes to the Mina Rara."

I knew he meant if my life, now in pawn for his comrades, were redeemed. But I refused to worry. I would believe I was going free until the messenger came back with fatal news. And so I took advantage of Lío's pensive mood.

"Domingo's very young. Could he stay at the mine with me and Sewa?"

Lío scowled. For the first time I felt his eyes raking me in a male questing. I couldn't help blushing but I didn't retreat, though he took a step forward till his brawny arm almost touched my breast.

"If you have such a penchant for Yaqui children, lady, you should get some of your own." He laughed. "They would be half-Yaqui anyway."

I didn't try to put distance between myself and Lío or answer his crude teasing. "Can Domingo come with me?" I persisted.

Lío shrugged. "You will have to ask Tula. And that will be easy. She's coming this way." He chuckled wickedly. "She's jealous, you know. She cannot believe that gratitude to your father was enough to make me let you go. And of course she's hoping the Mexicans will not exchange our comrades so that I will have to cut your throat." He turned to the lithe woman in my riding skirt, who was regarding me, hands on her slender hips, head tilted. "Tula, Señorita Greenleaf wishes to ask you a question."

I swore at him silently. Domingo would have done better at getting her consent. Now she might refuse out of sheer hostility to me.

"Oh?" Tula laughed in a brittle way. "Who could have guessed you were discussing me? You seemed absorbed in each other."

"In truth," drawled Lío, "we were speaking of Domingo."

"Domingo?" Her voice rose and her eyes slitted. "What of Domingo?"

Oh, damn Lío! There was little chance now, but I had to try. "He and Sewa are very fond of each other," I said carefully.

"Yes. *If* you get to go to the Mina Rara, I will care for her, if you like, and they can stay together."

That proposal startled me into blurting, "Could Domingo come with us?"

"What?" Her face grew terrible.

A cold sensation inched down my spine as I felt her almost palpable hatred. "He's so young," I pleaded. "You must want him to grow up, have something out of life except killing or being hunted."

"First and last, he is Yaqui."

"And what does that mean?"

"He must share the fate of our people."

"Some will live, surely, though some will die."

Lío interposed and a look passed between the two of them that made me catch my breath and realize the depth of their bond, a tie of pain shared in exile, comradeship in fighting, that far eclipsed the ordinary experience of love. "Tula means, lady, that Domingo must take his chance with our people, not shelter with outsiders. If he lives, God be praised. If he goes to Glory, he will meet his family there."

That was what Yaquis called heaven. Glory. It was like their love of flowers, brave in a harsh country, in such a cruel life.

"You will not let him choose?" I asked her slowly. "You, his sister, will not give him the chance to have at least a few years before he must fight?"

"There would be no problem if you had died by the train." Tula's lips pulled tight across her teeth. Suddenly she threw back her head and laughed. "We talk nonsense. If the Mexicans do not release our comrades, you will die. If I were you, I would not make too many plans for the future." She slipped her arm through Lío's, moved him away with her.

I watched the youngsters where they rested under a rock outcropping near the canyon mouth, ached with angry frustration and a sense of failure. What would become of them? If they were still alive in ten years, would they be like Lío and Tula? I tried to tell myself that at least they had the day, this time of being together, but somehow that only made it worse.

The messenger did not return that day, but late next afternoon, a silent message arrived when one of the lookouts led in the messenger's horse carrying what was left of him and, it proved, of several other men; after the first horrified shock, everyone realized that no man had eight hands or four heads or shriveled parts that looked like flesh-colored chilis strung on a thong.

"Here is your answer," Tula said to Lío, gaze crossing him to light on me. Her triumph was more horrible because it was plain she'd rather see her comrades dead than let me go.

Lío's face seemed carved from the mountain. "Yes," he said in Yaqui. "We have our answer."

"Then you must—" Tula began.

He gave her a look that stopped her words. "I know what I

must do. But leave the time to me, woman. Now we will bury our friends."

The heads, hands, and privates of the four men were collected and buried under a cairn of copper-streaked rocks at the western side of the basin where the morning sun would touch it daily. While the burial was taking place, I wandered numbly along the palisades.

Lío had to kill me. If he didn't, the others would. Would I die tonight? How? I hoped Sewa wouldn't have to watch. That made me wonder where she was. I hadn't seen her since morning when she and Domingo had gone walking.

They didn't know yet . . .

And now she would live with the fugitives for the hunted, harried weeks or months or years till soldiers cut them down. At least Domingo would have a care for her and the people, in their fashion, would be kind.

A small hand closed on mine. "Kawah!" greeted the raven, balancing on Sewa's shoulder.

"Domingo and I saw," the girl whispered though there was no one in earshot. Everyone was gathered at the western side of the valley. "We saw the lookout find the horse out on the plain."

"Do you think Mexicans trailed the horse in case it could lead them into the basin?"

"A couple of soldiers watched from a thicket while the horse grazed about all the morning. He was not going anyplace. Domingo showed our lookout where the soldiers were and he waited till they got disgusted and rode away, before he went down for the beast." The child shuddered. "He led it past us and we saw what was tied about the saddle."

"So you know Lío has to kill me."

Her grip on me tightened. "I will not let him!"

I bent and cradled the small fierce body. "Hush, *chiquita!* You'll have to live here after I'm gone. Don't make it harder for yourself. I made the bargain. It's not Lío's fault."

"Has he said when?" Her voice faltered and I found myself comforting her by trying to speak lightly.

"No. He doesn't want to. But whether that will make him delay or hurry to get it over with, who knows?"

She pondered, absently ruffling Ku's feathers. "Domingo is going to tell Cruz," she said at last. "Perhaps he can think of something. These Yaquis have heard of him, they know he is a *sabio* if not a witch. If Lío waits until tomorrow—"

What could Cruz do? But even a glimmer of reprieve sent my heart racing so that I laughed ruefully, understanding that the body cannot resign itself to death though the mind may. And, of course, I wondered if Trace would hear, if he would care. I wouldn't allow myself to build hope about him. He wouldn't have left me at Las Coronas without a word had he intended to help me. But Cruz . . .

So when Lío came to me while a subdued band ate supper that night, I had a different game to play than my earlier hopeless one that could aim only at dying with some style, show these Yaqui that someone else could be brave, at least for the few minutes it took to get through dying.

"Well," Lío said to me, dropping on his heels and tickling Ku's head. "Would you prefer another night, lady? Another sunrise? I cannot give you much, but I can permit that."

"You guarantee the sun will shine?" I asked in mock wonder.

He gave me a stare of surprise and then clapped his knee in a roar of appreciative laughter. "By God, even in Jonathan Greenleaf's daughter I had not expected such humor! You should have been a man."

I shrugged.

"Men are afraid that a woman with a sense of humor is laughing at them."

Lío chuckled. "If you can laugh at anyone now, lady, I am glad." He sobered. "I do not like what I must do."

"I know."

He hesitated, biting the edges of his moustache. "You understand, though, that I must."

My nerves, rubbed raw already, frayed and exploded. "Damn you, what do you want? We made a bargain. I'm not begging. But if you expect me to tell you that you're a fine fellow and I don't at all mind your killing me, why, damn you to hell. I want to live."

As he stared, jaw dropped, I gulped and set my teeth,

getting control. "I'll take the night," I said. "And that sunset you promise so confidently—every moment I can have."

He rose, head slightly lowered, and in spite of myself I did feel for him.

"Thank you, Lío," I said and held out my hand.

He gripped it in his callused ones, pressing the bones till they hurt. "Sleep well, lady. I promise that Sewa shall be like my daughter."

She dragged herself up, lame foot dangling, and her eyes smoldered like a trapped wild creature's. "I'll hate you, always hate you—"

His face closed. "Tula was right," he said. "Yaquis must stay with Yaquis or they lose Yaqui hearts. Good night then." He took a few steps away, halted, gazed around. "Where is Domingo?" he asked, turning back to Sewa.

Without blinking, she said, "He wanted to go to a cave that was too far for me to walk. He thought it might be a good hideout one day and wanted to see if there was another way out."

Lío frowned. "Where was this cave?"

"On the southern slope somewhere. He said he might spend the night there and to tell Tula not to worry."

"And did you?"

"I thought I would wait till dark."

"It is dark," Lío growled. "I will tell her, there's no use in your hobbling over."

As he strode away, Sewa let her breath go in a long sigh, only then betraying that she'd been nervous. "If Domingo can find Cruz, they should be back by morning," she said. "Domingo knows the box canyon. This band has stopped there for water."

"It was brave of him to go," I said. "Sewa, if he doesn't get back in time, tell him I leave my love and thanks."

"He'll get back." She threw her arms around me as if to defy the world. Strangely, vulnerable as I was, in as much danger, her embrace made me feel *safer* in some inner core of self, more loved and protected than I had ever been.

And so we settled Ku above us and went to sleep in each other's arms, and if it was to be the last night of my life, at least I had loved and been loved by this child. I wouldn't drop into the dark bottomless pool of death without leaving someone in the world.

I woke in faint gray light, my arm heavy from Sewa's weight, and shifted position gently, remembering in instant consciousness what was to happen that morning.

Domingo wasn't back. The camp was still except for the faint mewling of a baby who hushed even as I listened. Yaquis fed their children when they could, held and played with them; they didn't build character or develop lungs by leaving infants to wail alone.

For just a moment I thought of trying to slip away, almost as if it were a possibility confronting another person. I'd been around the Yaquis too long. I would keep the pledge I had made unless they remitted it—and that was not likely to happen, not after the hands and heads and severed sex organs.

So I lay watching the sky lighten above the palisades, the gold-red streaks color the waiting gray. A sunrise is so glorious that if one only occurred at a certain spot in the world once in a hundred years, throngs would travel oceans and pay vast sums to behold it.

One thing that death sentence gave me was a lasting appreciation of sunrise. I watched it happen and change and flower with the hunger of a person who must die before tasting sexual love and parenthood and the physical consummation we are born for, my unlived life. I thought of Trace. Of all the things I regretted, I was most sorry that somehow I hadn't gotten him to really make love to me. The virginity he had been so careful to save for my husband would now go to death. Another child waked, a dog barked, I heard muffled voices.

Raising myself with care so as not to wake Sewa, I saw Lío's squat figure, recognized the thin white-clad man as Cruz. Domingo stood to one side.

Lío let out a bellow that brought the camp scrambling. "Five dozen rifles. Five dozen. We can arm another band with those."

Cruz answered. I couldn't hear him, but Lío's tones carried far beyond the people who were gathering to listen. "Is the girl worth five dozen rifles? Of course she is not, I'd trade her for a dozen if that was all there was to it. I made a swearing, Cruz. I must kill her this very morning."

Cruz glanced about the crowd, seemed to be speaking to this person and that, then asked something that brought shifting, questions, a murmur of discussion.

"No," cried Tula, fists on her hips. "Keep your word, Lío. Remember our dead comrades, our slaughtered messenger."

"But five dozen rifles," one of the men shouted. "We can take many Mexican lives with those—avenge our comrades far better than by killing one woman."

A shout of approval. My heart swelled, began to pound with fearful hope, though all I could grasp was that Cruz was bartering rifles for my life.

"The woman must die," Tula cried. "It was a vow, Lío."

The group subsided and watched him. He stood, head bowed a moment, then thrust it back with bull-like strength. "It was a vow. But if you prefer guns and release me, I will not have broken my word and we will have five dozen of the best rifles of the U.S. Cavalry." He gazed around. "Those who prefer sixty rifles to a girl's life, keep standing. Those who want the life, sit down."

Even the slain messenger's woman and kinsmen stood, but Tula seated herself. When she read the silent choice, she leaped up and shouted, "Is this Yaqui honor, to hide men's blood under a heap of rifles and the smiling mouth of a gringa?"

Lío spat at her feet. "We need guns, not more honor," he said dryly. "The bargain is made, Tula."

"I do not release you," she screamed.

He only shrugged. She caught back her furious hands, held them to her sides. Each word glittered like obsidian, cut sharp and wicked. "I have made no bargain. As far as I am concerned, the woman's life is forfeit."

Lío stared at her. The anger, the sense of betrayal that ran between them were visible in his massive figure, in her slender one. "Fight the enemy," he told her roughly. "Do not fight me." He turned to Cruz. "The rifles?"

"A friend is bringing them from Arizona."

Trace?

Lío frowned. "When will they be here?"

"Within the month." Cruz shrugged. "As you know, such matters take time."

"When we have the rifles, Señorita Greenleaf may go," said Lío after a moment.

"I want her loosed now," Cruz said.

"There are no rifles," shrilled Tula. "It's a trick."

"I have helped you before," Cruz said, smiling. "Was that a trick?

Lío cut in. "Why should it matter if we hold the girl a few weeks longer?"

"Life is uncertain. And I think it may be uncertain for all of you until the señorita leaves this basin."

"Fraud!" shouted Tula. "She will leave and we will have nothing."

"We know where to find Cruz," Lío pointed out.

I slipped out of the hollow and hurried to the group. "Cruz! Cruz! I must talk to you."

Lío nodded consent and Cruz strolled with me out of earshot. "You look well, Miranda. How is the little flower?"

"You can see her." I caught his arm, searching those ash-gray eyes. "Cruz, you must not trade yourself for me. Are the rifles coming?"

"Yes."

"Truly?"

"As I see you." He patted my hand. "You must ride out of the canyon. Someone will meet you there, take you to Mina Rara. That seems the best place at the moment." He glanced at Sewa. "She goes with you?"

I nodded, too joyously relieved to speak. "I will greet her while you get ready," Cruz said, starting for our grotto. Domingo moved with him.

Tula was after him like a lynx, swinging him about, striking him across the face with all her strength. The boy staggered. Blood welled up on his mouth, trickled down his chin.

"Go with them," Tula shouted. "You are no brother of mine, no Yaqui."

She would have struck the unresisting wide-eyed boy again, but Lío seized her wrist, wrung it till she was forced almost to her knees. "Domingo is my brother if not yours, Tula. He may stay with us, in full honor, or go with the señorita."

"After what he has done?"

"Brought rifles for the life of his friend?" Lío laughed, showing his square big teeth. "He has shown courage, initiative, loyalty—fine qualities in either leader or follower. Well, Domingo?"

Domingo looked at me, glanced at Sewa, and I knew he longed to go with us, look after Sewa, play, and dream some of the childhood of which they'd been robbed. He sighed, then put back his thin shoulders.

"I will stay with you," he told Lío. "I am a Sierra Yaqui."

He didn't look at his sister, who caught her lip in her teeth and swung away. I took his hands. "Domingo, Domingo, there *is* no way to thank you."

His smile was very sweet. In a flash I saw him as he would look when he grew up—if he grew up—shy grace of a deer joined with the strength and control of a mountain lion. "I am your man for life, lady, because you helped Sewa. I know you will take care of her and so I do not ask it."

His young male dignity kept me from embracing and kissing him, and I pressed his hands and smiled at him through tears.

Twenty minutes later, Sewa and I were riding down the canyon with one of the men who was to bring back our horses when we met with whoever was to conduct us to Mina Rara.

Sewa startled me by laughing. When I raised a questioning eyebrow, she said, "You should be proud, Miranda! You are worth a lot of rifles!" She sobered. "Will Domingo ever come to see us?"

"I don't know. I hope so. Perhaps all this trouble will pass and Lío's band can go home."

"To land the Mexicans have taken?" Sewa's eyes were suddenly old and sad and wholly Yaqui. "Miranda, Lío's peace must be a grave, you know that."

Folly to argue. Lío and most of his band were outlaws many times over, but I hated to think that Domingo and the children were irrevocably locked in the bloody pattern.

"Perhaps Domingo can come to us in a year or two," I said. "I might get a ranch and he could someday be foreman. We could hire Yaquis and save some that way."

"But what of the others?" asked Sewa, and she was her suffering people, I the foolishly hopeful impotent child, speaking desires, not probabilities. She said to me with the first defiance she had ever shown, "If I had a sound foot and could be a help, not a hindrance, I would stay."

"I know you would," I said. All this grief and all this pain, and though I meant well, what could I do?

We rode down the canyon and the only sound was the hollow ring of our horses' hooves.

10

As we rode out of the shielded way into the canyon, I saw two tethered horses before I recognized the man who sheathed his rifle in his saddle scabbard and came out of the stirrups in one easy spring. He swept Sewa from her saddle, brought her around, and gathered me, so that we were all three together, bound and encompassed by his arms.

"So here are my sweethearts," he said, putting Sewa down, drawing back to gaze at me. "What a place to find you! Domingo says you were stolen off a train. What do you get up to when I turn my back?"

Dumbfounded anger eroded my delight. Coming through the narrow pass, I'd wondered who was escorting us to the mine, hadn't been able to completely repress a flickering dream that it might be Trace. Now here he stood. I was afraid to be as joyful as I felt, afraid to trust him.

Stepping back, I said coldly, "When you left Las Coronas without a word, I decided you didn't choose to be bothered with my troubles. No one could blame you for that."

Those incredible eyes, the blue of the sky mixed with sea green, widened in unmistakable shock. "Without a word?" he repeated. "Didn't Felipe tell you what I said?"

"No. In fact, a few days later, at my dear sister's bidding, he almost got me killed." Then a memory of Felipe's last tortured words drifted back. "Wait! After he was shot, he tried to tell me something—called your name."

"Belated conscience," said Trace, mouth twisting. "My God, Miranda, what you must have thought. So that's why you struck off on your own."

"There wasn't much choice. Reina wanted me dead."

Trace scowled. "Did she, the bitch? But Cruz and I understood from Domingo that you put your life in pawn for hers."

"I didn't think a military officer would sacrifice a rich woman like Reina for three guerrillas."

Trace shook his head. "I wouldn't have expected it either. Even so, love, you were a fool to risk your neck for hers after what she's done. Well, let's clear out. I have to ride straight on from the mine. I'm to fetch that five dozen rifles in case you hadn't guessed." He laughed. "Cruz finally asked me for a favor, but I still owe him since it's my woman I'm saving."

My woman. I repeated the words, loving their sound, though they weren't really true. His wife, his lawful woman, was across the Rio Grande. But for now I refused to worry about that. I was alive and with Trace. Sheer heaven.

He helped me up, swung Sewa and Ku on the other horse, and thanked our guard. The man smiled for the first time and I reckoned he was glad not to have to use the rifle in his saddle scabbard.

"God keep you," he said in Yaqui, and turned back up the canyon, leading the riderless mounts.

As we rode through the foothills, I told Trace what had happened since he brought Sewa and me back to the hacienda and he explained that he'd received an urgent message that night and had needed to ride at once, stopping only to ask Felipe to tell me he'd been called away but would be back.

"If he mentioned it to Reina, she'd have told him not to tell me," I said bitterly. "But why did you go?"

"My wife was in Hermosillo."

My heart seemed to stop up my throat. "And you went to her?"

"Yes. She was dying. She'd wound up in an El Paso whorehouse, and when she was too sick to work, they threw her out. She knew from friends in Texas that I'd drifted to Sonora, so she begged and 'worked' her way to Hermosillo. I'm fairly well known there, and when a woman claiming to be my wife turned up, a friend sent the message."

I remembered that he said she had loved to dance. "I'm terribly sorry," I said, ashamed of my jealousy.

"So am I." He was silent a moment. "At least I could make it a little easier. Out of all that anger and hurt I'd had, there wasn't any left. Or love, either. She was just a poor sick woman dying young."

We rode for a time without talking. Thoughts weltered. This changed everything. If he wanted to marry me, he could. Impossible to blurt out, yet it transformed the world. He had to perform his bargain, but after that we could start fresh.

"You can bet if I had time to find a safe place for you, I wouldn't leave you with Court Sanders," Trace said abruptly.

And if there had been time, I wouldn't have stayed. But since I saw no real choice, I resolved not to worry Trace with the things Court had said to me that night when I stopped his assault on Consuelo.

"Sanders has asked me to inspect the mine," I said matter-of-factly. "After all, it does belong to me."

Trace gave a wry laugh. "Court's been in charge so long that he probably thinks Mina Rara's his. Still, if he knows he'll have to answer to me for your well-being, I think he'll behave."

"You make him sound dangerous."

"Court loves women. Every chance he gets."

That I could believe, remembering Reina, the way his tawny eyes had rested on me, lingered like a touch that had waked even my angry and distrustful body.

"Sewa will be with me," I said. "And if he's too difficult, I can discharge him."

Trace laughed outright, shaking his head. "What a child you are, Miranda, a proper well-bred English child! Who could enforce such a discharge? Court's not the man to bow politely and obey. Don't fire him, don't threaten him, unless you have the means to make it stick."

"And when will that be?" I demanded.

"When I get back. Three weeks, maybe four. As soon as I can, I'll come to the mine and take you to my friends in Hermosillo. Keep peace with Court till then."

At noon we rested for an hour, chewing some jerky Trace had, and paused again in midafternoon. Sometimes our way climbed, but mostly we stayed in the arroyos twining through the small hills till late that afternoon, when we began to ascend into raw mountains scantily clad with jojoba, dwarf mesquite, and scrub. I glimpsed the narrow-gauge railroad twisting up the grade like a serpent, and we struck a road running beside it, marked by wheels and hooves. We reached the top of the mountain at sunset and looked down at the settlement scattered across the valley floor, seemingly spewed out of the vast hole in the mountain side, which literally shone.

"What is it?" I asked Trace.

"Fool's gold—pyrite. All that stuff is tailings, the useless matter washed off the ore." I stared at the two entrances to the mountain, the people gathered to harvest its depths, the loaded metal carts on the train track, and was filled with a surprise close to fear. This belonged to me, or would in a few months. In effect, dozens of people worked for me, drew their livelihood from the mine. I hadn't really given them a thought before: how they were fed or clothed, or the conditions under which they worked. I hadn't wanted to come here, but it was a good thing I had, for I was responsible for what went on at Mina Rara.

"Well, Miranda," said Trace. "What do you think of your kingdom?"

"I don't know. It doesn't seem real yet."

"It won't take long. Mines have a pretty convincing reality, though they're a world in themselves." He lifted his reins, starting his horse down the winding road spiraling down into the valley.

"You have to ride on?" I called.

He turned to look at me. It was as if the essence of our beings rushed together when our eyes met. "We should wait," he said. "I might get killed."

I shook my head. "Do you know what I was most sorry for

when I expected to die this morning? I wished that you had loved me."

"I do love you."

"You know what I mean."

His eyes were lit with inner burning. The long line of his jaw ridged. "*Chiquita*," he said to Sewa, who was catching up with us, "wait for us a short distance down the trail. There are some trees near a big rock."

She nodded and rode on. Trace took a side path that led behind gigantic tumbles of glittering rocks. We came to a shallow cave where the sand was fine-powdered, hued blue and gold and crimson. He hitched our horses and lifted me down.

I was ready for him almost immediately, moist and yieldingly eager. It was he who held back, kissed my breasts and eyes and mouth, caressed me till I moaned and drew him onto me. There was a sharp piercing hurt. I cried out. He stopped, kissed and stroked me till I relaxed, accepted that hard questing part of him that fitted slowly, breathtakingly deep deep into me. He lay like that, covering me completely, little shudders wracking him.

"I'll finish in a minute," he said. "First, Miranda my love, let's see to you."

Withdrawing, he began to kiss and gently touch between my legs, send his tongue over that tiny delicate center of feeling that soon engorged till my earlier hurt felt soothed.

"Your rosebud." He laughed, lifting his head.

I hadn't known people could talk while making love. That he was still Trace, caring, able to joke, made me wholly unafraid and happy. I stroked his hair and smiled, hoping he would go on with the exquisitely pleasurable thing he was doing.

"Let's make you bloom," he said.

He did. This time it was even lovelier than before because he could be my man and now I was a woman, his woman. I cried out with delight, and while I was still trembling and soft, he entered me again, surged to his own peak.

For a few moments we lay resting. I felt at peace, calm, completed. Whatever happened now, I belonged to Trace

Winslade. I wouldn't die without tasting this. When a flicker of fear shot through me as I remembered Court's warning that I had better be a virgin, I pushed it aside. Trace had claimed me; he would return. Court would hardly tamper with another man's intended wife.

I touched Trace's closed eyes. Starting, he raised on one elbow. "God, if we could stay here! If I could just take you and Sewa and get the hell out! But I've got to bring those rifles."

"I know. We'll be all right."

He kissed me, drew me to my feet. "Sure. Sure you will." He grinned ruefully. "I hope you want to marry me, Miranda. Because now that I'm free, I'm asking you, even if I'm poor."

"You'd better ask," I said sternly. "After all those lectures on saving myself for a marriageable man."

He helped me into the saddle and we rode down the trail.

Mina Rara. Company store, cantina, a tiny church with a belled steeple that seemed concocted of grimy frosting, a smithy, an infirmary, an office, two substantial houses and the homes of the workers honeycombed on the hill and valley opposite the mine.

We rode to the biggest house and Trace hitched our horses to the post railing, helped me down first, then lifted Sewa, steadying her as we went up a few steps to the large adobe with its massive doors.

A spicy odor wafted from inside and a woman's soft laughter floated out. "Sanders!" Trace called. "It's Winslade and some visitors."

"Come on in," boomed the answer. "If this visitor's as pretty as the last—" He broke off as I stepped into the room, dark as a cave after the light.

I stood, holding Sewa by the hand, waiting for my eyes to adjust. Court came forward, hands out. "Miranda! What in the world has happened to you? I heard you and the girl were on that train bandits looted."

"We were." I was too tired to go into it and felt reluctance to let him know any more about anything than was necessary. He seemed to have no self-consciousness about the last time we had been together. I tried to be equally relaxed. "Can we have a cool drink?"

"Raquel!" he shouted. "Bring wine and make some fresh coffee."

"Isn't there some water?" I asked.

"There is, but you won't like it. Full of minerals."

"Sewa needs something."

"We can flavor the water with a little wine," Trace said. "Sanders, I have to ride on. Can someone see to my horse while I have some of whatever that is that smells good?"

Court stepped to the front door, rang a bell, said a few words to the boy who answered. After Raquel, a large-eyed, voluptuous girl, brought water and wine, I briefly explained to Court what had happened.

"So Reina knows you're alive?" he asked, raising tawny brows.

"She saw me in the basin. But she'll probably learn that the Yaqui men were executed and believe that I was killed in reprisal."

Court studied for a moment, nodded. "I suppose you'd prefer she think that, at least until after your eighteenth birthday. Before then she could fetch you back to Las Coronas, and if I tried to stop her, she could get the *rurales*." He smiled, his golden eyes on me in an intimacy I found disturbing. "Mina Rara is a good place to be safely hidden away, Miranda. I'm glad you came."

"It's her mine, after all," said Trace. "I'll be back in three, four weeks. Then Miranda can stay with friends in Hermosillo till things settle down."

"Winslade, things aren't going to settle down, not till this country blows wide open and heals back together."

"Then Miranda will have to decide whether to stay or go to live in the United States or England." Trace looked directly at me, probing till I felt exposed, emotionally naked. "If you want to go to the United States, Miranda, I could take you across the border now."

Safety—distant from war and reprisal, beyond Reina's power. But it was not to live as a refugee that I'd left England. And my heart leaped as I thought this might be Trace's way of asking if I had changed my mind about marrying him.

"I want to stay," I said carefully. "I want to have a country. Besides, Trace, wives should be with their husbands."

"Wives?" Court's gaze leaped from me to Trace. Though when he spoke, his tone held a note of banter, there was a tension in him that frightened me in spite of all my arguments and reason. "Don't tell me you found a priest out in the brush?"

"No." Trace stared into those lazy topaz eyes. "But we'll be married in Hermosillo."

"When you return," amended Court smoothly. He inclined his head to me. "You're either valiant or foolhardy to marry in this country after what you've just escaped."

I took a long breath. Was he really accepting it so easily? Raquel and another girl brought trays that they placed on the drumlike rawhide table. Raquel served out bowls of thick stew and offered warm tortillas while the other girl brought wine and silver goblets.

"I like exquisite things when I can get them," Court said, pouring out and giving me the first goblet. "The trouble is that beauty is hard to find in this wilderness and harder to preserve." He raised his wine to me. "May your loveliness flourish, Miranda, even in this desert."

I poured half my wine into the water fetched for Sewa. "The desert is beautiful," I told Court. "And the sky, the sunrises and sunsets. Sometimes the mountains are melting fairy blue, or deep purple, almost black. Sometimes they're brown, and at sunset they can be ember red or glow as if fire blazed under their crust. I miss the green of England, but now it would be too lush, too verdant, too gentle."

Court tasted his wine, watching me speculatively. "I've been in Mexico too long. Nothing could ever be too lush or gentle or soft. I hunger for such things."

"No one would guess it," Trace said dryly. "There's nothing gentle in the way you run the mine."

"If there were, it wouldn't run." Court's half-smile challenged. "Are you lodging a complaint?"

Trace finished his food and drained his wine as he got to his feet. "Miranda has eyes. She'll use them. Thanks for the food,

Sanders. I'll be back in a few weeks and take her to my friends."

Court frowned. "This is her property. Why shouldn't she stay here?"

Without smiling, Trace said, "I don't see you as a likely chaperone, Sanders."

"In this country a beautiful woman needs a defender more than a prayer-chanting *dueña* who can only fulfill her duty if there's a strong hand to protect it."

"My friends can both defend and chaperone when I can't be with my wife," said Trace.

Rising, not quite as tall as Trace but broader, especially about the neck and shoulders, Court grinned. "Who knows? Maybe she'll stay."

"Then she'd better not let Reina know it till she's eighteen."

"You worry a good deal about this lady," Court said, still smiling. "You can leave it now, Winslade. I'll take care of her while you're running guns or whatever."

"I'm counting on that." Trace hugged Sewa, ruffled Ku's head feathers. "Good-bye," he told them. He took my hands in his. "Good-bye, Miranda my love." Releasing my fingers as if they'd grown into his flesh, he embraced Sewa and me with his eyes. "God keep you," he said in Yaqui, and strode quickly out, the heavy door creaking shut behind him.

I moved after, stepping into the veranda, lifting my hand as he rode off. Where was he going? Into danger, that was sure. Would he be back, ever, at all?

"He didn't see you," Court said. He had come noiselessly up beside me and took my still-raised hand in a gesture of pity. "He doesn't look back, not Winslade."

But he would now. He must. I loved him.

Holding the great door, Court took me inside, hand cradling my elbow. I didn't try to pull free; some instinct warned me that resistance on a small matter could trigger the violence he now held leashed. His brow wrinkled at Sewa as if he'd forgotten her existence and was annoyed to recognize it.

"There are a lot of Yaqui families at Mina Rara," he said. "Many of them would be glad to take the child. Shall I send for

some of the women so that you can select a good foster-
mother?"

I did break from his hand. "She is *my* child, Mr. Sanders. I
want her to make friends with her people, but unless she
chooses otherwise, she stays with me, sleeps in my room."

Court's eyes blazed for a moment. He took one quick step
after me, halted, picked up the wine decanter, filled my glass,
poured his own, and tossed it off.

"So," he said, grimacing. "You're intent on having the little
Indian with you, and that stinking raven, too, I suppose?"

"I slept with them on what I thought was the last night of my
life. Of course I want them with me."

"You'd better change your mind before you marry," Court
said. "No husband would share his room with that pair."

"Since I have no husband, that's not a worry," I said with an
acid sweetness I hoped would cover the strain I felt. Court's
touch and eyes sent a tingling sense of danger through me,
not totally unpleasant. My situation depended on how much
Court ruled his impulses. I told myself that he wouldn't play
too hard and fast, if only because Trace would be back, but I
wasn't soundly reassured.

"The guest room is ready," Court said. "I'll have a small bed
set up for the girl. You have no baggage, do you? One of the
women makes my shirts and does the mending. She could put
some clothes together for you out of goods from the company
store."

"That will be splendid," I said with genuine delight. "Sewa
can have some dresses, too. How kind of you to think of it, Mr.
Sanders."

He laughed outright. "My dear, it wasn't hard. The things
you're wearing look exactly as if you'd been abducted by
bandits and held in the wilds. How does a bath sound?"

"Like heaven," I sighed. "And Sewa needs one, too."

He led down the hall to the end of the way, opened the door
on his left. "The girls will bring water," he said. "Ask for
anything you need. When you're refreshed, I hope you'll join
me on the veranda."

It was a long narrow room with a fireplace, large bed, stern wooden armchair, dresser with a mirror, and a nail-studded leather-bound chest. Behind a Japanese screen painted with monkeys and birds was an elegant tub, fluted at either end to resemble a shell.

While Sewa and I undressed, the women brought pails of water and a stack of towels, a bar of perfumed soap. I couldn't imagine Court using it; in fact, this room, from laquered screen to rose satin bedspread, had an air of being used by women, and I doubted that they were there on mining business.

I washed Sewa's hair and helped her scrub and dry off while two boys carted out the tub and brought it back to be refilled. I apologized to Raquel for all the extra work. She shook back her long black hair and said it was nothing, of course we must bathe after our journey. And she carried off our stained things and returned with a shift for Sewa and what I guessed must be her own Sunday clothes, a white ruffled blouse and black full skirt.

Sewa was asleep in the bed the boys had set up in a corner by the time I had dressed and brushed my hair with a silver-backed brush from the dresser. I would have preferred to slip into the big high bed, lie between the white sheets that looked incredibly cool and inviting after weeks of sleeping rough, but the fact that I wanted to avoid seeing Court made me decide I must get it over with.

He'd been cordial, thoughtful of our comfort. And if I ran from him like a rabbit mightn't he prey on me like one? Against this lion, I had better try to seem at least an extremely agile deer, or a *burro* who could kick when harassed.

A headstrong tough little *burro* seemed the best bet. So I carried the image of Ratoncita with her lovely ears down the hall with me and out on the veranda.

It was full dark now. Outdoor cooking fires glowed from the ramadas of many of the miners' houses. Guitar notes and plaintive songs came faintly from the cantina and a lamp burned in the infirmary, revealing the occasional passage of a dark silhouette.

"A little world," said Court, rising. "Fairly cut off from the storms rising in Mexico. A good place for you to be, Miranda."

"I'm certainly glad to be here right now," I said, laughing. "The bath was marvelous, and a real bed—what luxury!"

He only came a step closer but cut out my view so completely that I felt overwhelmed, wished I hadn't mentioned the bed. "Sweet Miranda! If you're as innocent as you look, you don't know how luxurious a bed can be. Would you like more wine? Perhaps some peach brandy?"

"I'm so thirsty. Could I have water with just enough wine to cut the taste?"

"So you prefer to use wine to make plain water drinkable rather than take it full-bodied?" Court called an order, sat down across from me, far enough away to let me relax a little, too close to allow me to forget his physical immediacy, and again I experienced him as a great cat, watching its intended prey till its hunger reached a certain stage and the victim had strayed into proper range.

I would stay out of his reach if I could—do nothing to trigger a sudden spring. And hope that Trace came back before Court wearied of the subtle hunt.

Raquel brought water and wine, murmured a soft good night. "It was kind of you to loan the señorita your clothes," Court told her in the way one approved a child's generosity. "You shall have those earrings you've been wanting."

"*Gracias, señor.*" She ducked her head as if embarrassed and moved away, her bare feet making a gentle sound like small waves on a soft beach.

I was sure, from the casual intimacy of his tone, that he slept with Raquel, that it was on the same level as her serving him food. What she felt, I could not guess, but she'd displayed no jealousy. She didn't seem to fear him. Perhaps he was kind enough, provided he was not thwarted or challenged. I decided to appear a benign, sweet-tempered *burro* as long as he kept distance. If he got too close—well, Cruz had told me *burros* could fight off mountain lions.

Court poured the water and wine into a goblet, gave it to me, and sat in the chair nearest mine. "Miranda," he said. "You strike me as an intelligent young woman who can adjust to circumstances. When you see a situation is fixed, as in Reina's hatred of you, you don't exhaust yourself in battering at it. And in the Yaqui camp you must have made the best of what would have seemed brutalizing captivity to most women."

"I had Sewa and Domingo. And I had seen Yaquis after soldiers finished with them."

He made a brushing motion with his hand. "Nevertheless, few people are that philosophical."

I said nothing, uneasy at this reasoned approach.

Court's laugh, hard and small, cracked the silence. "Miranda, do you like your watered wine?"

Something in me contracted like an eye shocked by strident glare. "It quenches thirst."

"Not the kind I have."

I could think of no safe answer, tried to turn the subject completely. "If so many Yaquis work here, are they never bothered by federal authorities?"

"The Mina Rara Yaquis have been here for a quarter of a century. No fool, even a military or bureaucratic one, could pretend they are warlike, and they don't, most importantly, occupy land the Mexicans want."

I thought of Lío. "But they must have relations among the Sierra Yaqui."

"True, but for now the government is busy with killing or selling those Yaquis who are in the way or who are fighting. Mina Rara may remain self-contained and cut off from the troubles that are coming."

I shivered, remembering the slaughtered Yaquis, the massacre at the train. "But if there's a civil war—"

Court shrugged. "It won't be the kind you studied in school, my dear—Napoleon and Waterloo, large pitched battles involving huge armies. Mexico's revolution will be hundreds and hundreds of raids, skirmishes, looted trains. What are now smoldering grassfires will fan into blazes with the rising wind. There will be dozens of leaders, some patriots, some bandits. And the war will last for years, if not decades."

"If there's no strong central leadership, it would seem the federal troops could stamp out small rebellions."

"It can, so long as there are not too many. It would be simple for Don Porfirio if his foes were unified in one force, for he could surely put it down. It's the difference between chopping down one large tree or thousands of saplings scattered over thousands of miles. The strength of the revolutionaries lies in being elusive, small, far-flung. They will be a swarm of bees stinging the great bull, Don Porfirio, buzzing away from his assaults."

I considered. "You mean there will be groups like Lío's all over Mexico?"

"Yes. And after Díaz falls, the struggle will be between leaders while the country goes ungoverned. There will be anarchy for years. You are fortunate, Miranda, to have a quiet spot at Mina Rara."

"But I'm not staying."

"My sweet, of course you are."

"Trace will be back in a few weeks. Then he'll take me to his friends."

Court leaned forward. Before I could detect his motion in the dark, he had caught my wrists. "Trace will *not* come back, Miranda, unless you consent to be my woman and tell him that."

Those steel fingers tightened till I could have gasped with pain. It was like being pinned by a great cat, the soft parts of my body exposed. I tried to speak; it was only after several efforts that I could push around through my constricted throat.

"Your woman? I can never be that."

"You will."

"If this is your idea of courtship—"

He gave me a shake with enough violence in it to slice off my words. "I'm not courting you, Miranda. I'm revealing your situation, counting on that tough mind of yours to accept it." He gave a harsh laugh and his breath quickened. "I have eyes and ears. I know you fancy yourself in love with Winslade."

"I *do* love him."

"Then indeed you'll take me or he'll surely die."

That threat and the strength of this man, felt in the night, when I couldn't see his face, terrified me. And there was Cruz, who'd pledged the rifles for my life.

"You'd have Trace killed for nothing?"

"Not for nothing. For my love."

"Love. Call it something else."

"If it were only lust, my dear, I'd enjoy you and let you go to Winslade or the devil. But I want you in my life. To see you every day, hold you every night."

"When I hate you?"

"That's because I've put what you want out of reach," he said coolly. "Of course you'll tantrum like a child, but that'll pass. I can wake the fire that Winslade never fanned, make you live and die in my arms till they will be your real home, till I become your lover, not your master."

"No."

"Then Winslade won't come back. You condemn him to death."

"You—you unbelievable—"

He set his fingers over my mouth. "And it won't keep me from having you, Miranda. Nothing will. What we're debating is whether you put a good face on it and let Winslade live."

Sudden hope rose in me. "Is it the mine you want, Court? I'll make you co-owner if you'll let me go away with Trace."

"What if only sole title would comfort me for my loss?" he drawled.

Then I would be penniless, with Sewa to look after, dependent on the charity of Trace's friends. But for Trace to die—or for me to yield to Court . . .

"I'll sign it over to you as soon as I'm of age."

Court let me go and swore explosively before he calmed. "Well, Miranda, that means you really must love Winslade and have a strong dislike for me. It's not the mine I want and I swear that even if you marry me I won't use your money. But willing or fighting, married or not, I *will* have you. Soon."

"When Reina finds out—"

"She won't. She thinks you're dead, my sweetheart."

"How can she?" I demanded. "We all expected the commandant to let the Yaquis go instead of sending back their heads."

"Not Reina." His tone was grim. "One of my informants heard her send a messenger to the commandant to tell him to execute the prisoners since she had gotten away."

My head whirled. Reina had tried to hurt me before. But to cause my death when I was at risk for saving her. "You're lying!"

Turning my head, I retched, spewing out the watery wine and supper, wracked till my empty stomach heaved, humiliatingly conscious of Court holding my head, supporting my shoulders.

"Makes you sick, doesn't it?" He wiped my mouth with his handkerchief, called for Raquel, and scooped me up. "No, little fool, I'm not taking you to bed—or at least not with me. I was sick, too, when my man told me what that bitch had done. I was starting for Las Coronas, ready to choke the life out of her, when you rode in."

"So that's why you were so surprised."

He put me down in a big chair in the main room, sponged my face with clean water Raquel had brought. "Yes. And when I heard you were almost surely dead, that's when I knew what you were to me. My woman. You rode back to me from the dead. I'll never let you go again."

Weak and spent, I said desperately, as if I were shouting at him in a foreign language, "You don't love me or you'd care what I feel!"

"I do care. In a year you'll love me."

Even in that moment, when I hated him, my blood quickened as he smiled. I cried defiance as much to my treacherous body as to him. "I won't. I'll hate you more than I do now."

"We'll see." He cupped my chin and raised my face. I felt devoured by those tawny eyes. "You're tired, darling. Sleep now. You can give me your answer in the morning." At the hopeful lift of my head, he gave a thin little smile. "No, Winslade won't be out of reach. If I don't get him on the way to Arizona, my men will finish him before he rides through the pass into this valley. There's no way he can come unless I permit it."

With amazing tenderness Court helped me up, walked down the hall with his arm around me. At my door he said, "Good night, love," kissed my forehead, and swung quickly away.

It was almost better when he was menacing.

I couldn't let him kill Trace. But submit to those muscular, gold-haired arms? Let him do the things Trace had? And it wouldn't be for one time only, I was sure of that. Court might, after a season, let me go, but I had a frightening dread that if he possessed me long enough, he would drain me till I became his thing, his creature—that I wouldn't want to go, even if he allowed it and Trace would take me.

That possibility, not rape or death, was the real nightmare. But how could I resist him if that meant he would murder Trace?

11

During the next days Sewa and I grew acquainted with Mina Rara. Court was often with us, but when he was not, I felt we were watched. He hadn't pressed me further, and though his menace towered over me, tangible as the mountains about the mine, he seemed possessed of the certainty of ultimate success, which allowed him to wait. Meanwhile, he was a perfect host, indulgent, spicing his conversation with humor and fascinating lore.

He even produced a *burra* for Sewa, quickly beloved, cherished and named Cascos Lindos, Pretty Hooves, because its ears couldn't compare with those of Ratoncita. Ku, his leather nest fastened to the saddle, rode through the village, staring haughtily as a general reviewing troops.

About ninety men worked at Mina Rara, most of them Yaquis. The company doctor, Edwin Trent, gaunt, gruff, and given to drink, though he had been a minister before he turned to medicine, was the only other American. Not everyone worked at the mine. One Mexican family kept cows and lived by selling cheese and milk. Several widows baked bread, tortillas, and cakes for those who didn't want to bother as well as for the bachelors. There was a shoemaker and a man who hauled water around to the dwellings.

Services were held each Sunday in the little church by a Yaqui *maestro* and Court said the main *fiestas* were celebrated here just as they were in the Eight Sacred Pueblos.

"You've missed San Juan Bautista, June 23 and 24, when there are cockfights and horseracing," Court said. "San Ignacio's past. So is Virgen del Camino, July 1, when people often marry after maybe having lived together twenty years. The Easter ceremonies come to a crescendo Holy Week. The mine closes down from Good Friday till the Monday after Easter. A deer dancer comes from one of the pueblos, but Mina Rara has its own *maestro*, chanters, and *pascolas*, which are sort of clown dancers."

When he made assumptions like that, as if I would be there forever, I didn't argue. Better to make no resistance till I had to. Meanwhile, the mine was endlessly fascinating, though Miss Mattison would have fainted away with shock at the way the cantina filled every Saturday and Sunday with Mexican women up from Guaymas to help the miners spend their very good wages, eight pesos a day, compared to an average wage of thirty-five centavos plus rations for working on a hacienda.

Miners were paid in silver brought from the bank at Guaymas every two weeks, along with the mail, on the narrow-gauge train that ran from the main railroad to the mine. If a miner's money ran out before payday, he could get credit at the company store. Prices were high because of the difficulty of getting supplies, but I could detect no cheating. Meat wasn't expensive, for local ranchers brought it in nearly every day. I bought, or rather charged to Court, enough red and blue cotton to make dresses for Sewa and me, and the woman who made Court's shirts had us dressed respectably within the week, thanks to her sewing machine. Court wanted his things handmade, but I wasn't particular.

The mine itself was the passage to Pluto's dark, rich kingdom. A U-shaped tunnel went into the hill, with two surface entrances. At the bend of the U was a chamber, ventilated by a hole from above, with a hoist, compressor, and other equipment.

"The gold near the surface is found in this crumbly diorite rock," explained Court. "The gold deeper down lies in veins. Would you like to see?"

I glanced at Sewa, whose eyes shone eagerly. That decided me to go down in the depths. "Can someone carry Sewa?" I asked. Court summoned one of the miners and got two candles on sharp-pointed holders about a foot long.

"I have the workers on a short shift down here," explained Court. "There's no outside ventilation and it doesn't take long to get dizzy. We're dynamiting as we go along and it takes hours for the dust and smoke to settle after each explosion."

"It sounds dangerous."

"That's why the men get eight pesos a day."

"Have there been any bad accidents?"

Court gave me a surprised stare. "You bet! Someone had a cigarette too close to the dynamite last year and the explosion plastered twenty men all over the tunnel. We collected the bits in a sack and buried them all together. And then a few months ago there was an underground fire, probably started by a candle. It baked three men black. When I touched one, his skin peeled away as if it was greased."

We were approaching a shaft. I felt sick and took several long breaths before speaking. "What happened to the men's families?"

"Some went back to the pueblos. A few launder and cook for bachelors. Others, I reckon, earn their living on their backs."

"I want them—and the survivors of any man killed in the mine—to be given a lump sum or pension, whichever they prefer."

Court frowned and I braced myself for an argument, but he shrugged his wide shoulders and said smoothly, "If that's your wish. We'll work it out according to children, remarriage, and so on. Now take a good long breath. It's the last you'll get for a while."

Candle in one hand, he descended a ladder, steadied me as I followed to a ledge where another ladder went down into deeper twilight. Court braced the ladder for the miner with Sewa. We descended in increasing blackness, what Court said was three hundred feet down, till the shaft was a tiny patch far above and our candles threw yellow dusty light into the tunnel.

My lungs labored, pleading for oxygen, but I controlled the wish to gasp. After all, men *worked* down here. We wouldn't die for lack of air, though it certainly felt like it. The miner put Sewa down and I helped her follow Court. He held out his candle and it dazzled on gold.

Gold in patches, gold in thin leaves, gold twisted like sculptured wire. I'd had no idea it could come like this, in such clear, bright shining glory. Court pried a piece of corded metal loose with the edge of his candlestick, gave it to me.

"Keepsake of your first time down," he said.

"One for Sewa?" I asked, breathing fast in spite of all my efforts.

He pried off a filamented web the length of a finger, put it in Sewa's hand. "Let's get up," he said. "I'll go first to help with the child."

So we returned, ladder by ladder, to the comparative light and freshness of the equipment room. My head was ringing and I sat down dizzily on a box, gathering Sewa to me.

"Well," said Court, head thrown back, hands on his hips as he filled his lungs, "queen of the golden mountain, how do you like your treasure?"

"It's fantastic! But I hate for anyone to work down there. Isn't there any way to ventilate?"

"Not at that depth. But the ore shoot, which averages four feet thick, is raking north. It may eventually run out on the other side of the mountain, which is, in fact, the side of a canyon on its north face. Then there'd be air on that side and perhaps some draft between it and the shaft that ventilates this room, though that's a long way to travel."

"Can't you blast out to the surface?"

"Yes. But if we just barge ahead instead of following where the ore shoot goes, we may have to dynamite a whole new tunnel to get the ore and we might lose some through explosions."

"Do it anyway, please."

Court stared, jaw dropping.

"But the expense. After a charge goes off, I've told you nothing else can be done for a while. It could take a week to get through the mountain."

"But then the men could breathe."

"Hell, they aren't dying." Court shoved back his hair. "They pull a short shift down there. Double their money if you want. It'd be a lot cheaper than what you're suggesting."

"We're talking air, not money. Besides, it's my money. Isn't it?"

Those yellow eyes smoldered. Through my mind flashed the image of a giant cat, poised motionless except for its tail switching like a pendulum.

"If that's what you want," he said finally.

It was strange to watch him give on matters involving his professional judgment and large sums of money, while I knew he intended to have me in his bed one way or another. But at least he was giving me respite. During it, I had better make changes that would improve life for the workers. Besides, by exercising power affecting Mina Rara, I took up my work as a human being, began to create myself as a person in the outer world.

One thing was sure. I wouldn't, even if I got away, forget the place and leave its running up to Court or his successors while I spent the yield. In this one spot I could make a good life possible for some people, and though it was a wavering candle in a whirlwind night, some Yaquis were safe here.

Raquel had a younger sister, Chepa, who helped at the house and, as our stay lengthened, shyly made friends with Sewa. Chepa was a strong, chubby girl of thirteen, with big angelic brown eyes and a heart-shaped face. Court observed casually that in a few years she'd be a beauty. She led Sewa about on the *burra* and soon, by getting acquainted with Chepa's family, relatives, friends, and ceremonial kin, Sewa knew almost everyone, Mexican and Yaqui, in the village.

The religious *fiestas* were not the only celebrations. There was the novena, nine days after a person's death, rather like a wake, the *cumpleaño,* given on the anniversary of a person's death, and *fiestas* given simply because someone had made a promise to give one if a wish were granted.

There were three shifts at the mine, and when the seven A.M. to three P.M. got off, a lot of the men gathered at Chepa's house for cards and storytelling. Sewa brought home many stories, mostly true, some old, some recent.

There were tales of Yaqui generals, heroes, and traitors, of how the great Cajeme had a woman in each of the Eight Sacred Pueblos and stayed busy going from one to the other. Then there were reminiscences of a great earthquake when the sun shone through a mass of red clouds and everyone was afraid. Epidemics of cholera, smallpox, and yellow fever brought in by ships seemed to have ravaged the Río Yaqui pueblos almost yearly.

There were dozens of children in the village and I thought several times of starting a school, but it wasn't till I heard an uproar in the patio and investigated, finding that Sewa had just beaten half a dozen children at *monte* and that apparently she was developing a sinister genius at cards, that I was propelled into taking action.

"A schoolmarm, love?" teased Court. "Well, while we're blasting through the mountain would be a good time to get a school built."

"I could have classes in a ramada while it's hot," I suggested.

"All right," said Court. "First a ramada, then a real building. When the men know you want it, they'll put it up in a hurry." He gave me a measuring, slightly rueful look. "Since the pension plan was announced and especially since the men know you're blasting through the mountain so they can breathe, you're in danger of sainthood. But don't try to maneuver the men against me or ask them to help you get away. Trace Winslade's life is in my hand, and whether I smash it or put it in a safe place depends on the answer you must give me soon."

I looked away from him toward the glittering slope. In the long run I'd have no real choice. Perhaps my resistance whetted his desire. Could I strike a bargain with what I was bound to forfeit anyway, in a manner that would let me ride away with Trace?

"Court," I said slowly, forming each word and shoving it through my stiffened lips. "If I sleep with you till Trace comes, would you let Sewa and me go then?"

Though he didn't take an actual step nearer, he leaned forward, seemed to tower. A muscle throbbed in his jaw. He put his hands behind him and surveyed me in a way that sent hot blood to my face.

"An interesting proposition, Miranda. We'll talk about it later."

In a few days the ramada was built and I began classes. Chepa and Sewa were my only pupils for the first day, but on the second morning several of Sewa's friends ventured in.

Dr. Trent had donated a big globe and Court had produced some slates and chalk. I taught penmanship, or rather printing, till the children tired and then told them what I knew about different countries on the globe, using as much Yaqui as I could and learning, probably, more from the youngsters than they did from me.

"So your school's a success," Court said one evening while we were playing chess. "Perhaps now that it's running well you've had time to reconsider that fascinating offer you made me."

Coloring hotly, I muttered, "You mean being your—"

"Yes," he said. "Do you mean it?"

I could bear his glance only a moment. "Yes."

"And you don't think you should marry the man who ends your maidenhood?"

I remembered Trace with sweet despairing joy, that afternoon on the mountainside. Should I confess that to Court? My veins shrank inside me as I wondered what he would do when he learned I was no virgin, feared the vile tricks he had threatened to make me learn.

Fixing my gaze on the chessboard, I said huskily, "No matter what you do to me, I'll never marry you, Court."

His breath ejected in a barking laugh. "Who would expect such sentiments to come from a proper English school? What if you had a baby? Or is it in your mind to sleep quickly with Trace so you could name him the father?"

I hadn't even thought of a baby. That shocked me so that I

had no energy to resent his proposed solution. I just stared at him. He took my hands, carried them roughly to his face.

"You're a baby yourself, Miranda. What do you know of life? Love, either? I'll teach you but not on your terms, though I could play a game with your words. 'Till Trace comes back,' you said. Well, my dear, I could see to it that Trace never came back." As I flinched, he drew me closer. "But I won't play tricks with you. I don't want you for a few weeks. I want you always."

"How do you know?"

"I know."

This was more terrible, more hopeless, than anything I'd foreseen.

"You can't," I protested. "You might not like me at all."

He stopped my mouth with his, searing, demanding, pleading. "*Like* you," he breathed. "You little fool—I want to mold you, teach you, shape you, keep you forever. Why do you think I've been so patient?" Releasing me, he leaned against the wall. "If you're still so set on Winslade that you'd sacrifice your virginity to me in order to go with him, there's nothing to gain by letting you dream up more such foolishness."

I was afraid of what was coming, tried to ward it off. "Court—"

"We'll go riding early in the morning, Miranda. I want my answer then."

He strode away, toward the cantina. I watched him with hatred. Answer! What answer could I give? I'd have to be his mistress, but I wouldn't marry him, not if I had a dozen of his bastards. And I'd get away.

Somehow, someway, when he couldn't hurt Trace, I'd vanish. Even if it was down the mine shaft. And that gave me an idea.

When Raquel woke me next morning with a cup of chocolate and the news that the horses were ready and it was a beautiful day for riding, I refused the chocolate and asked her to tell Court I was sick. I was, in fact. The prospect of giving him an answer had twisted my stomach into a tight mass, cramped my nerves and muscles into a tight-wound internal rack.

I *was* sick. And I could stay so.

Sewa came over to me, closed my hand between hers. "Is it your head? Can I rub your neck?"

Her eyes were wide and troubled. "It's not important, little flower. I shall be all right. Why don't you ask Raquel for breakfast and then go for a ride with Pretty Hooves and Chepa?"

"I'd rather stay with you."

"That won't be necessary," came a voice from the door. "Run along, *chiquita*. I'll look after the señorita."

Sewa glanced at me. I managed a smile and touched her smooth brown cheek. "Get your breakfast. And see if you can find me some pretty rocks if you go riding."

She dressed quickly behind the Japanese screen, gave me a hug, and went out with a backward stare at Court. "Warning me, the little devil!" he said with a chuckle.

He came to my bed, laid his hand on my forehead, took my pulse, his finger listening for the trapped rhythm of my blood. I felt exposed, as if he could sense the workings of my body no matter what I did. I kept my eyes shut, knowing he was watching me, aware of my quick shallow breathing.

If he would just believe I was sick, go away and leave me!

"No fever, love," he said. "Your eyes are clear and your color divine. Let me see your tongue."

I didn't respond. He set thumb and finger in the lock of my jaws, forcing my mouth to open. "Pretty little kitten tongue," he said. "Pink and healthy."

With a lightning motion, he threw back the sheet. "Will you ride?" His voice was husky. He leaned so close that I felt the heat of his body. "Or shall I teach you a different gallop?"

Defeated, realizing with visceral impact that I could not evade this man, I shivered under his gaze. My thin shift might as well have not been there.

"Up!" he said. "Or I'll take you this minute with no song and dance."

I slid under his arm, scrambling up, snatching the clothes

Raquel had laid out. "You must have breakfast," he decreed as I moved behind the screen. "It'll be ready on the veranda in ten minutes."

Why did he drag out this game? Why hadn't I defied him, let him rape me and get it over? His patience was gone. It was only a matter of hours.

Still, it's nature to hope as long as one can, to run to the end of a closed tunnel, to fight till overwhelmed. And part of my fight was not to show how frightened I was.

Facing my mirror image, I made my hair smooth, rubbed color into my lips, and fixed my chin high, shoulders back. It helped. When I looked brave, I felt stronger. And though my heart thudded as I marched down the hall, I stepped onto the veranda as if I owned it.

As indeed I did.

That truth helped. I poured out for Court like a hostess, knew from the swift gleam of admiration in his eyes that he would let me appear in control for a while.

For a while. Till the lion sprang.

We rode along the railroad track as it twined from the valley, reached the top of the mountain and ribboned the crest. As the sun rose higher, we entered a crumbling diadem of rock that sprawled like a fortress over one ridge. Long grass fluffed high and yellow under mesquite and ironwood. Court stopped his horse and came to lift me down, holding me off the ground a moment, enjoying his power.

But he didn't gloat. Loosening the girths, he hobbled the horses and spread a serape for us, getting out the lunch Raquel had packed: roast beef, cheese, honey cakes, and a flask of wine. He ate with gusto, but I nibbled cheese and gazed northwest.

Trace was in that vastness. He should be done in Arizona by now, perhaps was on his way back, though he might seek out Lío before coming to Mina Rara.

Lío. Was Domingo becoming the kind of Sierra Yaqui to make his sister proud? And what was my own sister doing, my sister who had told the general to kill the Yaqui hostages when she knew it would mean my death?

"Penny for your thoughts?" asked Court. "Or perhaps they're worth gold nuggets! But what can a man offer the queen of the golden mountain?"

"I was wondering about the people I know. About Reina—"

"She's a witch," Court said, taking my hand. "But she can't hurt you now. No one can."

"Except you?"

He shrugged, mouth curving down. "I'll cherish you like the best and dearest part of my own body. And the pain that makes you a woman—there are ways to lessen that."

"That's not what I meant."

"No," he said impatiently, "you're choosing to feel martyred and abused. But that won't last long. So how shall it be, Miranda? Shall we marry? Will you take me for your lover? Or shall I send men to wait for Trace?"

The air was still and golden hot. A red *manzanita* twig seemed to bleed before my eyes. "What answer can I make?" I swallowed, willing my voice steady. "Of course I won't let Trace die. I'll be your mistress—and for all I care, you can take me now!" The words broke.

I stared into those golden eyes, might as well have searched for a soul in the eyes of a hawk. He straightened my clothes, bent his head, taking my mouth, opening it with his delving tongue. Holding me with one arm, he let his other hand find my breasts, my inner thighs. I was tense, not only because of his invasion but from fear of what he would do when he learned Trace had taken me. I held myself stiff, unyielding.

With an impatient sound, he opened my bodice, cupped my breasts, nipped them with soft little titillating bites, then plunged his head and sucked till it seemed he must be drawing out my very life.

His fingers pushed away my garments. When I tried to draw back, he held me, watching my face as he teased and played where only Trace had touched. Court didn't try to penetrate the moist pulsing hidden mouth his hand caressed, but I knew with frantic shame that he was aware of the building hunger in my loins, the pulsing beneath his skilled fingers.

"See, Miranda?" he said huskily. "You'll like it. You're ready for me now. You know that, don't you?"

"Court—"

"I won't take you here." Straightening my clothes, he drew me to my feet. "I'll have you in bed, with ease and comfort after Dr. Trent marries us. You're my lady, not a wench I found in the brush."

He bent to roll up the serape. I waited near the horses, aroused senses throbbing. No doubt at all that I'd respond to him, that he could own my body, do what he wished with it till I came to want whatever he did.

His rifle, as always, was in the scabbard. Stealthily, I moved toward it. His back was still turned. I grasped the rifle, sliding it free while holding the scabbard. Grasping the bolt, I pumped a cartridge in place as he heard and whirled.

When he saw the rifle, he laughed. "Put it down, love. You'll hurt yourself."

"I'll hurt you if you come closer."

He scratched his bleached hair, still grinning. "You've got the rifle, Miranda. Now what can you do with it? You know and I know you won't kill me if I stay put. But the second you try to ride away, I'll be on you. And you can't hold that gun forever. You'll get tired. You're tired already. Look how your hand's shaking." His tone was hypnotic, coaxing. "Drop it, Miranda. Drop it and we'll go home."

If there were some way to tie him up— I tried to imagine pulling the trigger, knew that I couldn't unless he rushed me. Damn him, all he had to do was wait! I hadn't gained a thing. Then I remembered the length of rawhide he'd used to tie up the serape.

"Take that rope and knot it around your ankles," I commanded.

He gave a long slow whistle. "And then what?" he asked, shaking his head as if grieved at my stupidity. "I can't tie my hands even if I wanted to and if you try—"

I didn't have that solved yet myself, but if his feet were secured, it would hamper him.

"Do it," I said.

With the air of a man humoring a maniac, he untied the rawhide and sat down, obligingly looped the cord around and about his ankles, making what seemed to be genuine knots. He looked up, laughing.

"All right, love. My hands?"

If I tried to stun him, there'd be a second he could lunge for me. I had to shoot him, hope my aim was good. I didn't want to kill him. But the right shoulder . . .

I sighted and fired. Eyes widening as he realized my intent, he flung himself forward, but the bullet was faster, took him in the upper right arm. The impact swung him around, carried him backward. The shot had gone right through his shoulder. There was a lot of blood on his white shirt. He seemed unconscious, though his eyes were partly open. His breathing was heavy, guttural.

I didn't want him to stop me, nor did I wish to leave him to bleed to death. Taking off my petticoat, I plugged both sides of the wound with flounces and wound the rest of the cloth around his shoulder.

"Court? Court!"

He didn't answer. His lips were pallid. "I'll leave your horse down the trail," I said, in case he could hear, understand. "And I'll send someone back."

But before you can do anything, I hope to be far, far away, with Trace warned.

I whirled my horse and rode, urging the gray along. The only plan I had was to ask one of the men to show me the way Trace would be coming and get there, with Sewa, before Court could catch us.

An hour and a half later, I tethered the gray to a mesquite and urged the mare on. How much time was I buying? Two hours? Five or six?

A shabby youngster was running up the trail. I didn't recognize Domingo till he raised his arms and cried, "Lady! Lady! Can you help us?"

Hanging on behind me, Domingo told his story as we rode down the winding trail to the village. The night before, Cruz had crawled into the basin, gasped a warning through bleeding lips. Federal troops were on their way, hundreds of them, assembled after pressure from Reina, who was determined to have Lío's head. Reina had been with soldiers who came to Cruz's hut and tortured him, trying to make him reveal the location of the band. He hadn't told, but through his control of bodily functions, he had made them believe him dead or near it, so they had left him in disgust. Reina had promised a thousand gold pesos to the man who brought her proof of Lío's death, and she rode with the troops.

Lío, Tula, and the fighting men had headed north, hoping to meet Trace and have the guns and ammunition that would give them some chance against the soldiers, but the women and children were hiding in the hills above Mina Rara, along with Cruz, who was in serious condition.

"Some have relatives who work at the mine," said Domingo. "They would take us in. But you should know, my lady, in case the soldiers come—"

The soldiers and Reina?

My head whirled with it all. Cruz injured, perhaps dying; Trace intercepted by Lío; hundreds of soldiers prowling the area; Court lying in his blood several miles up the trail . . .

"Of course your people can come," I said, "but they'd better wait till dark so only their relatives and friends will know. We can bring Cruz down now, though, take him to Señor Sanders' house. Señor Sanders is wounded. I'll have the doctor and some men fetch him while we go for Cruz."

Court would probably be in no shape to send assassins after Trace now, and even if he did, they'd have no chance against Lío's men. I wouldn't even attempt to guess the future, what would happen as Court recovered strength. With Sierra Yaquis hiding in the village and soldiers on the hunt, nothing was sure but trouble.

"Hold on!" I admonished Domingo, and urged my mare into a run as we reached more level ground.

I sent Domingo to tell Sewa what was happening while I rousted Dr. Trent out of his easy chair and told him Court was on top of the mountain, bleeding from a bullet wound.

"An accident," I said, though stuporous with brandy as he

was Dr. Trent seemed to accept the incident without much curiosity. "Better take a few men to carry him down."

I collected Domingo, gave Sewa a quick hug, and told Raquel to look after Señor Sanders, who would be home presently. "A friend of mine has been hurt," I explained. "I'm going to bring him back, so have a bed ready."

We got another horse for Domingo and Sewa insisted on coming, astride Pretty Hooves. "Domingo can ride back with me," she pointed out.

Two hours' brisk ride from the mine we found the women and children huddling under the washed-out side of a granite cliff. Cruz lay in the shade, twitching in fevered sleep. Blood matted his hair, his face was bruised, and when he raised his arms, I groaned and went sick.

His fingers had been cut off, some by a joint, some by two, some at the base. His healing, wise hands. Oh, damn those men! Damn Reina to hell, the cold bitch, to do such a thing!

Kneeling, wrenched with sobs, I held him in my arms, tried to lift him. Domingo and old Camilda helped. We got Cruz on my horse.

"We take Cruz now," I said in halting Yaqui. "The rest of you come tonight. Those who have no friends or relations at the mine must come to the big house of Señor Sanders and I will find you a place."

"What if soldiers come to the mine?" called one woman with a baby at her breast and a toddler at her skirts.

"We will have a lookout. If troops come, perhaps there'll be time to hide in the mountains. But let's pray that Trace Winslade and his guns reach Lío and the men in time to drive the soldiers away."

I got up behind Cruz, supporting him as best I could. Domingo, mounted, led my horse by the reins, while Sewa brought up the rear. We went back much slower than we'd come. It was almost sunset when we descended into the valley.

Domingo helped me get Cruz down the hall to the room Raquel had prepared. She came out of Court's chamber as we passed, gave me an accusing stare.

"How could you do it, señorita? He loved you! How could you?"

"Bring the doctor," I said curtly. "And can you make some strong broth? I will look in on the señor later. For now I must see to my friend."

Raquel flung away, weeping for the man who treated her as he might a pet. I had to admire her loyalty and believe she loved Court for himself, not just his presents.

As soon as we got Cruz in bed, I sent Domingo off with Sewa to the kitchen, for I was sure he was famished. Dr. Trent came puffing in while I was washing Cruz.

"You shoot this poor man, too?" he demanded, rubbing his mottled face. Then he saw the mutilated hands, gagged, and went to work.

If he wasn't quite sober when he started, he was when he finished. "This man's been kicked and beaten till it's a wonder he's alive," the doctor said. "May have some broken ribs and internal injuries. But he's tough. May do. I'll leave these morphine tablets in case he wakes up enough to feel what's happened. I'll look in on him when I check on Mr. Sanders."

I thanked Trent. After he was gone, I got a little water down Cruz's throat, and when Raquel sent broth by Domingo and Sewa, we got him to swallow a few spoonsful.

"A little at a time," I said at last. "Sewa, will you stay with him while Domingo and I watch for the women and children who have no place to stay?"

Five women and seven children came to Court's house, cautiously materializing out of the night. There was no way to conceal their presence from Raquel, since they would have to eat, so I enlisted her help in finding mats and blankets to bed them down in the storerooms connecting the main house and kitchen.

"Camilda and her daughter can cook for the group," I told Raquel. "Please be patient and helpful. If you are, you shall have the prettiest dress in Hermosillo and the longest earrings we can find."

"I do not care about that. Only that the señor shall be well and strong again."

It was not the time to tell her that he would have been in perfect health had he not threatened me with virtual rape and the death of the man I loved. "He'll be as good as new in a few weeks," I said. "Now let's see about a big pot of stew and some milk for the children."

A cousin of one of the refugees stood watch all night on the trail above the valley and was relieved at dawn by another Yaqui miner. To glance around the dwellings, no one would guess the population had increased by a third during the night. To strangers viewing Mina Rara, there was nothing suspicious. The children living in Court's storerooms were playing in the inner yard and no more than two women ventured out at once.

Still, in spite of outward calm, there was tension, suspense, the agony of waiting. . . .

I sat up all night with Cruz, dozing a bit now and then, giving him water when he seemed to rouse. While Dr. Trent was with him that morning, I looked in on Court, who was cradled against Raquel as she held a cup of coffee for him to sip.

His eyes kindled as he saw me. He pushed the cup away. "So you've hid Yaquis about the village," he said in a fatalistic tone. "And the fighting men are no doubt meeting Trace, so it's too late for me to send after him. I hope you know, Miranda, that you're jeopardizing not only your life and all you own, but everyone who works at Mina Rara. If soldiers find outlaw Yaqui here, the rest will be killed or deported, too. I'm surprised you can take it on your conscience."

"I don't see what else I could do. Anyway, if the men get the weapons Trace hoped to find, they could make things difficult for many times their number of soldiers."

"So now you're egging on rebels. How can you forget they were ready to kill you?"

"They only want their land, in peace."

"They'll never get it." Court's mouth hardened and I noticed, with shock, how haggard he was. "Even if they get away this time, they'll have to hide out in the sierra till they're killed or caught."

"There may be a revolution. You've said it yourself. That could get their land back or at least stop the deportations and extermination. No one has a guaranteed future." I paused and stared at him. "That includes you, Court. I want your promise not to betray the Yaquis."

"Or?" His yellow eyes smoldered and a faint smile twitched the edges of his mouth.

"If I have to shoot you again, I won't stop at a shoulder."

He laughed outright. "God damn you, sweetheart, I can't stand any more of your marksmanship!"

Raquel shielded him. "Hurt him more, señorita, and I cut your throat!" she hissed. He patted her arm.

"Don't be upset, *chiquita*," he said lazily. "Miss Miranda is a woman of principle and I have no intention of provoking her into further proof of it. Run along now, I want a few words alone with her."

Casting a warning glance at me, Raquel went out. Court watched me with one sun-bleached eyebrow raised. I felt an urge to run, though he was in no shape to be a menace.

"So you shot me, Miranda," he said conversationally. "How did it feel?"

"You've shot men."

"Yes, but I'm not you. Come, my dear, gratify my curiosity. How did you feel when I went over backward?"

"Awful."

He nodded. "That ought to tell you something about yourself, Miranda, that and the fact that you can't hold a grudge against those bandits who wanted to kill you a month ago. You don't belong in this country. When I'm well, I'll take you to the United States."

Astounded, I had to swallow a few times before I could speak. "You—you'll take me to the States? Court, you have to be out of your mind!"

"No, love. People will think you're out of yours. Crazed, you'll be, from what you've been through, and everyone will think me a devoted husband to care so tenderly for a demented wife who may at times insist she was abducted."

Somehow I managed to laugh. "*You're* demented, Court, to say what you hope to do. I suppose you'd bribe that poor old derelict, Dr. Trent, to marry us. And saying I was mad would explain anything, wouldn't it? But you're forgetting you're in no condition to make me do anything, and by the time you are—"

"You hope to be far away with Winslade?" Court asked silkily. "Well, *querida,* we all have plans. Let's see whose come true."

I advanced on him. "Court, you swore not to tell about the Yaquis."

"Neither shall I. But wherever Trace takes you, I'll find you. That's a promise, too, Miranda."

Cold foreboding gripped me. I had just thought ahead to getting to Trace's friends, being free of both Court and Reina. I had supposed Trace would be where he'd come to see me often. But if he were committed to stoking the fires of revolution, or if Court were really determined to hunt me down . . .

It came to me that while Court Sanders lived, I'd never be free of him. Yet I couldn't kill him while he was helpless. I stumbled toward the door.

"Thank you, Miranda," mocked Court, "for looking in on me."

12

The soldiers came at noon. I was spooning broth into Cruz, who was conscious now, while Sewa played the flute. Domingo came running in, bare feet spanking the tiles.

"*Federales!*" he panted. "The lookout just came in. He says they'll be here in an hour, at least two hundred."

My heart stopped, then tripped over and began to pound. To think the troops *might* come was one thing—to confront them was another. Would Court keep his word? Would Raquel stay silent? Had any of the Mexican miners noticed their neighbors' guests?

If only there were a hiding place, a safe secure spot big enough to hold the fifty-odd women and children . . .

And then it came. The mine shaft, the long tunnel eating through the mountain. The refugees could hide there. Putting the broth in Sewa's hands, I told her to feed Cruz, said I'd be back in a while, and hurried with Domingo to the storerooms.

There I told the women my plan and asked them to go swiftly to the house where their friends were and gather them at the new mine as soon as possible along with any bedding and food they could get.

The shifts wouldn't change till three and most of the Mexican workers were below now. With luck, the gathering of women and children wouldn't be observed by anyone likely to betray them, but I had a last-ditch strategy in case the soldiers did search the mine shaft.

I stopped in Court's office and put all the loose money in a small bag that I gave Domingo in case things went wrong. Then he and I loaded Cascos Lindos with water and food and urged her to the mine, where some Yaquis were already congregated in the supply room. Distributing candles, I led them down the ladders, left Domingo to instruct the others as they came, and ran back to the house as the first soldiers appeared on the trail.

As I glanced up, my blood turned to ice. I stood paralyzed for a moment. That was no soldier on the black horse at the head of the troops. That proud figure, red hair . . .

Reina!

It didn't seem likely that soldiers, without definite evidence, would search the house of a gringo mine superintendent, but I got Sewa and Raquel to help me move Cruz into my room, instructed Sewa to bolt the door, and went to sit with Court.

In spite of my threats, once Reina and the soldiers came, he would have me at his mercy. Would he keep his word? Darting him a troubled glance, I could read nothing on his calm face.

"Reina is with the troops," I said. "She's still my guardian. At the least I suppose she'll try to take me back to Las Coronas."

"At the least," he agreed. "Though seeing what you've done to me may cause her to think twice about your desirability as an unwilling guest."

"Oh," I blurted, "please don't—" I would beg but it wouldn't do any good.

Court's voice was rich with sarcasm. "You blew a half-inch hole right through me, beloved. Shall we pretend I have a fever?"

What else could I expect from him, even if he kept his word about the refugees?

"There's a way I'll lie for you," Court went on. "One way

only. Otherwise, your precious Yaquis, including that crippled brat, are as good as dead or slaves in Yucatán. And what
good is a slave with one foot? The troops might use her for
target practice."

The room seemed to heave. I hated him with a ferocity that
seemed to wrench my entrails into knots. "You," I choked,
"you unspeakable—"

"Save your breath," he advised. "You have one chance to
save the girl and all the others. If you hurry."

"What do you want?"

"Get Dr. Trent." Court's eyes traveled slowly, possessively
over me, as a potential buyer might sum up desirable qualities.
He smiled with his lips, but his gaze was cruel. "Tell him we
wish to be married. At once."

"Court, I'll sleep with you. I promise. But please—"

"You'll marry me. In the next few minutes."

My thoughts whirled crazily. Court had restrained himself
in order to have a virgin bride. If he knew I had been Trace's,
I was sure he wouldn't marry me. I was equally convinced that
if I told him that now, he would vent his outraged fury by
giving away the Yaquis. At last he had me trapped.

What he would do when he learned I'd given myself to
Trace was a nightmare I couldn't even think of now. I must
protect Cruz, Sewa, Domingo, all the others. After the soldiers
left—if they left—I would be confronted with a man who
could make my life hell. But first . . .

I stumbled to the door.

"Hurry, love," said Court. His laughter curled after me. I
pressed my hands to my ears and ran.

Dr. Trent pronounced the time-hallowed beautiful words
in a whiskey-slurred voice. I stood by Court's bed, responding
when prompted, inwardly screaming that it was a horrible
mocking travesty. In my heart and soul and body I had
become Trace's wife on the mountain.

But the words were said. I had promised to love, honor, and
obey a man I hated and meant to thwart in any and every way I
could. Court must have guessed my thoughts. His hand

tightened crushingly on mine as he slipped the signet ring he wore on his little finger on my third one.

With his other hand he brought my head down, held me to a taunting voracious kiss, a hard mouth that forced mine open, let his tongue thrust deeply, avidly. The display must have shocked even the befuddled Dr. Trent.

Mumbling his thanks for the gold piece Court tossed to him, the old man left as the sound of hooves became insistent, accented by the cadence of many marching feet.

Court released me with a complacent smile. "Try not to be impatient, darling. We'll have our whole lifetime."

Trembling with outrage and fear, I crossed to the end of the room. In that moment came footfalls. My sister stood in the doorway, her hair a glory, though her clothes and face were dusty from riding.

Her green eyes went wide when she saw me. "You! I thought Lío had slit your throat."

"No thanks to you, he didn't," I retorted.

She whirled to Court. "Why didn't you inform me? I'm this foolish child's guardian, responsible for her, even if she did repay my concern by running away."

"Concern?" His eyebrows crept almost to the thick fall of coarse golden hair over his forehead. "Is that what you call it?"

She advanced almost to the bed. "What do you mean?"

"Ordering a vaquero to loosen a cinch so the saddle turns under a rider is concern of a sort, perhaps. As was sending word to the commandant that he could execute the prisoners you knew your sister stood hostage for."

"Supposition," she said, regaining her calm, though her fingers bit white at her riding crop's handle. "Anyway, she goes with me when we ride out of here."

Court smiled. "But, dearest Reina, she's not your ward anymore."

"Of course she is! You can't change her birthday. Until Miranda is eighteen, I have her in charge."

"Not if she marries."

"What?" Reina's voice rose incredulously.

"She is my wife."

Reina whirled from Court to me. "You—you sneaked off

and married him? Why, you little idiot, he's only after your money."

"At least he wasn't trying to kill me. When I got away from the Yaquis, I had to go somewhere and Mina Rara does belong to me."

"I suppose Court pointed out to you that you could evade my guardianship by marrying?" Her lips curled. "Did your honeymoon raptures put him to bed? Is your love so fierce that you injured his shoulder?"

"Reina, what I do and why is no longer your affair."

Nostrils flaring, she tapped the whip against her boot. "It's my business, as a citizen, if you're harboring insurrectionists. Lío's outlaws went somewhere. Did you buy your release from him by promising refuge if his rebels ever needed it?"

"That wouldn't have been a bad idea," I said admiringly. "In fact, I was bought with a price, but it wasn't that."

Her eyes blazed. "Trace got you out. Where is he?"

"I don't know." That was true enough. "You've no right to ask me questions. Take those soldiers and get off my property."

"Not till we're sure the bandits aren't hiding here."

A uniformed officer, wiry and tall with a trim black moustache, loomed in the door, several men behind him. "The village is being thoroughly searched," he said, dark eyes going over me slowly before he bowed.

"Good," said Reina. "And, Major Ruiz, you had better search the house."

My heart lurched as I thought of Cruz in my room. I stepped forward.

"Major Ruiz, I own this mine and this house. I resent this invasion. While some excuse may be made for hunting through the village, there can be none for rifling my private dwelling."

"My wife is correct," said Court. "It is not valiant of you, Major, to ransack the house of a lady whose husband is in no physical condition to defend her rights."

Ruiz wavered. Reina strode forward, confronting him. "This is my sister, who ungratefully ran away from Las

Coronas and was seized by Yaquis. I thought they had killed her. Since they didn't, she must have bargained for her release, perhaps by offering the mine as shelter. Search the house, Major. You know your orders from the colonel."

He glanced unhappily from me to Court. "I crave your pardon," he said. "I have orders from my colonel to follow this lady's directions. I assure you there will be no damage."

"I cannot assure you there will be no damage to your career, Major, after I report this discourtesy to my friend, General Lobos," said Court. Ruiz winced.

"Señorita?" he appealed, turning to Reina.

"Lobos is in Mexico City." She shrugged disdainfully. "The colonel is in Guaymas. Conduct the search at once."

He spread his hands, bowed, and turned, began issuing instructions to the half-dozen soldiers at his heels. A desperate hope flashed through me. I swayed against the door.

"Court, dearest," I said loudly. "All this has made me faint. I have the start of a fearful migraine. You will forgive me if I retire to my room?"

"By all means, love," he said, frowning with worry.

As I moved down the hall, I heard him say in a man-to-man tone, "My wife, Major, is in a delicate state of health. I think you understand me? Her constitution is fragile anyway and now it is vital that she maintains serenity."

"I will be as considerate as possible, señor," replied the major stiffly. "Please comprehend that I only do my duty."

I went quickly into my room, decided against shooting the bolt since that would compel me to get up in case Ruiz absolutely demanded entrance. Tearing off my dress, I whispered to Sewa, who had come to her feet, flute in hand, Ku on her shoulder.

"Sewa, slip down to the mine and tell Domingo that if the soldiers start into the mine shaft, he must dynamite the passage. You must stand guard and tell him if they're coming. Stay with him. As soon as it's safe, we'll dig through and bring you all out."

"But, Miranda—"

"Hurry, darling." I gave her a quick hug. "I hope the

soldiers go away or that Lío comes, but an explosion can protect the people in the tunnel. Go out, fast, through the patio. Soldiers are searching the house."

She took her cane and fled, still holding Ku and her flute, limping only slightly. These soldiers were bound to make her remember the slaughter of her family. I hoped that they wouldn't stop her, that she would seem to them only an insignificant child.

Cruz's eyes were open and lucid as I got hastily under the coverlet. "Soldiers are here?" he murmured.

"Yes." I caught his arm as he tried to rise. "Lie as close to me as you can and let's fix the sheet so maybe they won't do more than peek in and get out."

"Miranda, you must not risk yourself." His eyes shut and his breath was shallow as he stored energy to say more. "What am I without fingers? A trunk without limbs or leaves. Let them have me."

"If they find you, they'll suspect the other Yaquis are here," I protested urgently. I embraced him, fighting tears. "Oh, Cruz, please let me hide you."

He didn't answer. His eyes had closed. I heard footsteps nearing, hastily arranged the bedclothes to disguise his presence as much as possible. The curtains were drawn so the room was dim.

If the searchers would only glance in and retreat in proper confusion from the sickbed of a lady . . .

There was a sharp rap. The door pushed inward. I raised on one elbow, holding my head as if it pained. I was, in fact, sick with apprehension.

"Your pardon," said Major Ruiz. "If we may just observe under your bed and inside the wardrobe?"

He didn't look directly at me and I prayed his followers wouldn't either. "Do what you must, Major," I complained. "But do be as quiet and quick as you can. This terrible headache—"

"I am unspeakably distressed," he muttered. "I will inspect your room myself, señora," He sent his men along the hall, bent to peer shamefacedly under my bed, then opened the wardrobe. Very little hung in it so he was immediately satisfied.

"Your pardon," he said again, bowing as he retreated.

"Pardon?" Reina strode in, eyes raking me, fixing on the disheveled bedding. "What is that in bed with you, Miranda? Surely you don't sleep with dolls? Not of that size."

With one strong jerk she flung back the covers. The pupils of her eyes swelled triumphantly. "So! You hide the Yaqui witch who must be a witch indeed. We left him for dead."

"He is my friend," I said, sitting up, shielding him. "He saved Sewa, if you remember. Of course I wanted to help him when he dragged himself to the mine."

"Along with a hundred Yaquis?" jeered Reina. "Major, take this wretch to the space by the cantina and have your men bring the grown people, all of them, to watch an entertainment. If the old man won't talk I think someone will."

"Don't!" I cried, holding Cruz as Ruiz gave orders and a pair of soldiers came toward us. "Can't you see he's almost dead? Look at his hands, you devils! Leave him alone!"

"Señora," said Ruiz. "If you do not remove your arms from that renegade witch, I must."

It was futile, but I clung to my friend. Ruiz, sighing, spoke to his men. He gripped my wrists while they dragged Cruz from my grasp, hustled him out of the room. Losing control, wild with fear, I struggled with the major. He laughed, eyes firing, and held me much closer then necessary to check my struggles, crushing my breasts on the buttons of his coat.

"Let my wife go," commanded Court from the door.

Ruiz released me so abruptly that I fell against the bed. His face was flushed and he spoke hoarsely. "Perhaps you will explain to her that she has done a very serious thing in hiding a criminal. I am not a vengeful man, but I cannot answer for what my colonel may do when I report." Bowing, he marched down the hall.

Reina smiled at me. "Well, Miranda? Will you hide under your pillows while we try to get some truth from that old scarecrow?"

"I will watch," I told her. "And you will pay for it."

Court's step was faltering as he came to me, but his good hand gripped my shoulder hard. "Stay here," he said. "You'll really be sick if you go out there. And if you do anything crazy, I can't help you with my arm crippled."

Wrenching free, dodging him, I snatched up my dress, struggled into it, and ran past my sister after the soldiers who half-carried the emaciated body of my friend.

Soldiers continued to scavenge through the village, though perhaps a score of them gathered to oversee the stone-silent group of people gathering by the cantina. Under orders, several miners had dragged up the pile of precious fuel, most of it chopped dry ocotillo and ironwood from each family's private supply. Cruz was tied to one of the paloverdes that had grown large from seepage from the watering trough. His eyes were closed. He seemed frail as a withered leaf, as if the vital part of him had already left his body. I knelt close by, heedless of the dust.

What did Reina plan? That heap of wood . . . Horrified, I refused to understand what was going to happen until Reina stopped in front of Cruz.

"Old man," she said, "I know what Yaquis do to witches. It will happen now if you don't say where Lío is."

He didn't speak.

She prodded him with her whip. "Do you hear?"

Slowly, his eyes opened. Their depths glowed as if all his remaining strength was hoarded in them. His lips curved in a faint smile. "Does one answer the hiss of a serpent?"

Gasping, Reina drew her arm, brought the whip stinging forward. I hurled myself forward in time to catch the worst of the blow across my upraised arm. The metal tips brought blood, but I didn't feel it. Outrage swept reason from me. All I could see was Reina's taunting face, the joyful glitter of her eyes. With an animal cry, I sprang at her, grappling for the whip. She was taller and stronger, but I was powered by fury.

Wresting the crop from her, I leaped back and snapped the lash against her face just as Ruiz reached me, forced me away. Reina snatched up the crop and lashed me across the breast.

"Stop that, señorita," snapped Ruiz, thrusting me among the soldiers for safekeeping. "Our business is not with your sister." He strode up to Cruz and Reina followed with a last murderous glance at me.

"Well, old man?" the major demanded. "Speak or burn. You have one minute."

Cruz was completely motionless. There was in him such self-possession that the soldiers Ruiz ordered forward didn't move for a moment, and when they reached the tree, they stopped.

"Lift him!" Ruiz commanded.

Fearfully, the men untied Cruz from the paloverde, fumbling the knots. His hands and feet were still bound together. "Kindle the fire," said the major.

In a moment the dry twigs spat and flamed, searing the heavier wood. Ruiz stepped close to the condemned man.

"Your last chance," he threatened.

Cruz said, "I am dancing." And I remembered what he had said months ago, about how even death must let a brave man do his last dance, reveal for one final time the essence of his nature.

"Dance in fire then," shouted Ruiz. He signaled his men.

They advanced on the blaze. There was screaming, my own, and I tore at the hard bodies around me, frenzied, unable to break through as the soldiers lifted Cruz, tossed him onto the pyre. The wood shifted, some breaking loose. There was the smell of burning hair, the flare of cloth, then, after what seemed an eternity, the acrid sizzling and scent of flesh.

No cries.

My knees gave way. I fell to the earth, retching. Someone put an arm around me, turning my face to his shoulder. "I think his neck broke when he struck the fire," Court said. "He's dead or he'd be coughing. Come to the house, Miranda."

One of the soldiers helped him raise me. Reina stood between the fire and the hushed crowd. "You see what happens to rebels," she shouted. "But I will reward anyone who can tell me where the outlaw Lío hides."

No one moved.

"We can build more fires," Ruiz said. "Or perhaps pulling out a few tongues would loosen those remaining."

"A hundred gold pesos!" cried Reina. "I will give that for Lío's whereabouts."

A woman stepped forward, muffled in a black shawl. I couldn't see her face, yet something about her was familiar, something in the free swing of her walk. She mumbled something beneath her breath.

Reina stared, then shrugged and moved toward the cantina. The woman followed her inside. The door creaked shut. Ruiz folded his arms.

"Come," urged Court.

I shook my head. "I have to know what happens."

Minutes passed. Cruz's body smoldered. Though I faced away from the fire, there was no way to avoid the smell of burning flesh, but I was so glad he was past pain that it scarcely mattered. At last, at Ruiz's order, a captain strode to the cantina, called.

There seemed to be no answer. He pushed through the door, gave a cry, and reeled backwards, clawing at the knife in his chest. At almost the same moment a tremendous blast echoed from the mine, reverberated from the hills, followed by a dull crashing sound like distant thunder.

After a frozen instant of shock, Ruiz ordered a squad to the cantina, the rest toward the mine. A figure was streaking from the rear of the cantina, dodging through the dwarfed trees and scrub. The major ordered his men to fire. Bullets hummed after a crash of firing. The running body leaped, turned around, and fell, arms swinging up as if to curse or embrace.

Tula!

Then the air came alive with hissing cartridges. From the low ridges and dusty thickets, men appeared, tattered wild men wearing bandoliers. Ruiz rallied his men, the bugler sounded, and the men straggling from the mine redoubled their pace, dropping some comrades, apparently wounded by the blast, in order to run forward and join the battle.

"Run!" Court hissed at me.

Lío's band? It almost had to be. But their shots could kill me as quickly as could the soldiers'. I ran with Court for the cantina, slid inside past the captain's body, and lay panting on the hard-packed earth a moment before I glanced around and sighted Reina.

She lay by the counter like a broken doll. When Court turned her over, her head lolled and I screamed; that slender throat was cut from side to side. Her green eyes stared in glazed disbelief. Tula, an advance spy for Lío's group, must have been rounded up with the villagers and taken her chance to kill the woman who had brought so much suffering on them.

"But they can't win," I groaned to Court. "There are so many soldiers."

"Maybe not so many," Court said dryly. "I didn't see near as many coming out of the mine as went in." He stared at me. "Was setting off that charge your idea?"

"I couldn't think of any other way to save the people if the soldiers started poking around in the place."

Court shook his head. "You're crazy, Miranda. Really crazy. If word gets out of what you've done, you'll be executed for treason."

"I'll worry about that if we live through the next hour." I shrugged. And for the first time it hit me. Trace had to be back with the ammunition and guns. He might even be with the attackers.

And he might be dead.

Court read my thoughts. "We'll know in a while," he grunted, staying low to the ground as he worked around the bar. "How about some wine?"

"I'd rather have water."

"It's wine or tequila."

I settled for a few sips of sour wine. At least it was wet. Bullets spanged against the cantina. One flew through a window, drilled into the opposite wall with a shower of flaked adobe.

"Damn!" said Court. "They're taking cover behind the cantina. If we're lucky, we can have them firing from both directions."

It was a nightmare; reality had stopped for me when Cruz

went into the fire. I wasn't afraid. All my interest was in what was happening outside.

Were the people in the mine safe? Did Lío's band have a chance? Where was Trace?

These things chased through my head till it throbbed. Another bullet whirred above us, spanked into adobe, ricocheted a palm's breadth from my head. Court swore.

Would the firing never stop? From the yells and shots, the fray ranged from the general store to the mine. Where we sheltered behind the bar, I could hear the steady strong beat of Court's heart, in strange counterpoint to the battle. Where our skin touched, it stuck with sweat. Even the earthen floor held little coolness.

A bullet whined over, struck the wall, splintered adobe, and bounced. Impact. Court's body lifted, shuddered.

"Court!" I tried to rise up, but he pushed me flat, collapsed so that his body shielded mine.

"Be still!" he panted. I could feel a thick warmth seeping from his hip. "I won't have you scarred, marked up. You're mine."

He would bleed to death. I rolled out from under what was almost dead weight, ripped off the flounce of my petticoat, made a pad, ripped the side of his trousers with a knife hidden under the bar. Blood pulsed from his upper thigh. I fitted the pad over the wound, bound it in place.

If the blood would stop! Court had done his best to protect me. I couldn't just let him die. Reaching for the wine bottle, I held it to his lips. He swallowed. His eyelids fluttered as I wiped the clammy moistness from his face.

"Lie down!" he breathed, exerting his last strength to bring me next to him. "Stay low, damn you!"

Pinned by his weight, I lay in the dust. Firing, shouts, and screams filled the air outside, now closer, now ebbing. Where was Sewa? Would she be safe in the tunnel with the women and children? Whatever happened outside, perhaps they might survive.

And Trace! He must be out there with Lío's men. If I could find a weapon . . .

Keeping as much as possible behind the wall and the fallen captain's crumpled body, I worked the heavy gun from his holster. It took both my hands to hold it. Aiming at the nearest soldiers spraddled behind some rocks near the cantina, I pulled the trigger.

It clicked on an empty chamber. But there were a dozen men clustered in easy range, their attention centered on the ragged Yaquis who seemed to be firing with those rifles, the ones with which Trace had bought my life.

Trace was out there somewhere.

With any luck, dense and close as they were, I could pick off one or two soldiers before they learned they had an enemy behind them.

I squeezed off a shot, wrist and fingers numbed by the recoil. A soldier pitched forward.

"Miranda!" It was Trace, over among some rocks. "Get down, you little fool."

He was alive. Till I saw him, I couldn't be sure. My heart swelled with thankfulness. I aimed once more. Then a mountain seemed to fall in on me as an explosion of pain was buried in unconsciousness.

13

When I tried to open my eyes, light stabbed through them to my brain in a way that made me moan and turn my face into the soft comfort of pillows. For a while I didn't know who I was, where I was, anything except that it hurt to be awake. Then drifts of remembering swelled; I would hear a voice, glimpse a face against my closed eyelids, figures outlined in blood-red so dark it was almost black.

There was a face I longed to see, not knowing whose it was, but it never appeared in my feverish half-dreams. If it did, I would know everything that my mind could not or would not retrieve. Till I remembered that face, I didn't want to rouse at all, open my eyes to the world around me, the owners of hands that brought me food and drink, dressed me, and attended my needs.

Reluctantly, I became aware of the hands. One pair was light and tentative, almost hesitant in the way they touched me. The other was strong, hard, deft. They held me more than was necessary, lingered in a way that, as I returned to reality, made my flesh chill. A voice that went with the hands talked at me. I couldn't hear the words. I kept my eyes shut. But a name kept knifing into the soothing haze, jarring me to consciousness.

"Miranda," said the deep voice that belonged with the caressing hands. "Miranda . . ."

My heart would seem to stop beating. And long warm fingers would stray over my face, my throat, pass to my breasts and down the rest of my body. What would they do if I came alive? I was afraid of the hands, though they cherished me. They didn't belong to the face I desperately groped to remember.

But the soft fuzziness muffling my thoughts and feelings began to fade. I began to want to see, even though it hurt. The face I wished for mightn't ever come, I might have to search for it. Only how was I to elude the hands that tended me?

"Why shouldn't I bed her, Doctor? It might help and it can't hurt!"

"A senseless woman!" protested a husky frayed tone interrupted by a harsh laugh.

"I've been patient. Six weeks married and still no consummation. I'll give it a few more days, but then I'll have her."

"If she stays like this, you should have the marriage annulled," said the other voice while I tried to understand the words.

The owner of the strong hands laughed again. "I won't lose her. I'd rather have her, even if she stayed just like this, than any other woman."

"That—that's obscene!"

The voices went away. I opened my eyes slowly, winced at the light, but fought to pierce the murky veil shrouding my vision. Pushing up on an elbow, I bit back a groan at the sledging ache in my head. When I could bear to move, I sat up fully, stared through weaving red shadows at the white-walled room, dresser, and elaborate screen.

Did I know this place?

Nothing stirred memories. If I could only see the face, then I'd know, then I'd remember.

Remember what? Sadness? My head throbbed, sending waves of nausea through me, and I lay back.

There was a sound. The hands gripped mine and the voice

that went with them said roughly, "Miranda, my darling. Miranda, my wife."

I looked up, through shifting mists to tawny eyes, a hard squarish face. I knew him.

He saw that I did.

But when a sound of pain tore from my lips as he bent over, jarring the bed, he said contritely, "Does it hurt so much, sweetheart? Never mind, just lying there as long as you have would make a person dizzy weak. Now you're awake, you'll soon feel good as new."

"Court," I said slowly. "Your name is Court. You—you were hurt."

He touched his thigh. "Healed." Strong white teeth showed for a moment. "And so is the hole you shot through my shoulder."

Then, as if parts of a scattered jigsaw suddenly fitted themselves together, I saw Reina dead, soldiers firing, and glimpsed, at last, the face I'd hunted in my fever dreams, a dark lean face with storm green eyes, as I'd seen it before something crashed in my head.

"Trace!" I said.

Court lost his smile. I felt a surge of longing and need for Trace, an equally strong fear of the big man leaning over me. His sun-bleached golden hair reminded me of a lion's mane. I felt exposed to him, my softness undefendable, as if he might lower his mouth to my throat and tear at it.

He did bend his head. I tried to move away, but he held me against the pillow, set his lips where the pulse leaped and pounded.

"You're my wife." His words muffled against my flesh. "I'll wait a few days more, help you get stronger. But then I'll make you forget every man but me."

Though I dreaded the reaction my question might bring, I had to know. "Where is Trace?" I asked. "The fight—what happened?"

Court released me abruptly, straightened, turned on his heel to the window. "Winslade's dead and buried."

"No."

"Lucky for him. Or he'd be slaving in Yucatán on some henequen plantation. He wouldn't last long. They'd beat him to death." As I stared in puzzled horror, Court explained, and each word woke echoes in my aroused memory.

Those of Lío's band who hadn't died in the battle were sent under heavy guard to Guaymas and shipped to Yucatán to be sold to great plantations, where they would work under brutal conditions till they died.

"Yaquis don't make good slaves," said Court. "I've heard two-thirds of them die inside the first year."

Another name stirred in the depths of my heart, a name I must call before I let myself think about Trace. "Sewa?"

"Your little pet got away along with the women and children you hid in the mine. They're back in the sierra." Court smiled indulgently. "You're thorough, sweetheart. It took the men two weeks to clear out the rocks and earth that dynamite shook loose." He paused. "Major Ruiz doesn't know you sheltered Yaqui families. I wouldn't give him an excuse, love, to take a closer interest in you. He's stationed here with a detachment that goes off Yaqui-hunting every week or so, but I believe he's far more preoccupied with you. Most punctilious he's been with his calls and courtesies. And unmistakably crestfallen at your slow recovery."

I scarcely heard all that. Sewa had escaped, and presumably so had Domingo. He'd look after her. The women and children would have a cruel time of it by themselves, but at least their men would not be attracting pursuit.

Their men. Dead or enslaved.

My man. Dead. Trace, to whom I was pledged with heart and body though drunken old Dr. Trent had spoken legal words binding me to this powerful man leaning over me. Court read my thoughts. His mouth twisted.

"He's dead, Miranda. Dead and tumbled in an arroyo where the soldiers tossed corpses and shoveled in the sides to cover them. By now worms will have eaten such of his brains as weren't blown away with the back of his head."

"Trace," I said. "Trace."

A vein stood out in Court's temple, but his voice was soft,

almost pitying. "Dead, Miranda. Dead and gone. Forget him. You'll get well and strong and be happy." His hand caressed my cheek. "I'll take good care of you."

I felt cold at the words, colder at his touch, coldest when I thought of the future. Live without Trace? It seemed impossible, yet I knew I could. A matter of getting through an hour at a time, a day at a time, till there was a week, then a month, at last a year. People did it all the time. So would I. Somehow.

But live with Court? I couldn't and wouldn't. I'd get away. Perhaps find Sewa again and Domingo, yet back to Las Coronas, and build some sort of life. . . .

Life without Trace. It kept coming back to that. I needed to weep, to mourn him, but my eyes were dry. The heaviness pressing on my heart seemed to crush all feeling. Or was it the pressure of Court's tawny eyes?

"Rest now," he said, trailing his fingers across my eyes. "You'll be better soon, darling. If you knew how hard it's been to wait—"

I could almost have laughed. He expected me to sympathize with his frustration? Did he think I could stop loving Trace, just like that, on the snap of a finger, because he was dead? I closed my eyes against the smoldering flame in Court's, but I couldn't evade his lingering hands, which both chilled and burned, like ice-fire. That was the awful, treacherous thing. I wasn't indifferent to him; in some hostile way he aroused my senses.

That frightened me more than the inevitability of being taken by him. So long as he took without my response or encouragement, I believed I could feel separate from it, not really there. But if I answered him, even to fight, he'd have trapped me in the body he could handle and use at will.

A sudden freezing question pierced my desperation. Court thought me a virgin. Only that had kept him from forcing me months ago. When he thrust for that membrane and found it gone, I doubted he'd believe I had lost it riding horseback or any of those other possible, implausible excuses.

My breath slowed till it almost stopped. Court's hand lay on my throat as a beast of prey might pin a victim. "We will be cautious," he said. "You will get back your strength a little each day." He buried his face against my belly and I felt his warm breath heat my skin. "For certain things, though, my energy will suffice at the moment."

Laughter rumbled deep in his chest. He kissed my mouth slowly, making it open to him. Then he went away.

My head still ached and I could go only a few steps without tiring, but I was recovering from what Dr. Trent called a serious concussion caused by a soldier clubbing me with a carbine butt.

Raquel and Chepa waited on me when Court was at the mine, Raquel with averted eyes and a resentful curve to her soft lips. When I was stronger, she might help me escape, but I dared not sound her out yet. When I asked Chepa if anything had been heard of Sewa or the others who'd hidden in the mine, Chepa gave a sad shake of her head.

"The soldiers line up our men every week to be sure no Sierra Yaqui have slipped in. Major Ruiz's order is that anyone giving food or shelter to the fighters will be hanged or sent to the henequen plantations."

"But Sewa's a child and crippled besides!"

"She's with the rebels. That's all Ruiz cares for." We shared a heavy silence before Chepa brightened. "Domingo will take care of Sewa. She's told me how brave and clever he is, that he will be a better leader even than Lío."

"Did Lío die?"

"No. It pleased Ruiz to send him as a slave to Yucatán."

Lío a slave? He wouldn't be one for long, I was sure of that. He would get away or resist till he was killed. Trace would have been the same; for the first time I was bitterly grateful that the man I loved had died quick and clean, been spared what Lío and the surviving men were enduring.

And Sewa, my chosen sister-child? Domingo would look after her, and so would old Camilda. The women and children would be safer in the mountains than in settlements where they might be arrested simply because they were Yaqui.

That evening Court helped me out on the veranda and filled goblets with wine. "To your recovery," he toasted. He pulled a rawhide bench so close that his long upper leg pressed mine. "You're beautiful again, Miranda. I'm rewarded for my patience."

"You've been kind."

"Be damned to that! I take care of my horses. Won't I do more for my wife?"

That was what I was if the words Dr. Trent had mumbled meant anything. Watching Court obliquely, I realized that if I were married to him in twenty cathedrals by twenty archbishops I'd still feel soiled and dishonored when he touched me. It wasn't only that I didn't love him—in my heart I belonged to Trace Winslade.

"I'm sorry I've been such trouble," I said, and changed the subject swiftly. "Court, everyone talks about slaves on the henequen plantations, but surely the Mexican constitution forbids that."

He stared, dumbfounded. "The constitution?"

"Yes. Miss Mattison had me study it. She didn't want me ignorant of my home country."

"As if reading a lot of high-flown words could teach you anything real!" Court scoffed when he finally stopped laughing. "All right, my earnest student. On paper, Article One, Section One, it says: 'In the Republic all are born free.' It even adds that slaves setting foot on Mexican territory become free with a claim to protection of their liberty. And it says that no one shall be made to work without just compensation and his full consent and that no compact shall be tolerated in which a man agrees to his own exile. But my sweet naïve darling, those words mean nothing."

"Then Lío and the others won't be released after a term? They can't be bought out?"

"Who'd buy them?"

"I will."

"Miranda! If you weren't my wife, you'd already be in serious trouble for sheltering Yaquis. If you don't want to be imprisoned, exiled, or have all you own confiscated, you'd better learn to mind your own business."

"It *is* my business when men are slaves and women and children are hunted and killed."

Court took my hands, gripped them hard. "The government is weary of these continual Yaqui rebellions. The Indians will either work peaceably on the lands left to them after Mexican colonization, or they will be exterminated. Nothing you do will change that."

"And later nothing could change that I did nothing."

"Lío and his men were rebels. Their death sentence is a slow one, that's all."

My head throbbed savagely. Closing my eyes for a few minutes, I made myself breathe slow and strong. "If a man can be bought, I think he can be sold. Tell me how this slave system works."

"It's an outgrowth of peonage. The victims aren't all Yaqui. If any Mexican incurs a debt he can't pay, his 'debt'—along with his body—can be acquired by anyone needing a laborer. Once he's caught, it's a simple matter to charge enough food, shelter, and clothing against his wage to make sure he never gets free."

"And the government allows it?"

Court laughed at my shock. "My very dear, the government is in the business. Ramón Corral, who used to be governor of Sonora, is Díaz's vice-president. It's said he gets three pesos for every Yaqui sent to Yucatán or Oaxaca. The Secretary of Development, Colonization, and Industry is Olegario Molina, the leading henequen hacendado of Yucatán. You see what a useful arrangement it is. The government, in sending Yaquis to the plantations, not only supplies cheap, replaceable labor to some of the richest, most powerful men in the country, but also opens up Yaqui lands to settlers, including large American interests, and it is solving the centuries-old problem of what to do with *indios* who will not become tractable peons."

"If the government permits such things, there *ought* to be a revolution."

"There will be. But don't say it so loudly. I don't think there are secret police among the soldiers, but one never knows."

"Secret police?"

Court touched my cheek gently, shaking his head. "I forget how innocent you are of the world and of Mexico, in particular. On top of the army, regular police, and both state and federal *rurales*, there are *acordadas*, secret assassins attached to each state. They put politically offensive people out of the way, along with personal enemies of ranking officials, and you may be sure no noise is made about their murdering."

We seemed to drop, conducted by Court's passionless voice, from one corruption to a worse. I stared at the lights of Mina Rara and wondered if it was for this that Juárez had driven out Maximilian and the encroaching European powers. Ironic that Díaz had fought the Austrian archduke but then opened his arms to foreign speculators who grew rich while untold numbers of Mexicans toiled for a bare existence!

How had my father been able to live here, accept profits to some degree made possible by such a wretchedly oppressive government? I knew my father had paid our miners well and doubtless he'd succored many families as he had Lío's, but all the same— The idealized picture I had of my father suffered a bit of tarnish and I began to understand why he'd hoped I'd stay in England.

And did I intend to give up everything I'd inherited because the government was rotten and helpless people were being enslaved or killed? I couldn't do anything about the abscessed core of the infection. That *would* take a revolution followed by careful building, courage, faith, and hope. But I must help my friends.

"What does a man cost in Yucatán?" The words seared my lips. I still couldn't believe such things happened.

"I'm not sure." Court frowned, watching me sharply. "I think it's about four hundred to one thousand dollars Mexican, but the big hacendados only pay sixty-five dollars apiece for Yaquis they can resell a month later for eight times that."

"I want to buy Lío out. And all of his men who went to Yucatán."

"You what?"

"You heard me."

Court studied me, eyes narrowing. "Lío and his guerrillas are rebels, not regular debt slaves. Even trying to buy them could bring trouble."

"It seems to me that money, used in the right places, can do almost anything here."

"You're learning," Court drawled. "And I have a few more lessons for you. When you married me, I acquired a half-part interest in your property. Though it may seem highly unjust, you cannot act independently in matters involving money."

It was a humiliation I hadn't imagined, though in England, too, a woman became her husband's chattel with no control of her own inheritance. Evidently Court had determined it was time to make his power recognized. As I tasted the bitterness of realizing that he could now interfere with me in economic matters simply because he was my husband, I reflected that married women were enslaved to a degree and all the teachings on equality I'd learned at Miss Mattison's rose to my lips.

Court's ironic smile made me stifle those appeals and arguments. Somehow I'd get away, be free of his domination. But for now I must persuade him to buy Lío and his men.

I raised my glass for more wine and managed a shaky laugh. "I don't understand all the legalities, Court, and I'm sure it would make my head ache if I tried. Lío saved my life. I want to save his. You understand these things. I'm sure you could bargain for him and his men."

"Why should I?"

He was playing with me. Very well. "Please, Court," I said tiredly. "Please do this for me. I'll be forever grateful."

"Will you?"

He let one hand drop from my shoulder to my breast, cupped it so that when he bent his head, he could tease the nipple with his tongue. I stiffened with a little cry. He raised his face slightly; a strange glow burned deep in those golden eyes so close to mine. I almost screamed as he buried his head between my breasts, devoured my throat and shoulders with hungry questing lips till at last he stopped, shaking his head as if he himself were dazed.

"Miranda, you're aware. And you're mine. Now I can—"

He broke off with a tremulous laugh, rising and pacing as if to keep his energy in check. "All right, my love. If what you want for your wedding gift is a gang of convict Yaquis, I'll see what can be done. Dr. Trent might go down, posing as a landowner willing to pay a premium for selected slaves. He may have to buy a few extra in case anyone notices he's taking Yaquis who know each other."

"But how will they get back here?"

"That's their problem. Trent will give them clothes and some food and money, but if they're caught wandering about without passports, they'll be sent straight back to the plantation. Their best bet is to hide out in the countryside and work their way back slowly."

"It sounds terribly dangerous."

"Dangerous!" Court burst into astonished laughter. "To *be* a Yaqui is dangerous. And for condemned rebels—" His broad shoulders moved in a careless shrug. "They'll have a chance, Miranda. It's more than they could dream of."

He had yielded with surprisingly good grace, but I sensed that pushing him could reverse his generous mood. "Could we talk to Dr. Trent this evening? Maybe he could leave tomorrow. Truly, Court, I'm very eager."

"Not as eager as I, love."

His gaze embraced me and I shrank inside as he started to sit by me. The time would come when he'd make love to me, when he'd learn he wasn't my first man. But I hoped to postpone that moment as long as I could, hoped above all that Dr. Trent would be irrevocably gone on his errand. Court wouldn't dare send a wire about something that might get him in trouble with the government. And it would be a solace, when Court vented his outrage on me, to know that at least I'd given a few brave men some chance for their lives.

There were voices approaching and I peered into the soft twilight that had just taken the gold sheen off the mountain. "Isn't that Dr. Trent?"

Court grumbled under his breath, kissed the palm of my hand slowly before he went to welcome the men coming up the walk. "Major Ruiz! Doctor. Come have a drink and see how well my wife is looking."

"Mustn't overdo, child," muttered the doctor, taking both my hands and patting them in his sweet, rather fuddled way.

"Lots of nice broth and chicken, that'll bring back your strength. You've got to be healthy to hold your own with the beef one gets down here." He chuckled at his joke while Ruiz stepped forward.

If Ruiz was remembering, as I was, how he'd held me as I struggled to run after Cruz when soldiers dragged him from my pretended sickbed, he gave no sign. His bow was punctilious, his clipped moustache and lips barely touched my hand.

"What a joy to find you so much better, señora. There has been much concern, I assure you, even from a toughened old soldier like myself."

I looked through his smile, his hard-planed face, and saw Cruz, Cruz burning. Rage and grief swelled in my throat.

"My wife is still not quite herself," explained Court. "But with the care I intend to give her, I'm sure she'll soon be in glorious health. Won't you drink to that, gentlemen, before she retires?"

"Pleasure!" said Dr. Trent. "Pleasure, sir!"

"Alas, I must still check my sentries," regretted Ruiz. "But I'll indulge in one glass of wine to salute your so exquisite wife."

Court sent Ruiz a quizzical look, but if he recognized some hint of masculine challenge it seemed to please him. Stepping inside, he returned in a moment with a bottle of whiskey, glasses, and a decanter of water.

A little water and a lot of whiskey went into the doctor's drink. Then Court filled my glass and his with wine again, filled the major's, and handed it to him.

"*Salud!*" said the soldier, lifting his goblet. "Your good health, señora! Your beauty and grace, may they comfort us in this desert as surely as a spring of water."

The doctor and Court drank, but Court's eyes stayed on Ruiz. "In the desert, Major, a spring is coveted. Men do not wish only to admire it. They must drink."

Ruiz raised a dark eyebrow. His uniform fitted perfectly, tailored in some city to flatter his rawhide lean body, hard-muscled thighs, and shoulders. If Court was a lion, Ruiz was a hawk. In either case, I was prey, no less afraid of beak and talons than of claws and teeth.

"In the desert, señor, a wise man does not deny a taste of water to the equally strong or he may find himself dispossessed."

"There is no equal strength once battle is joined," said Court. "As a soldier, you of all men know that. In every contest, there is finally a winner."

"Who may not long survive his hurts."

Court laughed. "But a winner, nonetheless. Tell us, Major, how long do you expect to be on duty here?"

Ruiz shrugged and sighed. "Who knows? Governor Yzábel is on a Yaqui hunt this fall. He seems set on killing all those he can't ship off to the henequen plantations, except, of course, for those he works on his haciendas. They might be better off in Yucatán. It is said that at his hacienda of La Europa he uses instruments of torture in addition to the ordinary beatings and punishments."

"Major," said Court with a protective glance at me. "My wife."

And indeed I was feeling sick. When the governor of Sonora was a monster supported by the federal government and the army, what chance did the Yaquis have? God, let the revolution come and quickly, even if it swept away my own class.

"If I could watch my friend burn alive," I said, staring with hatred into the major's imperturbable eyes, "I suppose I can hear about other barbarities."

"A tender heart is glory in a woman," returned the major so glibly that I would have liked to tear out his tongue. "It is a flaw in soldiers. You do not understand those *indios*, señora. They revolted against the Jesuits and Spain, then after Mexico became independent of Spain, they refused to pay taxes or allow colonization of their lands. They could get away with such defiance as long as Mexico was fighting foreign powers or trying to develop a strong central government. The state of Sonora has been especially chaotic and the Yaquis have contributed to that by insisting on remaining a state within a state."

"And what would be so wrong with that?" I demanded.

"They are excellent workers and farmers. If they were left alone, there would be no trouble."

"Mexico cannot tolerate their arrogance or claim to so much rich farmland. If they would submit peacefully, they could work their lands, señora."

"As serfs? Colonists in their own country?"

"My love," interposed Court, hand closing over mine. "You will develop a fever. Besides, we must not keep the major from his duties."

"I appreciate your concern," Ruiz said, nodding. As he slowly finished his wine, his eyes stayed on me and he smiled as if he knew some secret. "Thank you, señor and señora, for your most gracious hospitality." He rose to his feet. "I look forward to entertaining you, though a soldier's quarters lack refinement."

"They should be comfortable," said Court dryly, "since you have moved into the former assistant superintendent's house."

"Señor, I am not complaining!" Ruiz laughed. "After a tent, this is luxury. I thought only of your lady."

"That is kind of you but completely unnecessary, Major. You may be sure that I will have the utmost care for my wife's surroundings. She will not be exposed to any that I consider dangerous."

"That is wise of you," murmured Ruiz. "Doctor, señora, until we meet again." Inclining his dark head, he let his smile end on me and turned through the arch to the walk.

"Fancies himself," growled Court, settling back and taking the doctor's emptied glass. "When things quiet down a bit, I'll see if I can't get him transferred. If we must have soldiers at the mine, I don't want their commander after my wife."

"Machismo, my boy, pure machismo," soothed Trent. "If he ignored Miranda, now there would be your insult." He cleared his throat and looked hopefully at his glass.

"Doctor," said Court abruptly, "would you undertake an errand of mercy?"

"A what?" asked the doctor as if he couldn't have heard correctly.

Court grinned. "Oh, not for me! But Miranda has a softness

for Yaquis because of her pet cripple. And it seems that brigand Lío did his best to protect her—after he kidnapped her. She'd like to buy him and the survivors of his band out of the plantations. Would you try to do this?"

The doctor blinked. His red-veined eyes shifted unhappily from me to the whiskey and I knew he was thinking of all the reasons why he preferred to stay at Mina Rara.

"Please," I begged, leaning forward and touching his hand. "Please, Doctor, won't you try? I don't think I want to get well if I have to know Lío and the others are being beaten to death." He watched me from his sad old bleared eyes, and I strengthened my grasp on his sensitive fingers. "It's for Cruz," I whispered. "And Sewa. All the brave ones who deserve better than being ground into dust."

And for Trace. My love, my real husband, who died fighting for the Yaquis. Silence hung between us. The doctor's hand seemed lifeless in mine, the skin like a dry husk. Hope died in me.

Despairingly, I started to withdraw my hand. His tightened. "I'll go," he sighed. "Now give me a drink, in God's name, and let's figure how I'm to do it."

I hadn't realized I was holding my breath till my lungs filled spasmodically, everything blurred, and I felt myself slipping into soft waves of welcoming darkness.

14

The rich smell of coffee and fresh-baked bread stirred my senses so that I woke hungry for the first time since the battle. Raquel had been standing in my bedroom door. Now she came forward with a tray.

"Here is your breakfast," she said without looking at me. Her soft mouth curved down and I felt sympathy for her. It must be bitter hard to serve her lover's wife. "If you wish more or require help with dressing, ring the bell."

Her gaze traveled from my toes to my head, avoiding my face, and I was glad the coverlet hid my body. It would have been easier had she been like Reina, flamboyantly and crudely jealous, but I guessed that Raquel really loved Court and was desolate that he preferred someone else. She'd been a convenience, a pretty, useful servant to his body. I doubted he had even thought of her pain. This deepened my anger at him as it heightened my fear.

At the moment, he saw me as his gently reared, much-desired bride, a virgin. Because of his illusion, not because of me as a real person, he was wooing me. But when he was denied the breaking of my seal, his illusion would go, and with

223

it his consideration. Where he tormented Raquel out of insensitivity, he would hurt me with deliberation and calculated spite. He would bring me as low as he had set me high.

"Has Dr. Trent stopped this morning?" I asked.

Raquel paused on her way to the door. "He left for Hermosillo this morning. He has sudden business and will be gone for some weeks." She added almost hopefully, "You need him?"

"No, thank you."

She moved lightly into the corridor. I spread honey on a crisp roll and ate, spirits raised by the knowledge that the doctor was gone. It would be impossible for Court to call him back without calling notice to his own complicity in trying to free condemned rebels. And I thought the doctor would avoid or manage to misunderstand any countermanding of his instructions, for it was me he had promised, not Court.

Perhaps Court would be called away, maybe he'd have an accident . . . That was nonsense. I set my teeth and picked the most severe dress I had, made of cheap cloth from the company store. He'd be back and he would have me.

But let it not be till tonight. Please, let it not be till tonight. If it were in the darkness, it might not seem so real.

It happened at noon. Noon, with the shutters closed and the house quiet after the midday meal. Court had come in from the mine, greeted me where I sat reading one of the books loaned by Dr. Trent, and joined me after washing and changing into clean clothes. We had clear soup, cold chicken, and melon on the veranda, but I could scarcely eat. My nerves were screwing tighter by the moment and every muscle seemed to have gone rigid so that my motions were jerky and awkward.

Court, though, ate with good appetite. In the mine all the debris had been cleared and ore was coming out again. The blast, in fact, had opened a rich vein, so he was expecting increased profits, which he would share in now as my husband. When I thought about it, I knew that Court had made himself a wealthy man. He would enjoy that, but even more the power. It would have helped if I could have believed that was why he married me, but I was sure he loved me in a fiercely possessive way.

No amount of material riches would make up for what he would very shortly feel he'd been robbed of. Strange that should matter more than not having my love. I didn't think Trace would have minded much about my virginity so long as I loved him.

Court had finished his lunch. Small fires seemed to glow from the back of his eyes as he watched me sip the last wine from my goblet. I hoped frantically he would go back to the mine. Instead, he came around and raised me from the chair.

"Now, my love," he said, gathering me in his arms. "Now."

Through the corridor into my room. Still holding me, he bolted the door and drew the shutters. He sank down with me on the bed, kissing my throat. His fingers fumbled at the buttons of my dress. Losing patience, he ripped the cloth from my back, pulled off the ruined dress along with my chemise. I gave a cry as his hands closed on my breasts.

"It's all right, darling, all right. No matter what they taught you in England, you'll enjoy it, too. I'll teach you."

There was a tingling in my breasts and he laughed softly as he teased the nipples hard, began to caress my flanks as he slipped off my drawers and stockings, began to undress himself.

"Touch me," he breathed, pressing his hardness against my hand. "You have to learn to like him, Miranda. He adores you. He can scarcely wait to get into you." Taking my reluctant hand, Court made me stroke the quivering phallus with its swollen veins.

Court was shaking, too. With a groan, as if driven to a pitch he could no longer endure, he swung his leg over me. Then the stiff throbbing alien part that made him a man slid down to thrust lightly, then harder, plunging all the way in as I cried out, afraid of being smashed, afraid of being broken. . . .

"Why, you—" Court panted.

His loins spasmed. I thought he had climaxed. He rested

on me, almost a crushing weight, then raised on his hands, gold eyes piercing, while I felt him or my own nerves twitching within me. He stayed like that till my whole body ached and a silent screaming began to coil in my head.

"Who was it?" he asked coldly.

My mouth was dry. I couldn't speak.

He set his thumbs above my collarbone, fingers circling my neck. "Damn you, who was it?"

Trace was dead. He couldn't hurt Trace. As if he read my mind, Court ground out, "Winslade?"

I nodded. The thumbs dug in, the fingers tightened. Maybe I wouldn't survive after all. But I had my voice back and the screaming lashed out of me. "I belong to Trace, not you. I'll never belong to you."

Court lunged forward so hard that I screamed. His gentleness was gone. He gripped me beneath the head with one hand, grasped me under the buttocks with the other, holding me in a vise as he rammed and battered me senseless.

"I'll show you who you belong to," he gasped as my mind slipped into blackness. "I'll show you."

I roused with a heavy weight pinning my arm, shuddered as I saw Court's wiry hair beside me. I was bruised in many places from his hands but ached worst between my legs. As I tried to free my arm so I could get up and wash his odor from me, he stirred and flung one arm across me, fondling my breast.

"I'm not done with you," he said thickly. "Not by half. You've got some things to learn. A whore's tricks, since you are one." And he set his hand behind my head and forced it downward.

The afternoon nightmared into twilight. Still weakened from my long confinement, I lapsed into fleeting tortured dreams in between the times Court used me. After the first few attempts to fight, after my first shame and shock, I was numbed, longed for simple physical rest from his hands and mouth, sinewy legs, that incredibly renewed organ that came out of me limp but would breach me an hour later. Not that he relied solely on it for my subjection.

As the bars of light from the shutters dulled and muted voices sounded from the rest of the house, I grew inert, and as if he needed, if not my loving response, at least resistance, Court rolled from me, sat for a moment on the edge of the bed with his head in his hands.

"My wife," he said, as if he rinsed his mouth of foulness. "My innocent bride."

Getting to his feet, he dragged on his clothes, stood over me as he buckled his belt. "I suppose I shouldn't feel cheated. You have the makings of a pleasing whore. And that's what you'll be to me in our bed, though to the world I'll seem a fond-enough husband."

Speech was beyond me. I wanted only to slip back into comforting soft oblivion. It was one thing, still cherished and unmolested, to think I could divorce my spirit from what was happening to my body, resolve to live through it and escape. Now I had tasted to the roots of my being that what happened to my flesh happened to *me*, that interwoven total of mind, body, and soul.

If one afternoon could do this, strip me of will, physical courage, even normal response to outrage, what would happen in weeks, months, a year? Court seemed to guess what I was thinking.

"It will go better with you when you decide to use your energy to gratify rather than fight me," he said. "Be absolutely sure of this, Miranda: legally and in fact you are mine, utterly dependent on me for protection and all your needs. The sooner you fit your behavior and attitude to the realities, the sooner I'll be disposed to indulge you."

I kept my eyes closed, scarcely breathing. I felt his eyes burning my flesh, searing me with his ownership as cruelly as a heated brand.

"Chepa will bring you a tray," he said.

"I—I'm not hungry."

"Shall I feed you?"

I was silent again, beaten. After a long moment, his steps moved away.

Chepa's soft voice woke me from exhausted slumber. "Señora? I have brought rice and chicken and these are green corn tamales, very nice. My mother made them especially for you. Will you try them?"

The room was almost dark, gentle to my eyes as I raised slowly, stifling a moan. To my astonishment the food odors tantalized me. The short rest and, most of all, Court's absence had a bracing effect.

"Thank you, Chepa." I accepted the tray and began to eat slowly, propped against the pillows she plumped behind me.

Warmed by the delicately spiced food, my body slowly regained sensitivity now that it was safe to feel again, experience what was.

"Please heat water for a bath," I requested, setting down the tray.

"It is ready," Chepa murmured. The dark eyes in her piquant heart-shaped face would not look directly at me and I felt her pity. Perhaps I should have resented it but I didn't. We were both women, vulnerable to what had happened to me. I accepted her unspoken sympathy as a healing power that supported though it couldn't defend. "El señor said you would wish a bath and that I was to help you." She glanced in disappointment at the tray. "The tamales are so good, señora! Can you not have a few more bites?"

To please her, I dutifully ate the rest of one tamale. "That was delicious," I said. "Tell your mother I thank her."

Chepa smiled, nodding, and took away the tray. I lay back on the pillows. As if driven by their own volition, my hands groped over my body, finding bruises, weals, marks of teeth and nails for Court's passion was much like that of the stallion I'd watched that day Trace first kissed me but refused to finish lest he ruin me for my husband. I curled my lip at that, though it had proved a too-realistic objection.

Still, something deep and primitive screamed from my

center, from my loins and violated parts, that Trace was irrevocably my lover, my man, my promised husband. Court was the encroacher, the trespassing thief. And whatever happened, I rejoiced that I'd known the grace and strength of my true love, that he had possessed me completely, even though it made me a whore in Court's view, provoked him into debasing me.

I had loved a brave magnificent man, loved him still though he was dead, and he had loved me. That must be my armor against Court. I wouldn't let him defeat the woman Trace had loved. Somehow I'd live. Somehow I'd be free.

Wincing at the pain of movement, I pinned up my hair while Chepa readied the bath for me. Without being asked, she began to strip off the used sheets and put on fresh ones.

I thanked her and stepped into the hot water that stung every place, and there were many, where my skin was broken. I couldn't wash away what Court had done, but I could scrub off his scent.

The smell of him, a not-unpleasant man odor, for Court was fastidious, permeated my next days, seemed to fill and become the scent of my own body, for he spent each night with me and often part of the day.

Though sometimes he compelled me to the perversions of that first day, most often he simply took me repeatedly with an almost grim deliberation. He seemed to enjoy it little more than I did. I wondered if he hated me now, found me repugnant, but took this means of punishing me, keeping me physically aware of his domination.

I didn't dare ask if he'd tried to halt Dr. Trent's mission, but as weeks passed and the doctor didn't return early, I hoped that Court had either not tried or been unable to stop him.

Slowly, fearful of interference from Court, I resumed a patched, raggedy sort of life. Chepa helped me clean the school of wreckage from the battle and I began holding classes every morning. At first only a few children came, but gradually they all ventured back. Sometimes their mothers would stay for an hour or two, watching with pride as their children read aloud or spelled or did sums at the big slate.

I dreaded the scrutiny of the women for a time. Did they know anything of my life with Court? If they did, they showed nothing and treated me with shy respect.

When soldiers began to drop in, I could see only their uniforms and was nervous and on guard. Then I began to realize that many were very young, not much older than Domingo. They were bored, homesick, and listened intently to the lessons, particularly history and geography. The children stole suspicious glances at them the first few times they came, but then I noticed that the soldiers were walking home with the youngsters, sometimes playing with them.

One day Ruiz, now a colonel, came into the school. Three boy soldiers who were sitting at the back went rigid and rose, saluting. He smiled ironically, watched me for a long moment, dark eyes probing, then turned on his heel with a jerk of his head to the young men. They followed him like dogs about to be whipped.

Telling the children I'd be back shortly, I hurried after Ruiz, who had halted and was staring contemptuously at the soldiers, who looked like scarecrows indeed, with their ill-fitting uniforms and alarmed faces.

"Report to your sergeant," he ordered when he saw me. "Tell him I will be along in a few minutes."

They saluted and fled. Ruiz bowed, holding my hand almost to his lips for much too long. "I must apologize for those wretches, señora. Have no fear, they will not trouble you further."

"They are not a trouble," I said. "They seem to listen eagerly."

He lifted a bland eyebrow. "Ah, señora, who would not?"

"Colonel, please. Do not punish them. They are welcome. They—they're little more than children themselves and must miss their families."

"They must be soldiers. Have you thought what would happen if they become friendly with the schoolchildren? Then they would visit their homes and what would happen if it ever became necessary to enforce order at Mina Rara? Would you have these young soldiers you pity have to shoot their friends?"

"That—that won't happen! The Mina Rara Yaquis are not rebels."

"Not yet."

Fear gripped me, fear for the children and their parents. "These people have been here for years; some were born here. My father treated them well. They've been happy, had no reason to fight. This is true, Colonel! Ask Mr. Sanders."

"Yes. Your husband."

What did the major know of us, the truth of our marriage? Court had taught me to recognize the signs of desire in a man. Though the officer's manner was formally correct, his gaze made me flush, for it seemed to disrobe me with leisurely enjoyment.

"I am sorry that you think me severe," he said charmingly. "But there must be discipline. I will set my men at harder lessons."

"But—"

"Your concern does you credit, señora, but soft hearts are a luxury we soldiers cannot allow ourselves. May I say that I am delighted to see you in renewed health?"

"Thank you," I said mechanically. Argument would only provoke him to harsher management, but it was with a heavy heart that I went back to my hushed pupils.

I was telling them Sewa's story of the Ku bird, using its glorious features to teach them how to spell the colors of that fantastic borrowed plumage, when a tall broad figure shadowed the door.

For the second time that morning, the children froze. *"Fuera!"* Court snapped.

They were gone in a twinkling. Court strode forward, sent the globe spinning as he passed it. "What were you discussing so earnestly with Ruiz?" he demanded. "And those soldiers—I saw them scuttling out. Why were they here?"

"They—they like to listen! Court, they're only boys."

"Boys! If they had a chance, they'd prove differently." His

lips peeled back from his teeth. "You at least won't tell me that Ruiz is a child eager to learn his alphabet!"

"He made the soldiers leave."

"And you were sorry for them," Court guessed. "You followed him, begged him before the village to be easy with those insolent miscreants. Have you no sense of fitness, Miranda? Will you never learn your place?"

"My place?" I said scornfully, remembering that this was my mine and that Court would have still been an employee had he not used coercion. "And what is my place?"

"I'll show you, madam!" He caught my wrist, dragged me to the door before he stopped, obviously getting control of himself. "Will you walk to your place—our bed, my sweet—or shall I further entertain gapers by carrying you there?"

I regretted my proud words. I should've learned by now that defiance could only bring me pain, deeper humiliation. But Ruiz's treatment of the boy soldiers, the way he and Court had disrupted my school and frightened the children, provoked rebellion from deeper levels than reason could penetrate. Spine stiff, chin high, I walked to the house, Court's hand beneath my arm in a way that would look protectively cherishing to observers.

The moment we were inside the door, he swept me off my feet. Startled into panic, I did what I hadn't attempted in weeks, actively fought him, writhing to scratch, kick, bite, try to throw him off balance.

"And I thought you were tamed."

Laughing exultantly, though his face showed blood from my fingernails, Court gripped my bodice, tore off my dress and underthings. Tossing me on the bed, he clamped my arms and upper body beneath his thighs and legs while he grasped my hips and set his face deep, deep between my legs.

His thrusting greedy tongue flickered and teased, went searching. A great luminous wave crashed over me. I cried out in terror and unbearable ecstasy as the second wave slammed in.

Court wouldn't stop. When I tried to move, he found those hidden nerves, titillated me to a fresh paroxysm. Only after an endless succession of pleasures did he mount me and surge to his own climax, lie resting with one arm thrown over me in claiming.

"*This* is your place," he said when his breathing calmed. "I'll have you over and over, every way there is. You're learning."

"I don't want to learn."

"Liar!" He laid his palm on my belly, laughed as I moved involuntarily.

I couldn't guess whether he loved me or hated me; actually his feelings seemed to change abruptly. Sometimes he was almost tender, but a few hours later might tie my feet and hands to the brass bedstead and enter me without any preamble so that I felt torn and violated.

"When I get you with child we'll have to change our games," he said once. "So I'll use you to the utmost now."

I didn't want to tell him, but I almost certainly was pregnant, and it was my second skipped flow unless one had occurred while I was unconscious after the battle.

Could I be carrying Trace's baby?

When that possibility first flashed through my mind, I laughed with joy. Oh, if only that could be! A child of his would make up for some of the cruelty of Trace's death; he would live on in a fashion, joined with me in another being. Then I remembered Court.

If the child came before the time it could be counted his, what would he do? He would hate any reminder that I had been another man's. He might take the baby away from me. That I couldn't bear.

So my hope for Trace's child was mingled with dread. I wished Dr. Trent were back. Drunkard though he was, he exerted some influence on Court. A happier thought struck me then.

Court would never admit to the outside world that I had been impregnated by another man. Pride might force him to keep the child. I was repelled at the notion of Court pretending to be the father of Trace's baby, but that was clearly better than the alternatives.

So I taught the children, assumed nominal control of the

house, though it ran much as it had in Court's bachelor days, and tried not to think about those hours in the bedroom when Court explored the secrets of my treacherous body, brought me to physical pleasure that left me ashamed and angry.

Dr. Trent rode home one sunset when the mountain shone like gold. I was standing alone on the veranda, recognized the shape of his hat, the hunch of his shoulders as his horse jogged along.

Running to meet him, I caught his hand and squeezed it anxiously. "Did you find Lío, Doctor? Did you get him free?"

Grunting, the doctor slid down from his rawboned bay, turned it over to one of the boys who came running to earn a few centavos by rubbing down and watering the mount.

"Throat's parched, my dear," coughed the doctor.

"I'll give you some whiskey, anything you want," I cried in an agony of impatience, trying to hurry his steps. "But please tell me. Lío?"

"Drink first."

I flew ahead and got out whiskey and a glass, added water, and handed it to the doctor as he came through the arch. His hands shook, but after several deep swallows he looked better, sank down in one of the rawhide chairs.

"Did you find Lío?"

I thought I'd scream as Dr. Trent took several long swallows. He set down the glass and folded my hands in his trembly ones.

"Lío's dead, Miranda."

"Dead? You—you're sure?"

"You knew him. Can you imagine he would make a slave?"

"He might have if he thought he could get away sometime and fight again."

The doctor sighed, stroking my head as hot tears squeezed from my eyes. "He interfered with the whipping of a friend too sick to work, killed the manager, and was overwhelmed."

I bowed my head and wept. Lío had been a brave man and as tender as he dared. "But I bought out his men," the doctor went on. "Those that were left after the journey by boat and six weeks in the henequen hells. I bought fifteen men for eight hundred dollars each and brought them by train almost to Hermosillo, pretending that they were workers of mine. For a small bribe the train engineer stopped an hour outside Hermosillo and let me and my 'peons' off. I gave them food and water and advised them to get as far back into the sierra as they could and stay there."

"You warned them that Ruiz is stationed at the mine? If he knew they had come back—"

"He won't learn from me," the doctor vowed. "With Lío gone, I doubt they'll do much raiding. There'll be the women and children of their dead comrades to look after, and with winter coming on, they'll care more about surviving than harrowing the *federales.*"

My heart was sore for Lío, but I prayed that somehow, in the afterlife the Yaquis called "Glory," he could know his men were free and back in the sierra.

"The man for whom Lío killed the manager—did you buy him out?" I asked.

Dr. Trent shook his head. "That one escaped, God knows how. He must have had some outside help. Altogether strange how he got mixed up with them in the first place. He was an American who'd brought them guns—Miranda! What's wrong, child?"

"His name?" I felt as if I were choking, as if iron fingers pressed my throat and heart. "What was his name?"

"Winslade." Dr. Trent peered at me anxiously, forced me to take a sip of his whiskey. "Miranda, you look as if you have a fever. Come, my girl let me tuck you in—"

"I—I'm all right. It's just that I—I know this man. He got away? You're sure?"

"He escaped from the plantation. That was all anyone knew."

"I thought he was dead."

The doctor shrugged. "He may well be by now. That's wretched country and he'd have to hide from the authorities."

"But he may be alive." The blinding joy of that momentarily drove out all other concerns. Trace wasn't dead. He'd survived the battle, escaped the plantation. There was a chance I might see him again. Dr. Trent's watery gray eyes studied me shrewdly, touched my waist, then traveled back to my face.

"Miranda, aren't you going to have a baby?"

"I—I think so."

"Then shouldn't your husband be the first to know?" chuckled a voice from the arch. Court strode in and drew me to my feet. "Congratulations, love." Kissing me soundly, he held me close and laughed possessively as he turned to the doctor. "I'm glad you're back, sir, to help me take care of my wife. I could have wished this to be a year or so in the future, but one must needs rejoice in what is, wouldn't you say?"

"Oh, by all means," fuddled the doctor. "By all means."

"And we must drink to my son," proposed Court expansively. "For it *will* be a son." He filled the doctor's glass, made a drink for himself, and the two of them toasted me while I shrank against the wall.

A baby. Yes, I was to have a baby. It might be Trace's. And Trace was alive—or at least, he might be. He hadn't died in the battle.

Court had lied to me. He had cruelly let me think Trace was dead. In that moment I loathed the tall handsome man who had let the one he knew I loved be sent to Yucatán. While Court had made love to me, yes, even sometimes when I was responding to his skill, Trace was being beaten or forced to brutal labor. Court had known. Known all the time.

He was asking the doctor about his errand, nodding approval that it was completed. "I'm glad Lío's dead. The others shouldn't create a problem, especially not after they've had a taste of Yucatán, eh?"

I leaned against the door, fighting waves of nausea, hatred so bitter that it left a taste like alum in my mouth. "Court, I must speak with you."

"Of course, darling." How that proud husbandly smile made me despise him! "I'll join you in a moment and you can give me your news. Here, Doctor, tell me what you thought of Yucatán. Those hacendados live in great state, I'm told. American Cordage Trust buys half the henequen output of

Yucatán, and from the way those plantations go through slaves, the demand must be holding up."

My knees threatened to give way. There was scalding acridness in my throat. I fled to my room and was rackingly sick, vomiting into the washbasin till spasmodic heaving brought up only bile. I was still crouched there when Court came in.

"What, my love? Morning sickness in the evening?" He wet a towel and sponged my face, guided me to the bed. "Lie down. I'll call Chepa to tidy up. Do you want the doctor?"

"N-no," I managed.

"You had better have just clear broth tonight," Court worried, drawing a chair up by the bed and taking my hand. "I don't suppose you know much more about this than I do. We'll have to rely on the doctor and take great care of you."

Skin crawling at his touch, I jerked my hand away and sat up, strengthened by a furious sense of betrayal. "You lied to me, Court. You told me Trace was dead."

Golden eyes dilated and the edges of Court's nostrils went white. "Isn't he?"

"You knew he wasn't killed in the fight. You knew he was sent to Yucatán."

"He was?" There was no doubt that Court was as shocked as I had been earlier. Suddenly, he swore. "Why, that money-loving bastard. He sold the same man twice."

"What do you mean?"

Court didn't answer, but I understood. "You—you paid someone to kill him. He lived through the battle, but you wanted to be sure he was dead."

"Yes. Not that I wouldn't have been glad for him to taste the lash and crawl, but I preferred to be sure he was out of the way for good." Court stiffened. "My God, that fool doctor didn't buy him out?"

"No. He got away."

Court shrugged and looked relieved. "Then he *is* dead. No one comes back from Yucatán. He'll starve or be caught and turned in for the reward paid for runaway slaves. Better for him if Ruiz had ordered him cleanly killed."

"He's alive. I'll believe that from now on till I see his body."

"Believe what you please." Court shrugged. "What difference does it make?"

That mocking question, my impotence, and the danger of Trace's position if indeed he still lived wrung from me the snarling moan of a trapped, defiant animal. "I'll hate you more than ever. And despise you, too, for taking a woman you knew belonged to someone else."

Court paled, though he retained his jeering smile. "Your ferocity will ebb as your womb grows with my child. A woman needs protection at such a time, a safe nest for her baby. You'll be glad then that you're here with me, not in the sierra with convicts."

"It may not be your child," I hissed. "Have you thought of that?"

"Whore!" He brought back his hand, slapped me so hard I reeled backward, fell on the bed. "It is my child. My child, do you hear?"

"Hearing has nothing to do with it." Raising on one arm, I laughed in his face in spite of the slow warm blood trickling from my cut lip. "Being pregnant by you should sicken me, but not this quickly, I think."

Court shook me till my wild laughter splintered to silence in my throat. Holding me in his bruising fingers, he spoke in a jerky guttural way. "This will be my child, damn you! And you will never hint again that it isn't."

Though I was frightened and in pain from his hands, the hope that Trace lived gave me courage. "You think too little of my love," I said. "And too much of your power."

"Do I?" The pupils widened till only a rim of hot gold showed around them. He laughed savagely. "Oh, no, beloved. It is you who hasn't understood."

"Understood what?"

"You will stay with me. You will bear my child. You will study to please me and deserve my favor and forgiveness."

"I—will—not!"

"But you will, Miranda." His tone was caressing but edged with steely finality. "This is why. Listen for I won't explain again. Comport yourself as an obedient wife and mother of my child, or I'll tell Ruiz certain rebel Yaquis are in the mountains, and I'll offer an irresistible reward for the head of a certain *tejano*. This time there will be no survivors, not even that little cripple you doted on."

I stared at him, wanting to protest, to cry out that he wouldn't do it. But I knew he would. He would kill my love, grind Sewa in the dust, slaughter Lío's remaining band.

So I must obey him.

The only comfort I had was that Trace might live and that his child was almost surely growing in me. Court placed one hand on my breast.

It was the motion of a lion claiming its prey.

Two

Trace

15

Man is a counting animal. At first Trace counted days. Four days packed in a government ship from Guaymas to San Blas. Twenty days of being driven on foot through the mountains from the port of San Marcos, then crammed into trains that traveled to Mexico City and changed lines for Veracruz. Three days from Veracruz to Progreso in a freight steamer. One day more to the plantation, Mariposa.

Thirty-six days from Mina Rara to Yucatán, from being free to being a slave, from counting days to counting henequen leaves, the lashes that fell on a man's back before he fainted.

Two thousand leaves a day, or the lash. That was the kind of mathematics learned quickly by even the dullest mal-nourished man. Or woman or child, for they, too, hacked at the thick, saw-toothed leaves.

Forty-two leaves on a henequen plant. Twelve to be cut off at the root, the spearlike tip and edges trimmed and placed in a bundle, which, when big enough, was carried to the end of the row to be collected by a movable-track mule-car line.

Thirty leaves exactly must be left on each plant. You were

beaten for twenty-nine, beaten for thirty-one. Other plantation counting was simpler. Hours were from the dimmest
morning light to the faintest twilight. There was one meal a
day and a lump of fermented dough.

No, the important numbers—two thousand leaves a day,
twelve from each plant—were taught in the field by the
foreman or *capataz's* cane. More advanced lessons were given
in the clearing by the living quarters.

The whips were made of henequen, braided thick and
heavy for their special work, dipped in water to make them cut
deeper. It was the fifth morning after Lío's band arrived at
Mariposa that Trace counted lashes.

They'd been given three days to learn their task before the
full stint was required of them. On this day of their expected
"graduation" they gathered in the clearing for roll call after
the bell sounded at a time Trace knew was not yet four.

Lanterns hung from the commissary, flickering on the
hundreds of slaves. Eight hundred, someone had said. Most
were Mayas, descendants of the people who had once ruled
this part of Mexico, but several hundred were Yaquis and
there were perhaps forty Chinese. And one stupid gringo,
Trace thought dourly. He ached all over from hacking
henequen sixteen hours at a stretch, but he'd done his two
thousand leaves yesterday, damn them, and he'd do whatever
he had to in order to live and get out of this place.

Live to see Miranda. Hold her again. Fear gripped him as it
always did when he remembered how she'd fallen, struck
down by a clubbed rifle. He was trying to reach her when he'd
been creased by a bullet. When he'd roused, guarded with the
rest of the prisoners, he'd asked how she was, but the soldiers
weren't answering questions.

She was alive, though. Had to be. For he was going back,
sometime, somehow. A whispering ran through the ragged
crew.

"Going to be a cleaning up," muttered the thin pockmarked
man beside him.

The top bastards stood up front, facing the listless workers.
Maybe thirty men with the power to beat, starve, or kill any or

all of the slaves: the *administrador*, or manager, with his neat moustache; the *mayordomo primero*, or superintendent; his assistants, the *mayordomos segundos*; and the *capataces*, including the one who had already raised a weal on Trace's shoulders for faulty trimming of a leaf.

We ought to rush them, he thought.

Trace looked around. Was it only because he knew Lío's men that they retained individuality for him? The old-time hands—tall, short, Chinese, Maya, or Yaqui—seemed to wear masks, or perhaps the masks had become their faces. Hopeless and, except for the Yaquis, trained from childhood to work and obey, they would, at a word from their masters, overwhelm any rebels. Even Trace knew that killing overseers would bring ruthless retaliation from Army and police. If a man had to die, he might as well take along a few of those smug sons of bitches. But a man hoped not to die. . . .

Miranda. Miranda. Sweet and bracing as the scent of acacia after rain in the desert. Till he came to this thick-aired muggy green hell, he hadn't guessed how the harsh clean beauty of the desert had entered his soul. And Miranda was honey in the rocks, a bloom among the thorns.

"Lío Tercero," called the *administrador*, "step forward!"

Lío came out the crowd, squarish head high. Not a slave, Trace thought with a thrill of admiration. That one will never be a slave. And he understood why two-thirds of the Yaquis died during their first year on the plantations.

"Take off your shirt," ordered the *administrador*. "You have not fulfilled your stint, lazy dog. But you will learn."

Lío didn't move. Several foremen tore off his flimsy white shirt. The *administrador* barked another name. A Chinese of immense proportions stepped into the clearing. He towered for a moment over Lío; then, face impassive, he stooped, gripped Lío by the wrists, and straightened.

Trace understood then.

The *majador*, or whipper, bent over a bucket and dragged out three dripping ropes. He chose one, dropped the others back.

No one was sleepy now. At sight of the whip, a moaning gasp stirred through the men as if their scarred backs cringed from that three-foot-long rope plaited from the fiber they slaved to harvest.

The *administrador* pulled out his watch, motioned with one slim finger. The *majador* lifted his arm, brought the whip down with slashing force. Lío's body convulsed, a sighing breath rose from the slaves whose bodies seemed to sway in an echo of that blow.

The inside of Trace's mouth filled with blood. He was biting the inside of his cheeks, clenching his fists. It seemed forever before the *administrador* signaled the second blow. More of the plantation's arithmetic, Trace decided, as he realized there was a precise space between each descent of the rope. It must hurt more that way, drag out the torment.

How long would it last? Lío had not made a sound, though his body, unsupported by his feet, contracted involuntarily with each blow. On the sixth lash the brown skin showed flecks of blood that expanded into trickles. On the seventh, Lío's back seemed to spasm, go into muscular twitches as if it had become something separate from the man.

On the eighth . . .

Trace didn't know how he reached the *majador*. Only that he had wrenched the whip away, lashed out with it at his own *capataz*, who closed in on him with the *mayordomos* and other foremen.

For a moment he held them at bay with the rope before he cracked it into the snarling face of the nearest man, let it drop and felled his *capataz* with a blow in the windpipe.

Heedless of the canes that whistled down around his head and shoulders, Trace fought savagely. He'd pay for this, they might kill him. So he'd better make it good. If he could just get through to that damned *administrador* with his needle-thin moustache and gold watch, his almost dainty finger that signaled down the rope till it dripped with blood as well as water.

Over the shouting men, the *administrador*'s black eyes met Trace's, held a gleam of—mockery? Excitement? Then something struck the back of Trace's head. He felt his legs dissolve, fell forward under a hail of blows and kicks.

Incredible pain seared his back, pierced him awake with his

own cry. In spite of blurred vision and the sledging ache in his head, he knew where he was even before his mouth tasted the sweat of the back it pressed against. He ground back a scream, heard a swish close by, the unmistakable impact, once heard, of wet rope on flesh. Through a weaving red mist, Trace saw Lío, still on the Chinese's broad back. A *capataz* had taken over the whip.

That meant . . .

The third blow. Trace's body jerked. Was he bleeding yet? How many lashes?

Four. Trace felt as if his back were on fire. The nerves and muscles convulsed. He chewed his lip, blind with agony. If the blows came faster, he'd merge with them, drown in the black flaming sea.

But that *administrador*—he had a watch. He counted. Signaled. Enough time between to make you feel each blow to the utmost, no running them mercifully together.

A strange metallic rasping came from Lío. He didn't cry out as the blows fell, but that strange inhuman sound came after every lash, and as it came, so did the rope on Trace. He set all will on not screaming.

Then he lay in a heap in the trampled grass. Something prodded him. He looked up at the *administrador*. "*Norteño* eyes," murmured the immaculately groomed slender man. "Well—we shall see, gringo. See how you tame."

Trace watched his polished shoes move away. His *capataz*, face wealed by the rope, came up and delivered a kick that sent Trace halfway over.

"Up! Since you've energy for brawling, you'll cut an extra five hundred leaves today or taste the whip again."

Trace crawled up, pulled on his shirt. His bloody back would stick to it, but it would be some protection from insects. Lío was moving away with the other workers. Someone handed Trace the ball of soured cornmeal dough that was all he'd taste till supper. His stomach revolted. He started to refuse.

"Take it," muttered one of the old-timers. "Right now you think you cannot eat, but an hour in the fields will change that. You're going to need your strength. They'll be after you now."

If the other days had been forced, driven labor, this one was torture. Each swing of the machete, each bending to add to or pick up a bundle sent pain twisting through his bruised, broken flesh. His head throbbed and the *capataz* never passed without slashing him with the stinging limber cane.

"Five hundred extra leaves, gringo. And mind you trim them well."

An impossible stint even for an experienced worker in good condition. Hell! thought Trace, startled at his own bitter amazement. Gives me something to think about besides how I'd like to kill those bastards. Especially that foppy *administrador*—break his signal finger and cram that watch right down his throat!

Lío, several rows over, worked doggedly. He and Trace had the same goal—not to be whipped again till their backs healed. The thought of that rope laid across raw wounds made Trace sweat. If he died from the whip, that would be one thing; but what he dreaded was to be reduced to a groveling wreck whose only aim was to escape punishment.

If he saw that coming, he'd attack the bosses in such a way that they'd have to kill him. But could a man tell when he was breaking? Which whipping would be the one that snapped his hold on pride, every dream and hope that made him able to keep his spirit free?

Trace didn't know what was happening till he came on the bundle of twelve neatly trimmed leaves, stared in amazement at the adjacent plant.

"There are thirty leaves left, exactly," muttered the man in the next row, Tomás, one of Lío's Yaquis. "Rosalio and I worked it while the foremen were at the other end of the field and couldn't tell which rows we were working on."

As Trace gaped, Rosalio, a small tough little man, whispered sharply. "Get to work, *norteño!* None of us can waste time if you're to pile up that two thousand five hundred leaves!"

"Lío—he's going slower."

"The men next to his row are helping." Tomás hacked off a leaf, began trimming the spikelike point. "He'll make it.

You're the one who's in trouble. Five hundred extra leaves."

At noon the soured dough was gone and Trace was glad the long-time slave had urged him into taking it. Salt sweat stung his wounds but at least there was no chance of getting stiff from inaction.

And thanks to Tomás and Rosalio, who were getting some help on their stints from neighbors on their other sides, Trace had thirteen hundred leaves to his tally, a figure that made the *capataz* scowl and shake his head in disbelief.

"If a cleaning up makes you work this fast, gringo, maybe we should give you rope for breakfast every day."

Trace went dizzy. What if he was given this number of leaves daily? Tomás and Rosalio might help for a while, but they couldn't indefinitely drive themselves that much harder without collapsing.

Eight hours later he staggered from the field, legs feeling like a hay-stuffed scarecrow's. His back was an itching throbbing misery. But his extra five hundred leaves were done and Lío had met his quota. The sweating, tedious, backbreaking work their companions had done to help them created an even stronger bond than having fought together.

About half the workers were married and lived in one-room huts scattered around the center of the plantation, where were located the commissary, factory, drying yard, stable, jail, corrals, stables, and homes of the *administrador* and *mayor-domos,* as well as a little chapel. The unmarried men, about four hundred of them, slept in closely hung hammocks in a large stone building surrounded by a wall twice as high as a tall man, with broken glass mortared on top. At the single entrance stood a guard armed with a club, sword, and a pistol.

Behind the sleeping quarters were a half-dozen crude stoves where women were serving out the single meal of the day. Being one of the last out of the field, Trace didn't have to stand in line long, for most of the laborers were already squatting or leaning against the wall as they devoured their tortillas and bowls of putrid fish and beans.

On the night of their arrival at Mariposa, Trace had believed he could never force down the stinking rotten fish, but now he took his bowl eagerly, sat down where his back wasn't likely to be jarred against, and scooped a folded tortilla into the beans.

Lío joined him a few minutes later. "I think my back will heal faster than yours. It won't help anyone, *norteño*, to ask for a whipping."

Trace nodded. Hell, he knew that. He hadn't wanted to tackle the *majador*. It had just happened.

"I won't even try to defend you if you earn another beating," Lío growled from the corner of his mouth. "My aim is to stay as strong as I can in order to get away—go back to the sierra and fight for Yaqui lands."

"Sure," said Trace. "I'm going to get away, too."

"Not if you mix into every cleaning up."

"I've learned." Trace grinned hardily. "They can cut you in strips, hang you to dry for jerky, and I won't bat an eye."

"That's it," grunted Lío approvingly. He winced. "Don't make me laugh. Cracks open the scabs." But he laughed anyway.

Blessedly next day was Sunday. Trace and Lío rubbed each other's lashes with crushed aloe vera pulp one of the cooking women gave them. It stung at first but then had a soothing, drawing effect. The worst thing about open sores was attracting insects, which often ate their way half through a foot or hand. A Maya had died of blood poisoning caused by insects the day Trace arrived, and another lay in his hammock with one foot swollen to double size, already full of maggots.

Trace remembered how Cruz had saved Sewa from gangrene by taking off her foot, but even if there had been someone to do the operation, this man seemed too far gone.

Two more slaves died that week and were buried hastily in the graveyard edging the uncleared tropical growth outside the huts of the married people. The *campo santo* by the chapel was reserved for *administradores*, *mayordomos*, and *capataces*. A priest made a circuit of the plantations in the area, but except for mass solemnization of existing or planned marriages among the workers and baptism of any handy infants, he wasted no time in exhorting the plantation force to meekness. The soaked rope whip preached its message.

"You'd think that just to protect his investment, the owner would feed us better and drive us less," said Trace one evening when the fish seemed even ranker than usual.

Rosalio shrugged. He had grown even more thin and wizened so that he resembled an elongated hairless monkey. "Yaquis only cost sixty-five dollars when the Secretary of War sells us to his good friends, and there are thousands left."

"But not many are fighting."

"No, they're working at mines or ranches or railroads, or trying to hold on to their lands in the Eight Sacred Pueblos," spat Lío. "And so they will be marched away by the soldiers till not a Yaqui is left in all the rich river country that was marked out for us ages ago in the singing of the saints."

"If our women and children escaped to the mountains, perhaps they can hide till times change," said Tomás dreamily.

"From Torres to Yzábal to Corral and all over again?" scoffed Lío. "That gang have run Sonora all my life, taking turns as governor. With Corral as Díaz's vice-president, the federal buzzards simply devour what the Sonora wolves leave. Only a revolution will help the Yaquis."

"You think a different government would protect Yaqui lands?" Trace asked incredulously.

Lío's strong teeth flashed. "No. It would be my hope that the revolutionists and *federales* would keep each other so occupied that they'd have no time to civilize us or lust after our delta soil. That's why we've held our Eight Sacred Pueblos so long, *norteño*. First there was war against Spain and then against France and general brawling for power. It is only when the central government grows strong that there is time and energy to bother us."

"But I thought Yaquis fought in the other wars."

"To be sure," said Rosalio. "Very often we fought on both sides, too, depending on who made us the best promises. It's nothing to us who governs from Mexico City as long as they leave us in peace. We have our own laws, our own warrior societies, our own ways. We shall keep them as long as we live."

"Not when we are slaves," said Tomás bitterly. "How would we give the Easter celebration here? Or hold a novena or even make a decent funeral? And though there are many Yaquis here, you will notice that the families have all been broken up and Yaquis cannot marry each other. The women, even those with living husbands, are forced to marry Chinese, and if any of us were allowed a wife, she would be Maya. The government wants to destroy us as a nation."

"They will not do it," vowed Lío. "Our pueblos are holy, each located according to a vision. Prophets sang the boundaries of our land. It is not the government's right to change them."

Trace didn't say anything. That was how Indians in the United States had felt, but all of them, even the ones left in their homelands like the Navaho and Papago and Hopi, had been forced to terms with a completely alien government.

The Yaquis talked on about their home pueblos, about their great military leaders. And you? Trace asked himself. Where's your homeland, your sacred boundary, your holy city?

Texas? He belonged to his birthplace as he did to his family, but he doubted he'd ever go back. Las Coronas? Jonathan Greenleaf and Doña Luisa were dead. If he were ever to go back, he'd have to start all over to make it seem home. Yet there was a center to him and he suddenly knew what it was.

Miranda. She was his homeland, rest, the heart of his life. The song and boundary, his blessed place. Was she alive? Surely he could feel it if she weren't. Court Sanders would look out for her.

Too well?

Trace clenched his jaw. Couldn't think about such things. No. Just of Miranda, the fierce beautiful way she'd given herself to him, the sweetness of her. Dream about that and stay alive. Alive to go back.

Both he and Lío had been lucky. The rope wounds healed clean. And at the next whipping, of a Maya for missing roll call, Trace stayed at the back of the crowd and managed not to look, though there was no way he could shut out the sound of wet rope on flesh, the screams that began with the third lash and dwindled to gasping whines. Each blow reverberated through Trace's body. His guts twisted and sweat broke out as he fought the need to retch.

How long could this go on? Trace had thought measuring of the time between strokes by a watch was hideous, but this enjoyment of a cigar while a man was beaten. . . .

God damn the little bastard *administrador*—

With a flip of his wrist, the manager tossed away the cigar. The lashing stopped. A sigh floated up from the hypnotized throng. The *administrador*'s gaze hooked abruptly into Trace's. Above the heads of scores of workers, beginning to shuffle toward the fields, Trace felt those dark eyes pushing, appraising.

Turning swiftly, Trace started off with his fellow slaves, but before he could sever the first leaf, his *capataz* approached with an envying sneer.

"Don Enrique commands that you report to his house."

"Don Enrique?"

"The *administrador*, dolt."

Trace went cold. Had that runty little dandy decided to punish a gringo for looking disgusted at his entertainment? "Get moving!" snapped the *capataz*.

Questions would bring the long slender cane. Anyway, whatever the bad news was, Trace knew he'd get it soon enough. "The largest house," instructed the *capataz*. "Opposite the chapel."

A private whipping? Some more elaborate torture? Trace had heard there was a small dungeon at Mariposa, a cave where rebellious slaves were thrown to repent or die. They usually died after being hung up by their thumbs for a day or two.

The capataz took his machete. "You won't need this." He chuckled, running his tongue over his lips, again darting that curious half-jealous glance at Trace. "Get along now. Don Enrique's not a patient man."

Ordinarily an order repeated twice was accompanied by a few slashes of the cane. Trace moved off, puzzled by the foreman's manner but too apprehensive to think much about it. He passed the corrals and the factory, where an elevator sent henequen leaves down a long chute to the stripping machine that tore them apart, yielding strands of green fiber that would turn golden in the drying yard before it was baled and sent to the port where United States interests would buy most of it.

Trace grimaced to think of all the rope he'd used, never dreaming of where it came from, of the misery of those who harvested the raw material. He was sure that very few southern slaves had led such cruel lives. Slaves had been costly in the United States; there hadn't been an unending supply of cheap new ones provided by the government. Sharecroppers, white or black, often barely scratched out a living, but they couldn't be flogged to death. No, the henequen plantations were like vast prison-punishment farms; he didn't think they had improved a bit since the sixteenth century. Yet foreigners thought Díaz had brought such prosperity and advancement to this country.

Díaz's age was golden for the rich and powerful; for all but that handful, it was perpetual hardship, and for many it meant slavery for debt, serfdom as savage as that of the Middle Ages.

Trace saw the sick laborers working in the drying yard along with small boys. He knew this was Mariposa's hospital; those with fever or other ailments could work here at half-pay. Not that pay mattered since it was absorbed by food and lodging. No one had ever paid off his "debt" and regained his freedom.

The *administrador*'s stone house was the most imposing building on the plantation. The owner didn't live here, of course, but had a mansion in Mérida and seldom visited the several green hells from which his luxuries came. A young barefoot girl dressed in a flowing white dress, embroidered in blue about the hem, stepped out on the long veranda and said softly, "Come."

Small and graceful, she had olive skin and the Mayan features that Trace thought were like a mingling of Egyptian, Indian, and Chinese. She was no taller than Sewa, but firm little breasts suggested that she was biologically a woman. She led Trace through a broad hall and into a bedroom where a copper tub of water set on a rug near pails of water and a bench where towels were folded next to soap and a brush.

"Bathe yourself," said the girl, eyes downcast, keeping her distance as if afraid of him. "Then put on these." She touched soft dove-gray trousers and a linen shirt draped over a chair. Trace stared from the tub to the gentleman's garments. "What is this, little one?" he asked, keeping his tone gentle so as not to frighten her.

"Hurry," she begged. "Or he will think it's my fault, he'll whip me."

Whip this fragile little butterfly? She backed out of the room and her alarmed face lingered in Trace's mind as he peeled off his filthy shirt and trousers and stepped into the tub. Whatever happened, it was wonderful to get clean again! He dried on the thick soft towels and pulled on the clothes. Almost a perfect fit. Now how did that happen? Though the clothes were in excellent condition, they weren't new. Which made Trace even more uneasy. Even the woven sandals fit fairly well.

Glancing around the room, he tried to find some clue to its occupant, but there were no personal belongings visible. The bed and dresser were of mahogany and the coverlet and curtains were white.

An anonymous room. Why had he been brought here?

Thirstily he drank from one of the pails, sure that it was cleaner than the water put in cans for the slaves, and certainly much cooler. A tap came at the door. Answering, he saw the girl, who blinked at the change in his appearance.

"Better?" He grinned.

She tittered behind one slim hand and motioned him to follow. In a large pleasant room facing a patio where a fountain played among lush trees and flaming hibiscus and bougainvillea, Don Enrique sat in an easy chair, shapely feet extended on a large footstool. On a table next to him was a basket of fruit; a bottle of wine stood by two goblets. But what really caught Trace's eyes and set up a clamoring in his belly was a small tray of sliced chicken and fresh-baked rolls.

"Be seated," said the manager with a wave of that hand that

could signal beatings. "I am sure you would relish some refreshment. Will you have wine?"

"Thank you, no." Trace sat down in the empty chair on the other side of the table.

What was the manager's game? Trace would think he was being set up as a spy, only that didn't make sense. Scores of them could have been bought by adding a little better food, a shorter stint in the field. Maybe Don Enrique thought the U.S. government or Trace's family might pay a nice ransom.

"Your Spanish is good," he said as Trace polished off the last of the chicken. "But you are not Mexican, nor, I think, a ruffian who deserves this fate. I would like to help you."

The opening to say his great-aunt Minerva would pay thousands to free him? Trace shrugged; at least he'd had a good meal and bath.

"I appreciate your concern, señor," he said dryly. "I regret I have no way to repay it."

Don Enrique smiled. "But you do! You have the look of an educated man. Can you keep accounts?"

"I suppose so, but—"

"Then you will be my secretary. You will live here and in addition to food and clothing, you will receive a salary. In a matter of years, you might save enough to purchase your freedom." Don Enrique beamed, awaiting jubilant acceptance, but Trace hesitated.

He wanted to escape. If he became of extra value, more effort would be made to track him down. Anyway, though the manager was presently so affable, Trace remembered him that morning, enjoying his cigar while a man was beaten. Trace didn't care to owe such a man favors or be around him more than was necessary.

"You will be my companion," Don Enrique went on expansively, "Life is dull here for a person of cultivated tastes. I perish of boredom. And do you know why I am here instead of Mérida or Mexico City like my father's other sons?"

"Señor—" began Trace, afraid he was going to hear things he'd later be hated for knowing.

"It is because I am illegitimate!" growled Don Enrique,

nervously smoothing his moustache. "So I must work like an exile in this remote hole while the others idle about—an employee while they are owners." Pouring out a glass of wine, he tossed it down, breathing heavily, assumed a smile that looked eerily like an ill-fitting mask. "But that's the world, no? And my misfortune is your luck since my need for your skills can give you really quite a comfortable life."

He smiled and leaned forward. "So long as you please me," he added softly. His hand fell on Trace's shoulder, moved slowly down, caressing the muscular curve.

Trace stared at him in fascinated revulsion, understood at last. He got to his feet. Don Enrique sprang up, too, barring his way. "You—don't have to do anything," he gabbled wildly. "You will like it. The most *macho* do."

At Trace's look he gave a despairing cry of humiliation and thwarted lust, snatched a braided leather riding whip from the wall as he struck a brass gong that echoed through the house. Trace tore the whip from the manager's uplifted hand, twisted it around his throat like a garrote, but before he could snap Don Enrique's neck, two huge men loomed in the door and sprang at Trace.

"You fools," he shouted, knocking one backward and trying to dodge the other. "Help me kill him and we'll run for it!"

The heavy butt of the whip struck him on the side of the head. He staggered and the second man tripped him over one foot while felling him with a heavy blow at the back of the neck. The lash descended.

He surfaced in humid fog, brain exploding when he moved his head. The pain was so great that he fainted. When he roused again, something cool yet stinging was being applied to his lacerations.

"Be still a little moment," came a woman's voice. It was Luisa, one of the cooks. The woman sighed. "He will kill you, you know. It happened once before with a young very beautiful man who would not be Don Enrique's toy. He was whipped every day and in a month he was dead."

"Maybe I can kill him first."

"You will not get the chance. He is a coward, that one. Bodyguards in his house, wherever he goes."

I was stupid, Trace thought. Should have pretended to accept his proposition, then strangled him when he wasn't expecting it.

Luisa bound the aloe vera poultice on with an old shirt, helped Trace slip into his. She brought him a drink in a gourd, washed his face with a sour-smelling clout. But her kindness was better for Trace than the most medically perfect care. In spite of this brutal life, she had stayed human; in their common misery, she comforted him. Now she handed him a lump of dough.

"You had better go back to the field if you can. Otherwise the *capataz* will fetch you."

Trace pushed to his feet, leaned for a moment against the wall of the big stone sleeping room. His body had a strange light boneless feeling, as if he were nothing but waves of pain.

Luisa's anxious pitying face took shape in the mists. "God help you, *norteño*."

"You have." He tried to smile but knew it was an uncontrolled twitching of muscles. "Thank you, Luisa."

One step. Two. He paused, sucking the pain through him, breathing with it after a moment. He would get to the field in order to live. He would live in order to kill the *administrador*. Trace no longer dreamed the fantastic—getting away, loving Miranda. He had become a slave in hell; there was no way back to the land of the living.

Somehow, with the help of Tomás and Rosalio, Trace cut his two thousand spiky leaves. The *capataz* regarded him with jeering awe. "If I had your chance! But he likes handsome ones. You're not so handsome now, gringo." The foreman didn't use his cane on Trace that day, which suggested that even an insensitive brute shrank from adding more punishment to what was coming to Trace.

If they whip me in the morning, I will die, Trace thought.

Don Enrique waited three days, till the wounds were scabbed and cracked with every motion till night gave them a chance to crust over again. On the fourth morning at roll call, Trace was called out.

No way to get at Don Enrique, who was flanked by his men. No weapon in reach. The *mayordomos* were coming forward to rip his shirt off. Trace motioned them back.

How did you show pride while being whipped? No way. But by keeping as much control of the torture as he could, he felt more a man, less a cowering object, though he felt sick at what was coming. He took off his shirt, held out his wrists to the big Chinese, who stooped to lift him.

Before he shut his eyes, he saw Don Enrique's elegant finger signal.

Lío said he was delirious for two days. On the third morning, the fever broke and he walked to roll call with an unsteady gait. As soon as Don Enrique's searching gaze fell on him, Trace knew he had made a lethal mistake, for the manager barked out his name.

For a moment Trace's legs refused to move. A murmur ran through the laborers. Then, as Trace took the first step, Lío strode past him to confront the manager.

"Let me take his whipping, señor."

"Lío, no!" cried Trace, moving forward.

Don Enrique glanced from one to the other, a bitter smile curving his lips. "Such love!" he derided. "Well, you were whipped together once. We can oblige you again."

Springing forward, Lío grasped the manager's head, snapped it sideways, and kicked Don Enrique as he collapsed. It was done in seconds. Lío was overwhelmed an eye's blink later by overseers and guards, but the *administrador* stared unseeing, and his neck was jackknifed on his shoulder.

Lío was lucky. A machete had almost severed his head as he went down. Dead quick and clean.

Trace looked around in wild hope that the slaves might be swelling across the clearing to slaughter their oppressors, but they seemed paralyzed with shock. And the chief *mayordomo* took over so quickly that he must have rehearsed a similar emergency in his mind.

"Get to work!" he ordered. "Hurry, dogs!"

Capataces and lesser *mayordomos* brandished their canes, herding the laborers to the fields. Trace stood dazed, looking at his friend—dead in his place. Don Enrique's bodyguards were carrying him away.

"Bury that Yaqui," ordered the *mayordomo*. His hard eyes ran over Trace. "Then work in the drying yard till you're well." He slanted a triumphant smile after the manager's corpse. "Slaves are for working. I don't beat them to death for my entertainment."

He spat on the bloody ground and walked away.

It tormented Trace that Lío had died for him. When he closed his eyes he saw his friend's almost-severed head. Lío had always believed he'd go home again, home to win back the Eight Sacred Pueblos. Now his body would rot in the steamy rank soil of Yucatán.

"He managed to kill that abomination of an *administrador,*" pointed out Rosalio. "He died like a warrior. It was a good death, *norteño*. Do not brood so much."

"He should not have died for me."

"Who can say that? It is the will of God."

"God?" mocked Trace.

"Indeed." Rosalio scratched his ear, looking more than ever like a sad-faced monkey. "God willed that Lío should die here rather than in our sierra. Perhaps He wills that you take Lío's place."

"How can I? I'm not Yaqui."

"Nor was it Lío who was called out for a whipping a few mornings ago."

Trace fell silent. And though part of him rebelled against trying to fight another man's battle, the idea had the power of offering a way to pay his debt to Lío. It was plain, too, that Lío's men, especially Tomás and Rosalio, who had driven themselves to help Trace fulfill his stints, expected him to assume Lío's responsibilities. For a while, at least, these would fit with Trace's personal aims, so he stopped wrestling with the commitment. There was no doubt that Lío had saved his life; and after this advanced education in governmental graft and cruelty, Trace burned to fight Díaz's tyranny. No one had suffered more from it than the Yaquis. He might as well throw in with them.

But Miranda? He couldn't expect her to live in hiding, become outlawed to stay with him. He could see her sometimes. Yaqui warfare was the sporadic, guerrilla-style. But what was that to offer a woman?

Then he would come back to the monotonous work of the drying yard, spreading the hairlike fiber, gathering it when it was dry, stuffing it into bales. He had lofty aims for a slave who still carried weals from his last beating. But he was sure he would escape. He had Lío's life to fulfill now as well as his own.

Studying the chances of escape always led to one unsolvable problem: help after getting off the plantation, food, safe shelter, a change of clothes so that one's appearance didn't immediately suggest a runaway. So little, really. And yet so much.

Trace, as his strength returned, became obsessed with breaking free. An overseer came by the drying yard at frequent intervals, but since the men working there were sick, it wasn't necessary to watch them so closely. The workers changed from day to day, some dying, some returning to the fields; so it would be easier to disappear unnoticed during this time.

But then what? He knew nothing of the region, had no money, friends, or place of refuge, and even if he half-starved, he couldn't save more than a few days' supply of sour cornmeal dough before it grew inedible and the other food, beans and spoiled fish, wouldn't keep at all. As Trace spread the wet green fiber, collected it when it was dried yellow, he pretended to be weaker than he was, trying desperately to think of some way to avoid being picked up or dying of exposure if he did manage to slip away.

When the laborers had to relieve themselves, they stepped outside the drying yard near the corrals. Trace was fastening his loose once-white trousers when a voice called softly.

"Señor! Don Trace!"

A trap? Didn't seem likely with Don Enrique gone, along with his thirst for vengeance. He replied in a low tone, "Who is it?"

"Sewa." Before he could take that in, the girl went on breathlessly. She was hidden in a broken-down mule car that stood with a jumble of wagons, carts, and old machinery. "Domingo and I have food and clothes and money. When you can, come this way and go straight through the brush till you reach an overgrown ditch. I'll wait for you there."

Sewa! Domingo! How in the hell had those two youngsters got down there? A warm rush of hope surged through Trace; Miranda must have sent them. That had to be it! Which meant she was still alive. . . .

No time to sort it out now; he'd better get back before the wandering foreman noticed he was gone overlong. "I'll meet you as soon as I can," he whispered. "God bless you, Sewa."

Compelling himself not to glance toward her hiding place, he went back to the yard and resumed the unending task. If he got away from here, he never wanted to see another piece of rope. But his blood hummed and pulsed as if coming alive again.

In spite of their agreement that anyone who got a break should take it, Trace felt sorry for leaving his friends, especially Tomás and Rosalio. But there might be a way of breaking them out later. What he'd like to do would be to free all the slaves, wreck the whole damned system, but that was work for a revolution.

After he'd talked with Sewa and Domingo and knew the situation at Mina Rara, he could decide what to do. He spread damp fiber while the foreman watched, but as soon as he was out of sight, Trace left the drying yard, hand to his belly as if wracked with dysentery. Squatting, he glanced about.

Not a soul around. Rising, he crept as far as he could in the cover of the wagons and equipment, then, doubling, he ran for the underbrush, dived into its cover, and lay on the ground, panting.

No commotion. No sound of pursuit or discovery. Keeping

as straight a course as he could, he moved through heavy growth, breaking entangling vines, trying not to trip over exposed roots. He sighted the old ditch, probably some ancient canal, at the same instant that a small lithe figure rose with a taller gangly one behind it.

Trace hugged Sewa, almost sweeping her off her feet, gave Domingo the male *abrazo*. The young Yaqui didn't return the embrace and back-patting but produced a bundle.

"You had best change into these," the boy said austerely. "And then let us get as far away as we can as fast as we can. We have food and sleeping mats hidden in an abandoned hut a few hours from here, and we can be in Mérida tomorrow night and catch a train."

"A train?" frowned Trace, shedding his stained rags and longing for a bath. It seemed close to sacrilege to fit his dirty body into the well-cut dark-gray suit and white shirt. "Isn't that risky?"

"There is a razor in the hut," said Domingo. "In these clothes you look like a well-to-do businessman or engineer." His young straight mouth curled a trifle bitterly. "No one will molest a well-dressed American, even *if* he is traveling with two Indians."

"Try the boots," Sewa urged, crescent brows puckering her smooth brown skin. "We brought an extra pair of socks in case they are too big."

"And if they're too little, we cut off a toe, eh?" teased Trace and then could have bitten his tongue, remembering that Sewa, poor pretty little girl, had lost her whole foot. But she seemed not to notice, though Domingo shot him a scowl.

Damned if that young tiger doesn't love the child! Trace thought, and smothered his amusement. Domingo was old enough to fight and die, old enough, at Mariposa, to be held accountable for a man's stint in the field. Sewa couldn't be more than thirteen, but she'd grow.

"Miranda?" Trace asked, caressing the name. "She sent you?"

Domingo blinked. Sewa's eyes grew even bigger and her chin trembled. "No. We have not seen her since she sent us to the mine before the battle."

Trace stopped working his foot into a boot. "You haven't seen her? Is she alive?"

"Yes, señor, but Chepa—she's my friend who works in Señor Sander's house—Chepa says that Miranda was hurt during the battle and Dr. Trent said it might be weeks before she woke up."

"Did you see her?" Trace demanded, fear clutching at his heart. Sounded like concussion. And if she lived, her mind might be damaged. From the hurt look on Sewa's face, he knew he'd sounded accusing.

"Chepa sneaked me in to look at her," the girl said with wistful sadness. "But I could not stay there. Major Ruiz and his soldiers are at Mina Rara. If they knew a lot of Yaquis had escaped, even though they are mostly women and children, the soldiers would have hounded them down."

"Dr. Trent is a kind man," Trace reassured himself. "He'll do all he can for her."

"Of course." Sewa nodded more brightly. "How are the boots?"

"Just fine," Trace said, grinning, resolving to pull himself together. These kids had risked a lot for him and they still had a long way to go. He'd believe that Miranda was all right until he knew otherwise.

"Then let's go, señor!" Domingo took the lead. Trace put Sewa in the middle and they moved through the thick scrubby growth on a trail that must have been worn by animals. A trail away from Nariposa. And to Miranda.

There were straw mats in the hut and food. Wonderful food it was to Trace: cheese, tortillas, coffee, chicken stewed with rice, sweet rolls crusted with nuts. He told Domingo and Sewa how Lío had died and how Tomás and Rosalio had helped him, Trace, fill his quota of henequen leaves, but he didn't want to talk about the plantation. In turn, the youngsters told him how the remnants of the band—not a fighting-age man among them, except for Domingo (who must be all of fifteen, Trace thought grimly)—were living in their old palisaded mountain, making homes and cultivating small plots. Friends and relations at Mina Rara had stolen a few chickens and goats for them. With their men dead or enslaved, the women were prepared to live in the sierra as long as necessary, perhaps the rest of their lives.

"I'll get their men free somehow," Trace said. "Maybe I can find a few men to come back here with me and break them out. We'll have to organize. Twenty can't get away as simply as one. The real problem will be avoiding recapture."

"I will help," said Domingo. His golden-brown eyes glowed in a face much too severe for his age. But he had seen—Trace didn't like to think of all these children had watched and lived through. "When the men are back, we will raid again. You will be with us, Don Trace?"

"Whatever Lío would have done, I will do my best to perform," Trace said, but he felt unutterably weary. What then of Miranda?

Sewa had been so quiet, shying away from any mention of Mina Rara, that Trace grew increasingly worried. The girl knew something she didn't want to tell him. He had a terrible fear that it concerned Miranda.

"Sewa." She lifted her oval face, eyes like a fawn's. She was going to be a lovely woman, and he realized with a shock that it wouldn't be long. "You seem troubled about something," he said as gently as he could. Astonishing strength behind that fragile look—strength to come this long dangerous way, plan his escape! He respected her as he had respected few men in his life. "Is it Miranda?" he went on, watching the child's face closely. "Was she injured beyond what you have told me?"

"Truly, Don Trace, she was sleeping when I saw her, but Chepa did not know of any hurt except the blow on her head."

"Her sister? Does Reina mean her harm?"

Sewa winced as if at old pain. "Don Trace, the señorita was killed by Tula, who also died in the battle." Trace drew in his breath. Reina dead? That tigress, Tula? Both women had possessed such blazing vitality that it was hard to believe they were extinguished, blown out like torches. And Reina— He had thought once he loved her, and even when her streak of cruelty repelled him, he had gone on taking her when she put herself tauntingly in his way. With a heavy shrug he pushed thoughts of her away.

"Then what is wrong?" he persisted.

The way she stared at the dirt floor convinced him. His breath wedged solid so that when he managed to speak he didn't recognize his own voice.

"Tell me, Sewa."

"He will find out," Domingo said resignedly. "He might as well know now."

"What?" Trace felt as if his body were clenched as tight as his fists.

Slowly, Sewa lifted her drooping head. "Oh, Don Trace, I don't know how to say it—" She made an inarticulate cry and turned away. Domingo stepped protectively in front of her. "Our lady Miranda has married Court Sanders."

And he had thought the rope lash agony. "Married? Sanders?"

Domingo nodded.

For a moment Trace's head spun. It couldn't be. She hadn't even seemed to like or trust the mine superintendent. *And she loved me!* But over that inner cry jeered doubt and logic.

Sanders was an attractive man. He'd had weeks in which to court Miranda. A woman alone in Mexico, especially an heiress, needed a strong husband. Trace certainly hadn't anything to give her. Not when he was vowed to war for the Yaqui in Lío's place. Except for his love, the worship of his body. . . . Which remembered her now; in every nerve and muscle, remembered how sweetly she had given herself to him that day on the mountain.

Miranda, oh, Miranda! You belonged to me. How could you take another man?

Trace sat in silence for a long time while Domingo hunkered next to Sewa, his arm around her in sturdy comfort. One moment Trace felt as if he were bleeding inwardly, as if his force and manhood were draining away; the next instant he was gripped with rage, jealousy, furious hurt. But through the tumult, cold reason asked if he expected her to hide in the sierra with him or be content with the occasional furtive visit he could pay. His life for a while was not his own; he owed a blood debt. In a way he should be relieved she had a capable man to look after her, especially if the damned Army was going to quarter troops at the mine.

But— Goddammit anyway! While he had dreamed of her and when they could be together, she had been in Sanders' arms. Sanders would know how to make her completely his.

But I had her first, some fierce despairingly exultant voice insisted. She loved me first.

How could she? How could she marry him?

At last, rousing himself, Trace got to his feet. "We'd better sleep," he said. "It's a long way to Sonora."

Three

La Grulla

16

It was hard to get Jon to bed that night. How one small body could contain so much energy was beyond me. Kneeling by his bed, I regarded my son with a mixture of irritation and bemused tenderness. How like Trace he was! Straight black hair falling into storm-blue eyes, cleft chin, a sudden smile that dissolved any sternness he was about to encounter.

"I'm a big boy!" he was saying indignantly. "Almost *cinco años*. I want to stay up and see Papa."

Would I never get used to his calling Court that, ever stop wanting to cry out the truth? After that single outburst when Court had learned I was pregnant, I'd schooled my tongue for the sake of Trace's baby. At least the man I loved wouldn't utterly perish if I could preserve his child, though as time passed and I heard nothing of Trace, I was forced to believe he'd died during his attempted escape from Yucatán. Surely if he'd come back to Sonora, he'd have found some way to meet me or send a message.

And Sewa? Domingo?

Ruiz and Court mentioned rumors of a beautiful young Yaqui woman called La Grulla, the Crane, because she perched like one on an artificial foot. She led raids with her young lover, but the band's operations were down in the traditional Yaqui country. They struck from the mountains, killing soldiers, seizing supplies. Even the dreaded *rurales* had pursued them, but this group seemed to have separated itself from families and couldn't be tracked to any permanent retreat.

"I want to see what Papa's going to bring me from Hermosillo," insisted Jon. "Let me stay up, Mama. Please? *Por favor? Por el amor de Dios, una horita más.*"

When he couldn't get his way in one language, Jon always used a second. He had tried persuasion in Seri, as well, till he realized no one understood it except Caguama, the brawny young soldier who had taught it to him. Caguama had wanted to learn so much that he'd come back to the school after Ruiz forbade such visits. Alarmed for him and touched by his loneliness, for as one of the primitive Seris he was shunned by his fellows, I'd got Court, indulgent because of my pregnancy, to buy Caguama's way out of the Army.

Since then, while learning to read and write, Caguama had done my errands, worked in the gardens I hopefully tried to nourish, and after Jon's infancy, had assumed more and more of the boy's care.

He taught him to shoot a bow and arrow, made a small harpoon with which Jon spent hours trying to spear quarry in the puddles left by thundershowers. On a leather thong around his neck, Jon wore a bone amulet taken from a giant sea turtle's flipper and shaped like a dolphin. Caguama said proudly that it would keep Jon free and happy like those sportive creatures I'd heard of but never seen.

Strange. Caguama told me stories of Tiburón Island, sang the songs his people used to call up whales and seals and fish, and I told him about England and the queen's funeral and sang ballads and snatches of Gilbert and Sullivan. I had to smile at the contrast but then put on a severe look and drew the covers up beneath my rebellious son's chin.

"Love of God indeed, you little rascal! Court may not be home till tomorrow, or even next day. It's bedtime, and if you wriggle out one more time—"

Jon went suddenly boneless and yielding as a puppy,

cuddling against my arm. "I'll go to sleep if you tell me about the Ku bird," he wheedled.

He had learned that even when I was very tired or cross I could be coaxed into reciting that particular story. And sure enough, as he nestled against me, I began the words he knew by heart, the litany that eased him into shimmering bright dreams.

"Once there was a bird so very poor that he had no feathers, no, not one . . ."

Ten minutes later, Jon's long black lashes didn't flutter when I gently disengaged myself and got to my feet. Probably I spoiled him. Yet in an odd way, the lonely child inside me was comforted by mothering him. I'd been only a little older than Jon when I was taken to Miss Mattison's. The very idea of being separated from Jon made me go ice-cold. But that was nonsense, it wouldn't happen.

Tears filled my eyes as I thought of that other child I'd loved, the one who had taught me the Ku bird story. Sewa was gone—it was all too possible she was dead or enslaved, all too likely we would never meet this side of Glory. If Sewa had become that lightning raider they called La Grulla, perhaps she had come to hate all foreigners.

Let her be alive and well. It was the prayer I made whenever I thought of my foster-sister-daughter. Blowing out the lamp, I decided to have a cup of tea before going to bed. Unlike Jon, I preferred to be asleep, or feigning it, when Court returned.

As long as he was at Mina Rara, he mightn't visit my bed for several nights, but if he made a trip, even for a day, his first act, sometimes before eating or bathing, was to possess me. It was as if absence drove him to prove to us both that he owned me. If he came back tonight, my sleep wouldn't delay his asserting mastery, but I'd feel it less, be able to merge it into a nightmare.

Court baffled me as much as ever. Though I was in fact a prisoner, most of the time he behaved like a doting husband. He *must* see daily that Jon was Trace's child, yet he seemed proud of the boy and indulged him at every turn. In these ordinary periods life was calm, and when Court came to my bed, he made love with quick efficiency. But every month or so, sometimes when he was drinking, sometimes not, he would lock the door and proceed to behave as if he'd just paid for every service of a skilled whore. Resistance excited him more. It was best to do as he said, get it over with, try to exhaust him. These were the nightmares—and the worst was when my body responded to him, when he made me want him and taunted me with that.

There had not been another baby. Dr. Trent said that my womb was tilted and that it would be difficult to conceive, which made it all the stranger that Trace had got me with child that one first time he'd had me along the mountain trail.

Oh, my love, I thought. You must be dead, I'll never see you again, you'll never see our son. But my dear love . . .

The sound of footsteps roused me. Court's, lightly deliberate. Too late to escape to my room. He stood in the kitchen door a moment, golden eyes examining me. I flinched inwardly at that look I knew so well, the honed, voracious expression. I could never feed his spirit, give him what he desired.

Why wouldn't he let me go? I wished I could believe it was because he enjoyed the use of my wealth and property, which he did, but that wasn't the reason he kept me at Mina Rara, wouldn't let me take Jon and live elsewhere. With a certain amount of pity, I knew that just as I was Court's prisoner, he was mine. The ironic part was that if I'd loved him in the whole-souled, self-abasing fashion that Raquel did, he would surely have tired of me long ago and I could have bought my way out of the marriage.

"Tea, love?" He smiled. "The eternal English." He started to pull the cord attached to a bell in Raquel's room, but I rose quickly. "Don't call her. I can heat the coffee in a few minutes and there's chicken stewed with rice that just needs warming."

He sank down in a leather chair by the fireplace, worked off his boots, and sighed. "You're funny, darling. Servants are supposed to do what's needed, it's what they're for."

It was probably his total disregard for other people's needs and feelings that kept me from developing some affection for

Court. In some odd way, he'd incorporated me into himself so that he was exaggeratedly considerate of me except for those occasions in the bedroom, and by some feat of self-delusion for which I knew I should be grateful, he had included Jon in his self-love, insisting the boy was his. It was a maddening attitude but the thought of what could happen if he repudiated my child clamped a heavy weight on my scorn.

I lit two burners of the kerosene cookstove and set on coffee and a skillet of the spicy chicken. Court closed his eyes, feet resting on an ottoman covered with the skin of a panther he'd shot.

"How's Jon?" he asked when I sweetened his coffee and handed him the mug.

"Begging to go to the beach so he can harpoon sea turtles," I said, glad to lighten the silence with something entertaining.

But Court didn't laugh. "He's becoming a savage, Miranda, constantly with that Caguama or the miners' brats. With your education and background I don't see how you can permit it."

"Jon lives in a Sonora mining camp. He'll grow up understanding the people and language, and what Caguama teaches him will be very useful." I didn't like the trend of this conversation and shifted it. "How did you find things in Hermosillo?"

"In an uproar. That damned fool Madero is chasing around Mexico forming Anti-Reelectionist Clubs. He didn't get into real trouble till he hit Sonora, and what could he expect in Ramón Corral's home state, and Corral Díaz's vice-president?"

Though Court didn't like to talk politics, Dr. Trent did; so, remote though Mina Rara was, I knew something of the pressures mounting to explosive force in spite of Díaz's iron grip. Dr. Trent had loaned me his copy of the February 1908 *Imparcial*, which carried a translation of James Creelman's interview with Díaz, which had been published in *Pearson's Magazine*. Díaz had emphatically announced that he wouldn't run for office again, that he had made Mexico strong and prosperous enough for democracy, and that he would now welcome active political parties and the formation of a representative government.

Perhaps he'd never meant these sentiments to be translated into his native language, but his countrymen eagerly took him at his word and prepared for the election that would take place this year, in 1910. Even if Díaz didn't step down, he was eighty. The post of vice-president was vitally important, since the man elected to it would almost surely be the next president.

Not long after Dr. Trent lent me the Creelman translation, he let me read his copy of *La Sucesión Presidencial en 1910* by the same Francisco Madero, who was presently provoking the wrath of Sonora's political *jefes*, that same cruel and greedy lot who alternated in the governor's seat and hounded Yaquis: Luis and Lorenzo Torres, Rafael Yzábal, and Corral himself.

Madero, a gentle idealist, a typical son of a wealthy Coahuila family, had worked for years to improve conditions for workers on his family's haciendas and to educate the children. When he tried to improve the lot of his poorer countrymen beyond the family's holdings, he ran into opposition that convinced him Mexico's political system must change. In his famous book on the presidential succession he pointed to the corruptions of the Díaz regime, insisted that there be no reelection, called for effective suffrage, and kept reminding people of the constitution, for which he had a lover's ardor.

If he, or someone like him, could be elected, peace with justice might come to Mexico, there might not have to be the horrors of a revolution already foretold by the bloodily suppressed strike at the cotton mill of Río Blanco in Veracruz, where the flat cars of mangled bodies had been dumped in the harbor for sharks, and Cananea, in the north of this state of Sonora, where *rurales*, Arizona Rangers, and soldiers put down the copper strikers. The American owner of the mine had brought in a force of several hundred volunteers from Douglas and Bisbee, Arizona, who came in the belief they were defending helpless American women and children from a rampaging mob. Governor Yzábal in person had helped crush that revolt.

Bloody, turbulent times. But if Madero could be elected, if he could fulfill the promises of the constitution, the dreams of Hidalgo and Juárez might at last come true, a hundred years after Mexico declared independence from Spain. But the good, like Jesus, often do die young and I was worried about Madero.

"Is Madero being threatened?" I asked as I put Court's plate before him on a small table.

"You might say he's being made unwelcome. In Alamos his hotel refused to put him up and the *jefe político* wouldn't let him hold a meeting of more than two. He got around that by getting a follower to have a dance and invite only possible sympathizers. *Rurales* trailed him out of Alamos."

Rurales, many of them recruited from banditry, were known for their use of the *ley fuga*—more of their victims were "shot while trying to escape" than were ever brought to trail.

"They didn't arrest Madero?"

"No. He held a rally yesterday in Hermosillo—or that is, he tried to. The local authorities didn't refuse to let him speak, but police tried to break up the gathering crowd and hired thugs heckled the speakers and threw rotton fruit. Part of the audience was lured away with the offer of free drinks. Madero gave up and rescheduled the meeting for today, but he probably won't have any better luck."

"Then his trip to Sonora was useless?"

"Oh, he had a chance to weep over the Yaquis and he got together with some powerful men who hate the Díaz government only a bit less than they loathe Corral." Court yawned and stretched. "The hell with it! Madero's too starry-eyed. He'll get himself killed."

Getting to his feet, this man who was my husband stroked my breast, laughed as I went very still. "Come, Miranda. Show me how glad you are to have me home again."

Jon was delighted with the silver-handled whip Court had bought for him and ran outside after breakfast to crack it at Cascos Lindos, once Sewa's beloved *burra,* who stared calmly at him and went on seeking forage. He seemed to be considering really hitting her with it and I called from the dining-room window.

"Jon! That's not for using on live things. You'll hurt them."

He looked from his handsome whip to the *burra,* shook his head earnestly. "Don't want to hurt Lindos. But trees and rocks can't feel, Mama. It's no use whipping them."

"Practice knocking a can off the porch," I suggested. "This summer when the flies are bad, you can kill all of them."

Court laughed, circling my wrist with his hand. "You're as softheaded as Madero, my sweetheart! Delightful in a woman, but such fidgets won't do for a man. Jon's a realist. Whips are made for hurting."

I never thought of whipping without remembering how Lío had died, trying to save Trace from a beating. Though I knew it was dangerous to anger Court, I twisted free.

"I hate whips. Why couldn't you have picked something else?"

Court rose, towering over me. His tawny eyes narrowed, and a heavy pulse throbbed in his neck and temple. An almost palpable desire radiated from him, setting off in me a sort of bitter gratification that I could make him feel so powerfully.

"Maybe I should use a whip on you, Miranda," he said softly. "Perhaps then I could pierce to the core of you, through your pain."

I stared at him defiantly, though fear made ice of my vitals. He had used me cruelly, roughly, sometimes left my body bruised from his hands, but he had never struck or beaten me. He dragged in a ragged choking breath.

"Come!" he said thickly.

He caught me high in his arms as I tried to evade him, carried me down the hall with his mouth pressed so hungrily to my throat that I felt as if he had tapped my blood.

He never left me all day long.

Even for those of us who knew that the heavenly body glaring in the sky that spring was Halley's Comet and that it would duly pass from sight, its brilliance was disturbing. The workers muttered, and though I explained it to my pupils and to Chepa and Raquel and the household, they obviously pitied my educated ignorance and went on believing that the comet meant war, famine, death, and plague.

Court traveled down to Las Coronas to reassure the people and make one of his periodic inspections. I hadn't been back since I ran away that night with Sewa. Lázaro Pérez was foreman now. Soon I must start taking Jon there, acquainting him with the people and the work, for it would one day be his. But the place held unhappy memories for me, of Mother's dying, of Reina, whom I had so longed to love, and I had never asked Court to let me accompany him.

I endured Court's unpredictable cycle of remote courtesy and unleashed sensuality, ignored Ruiz's gallantries, and absorbed myself in Jon and the little school. I knew most of the mothers by now, and though our communication was mostly silent, I felt that it was warm.

Except for rare, shamefully frightening responses to Court, the woman part of me seemed dead, blighted by the bitter realization that Trace wasn't coming back. I was Jon's mother and *la señora*, but the Miranda who had fiercely desired and loved a man seemed as dead as the other people in my past.

In 1910, though, things were changing, perhaps because Jon spent more time with Caguama and his playmates, perhaps because the comet above lit up the dark recesses of hearts and minds, perhaps because of the restlessness pervading all Mexico that year of the centennial, when people remembered how ill the promises of the revolution against Spain, the dreams and laws of Juárez, had been kept.

Dr. Trent had lent me a book published in 1909 by Andrés Molina Enríquez. *Los Grandes Problemas Nacionales* put into words the terrible inequities of life under Díaz. He had said only three occupations were open to educated mestizos: governmental employment, the professions, and revolution. To an increasing number of even these comparatively fortunate Mexicans, the last option seemed to offer their best hope.

No one, not even Madero, seriously expected Díaz to lose

the election that summer. The practical question was who would be vice-president and take over when death finally claimed the Strong Man. Limantour, the Secretary of Finance, had hopes. So did handsome General Bernardo Reyes, favorite of the military, university students, jobless professionals, the remaining old Juárez liberals, and businessmen who lacked entrée to the present rulers.

Madero continued to travel and speak to enthusiastic crowds whenever he could thwart official repression. I began to hear other names from Court, Ruiz, and Dr. Trent. Álvaro Obregón, a ranchero and mechanic, was rousing people in his part of Sonora, and down in Morelos the big sugar hacendados began to feel nervous about young, surly Emiliano Zapata, who made no bones about his fury that some of his village's land had been taken over by one of the large owners.

Ironically, as conditions grew unbearable for more Mexicans, the situation had improved a little for the Yaquis. In 1907 there had been orders to deport all Yaquis north of Hermosillo. Only about two thousand were left in the valley of the Eight Sacred Pueblos. There were possibly 150 rebels in the sierra. Thousands had been killed or sent to Yucatán. The rest had settled in the northern provinces or escaped into Arizona. Former Governor Yzábal ferreted out hundreds of peaceable men and women and sent them to bondage, but in 1908 a banking crisis affected business and cut the demand for henequen and slaves to harvest it. This same crisis brought competition for jobs in Arizona and the United States agreed to deport back to Mexico all illegally entered Yaquis.

During 1908 Governor Torres tried to bargain with the rebels to make peace, dealing with Luis Bule, one of the leaders. Succumbing to pressure from Sonoran hacendados and employers, Torres halted deportation except for punishment; any raid would be followed by the shipping away of five hundred Yaquis.

By 1909 Bule had made peace for the Yaquis and passports were issued. Bule's men were put in Special Forces groups in the Army to hunt out those of their comrades who still persisted in defiance, but at least indiscriminant persecution of the Yaquis had stopped for the time. As always, when the country was in turmoil, the Indians fared best.

Spring came with the Easter ceremonies performed by the Yaqui workers of Mina Rara. The processions began on Ash Wednesday and accelerated week by week as the soldiers of Pilate and masked *fariseos* with their wooden swords pursued Jesus. Tantalizing smells of stew, beans, and tortillas floated from the outdoor communal kitchen where even the Mexican soldiers were fed, for this most important of celebrations was open to all. Those giving it gained "flower" or spiritual grace.

Jon loved to go and I often attended with him and Caguama, laughing at the *pascolas,* clown dancers who kept the ceremonies moving and made ribald jokes, or admiring the flag girls and the *matachines* crowned with flowers who danced for Mary, but most of all delighting in the ancient rite of the deer dancer who embodied the primeval wild spirits.

On Saturday, after Jesus had been betrayed and killed, there was a battle between the forces of evil and good who fought swords with flowers. When the flowers won, the *fariseos'* masks and swords were burned in a great fire where an effigy of Judas also blazed, but I never stayed for that. It reminded me too much of Cruz. But I never missed Easter morning when San Juan bowed to Mary and told her that her Son was not dead, but was down there in the fiesta and Mary cried out to all her followers, "Let's go see my loving Son and meet Him in the middle of the road."

To a people that had lost so many sons and daughters, the hope of reunion was especially poignant and I envied their faith, for I couldn't believe I'd ever see Trace again, and our meeting in some heavenly fiesta couldn't help me now. I longed for him in the flesh with my flesh, wanted him to know our son, be his father and my man. I had no other, no matter how many years I was married to Court.

Summer followed Easter and unrest grew. In Sonora, newsmen critical of the Díaz government were jailed as were the officers of the Cananea Anti-Reelectionist Club. In San

Luis Potosí, Coahuila, Aguascalientes, and Nuevo León, Maderista rallies were forbidden and all anti-Díaz publicity was banned.

Hundreds of Madero supporters were in jail all over Mexico, and Court predicted that their leader would shortly join them if he wasn't assassinated first. I prayed for the life of that small, gentle man as I had for nothing since I abandoned hope for Trace. Madero was a chance for justice with peace in Mexico—a bloodless revolution. If he died, whirlwinds would rage, destroying the oppressed with the oppressors.

Early in June, Madero was imprisoned in Monterrey. Fearing he'd be secretly murdered, his wife stayed in jail with him. At the same time there were uprisings in Yucatán, which were ruthlessly crushed. The primary election would be held June 26 and there was absolutely no doubt that Díaz intended to win.

I told Court I would like Jon to have his birthday at Las Coronas. Mexican-style, we celebrated his saint's name day rather than his actual birth date in May. The Day of San Juan was also Midsummer's Night, June 24, and the best of feasts for a boy on a ranch because there were contests of vaquero skills. I had never seen the merrymaking, but this year I wished to take my son and make him known to the leather-tough men who would greet him one day as *dueño*—if our world lasted.

Court considered my request. I seldom asked for anything. When I did, it gave him a sensation of power he savored to the utmost, a subtle tyranny that pleased him more than the physical dominance he could exert over my will.

"An excellent idea, my love." His tawny eyes were unreadable and I had learned long ago that a smile on that long well-shaped mouth meant nothing. "As you say, he should become acquainted with Las Coronas. It will give him something to remember."

Though my lips smiled on, something cold fixed about my heart. "Of course, it won't be long before we should go again. He needs to understand the life of the ranch, since he'll own it one day."

"Don't be old-fashioned, Miranda," Court said, yawning.

"He can hire a foreman if the place is still in the family when he grows up. What he needs now is a gentleman's education."

I stared. The chill had entered my heart and seemed to freeze it to stillness. "I—I teach him. And he's very young."

"So were you."

Just that. For seconds, I couldn't, wouldn't, comprehend.

"You were Jon's age when your father took you to that English school," Court said blandly.

"England? Court, you—you won't."

"No need for that," he agreed kindly, rising to help me sit down and keeping my hand in his steel-hard fingers. "There are good schools in New England. An excellent one in a town where I have a maiden aunt. I'm sure she'll be delighted to have him for weekends now and then. And he can come to us for long holidays, naturally."

A maiden aunt of Court's instead of Caguama and his playmates, a village and household that loved and indulged him? Remembering my own lonely childhood exile, I made an animal sound.

"Court, you can't mean this! It—it's cruel!"

He laughed. "Was the sainted Jonathan Greenleaf cruel then?"

"That—that was different! He was English. He hoped I'd stay in England. But he'd never have done it if he'd known how lost and afraid I felt."

"What you say confirms my fears, darling. You spoil the boy. Clinging to a mother's skirts is very well for a girl, but a boy must learn to keep his chin up even if he is lonely."

Clenching my hands, I tried to think of some appeal, some argument to reach this man. I knew he was enjoying my distress and I hated him for that, hated the complete control he had over my life. Open defiance would only harden his resolve.

Swallowing, I said thickly, "Could I go with him? He could live with me and go to day school."

"You'd like that, wouldn't you?" drawled Court, idly tracing the line of my jaw. "No, dear wife, I'll never let you go."

Something snapped. "You—you're jealous of him," I blazed. "You can't bear me to love him!"

Court gazed at me, eyes dilating till the gold was almost obscured. I feared him, but hate was stronger. I spat the words at him. "You know he's not yours. You know—"

Court slapped me so hard that my ears rang. Blood trickled from the side of my mouth. Calmly, he produced a snowy handkerchief and stopped the flow.

"I'm sorry, my dear, but when you exhibit such hysteria, I must check it. Jon, of course, is my son. Fortunately." His eyes gripped mine; I could scarcely breathe. Court went on in velvet tones more terrifying than rage. "If Jon were not mine, he wouldn't be celebrating his feast day this month. There are countless poor women who will nurture a child for a few pesos and I fear even a mother would never find him."

Would there never be a time he couldn't gag me, force me to bow to his will? If I made continuing trouble about Jon's being sent to the United States, my son could vanish. I knew well enough I'd been incredibly lucky that Court had decided to acknowledge him.

Open battle would bring disaster. I must play for time and think.

"Surely he needn't leave for school till fall," I said.

Court looked surprised but relaxed slightly. "There's more to it than simply school, Miranda. When Díaz is reelected, as he will be, all hell will cut loose unless he names an acceptable vice-president. We'd better get Jon out of the country while we can."

"But—but he can have his day of San Juan at the ranch?"

Court kissed me, and when I was quiet, he lifted me in his arms. "Yes, love. We'll celebrate his feast, and then as quickly as possible, we'd better get him off to New England."

That was one of Court's more inventive nights, but though I obeyed his wishes as if drugged, I couldn't think of anything except that I was losing Jon.

Unless I could think of something. Unless I could find a way . . .

17

We arrived at Las Coronas the night before San Juan and attended Mass early on the saint's day, with Jon squirming between us in the suede *charro* suit old Emilio had lovingly hand-stitched and adorned with silver braid and conchos. Jon was impatient to mix with these people who called him Juanito and were already by way of spoiling him. Enrique, married now to Consuelo who had two little boys, had promised to teach Jon roping. Lázaro, the foreman, had a pony gentled for him, and Catalina, Consuelo, Lupe, and the other women were stuffing him on *pan dulce*, brown sugar candy, and orange conserve.

The chapel was crowded with folk of the hacienda, most strangers, all clean and dressed in their best. After Mass, guitars sounded from the shade and girls tucked flowers in their long shining hair while several beefs and two young goats barbecued over smoldering pit fires down in the clearing by the main corrals.

I'd explained to Enrique that Caguama was Jon's companion and asked the vaquero to make sure he was well received. Seris, because of their reputed cannibalism and lack of exposure to Christianity, were despised and feared by Mexicans, and Jon was so enthralled with new sights and people that his five-year-old sense of responsibility for his big friend might not be dependable.

Enrique assured me he'd look after both Jon and Caguama. "I am your man forever, lady," he said extravagantly. We both evidently felt it would be poor taste to recall that I had protected his wife from casual rape by the man who was now my husband.

I would have liked to forbid the cock fights, but Court pointed out that if I banned them from the *fiesta*, they'd simply take place in secret. The racing and roping and bull-tailing would be better held after the heat of the day, so while Court strode about playing *patrón*, I went to chat with Consuelo and Catalina, who were making tortillas by the dozen.

Time had gnarled Catalina even more, but Consuelo was plump and matronly, very happy, she confided, with Enrique, who never got drunk or beat her or chased other women. It was almost six years since I'd seen them and I let them do most of the talking, for I had no wish to explain why Reina had been at Mina Rara when she died, or how she'd betrayed me after I went surety for her, or how Trace had vanished in Yucatán and why I was married to Court Sanders.

"Ay, señora, when we heard the Yaquis had you, we burned many candles," remembered Catalina, shaking her gray head. "We were glad to hear you were at the mine, though we wished you were with us. However, one must live with one's husband. It is a joy to see the little Jonathan. You named him for your good father?"

"Yes," I replied, a tight feeling in my throat. I always grew sad when I thought of how much father would have loved his grandson.

Catalina nodded. "There is your father's way of holding his head. But those green-blue eyes, *ay de mí!* And the hair black as a raven!"

Consuelo was frowning. "I only knew one with eyes like that. The *tejano*, Trace Winslade." Her own eyes widened as she glanced up at me, startled at what her unthinking remark suggested.

"No doubt it is a common color among the English," her mother said quickly while my face burned.

I was extremely grateful that Court hadn't overheard. If others observed Jon's striking resemblance to Trace and whispers grew to rumor, I was terrified at what he might do.

No, even if he hadn't determined to send Jon away, the days of comparative peace were over. I must get away with Jon. Somehow. But where?

Bitter, bitter, that I couldn't take refuge in my own ranch. Supposing I announced to Court that I would remain at Las Coronas with my son? Legally he was my master; he could make me leave, and if those who remembered my parents resisted, he would see they died for it.

There was one way. I could murder him. Or Enrique might do it for me. My heart leaped at the thought of freedom even as it chilled at the means. I would kill Court if he threatened Jon or was a serious danger to him, but it was not in me to kill in cold blood and I wouldnt't put it on someone else.

The only thing for it was to run away with Jon. And at that point my brain whirred like faulty machinery. Who could help? Dr. Trent was too old, even if his drinking hadn't made him a dubious support. I had no money but it seemed reasonable that I could get some in exchange for bits of the curious twisted pieces of almost solid gold Court kept in a specimen case, locked in his office. He never made any effort to hide his keys from me.

I was less worried about money than where to go. Court would find me in any Mexican city and had enough business contacts in Arizona to make that nearby part of the United States seem hazardous. California appealed to me most. The thin strip of northern Mexico leading toward it was desolate and wild, but Court would never dream of my attempting that route.

Nor could I, without a guide.

For a desperate moment I thought of asking Enrique, but discarded the notion at once. He didn't know that region. Besides, there was a chance we'd be caught, and though I'd already tasted the worst Court could do to me, he'd kill anyone who tried to help me.

Consuelo's words drew me back to the present. " . . . if she could be the child you sheltered? Very beautiful, they say, but La Grulla has only one foot."

"La Grulla?" I questioned, heart thudding. "Has she been to Las Coronas?"

"Not that we know of!" Catalina crossed herself. "She and her man made very cunning raids on the railroad and other haciendas but never here. And they have not raided at all since the ruling that five hundred *pacíficos* would be deported for each attack." She lifted one thin hunched shoulder as she expertly slapped a tortilla thin. "Who knows? Perhaps La Grulla is dead. Perhaps she had a baby and stopped fighting like a man."

By no stretch of mind could I imagine Sewa killing people, but La Grulla's sparing of Las Coronas sounded as if the legendary leader might indeed be my onetime beloved sister-child. Once again I had a brief spurt of hope, of trying to escape to the old stronghold and beg refuge.

But Court might think of that; if he pushed Ruiz, there could be an all-out effort to crush the little band. Another thing to remember: when I left, I must leave a note or message telling Court I was leaving Mexico so he wouldn't harass my friends.

Smiling crookedly to myself, I decided to tell a prodigious lie while I was at it, say I was returning to England and that he was welcome to divorce me for desertion. But the sharp spur of urgency deflated such grandiose plans. First—and within a few weeks—I must find a way to escape Mina Rara.

Musicians were tuning up outside, playing guitars and fiddles, tooting out bright brassy music on their trumpets.

> He is a little purple bull,
> And has a dun back.
> They have not been able to rope him
> And they blame it on the horse.

As the most oppressive heat waned, the races began. Fleet horses, skillful riders. I remembered when Trace had taken me to see the *manadas*, and even now a warm languorous sensation ran from my center through my thighs and legs. Trace, my lover, my man. I would never love again as I had loved him; I did not think that I would love at all.

Enrique won the races with a rangy coyote dun. Lázaro had asked me to present the prizes, and it was a special pleasure to give an old friend a pair of ornate silver spurs. He was so fine a horseman they would be mostly for show.

Next the men tailed bulls, flipping them if they were lucky, coming out of the saddle into churning dust and a fast scramble from sharp horns if they were not. That prize, a silver-trimmed *fiesta* hat, went to Angel Contreras; Consuelo whispered that he was the oldest son of Felipe, the man who had loosened my girth at Reina's order but then died trying to defend me at the train robbery.

And as dust turned the sunset orange-crimson, rawhide reatas looped on the forefeet of untamed mares. Lázaro Pérez, as might be expected of one so long in charge of horses, bowed deep, teeth flashing beneath his graying moustache, as he claimed a suede vest with silver buttons.

The long twilight settled in. Music grew louder and barrels of tequila and pulque were opened while all the hacienda people feasted. Ordinarily I had little appetite, but this night I hungered for a plate of barbecue beans, and tamales with some of Catalina's good tortillas. Court indulged me and we sat on a serape-spread bench while Jon ate with Enrique and Consuelo's boys. I didn't see Caguama and was deciding to have a look around for him after the meal when a commotion broke out down by the dark corrals.

"Only tequila and some real or imagined insult," Court said in my ear, taking my wrist as I started to rise instinctively. "Don't fret about it, love! This is *fiesta!*"

But it sounded more desperate than that. Then I saw Jon diving into the shadows, shouting outrage. Wresting free of Court, I ran after my son as Lázaro, Enrique, and several other vaqueros hurried to the brawl.

Caguama lay crumpled by the corral. Three young men crouched dazedly as Jon laid into them with the whip Court had given him. I dragged him back. He struggled and sobbed against me. "They were kicking Caguama," he cried furiously.

"I'll kill them, Mama. Let me go." Glimpsing Court, who was close behind, Jon panted sobbingly, "You'll let me whip them, won't you, Papa?"

"Hush!" I scarcely knew my own voice—or my child. I wrung the whip from him, dropping to my knees. "Oh, Jon! Jon! Will you hit men who can't hit back?"

His breath jerked his small chest, and even in the shadows I knew those eyes, glinting turquoise; oh, God, I knew those eyes and I heard Court chuckling, knew the vaqueros waited, and I thought bleakly, *Trace, why did you leave me a son if you couldn't help me raise him?* What if Court took the force inherited from Trace and warped it to cruelty, to imperious self-will?

Jon pointed to the men who stood shamed in the flickering light cast from the fires of the merrymaking. "They hit Caguama, Mama. They knocked him down and kicked him because he's a Seri." He blinked manfully at tears he couldn't stop. "Mama, I have to take care of Caguama."

"Of course," I agreed. "And you were right to stop the vaqueros. But a word from you would have done it. You didn't need the whip."

He stared at it longingly. "I wanted it. I wanted to hurt them. I still do." Again he looked past me to Court. "I can whip them, Papa? Or you will?"

Court lifted amused eyebrows. "Well, my love?" he asked softly. "The boy has more aptitude for this country than you will ever learn. Don't you think he should demonstrate that his servants are not to be mistreated?"

"The vaqueros are his people, too, Court. Will you let him, at five, think he can beat men who displease him?" It conjured up those old nightmares—of Trace being whipped, of Lío dying—and white-hot anger mixed with grief as I threw words at Court with as much intent and precision as if they'd been knives. "Why are you doing this? If you think that ruining my son will break my heart, you're right, but I don't think you'll care for the other results."

"Careful, my dear," warned my husband.

I turned to Lázaro. "These men who attacked a stranger

shall have no more share in the *fiesta*. They shall go at once to their homes."

Lázaro bowed and spoke sharply to the skulking men who ducked their heads toward me and faded into the night. Caguama had risen now and put his hand on Jon's shoulder.

"Thank you, Juanito," he said slowly. "I do not argue with your mother. She is right. The others, these of Las Coronas, are your men, too. It is not good to begin as *dueño*, on your first feast day here, by using the whip."

His face was bloody. I sent him to wash up and get salve from Catalina. Lázaro and Enrique went with him, evidently constituting themselves as a bodyguard to see no more roisterers took out their high spirits on Jon's companion. Jon glanced from Court to me, still scowling.

"If they do it again—"

"If you had kept Caguama with you instead of taking up with your new friends and making him feel awkward, this wouldn't have happened," I said firmly. "Go back to the *fiesta* or to bed, if you're tired."

He dug his boot in the ground, very winning in his soft leather and silver. "May I have my whip?"

Before I could say no, Court took it from me and restored it to Jon, who was sensible enough not to cast me a look of triumph as he ran off.

"You should admire the way Jon defended his servant," Court observed.

"I'm glad he defended his friend, but not that he was ready to use the whip once the men had stopped their bullying."

Court shrugged. "He will have power. He must learn to use it."

"Exactly."

Sweeping my stiff body into his arms, Court nuzzled my ear. "Well, then, sweetheart, don't you see you're far more likely to get the gentleman you want by sending him east? In the long run, you'll be pleased with the outcome. Shall we dance for a while in the firelight before I take you to that incredible Spanish bed with its pillars that could hold up a roof instead of a canopy?"

I danced because I knew the people would like it, and it was in my mind that I might never be back, though I hoped Jon would someday come to claim his heritage. So I danced with Court, clapped and laughed and sang with my people, and even managed a smile when Court rose, his fingers tight on the pulse of my wrist, and led me to the house.

We got back to Mina Rara to learn that, predictably, Díaz had won the election, with Corral for his running mate. "Díaz and Death" was what that combination was popularly called, but Madero and other liberals were trying to persuade Díaz to name a more acceptable vice-president before time to take new office on October 4.

Dr. Trent thought Díaz would have to listen, but Court scoffed. "Not the Strong Man! Corral's his boy and he'll keep him. There'll be an explosion. We'll just have to hope Díaz can ride it out and that the revolutionaries are all as softhearted and dreamy as Madero, or too damn disorganized to pull down the government."

"Corral's dying of syphilis," said the doctor. "Two years at most, I've heard. The pair of them may die soon enough to head off real trouble." He snorted. "Looks like that's the only way Mexico will ever be rid of Díaz and his slave-selling whoremaster—begging your pardon, Miranda."

After Dr. Trent had gone to his quarters, Court rose to stare out at the night. "We'd better get Jon settled as soon as possible. We'll have to get new clothes for him in the United States, so you needn't pack much. Can't have him wearing leather breeches and boots at a proper New England school." Turning, hands behind him, Court looked at me in a way that forbade argument. "Can you be ready next week?"

If I yielded too readily, he might grow suspicious. I'd be ready next week—had to be—but not for what Court intended. For a long moment, as if debating argument, I gazed into those golden eyes and found them alien and remote as a hawk's. I was no longer angry with him; since my decision to run away, he'd become less a human enemy and more an obstacle like the long, arduous miles between here and California. I wouldn't try to plead or reason or consider him anymore except as a hazard that had to be assessed as coolly as possible, then coped with.

At last, when Court's mouth hardened and he took a step forward, I inclined my head. "As you say, I won't need to pack much. We can be ready."

"That's my darling," he approved, caressing my cheek. "We'll stop in New York and give you a few days in the shops, eh? Anything you want."

I didn't point out that he was being generous with my money. The less energy I spent on minor quarrels, the better. I felt I was scarcely there when he swept me up and carried me to our room.

I had to get away. By next week. But how?

Jon protested, first angrily, then with tears, when Court told him about school. "Can I take Cascos Lindos and my pony?" he demanded.

"No, son. They'll be better off waiting for you here."

Jon gnawed his lips and blinked mightily before he tried again. "But Caguama, he can stay with me, Papa?"

Court shook his head in sympathetic amusement. "No, Jon. He's too old and you'll have your lessons and new friends. My aunt will spoil you terribly, I imagine."

Jon's sniff left little doubt of his valuation of aunts. "I can't leave Caguama. You've got Mama, Papa, but he doesn't have anyone but me." He glanced appealingly in my direction.

Feeling treacherous, I said nothing. It would be too dangerous to tell him he wasn't going north, not if I could help it; for the time he must believe he was indeed bound for school in the United States.

"I'll hate it," he said wildly. "I—I'll be so bad and stupid they'll send me back. I will, I will—"

Court had never struck or spanked Jon. Now, as if maddened, he slapped the child. Not hard, but the finger-marks stood out livid on Jon's reddened cheek. Gasping, Jon slipped from his chair and dodged past Court, running outside. I started after him, but Court caught my arm.

"It's high time he had some discipline, Miranda. Let him come to terms with what has to be."

"Strange that the only time you think he needs discipline is when he defies you," I couldn't resist saying, furious at the unnecessary brutality.

Court flushed. His broad shoulders hunched defensively. I suspected he was beginning to admit the truth of Jon's fathering, if only beneath the level of rational thought. How could it be otherwise when Jon was every day a more faithful mirroring of Trace?

"Be ready Wednesday," Court said, turning.

Resigned to a fate he didn't fully comprehend, Jon kept slipping treasures into the leather trunk standing open in his room. Bits of ore, the harpoon Caguama had made him, his rawhide reata, the old stuffed bunny he slept with, and, of course, that damned whip. I was tempted several times to clear his woebegone face by telling him he wasn't going to the school, but I still had found no means of escape and time was getting terrifyingly short.

Then one evening when Colonel Ruiz stopped for a drink and Court said that we were taking Jon to the United States, the colonel's elegantly expressed regret at our coming absence gave me sudden inspiration. I knew Ruiz had at least the obligatory *macho* interest in me. Could that, without too much risk, be nurtured into his preventing our departure in the name of national security, our own safety, or some such excuse?

A frail hope, but my only apparent one. Delay while I looked for some means of escape, someone to help. If that failed, my only desperate alternative was to plunge myself into the wilderness and hope it took Court a long time to find me. I couldn't take Jon on such a dangerous flight, but it might jolt Court into realizing that his only way to keep me was not to send away my son. And it might also harden his resolve; he could send Jon north and keep me virtually a prisoner.

The circular maze always fetched me back to the grim knowledge that none of my choices were good. But I would start with Ruiz. The morning after he'd stopped by, I went to visit Chepa's mother, who lived near the small garrison. The soldiers had built adobe barracks for themselves, a storehouse, and headquarters, on the slope above the miners' homes. Anytime I was in the area, Ruiz usually appeared as if by chance and escorted me home after my errand or call. This kept me away from the village, except for sickness, births, deaths, or weddings, but today I drew a dizzying breath of relief when I saw him coming out of headquarters, saying something to the sentry that made the young man straighten as if he had a bayonet for a spine.

Saying good-bye to Chepa's mother, a widow who supported her younger children by doing laundry for both soldiers and miners, I started homeward, pretending surprise when the colonel called my name.

He bowed over my hand, which I didn't withdraw. "I am devastated, señor, that you will be gone for what will seem eternities." His white teeth flashed and his dark eyes clung to my mouth. *"Por favor*, entice your husband to bring you again to your own land as quickly as may be."

I sighed. "Colonel, if my powers of enticement were as great as you flatteringly seem to think them, we would not be making this trip at all."

"Indeed, señora?" He knit his brow and I could almost see the lightning play of speculation in his mind. "Then I both condole with and envy your husband."

"Colonel?"

He smiled, in his lean ranginess reminding me of a black panther so controlled that one was prone to treat him like a house pet till the claws arced into their prey. "Who would not envy the husband of such a beautiful lady?" he murmured. "And who would not pity him for incurring her displeasure, though doubtless for a necessary end?"

"Forgive me, Colonel, but I cannot feel it necessary to have Jon educated in a foreign country. This is home. I believe he should grow up here."

"Your patriotism does you credit," said Ruiz, scanning me carefully.

I gave him a look full of suffering and wistfulness. "Alas, sir, I know the pain of being alien in two countries. I would spare Jon that."

He pondered as we walked along. "Since the election there

is much unrest," he mused. "Not a good time for traveling.
And if foreign investors appear to be leaving Mexico, it would
not be healthy for the economy."

"That's true." I nodded, hardly daring to breathe while I
looked vastly impressed with his grasp of the situation.

We passed the school, the store, the doctor's house, paused
at the entrance of my home. "I will think about it," Ruiz said.
He bent his dark handsome head over my hand, which I felt
like jerking free in a stinging rush of disappointment and
chagrin.

"There's not much time, Colonel Ruiz. This is Monday. We
are to leave very early Wednesday."

"That *is* soon," he agreed. His fleeting smile showed that he
knew quite well that I'd been maneuvering for his help.
"Perhaps, most charming lady, if we both think on the
problem, we will be inspired. I would be glad, of course, to
reason with your husband, point out the difficulties—"

"You know he'd ignore that!"

Ruiz shrugged. "You are doubtless correct, señora. A man
who will not be moved by your wishes could scarcely heed a
plain soldier's unofficial advice."

Now . . .

Forced to it, I tried to frame words while he watched me
blandly. "You have said there might be undesirable results
from our going, Colonel, apart from our personal safety. Do
you not have discretion to prohibit acts you judge contrary to
the country's interests?"

"Oh, I can prohibit. But your husband would go over my
head and no doubt he could present the matter so that it
would sound beneficial to Mexico."

I knew that but had frantically searched for even a delay.
Defeat sour in my mouth, I kept my head high and managed a
smile. "Thank you for your concern, Colonel. If you will
excuse me, I must be about our packing."

"But there might be other circumstances," he went on.

I halted. "What?"

His eyes caressed my throat and breasts as he gave a lazy lift
of his shoulder. "Perhaps you have noticed irregularities in
the señor's conduct? Mysterious visitors, puzzling details it

should not be too hard to get servants to vouch for?"

"You mean Court is spying? Smuggling?" At Ruiz's amusedly patronizing smile, I straightened with shock. "Colonel, I won't falsely accuse a man of such charges."

"Even if he is about to separate you and your small son?"

I stared back coldly.

"An interesting thought," Ruiz amused. "Americans have unusual temptations and opportunities in Mexico. It would almost be a wonder if the señor had not erred now and again."

It was one thing to hope Ruiz might block our departure, quite another to connive at Court's imprisonment. And my revulsion at the scheme was not totally on his behalf, once I had a chance to think about it.

Simple for a commander to see that a suspect is shot "while escaping"—easy to plant evidence and buy witnesses. And if I were left a sudden widow . . . I shivered at the officer's eyes, which flickered as if coals burned far back in their darkness. I'd been forced into one marriage. I didn't want there to be a second.

"Please, Colonel." I laid my hand on his arm. "I'm sorry to have troubled you with private matters. Thank you, but put this out of your mind."

"Dear lady, the matter seems not so private after all. Be assured I will carry out my duty." His face was expressionless as he turned away, but I sensed a ruthlessness I hadn't seen unleashed since Cruz burned.

Staring after him, I felt overwhelming panic. What had I set in motion? How could I stop it? I didn't completely hate Court; in his way he'd taken care of me and been father to Jon. I didn't want to be responsible for his death and I feared that was what it came to, for Ruiz must be sure he covered his tracks. Holding Court on charges would be too risky, but apprehending a smuggler in the act, an American perhaps distributing rifles and ammunition to rebels . . .

Oh, Ruiz could concoct almost any story and make it credible. Unlikely that my word would be taken over his, even if there were not horrid probabilities of his ensuring my silence by threats to Jon or the peaceable Yaqui miners.

How could I have blundered so badly? The man I'd thought

to dominate with a smile had now become infinitely more dangerous than Court, who at least would not hurt Jon.

As Trace would have put it, I had played hell. Now I must run across the coals and try to ward off an avalanche of brimstone. I was starting for Court's office when I saw him coming down the walk. For the first time in all our married life I went to meet him.

The pleased surprise that had shone on his face dimmed as Court looked down at me and his bleached heavy brows drew together. "What's wrong, love? Jon—"

I shook my head, my throat so constricted with guilt and dread that I couldn't speak. Court swept me toward the house, his arm around me, made me sit down and poured wine.

"If it's not Jon, it can't be too bad," he soothed. "Drink up, sweet, and let's have it." His head jerked back suddenly and his eyes went hard as polished brass. "I saw Ruiz leave you. Miranda. Did he dare—"

"He didn't bother me," I blurted. "But I—I'm afraid he means to accuse you of smuggling or something like it. He said Americans have many temptations and opportunities."

"Hell, would I smuggle?" demanded Court. "He can't have any proof, because there isn't any! I'll go have it out with that crazy one right now."

I caught his wrist as he swung toward the arch. "No, Court. He won't *care* that it's a lie. Don't you see? He can shoot you if you argue or try to get away."

For seconds, Court gazed at me as if I'd gone mad, before belief gradually dawned. "By God, he *could* get away with it, couldn't he? With the whole country in turmoil, uprisings everywhere, no one's going to worry much about an American killed for resisting arrest for running guns. Neat. I'm surprised he's not gone higher than colonel." To my utter confusion, Court burst into laughter, head lifting back on his powerful neck, before he sobered. "I admire ambition, but I don't mean to be Ruiz's stepping-stone," he growled. "Especially not when it's clear he's crazy for you and would try to console your loneliness before I was properly cold." Rubbing his chin, Court stared toward the garrison, the Mexican flag rippling green, red, and white in the breeze. "Have any idea when he'll start his comedy?"

"Soon, I think. He may guess I've told you."

"Strange he'd hint his plan to you." Court frowned. "What did he say exactly?"

"He asked if you had any mysterious visitors, if your behavior was unusual." Guiltily, I used the truth, though not all of it. "And then he said what I told you about opportunities."

Court deliberated. I knew that his quick shrewd mind was trying out positions, discarding, altering, testing. "It's the devil of a mess," he said after what seemed a long time. "I don't have enough weapons to arm our miners and they'd be no match for soldiers anyway. If we could make it to Las Coronas, we could stand him off till I could get word to friends who'd settle his little game. But I can't leave you and Jon and he's bound to have sentries watching now he's tipped his hand." Court slapped his hand to his knee. "Hell, I'll give the bastard a dose of his own physic."

"What do you mean?"

Court gave a wolf smile. "I'm going to do the government a big favor by locking up an officer who's plotting to throw in with rebels. His men don't love him, and some would sell their grandmothers for a few pesos. There'll be witnesses."

"But what if he disproves the charge?"

Court shrugged. "All I care about at the moment is putting him where he can't get at me. And a bribe or two can ensure he isn't reassigned to Mina Rara even if he can beat the treason count, which I doubt. His family have no money or influence."

"But how will you lock him up?"

"I'll walk into headquarters and have a gun on him before he can blink. Once Ruiz is my prisoner, the rest is child's play. Captain Ortega, his second in command, might even file the charges if I made it worth his while." Court brushed a kiss on my cheek as he concealed his Colt .38 beneath his shirt and pulled on a loose vest. "Don't fret, love. I'll have this gun in his ribs before he can say 'Buenos días.' "

He strode out, whistling. If he had any doubt of the

outcome, it didn't show. I had to admire him. I also had to think what to do whichever way the encounter went.

If Court subjugated Ruiz, he might have to stay in Mexico long enough to push the officer's trial. If Ruiz killed Court, I had better take Jon, with whatever supplies I could gather, and get away. But if Court was arrested, locked up till an opportune time for slaughter . . . Damn it, I would have to try to free him since I'd caused the mess.

My head whirled, but I put down the wine and hurriedly began to assemble, for immediate flight, necessities I'd been secreting. I sent Chepa for Caguama. He could have Cascos Lindos and another sturdy *burro* waiting behind the stables along with dried meat, dried peaches and quinces, rice and beans, blankets, two changes of clothing for Jon and me, and other necessities stowed into packs that could be tied behind the *burros'* saddles. Water would be our most important need, but was heavy.

Two water skins? Three? My head throbbed and I tried not to panic as I wondered what was happening at the headquarters.

Caguama came while I was slipping the twisted pieces of gold into a leather pouch containing my jewels. I always wore my mother's crucifix, of course, with its turquoise the color of my dead love's eyes. I had only a few coins, but hoped the cheaper jewelry would serve for barter till I reached a place where I could sell the gold and the truly valuable ornaments.

Caguama's first loyalty was to Jon, his second to me. He wouldn't give away my plans, if they could be dignified with that name. So I told him what was needed, but though he nodded understanding, he didn't go at once but stood shifting his feet.

"Well?" I asked sharply.

"You go away, lady? You and Juanito?"

"Yes, my friend. You know my husband wishes to send Jon far away to school."

"So Juanito has told me, lady. You run to keep Juanito with you. But you have no guide, no men?"

"I did not know whom to trust."

Caguama glared at me accusingly. "You can trust me."

"But the señor will be very angry," I protested. "If he catches us, he might even kill anyone who helped us."

The young Seri's grin exposed the gap in his teeth. "He must first catch, lady. Where do you go?"

I told him my vague notions of how to reach California. He shook his head, appalled. "I can take you. That is my country, at least part. But alone! You and the child? Oh, lady, you would die!"

"If you take us, the señor would put a price on you."

He laughed and scratched his ear. "Then I would be worth something, *pero no*? To escape along the coast, lady, you are better with one Seri than with fifty soldiers or vaqueros."

His confidence raised my spirits. "If we get away safe, my friend, we will owe you much."

"I wish one thing." The smile faded from his broad features. "To be with Juanito." He began to collect the supplies and said he'd see to water and *burros*, after we arranged that I'd slip away with Jon as early as possible that evening.

"Juanito does not know yet?" the Seri asked.

I explained briefly about Ruiz and Court. "It has all happened fast, Caguama. If the colonel locks the señor up, I must try to free him. But whether we run from my husband or the commander, we had better run tonight."

"I will be ready." He hesitated. "If Señor Sanders does not return soon, do you wish me to find out what has happened?"

"I—I don't know, Caguama. Be watchful, but don't go to the garrison unless I ask you."

He went out and I ran to the veranda, peered toward the headquarters. Sentries patrolled and a squad was drilling, but I could see nothing unusual.

What was going on? Surely Court would move quickly since surprise was his chief ally. If he pulled off the audacious play, he'd have to win Captain Ortega, make sure there'd be no problems from the garrison. It seemed to me that he'd been gone longer than all that could have taken.

Inwardly chilled in spite of the July heat, I leaned my face against the wall and tried to think what to do if Court was gone much longer, for that would mean Ruiz had taken him.

Should I go to headquarters and try to make some bargain with the colonel? Or let Caguama determine where Court was being held and then somehow get him loose? If only I'd never tried to influence Ruiz to block our journey! I was resolved now to escape, whatever happened, but by bringing Ruiz into the situation, I had multiplied the problems. Now I had two men to elude, one of whom, my husband—no matter how ill he'd used me—I couldn't leave under virtual death sentence.

Jon darted in with several small friends and I told them to go get lunch from Raquel or Chepa. My heart contracted as shouts and laughter rang back down the hall. Jon had never been hungry or thirsty, and if anyone in the world wasn't his friend, he was happily oblivious to it.

Suppose I took him to his death? What if we were lost or robbed because I wouldn't let him be sent away? Was I being selfish to risk him?

My thoughts roved back to when I was his age, when I begged my father and mother to let me stay with them. Offered a choice of England or a trip such as the desperate one I'd planned, which would I have chosen? The trip, of course.

He would have one parent, one friend, and one burro. Trace, am I doing right? No answer—there never had been in all these years that I had hoped for some sense of communication.

With growing dread I watched the distant garrison. And then my heart froze as a man came out of headquarters, saluted the guard, and started in my direction.

The colonel, and he was not waiting till dark.

18

My impulse was to run to my room, but I forced it down. I would go to meet him, demand to see my husband. Instinctively I knew if I showed fear, Ruiz would pounce. He would anyway, but boldness, all the cool imperiousness I could muster, might fend him off till I could do something for Court and escape with Jon and Caguama. I refused to even think that Court might be past help; there had been no shots. Ruiz probably needed time to think before his final action.

Walking rapidly but without flurry, I met the colonel by the school. "Where is my husband?" I asked flatly.

"Under guard in my office." Ruiz permitted himself a slight smile. "I must admit I was startled to be facing a revolver, but fortunately, my aide walked in and stretched the señor out with his rifle butt." Dark eyes played over me, gathering heat. "I was amazed, Doña Miranda, that you told the señor of our plans."

"Arresting him was not my plan, Colonel. I had hoped you might forbid our departure on grounds of safety or national interest. I am horrified at what has happened and feel much to blame."

"For that I have much sorrow, but when you see the advantages you should be reconciled."

"I will not be reconciled if harm befalls my husband. I wish to see him."

Ruiz shook his head, sighed eloquently. "Ladies! Never knowing what they want. First this, then that, changeable as mists." His tone lost its playfulness. "Perhaps they need a man to tell them what they want and make them like it."

"Speaking for myself only, Colonel, I know perfectly what I want in this case—the señor's release."

"I am grieved not to oblige you, Doña Miranda, but I have my duty."

"Which is to investigate suspicions. When you discover these to be unfounded, Colonel, you will naturally release my husband, who, also naturally, will be most grateful."

I could amost trace his thoughts as he studied me, eyes narrowed. He could put Court out of the way, actually rape me if his blandishments didn't work, but he couldn't be sure that I'd marry him. It was even possible that I'd kill myself, and he'd have had considerable annoyance for nothing.

He desired me, but he also had visions of wealth. At this point I wasn't going to balk at hints that might swing the balance. "Yes," I repeated. "The señor would be grateful. As would I, Colonel, though I would express my gratitude in a different manner."

He caught his breath. Passion radiated from him. "Doña Miranda, if I could believe that—" His thin hawk face appeared to swell, and he touched his tongue to his lips. "Not that I doubt your word, but once your husband is released certain things might prove difficult." He bowed over my hand, but turned up the palm and kissed it lingeringly. "Let me pursue my investigation this afternoon. Then if you will allow me to call this evening, we can discuss it thoroughly."

He meant to collect in advance. And there was no way to ensure he'd keep the bargain. But I thought of the *burros* and Caguama and steeled myself to do whatever was required in order to leave with a clear conscience about Court. Strange, I was his wife, he was the only man who had ever had me except for that single time with Trace, yet it wasn't to him I felt unfaithful, but to Trace, when I thought of sleeping with Ruiz.

"May I see my husband?" I asked again.

Ruiz laughed. "There will be time for that when my investigation is complete. But in all other things, beautiful lady, I am at your orders."

Stifling a rude one, I turned and walked back to the house. I had made a grand muddle, but at least Court's death wouldn't be on my head and I would tell the Seri to be ready to leave at any moment after dark, though the heavy doomed feeling weighing down on me made me admit Ruiz might not leave till morning.

I would ask him to write an order for Court's release and request that I might be allowed to surprise Court with it. That way I could leave the order with Dr. Trent and ask him to deliver it after I'd been gone at least eight hours.

Crossing to the patio, I found Caguama showing Jon and a friend how to make harpoon barbs of ironwood. "You killed a sea turtle as big as *you*?" Jon was asking, round-eyed.

"Tall as me and much fatter." Caguama grinned. Leaving the boys to admire the sculptured prong, he rose and came to me.

I explained in a few words that Court was under military arrest, but that I hoped to arrange his freedom that evening with Colonel Ruiz and as soon as that was done, we would leave.

"Do not worry," the young Indian said. "I have the *burros* in the stable, and everything ready. I will sleep at the door of Juanito's room, lady, and carry him out when you are ready."

If he had any notion of what arranging I must do with Ruiz, he mercifully gave no hint, though his light brown eyes were concerned. "Try to sleep," he urged. "You need to be strong tonight."

More than he knew. But along with my dread of that interlude with Ruiz and anxieties about the arduous journey, exhilaration—a sense of life, returning freedom—was waking in me. It was as if after years of numbed existence with Court I was starting to breathe again, feel blood pulsing fresh and eager.

If only Trace were alive! But at least I had his son. And tonight or early tomorrow we would leave what had been a singular kind of prison. I filled my lungs with air, hugged Jon as he ran to show me the harpoon barb, and went to write one letter to Court and another to Dr. Trent.

In the message to Court I said that I was taking Jon to the United States and that he should no longer consider me his wife. In time my legal representative would contact him about divorce and a division of property. "You know Jon is not your son," I wrote. "I believe this is really why you wish to send him away. The antipathy could only grow as he becomes older and embitter all our lives. You forced me to marriage but you've been kind to Jon. Let's cry quits and wish each other well."

I asked Dr. Trent to try to reconcile Court to my permanent absence, thanked him for his friendship during the years at Mina Rara, and put Court's letter inside his for delivery.

Pausing, I checked preparations. In the armoire my divided leather riding skirt, copied after the one Tula had taken from me, hung with a cotton shirt above my oldest and most comfortable boots, wide-brimmed felt hat, and the pouch of jewelry and gold. Jon's travel clothes were ready on a shelf in his room. I could help him dress, briefly explaining the journey, while Caguama got the burros loaded.

That left getting Court's release and the letters to Dr. Trent. I decided to entrust that trip to Raquel. No danger of her trying to stop my flight. She'd be delighted to have Court to herself and she could also be relied on to see that the doctor carried out his mission promptly, though again she wouldn't rush Court's freedom prematurely for fear of his overtaking me. How perfectly her interests and mine coincided! I could almost chuckle over it as I sought her out.

She assumed that I was riding to Hermosillo and from there would take a train to Arizona. That would be a useful impression for Court, so I didn't correct it. Her distress over

Court's detention was slightly overbalanced by my assurances that he would be released and by my plans to go away. This she plainly considered lunacy, but it was not her duty to remonstrate with the mad.

Dr. Trent appeared late that afternoon, slightly disheveled, for he'd come straight from the cantina where rumors of Court's arrest were rife. He hadn't had time to drink to befuddlement, so I explained that I was sure the colonel would release Court by the next day.

"*La mordida*, hey?" rumbled the doctor. "A bribe? Disgusting, but a wonder it hasn't happened before, what with the mine working quite a few Yaquis." His face clouded suddenly and his watery eyes fixed on me with unusual sharpness. "Ruiz has always fancied you, Miranda. Is that beggar—"

"He's not asking what I can't give."

After six years with a man I didn't love, another night wouldn't kill me. I'd learned to handle the unthinkable by not thinking about it—not a good choice for free people, but a way for prisoners to at least endure.

I was tempted to tell this old man who'd shared his books and thoughts with me, much lightening my captivity, that I was going away, but I feared he'd never understand and might feel he had a responsibility either to stop me or to come along. So I gave him cakes and tea and kissed him affectionately on the cheek when he departed.

"Bless us!" he said in pleased confusion. "If having old Court off the scene gets me treats like that, I don't know why I'm worrying about it. But if you have any trouble with the colonel, Miranda, break a window or scream or something."

I laughed and kissed him again. "There won't be any trouble, Doctor."

That was more confident than I felt.

Court was often needed at the mine mealtimes, so when Jon asked where he was, he accepted my answer that Court was busy. We had a simple meal of soup, chicken, and fruit in the patio, I read him a story, and by twilight he was rubbing his eyes and only put up a token argument when I tucked him in. Later, after Chepa and Raquel retired, Caguama would spread his mat by Jon's door.

I had believed myself stoically able to receive Ruiz, but as the house darkened and voices ceased, a kind of horror grew in me, dread of the colonel, fear that he might trick me, fear of the journey we faced even if everything else went smoothly; mounting irrational terror where night and Ruiz and the unknown all mingled in cold threatening darkness, surging against my intelligence and will. Each time I fought it back, a bit more of my strength crumbled, and before I could brace myself firmly, it overwhelmed me.

Lighting lamps in the *sala,* I poured myself a shot of straight whiskey, though usually I didn't drink except for wine, paced out on the veranda, and sipped it, welcoming the stinging warmth that spread from throat to belly.

Better, much better. I didn't feel so cold. How did Ruiz expect the tryst to go? I still wore my daytime dress, but a robe and some perfume might hasten the inevitable.

The only part of the impending call that I'd prepared for was pen and paper prominently laid out on a table near the decanters. If Ruiz was willing to blackmail his way into my bed, he'd hardly expect an air of high romance.

Still, appearing too much the bookkeeper might push him into reverting to his original gamble for higher stakes. I must give him enough without enflaming him to try for more by murdering Court. God, how I wished it were over, with Court's release signed and the colonel gone! Once the journey started, this last price of freedom would fade into the limbo of the last years, become a vague bad dream no worse than many others, not as bad as some.

Why didn't Ruiz appear? Tenseness building every second, I changed into a flowing robe of ivory satin and lace, took down my hair and brushed it. My anxiety was by now so great that I longed for the officer to come, end this suspense during which I could do nothing but wait.

Another drink might help. My hand shook as I poured the little glass half full and went back to the veranda. My eyes smarted as liquid fire burned down through my body, but by the time I'd taken a couple of swallows my head felt ridiculously light and warmth dissolved some of the icy dread in the pit of my stomach. I felt slowed, fuzzy, almost comfortable, but my legs were treacherously refusing to support me.

Then a figure took on solidity against the shadows, wavering as I stared, mind suddenly clear, though my head spun and my pace was unsteady as I moved toward the arch.

"Good evening, Colonel. May I offer you refreshment? Fruit, perhaps? Coffee, brandy?"

In the dim veranda his eyes glowed. "Your presence is refreshment enough, Doña Miranda, but I could enjoy savoring some brandy along with your beauty."

With tremendous effort I managed to keep my balance as I preceded him into the *sala*, gestured to the array of decanters. "Have what you wish, Colonel."

"Then I would wish that you call me Armando." He smiled, glancing at the pen and paper as he poured brandy into a crystal snifter. Saluting me with his drink, he watched me as he took a slow sip. "Now let me prove, most lovely lady, that where you are concerned I am clairvoyant."

My heart skipped, then thudded painfully. Could he have learned that I intended to vanish, that there would never be any repetition of this night? He picked up the pen, wrote, and handed the paper to me.

It was a note to Captain Ortega, ordering Court's release, since Ruiz's investigation had established innocence. "Does it content you, little dove?" asked the colonel. "See, your husband's freedom is guaranteed even if I should be sleeping late in the morning, even if I should die of joy this night." Taking the order from me, he put it beneath a bowl on the bookcase and came to stand by me, noticing the glass in my hand.

"Whiskey?" he asked, frowning. "But surely that is not your usual drink."

I had to laugh at his disapproval. "This is not my usual way to pass an evening, Colonel."

"Armando, *por favor.*"

"Armando, Colonel, señor, Commandante, Excellence." I curtsied shakily. "Have any name you desire."

His breath sucked in. "You are drunk. Drunk, by God! So *that* is how you prepare for me." He struck the glass from my hand. It shattered on the tiles. He caught me up with a brutal laugh. "Then let's find your bed, *querida*. Once I have you there, it won't matter if you are tipsy or sober."

He tore the robe off my shoulder, burning my throat with his lips. I moaned and struggled involuntarily as his mouth settled on my breast and he ripped the satin from my body, caressing me with savagely questing hands.

"I will make you drunk indeed," he whispered, laughing deep in his throat. "Fight if you like, Mirandita, it makes your honey sweeter. Ah, that honey! Soon I will have the taste of all of you—"

There was impact I heard and felt, a convulsion of his body, a tightening of his arms before he half-turned, dropped me, pitched forward on his face.

Caguama stood there, a rough ironwood mallet in his hand. Ruiz twitched forward, head lolling. Caguama struck him again at the base of the neck. The officer's whole body shuddered and went still.

"You are not hurt, lady?" asked Caguama.

"No." And I couldn't be sorry Ruiz was dead. My thoughts flew past him to what must be done. "It would be well if Ruiz's death seems an accident. Put a bottle of whiskey in his hand and tumble him off the nearest slope. I'll dress and get Jon ready and we'll go as quickly as we can."

"The señor?"

I took the relase order from the bookcase. "In the morning Dr. Trent will take this to Captain Ortega, who, I imagine, will be glad to have Señor Sanders out of his custody so neatly." I wondered that I felt no regret or horror as I passed Ruiz's corpse, but instead a trick of memory put me back in the crowd, unable to help, the day Cruz burned; he had made no sound, but the smell filled my nostrils till I forced that image away and tapped on Raquel's door.

Half an hour later, Caguama holding a drowsy Jon in Cascos Lindos' saddle, we struck northwest, avoiding the garrison and village, where a few lights and fires glowed.

Waterskins sloshed and I often got off and walked. We weren't trying for speed. Court would almost surely echo Raquel's assumption that we were bound for Hermosillo and then Arizona. By the time he cooled on that scent, I hoped to be in California. Caguama obliterated our tracks by dragging an acacia bough over them, a precaution I thought we could safely drop after we'd traveled ten miles.

It had been a problem, what to tell Jon. Court to him was an indulgent demigod but not involved in his intimate small-boy life. I certainly couldn't tell Jon, not for years if ever, the real story of my marriage, though I planned someday to tell him about his true father. It seemed best to stick to a few facts, answer questions honestly, and hope that Jon was so young that this flight would make sense to him.

I had told him as I helped him dress that Caguama was showing us the way to California because I couldn't agree with Papa that he should go away to school.

"Papa will be angry," Jon remarked.

"Yes, he will, but I don't think he has the right to make such a decision." A sudden thought struck me and I caught his hands. "Would you rather do what he says, Jon? Are you afraid to go with me?"

"Cauguama's going?"

"Yes." Court would be furious to know that a Seri led him in his supposed son's affections.

Jon hugged me hard. "I want to go with you, Mama. Don't worry, I'll take care of you. Maybe we can kill a shark with my harpoon."

"Gracious, I hope not. Here, stamp down hard in the boot."

Ruiz's killing and the need for immediate action had dispelled my slight tipsiness. The air was cool and the summer heat wouldn't become formidable till late morning when it should be safe enough to rest. The full moon washed rocks, brush, stunted trees, and cholla with luminous silver. We seemed to move in a dream across an eerie landscape that stayed remarkably the same, exchanging one line of small jagged hills for another as we kept to the passes or high plateaus.

Yet, though the surroundings seemed unreal, that sense of awakened life after years of mechanical functioning permeated every tissue of my body and brain. I breathed deep; my blood tingled, objects stood out in sharp relief. Could it make so much difference, acting from my own will rather than Court's?

It seemed to. I was excited and eager more than afraid. Jon perked up and chatted with Caguama for a while, demanding to hear tales of the country we would traverse, before he nodded off to sleep again, secure on the back of his beloved *burro*. That reminded me of Cascos Lindos' first owner, Sewa. Strange to think that a leader of warriors had once doted on a little donkey called Ratoncita, shot by Reina and replaced by the sturdy animal clopping surefootedly along.

Did Sewa remember those days? How did she think of me? In my rush of revived feeling, I ached to see her and wondered if that could ever be. If Court divorced me and lost his legal authority over me, it would be possible to return to Mexico, possible, perhaps, to find Sewa again. If she wanted to be found. Was she truly La Grulla?

But that lay far ahead. I walked till my feet hurt, rode till my thighs ached, then walked some more while the Big Dipper swung slowly around and the Polestar glittered. Out here one was very conscious of the sky.

At last I had to call a halt. Caguama could probably have walked till this time tomorrow night, but I mustn't exhaust myself and be a hindrance later. We ate and drank sparingly, rested a half-hour, and started on, paused again at sunrise, took off the animals' packs, and let them browse for an hour. I worried about their water, but Caguama said there was a seep-filled spring halfway through the next defile, and anyway the *burros* could last for several waterless days.

It was by this little water hole nestled between steep canyon walls that we made our long stop shortly before noon. The *burros* sucked up water and rolled in the sand, meandered along the valley, browsing off trees and shrubs. Even after six years in Mexico, I couldn't believe how animals subsisted, and wondered what they'd do if they were miraculously set down in a lush English meadow.

Wetting a cloth in the seep, I washed Jon and told him to lie on the blanket Caguama had spread under a rock outcropping shielded by an ironwood tree. After I had cleaned off my own top layer of dust and perspiration, I wrung out the cloth in more water and stretched it over Jon's forehead. He was flushed and there was no breeze at all.

I poured some of our drinking water on the dried fruit to soften and swell it. Caguama said that the seep water, though drinkable, could give us stomach cramps and that we should use our own supply since we'd reach sweet water in two days and could refill our bags then.

I looked at him with great respect and thankfulness, laughed ruefully. "Caguama, it's good to know there's water two days from here, and that you can find it. If you hadn't come with us, I'm afraid that right about now is when I'd decide that I mustn't risk causing Jon's death and I'd turn back."

"But I am here," Caguama pointed out. "And my people have lived along this coast since the world was set up, when the great turtle raised up the land on her back. We know what we must know to stay alive."

We ate softened fruit and chewed the leathery dried meat. "Sleep, lady," urged Caguama. "I will rest down the canyon a little way so that I will hear anything approaching."

I scrambled under the ledge beside Jon, made a hollow in the fine silt for my hip, and was asleep before I could feel uncomfortable.

It seemed only minutes before I roused to the muffled sound of the *burros'* feet. They were drinking again. Lifting Jon, I gave Caguama the blanket to go into a pack and helped Jon get on his boots. The sun was still two handbreadths above the horizon, but the grilling heat was over till next morning.

Freshened by his nap, Jon peppered Caguama with rapid-fire questions. How far was the sea? Would we meet Caguama's family? Would he make a boat? Where were the sharks? To this flood of queries Caguama responded with patience, promising that when we reached the sea we would feast.

Cabrilla, pompano, pargo flamenco, blanquillo, ronco, sardina, salema, corvina—hundreds of kinds of fish whose names made a song; lobster, turtles, and there were clams to be picked up, scallops pried from rocks in the sea.

"We never understood why people bother with cattle and plowing when there is so much to eat in the sea," said Caguama, grinning. "Ever since the Ancient of All Pelicans flapped his wings, there have been sea and sky. It was only later that the giant sea turtle heaved up from the sea to make land." He added, being fair, "Of course, along the coast there is not much for cows to eat and the land is not good to farm. Those who want herds and crops must go inland, where they can't watch the sea."

The note of longing made me say, "You must have missed it very much, Caguama."

"Yes. I was taken by the Army while I was working for a rancher near Caborca, saving for a bride. Brides are expensive. I thought to pay in silver rather than by working for her family for many years."

"Do you think she will still be unmarried?"

"For sure she is gone by now. But I have saved most of my wages. If I go back to my people one day, I can have the prettiest girl to be found."

"You won't go back soon, Caguama?" beseeched Jon. "I'd be lonesome without you, especially since we've left Mina Rara."

"Jon, don't be selfish," I admonished, but Caguama grinned pleasedly and gave Jon's head a caress.

"I will stay till you no longer need me," he promised. "The sea will wait. But it will be good to smell the water again and eat what we'll catch in my net. I'll show you how to cast it, Juanito."

Jon gave a wriggle of excitement and I was glad he had the promise of adventures to help him endure the relentless traveling we must keep to for at least a few more days.

We rested that day in a cave hollowed by the elements in the side of a craggy mountain. Down in a wash Caguama dug in the silt till he reached wet sand. Gradually it filled with water, and the burros could drink.

"It's the rainy season," Caguama explained. "Water runs off fast, but some sinks down and it's not too hard to reach it now. In dry time—" He shrugged expressively.

When Jon and I woke, a breeze was stirring the heat, breaking its suffocating intensity and there was something else different, a tantalizing odor of a fragrant mesquite fire.

Jon sprang up, sniffing, and would have made for the small fire over which browning meat sputtered on a wood spit if I hadn't hauled him back to put on his boots.

"Didn't you sleep?" I reproached Caguama, pulling on my own boots and pushing back my hair. How stiff and dirty it felt! When we reached that good plentiful water promised for tomorrow, I would wash my hair and bathe. I had brought two bars of perfumed soap.

"I set a snare." He laughed. "It took a rabbit while I dreamed of harpooning turtles."

Very good rabbit it was, flavored with wild herbs, and we had dessert, too, for after we started out we found wild fig trees, roots white and gnarled as their trunks, exposed for a hundred feet down the side of the cliff. Caguama scaled up and brought down several handfuls of small figs. We munched some and saved the rest.

We had a rifle, but Caguama didn't want to use it for fear of attracting attention. "Wild pig is good meat," he said. "But not worth using a rifle and I don't have a bow." He touched the ironwood mallet with which he'd killed Ruiz. "I might kill pig with this, but they are mean and have very wicked teeth."

"We have plenty of food," I comforted. "Besides, won't we soon be eating those wonderful fish?"

Next day, when the noon heat was making Jon look alarmingly flushed and my lips were so cracked and sore that I could scarcely move them, we ascended a ravine that dropped away into a small high amphitheater of rocks. Strange formations reared among clumps of real grass and several large mesquite trees cast inviting shade. Most delicious of all was a series of small pools scattered in rock hollows and fed from a spring in the cliff.

The burros slanted their ears and made for the water. Jon pulled off his boots and clambered into a small pool, willing to be clean it if meant cool. Caguama sloshed water over his face and arms. So did I, promising myself a bath and shampoo later. We all drank, cupping our hands and catching up the laughing crystalline water flowing out of grim rock. Only those who live in the desert can value water at its true worth. After this journey I would always prefer it to any other drink.

After we'd eaten our water-softened fruit and tough dry meat, Jon and Caguama lay down under one big mesquite and I luxuriated in soaping my hair and naked body in the lowest pool, rinsing off as new water tumbled down the haphazard incline. There were many tracks around the pool; deer, coyote, others I didn't recognize. We wouldn't keep the wild creatures from their water long and I was glad Caguama didn't want to use the rifle. It seemed unfair to kill animals coming to drink, thirsty as we had been thirsty.

I dried in the sun, tossing my hair in my hands till it was only faintly damp. Then I lay on the blanket Caguama had spread for me under another mesquite, reveling in the pleasure of being clean and comfortable. We slept till the sun was down and all of us, including the *burros*, were sorry to leave the clear water, trees, and grass.

As we journeyed in the trancelike moonlit hours, the country began to alter. The ground was flintier, crumbled disconcertingly; cardones were much larger than any tree; ocotillos were thorned, graceful, small-leaved fountains shooting from the ground, rippled in the breeze. Some kinds of cholla seemed furred with silver while others resembled many-pronged stag antlers or massed grapes drooping from overburdened limbs.

The breeze was almost chill. There was something different in it, a stinging tanginess. Caguama stopped, breathing long and deep.

"The sea." He might have been called a loved one's name. "I feel it again, smell it. We have almost reached the sea."

His home. I was glad for him, glad that Jon gave him an ecstatic hug. But at the same time I wondered if my son and I could find a home, ever, anywhere, without Trace. There would be places to live, of course, and in time I hoped we could return to Las Coronas. But without Trace, at least for me, there would be no true home.

We rested for a while, traveled on, and when the sun rose from hills on our right, it glimmered on the sea, vast, still, and turquoise, the very shade of my one love's eyes.

19

We traveled through small hills and piled sandstone cliffs above the sea, and the burros found what they could. We still rested in the heat of the day, but we also slept at night, relaxing the grueling pace of the first days. Most of our day stops were spent along the beach and each brought the waves' bounty. It seemed to me we ate scores of kinds of fish, broiled over coals till they were crisp and golden.

Jon was disappointed that no huge turtles appeared for him to harpoon, but he learned to swing a small net and grew skillful with the small harpoon Caguama made for him to replace the one left at Mina Rara.

I loved to wade in the tide pools, admire shells of all sizes and shapes gleaming against the rocks and moss. Sand dollars and sea urchins, sea cucumbers, starfish, and red, white, yellow, and green seaweed washed in, too; I found it endlessly fascinating to perch where the waves churned up and admire what they left behind. My favorite shells were the small white spirals, worn away to ivory-lime hollow ornaments. I felt myself rather like a bit of driftwood or clean-rinsed shell that rested on the sand after a wild storm.

One day we came upon dozens of brown sea lions basking

on white reefs. They barked at us and dived into the water. Caguama laughed. He sang to them, high and sweet and deep and low, and they played and cavorted, coming up to Jon as he splashed gleefully among them, as curious about him as he was about them.

That was the same day we saw a whale spouting and scores of dolphins leaping into the air. There were nearly always dolphins or porpoises, which Caguama said meant that no sharks were in the area. There were many kinds of whales, he said, and numerous sharks. Stingrays had to be watched for and jellyfish could give painful stings.

Sometimes, while we rested, Caguama taught us the songs he sang to seals and whales and told us how in the beginning all animals and people could speak together and lived in peace.

"In the evenings, they would all come in to the campfire—the badger, raccoon, puma, bighorn, deer, coyote, wolf, birds, too, and seals, while whales and dolphins and even sharks swam close in the waters to hear and tell stories. The great sea turtles still know our language, and when one lets herself be caught, she is brought to camp, her shell is painted, and she is entertained with songs and dancing and games for four days before she is eaten."

"Eaten," I said, recoiling at this pragmatic end to an idyll.

"She is caught by her own will," Caguama explained. "She comes to renew our people."

"It's like eating the sacrament, Mama," put in Jon loyally, though he'd looked as shocked and distressed as I. Then as if he could no longer restrain himself, he blurted, "Caguama, did—did you ever eat anybody?"

"Jon!" I cried, but Caguama, after a startled look, simply shrugged and laughed.

"Who knows what goes in cook pots?" he inquired guilelessly. "I have certainly eaten the great sea turtle and we consider her divine."

Jon's eyes had gone absolutely round. "But a man—"

"Jon," I said firmly, "this is one thing that is absolutely none of your business. Would you sing that whale song again, Caguama?"

The late sun turned the sea to winy gold and Jon cuddled in the Seri's arms as Caguama made soft humming sounds and began his song.

> In warm sun I play
> with many companions.
> In warm air spout
> many clouds of vapor.
> All of them are happy. . . .

So we journeyed along the Sea of Cortez, the Vermilion Sea, clambered over lava spills that were gray-black and criss-crossed with sparkling quartz, pinkish sculptured masses that might have been mud hurled by a giant child and left to harden in weird shapes.

We glimpsed bighorns on high pinnacles and, of course, there were circling buzzards and hawks. I had a strong sense of life in the air, on the land, in the water, with humans only a small part of it. We didn't meet any of Caguama's wandering tribesmen. He thought most of them must be at Tiburón, the shark-surrounded Seri island homeland shaped by the great turtle's shell ages ago. Our only sight of people was several fishermen in what Caguama said was a Seri boat, formed of reeds lashed together with mesquite root fiber. Though they must have seen us, the men didn't come in to shore.

I worried about that, but Caguama seemed unperturbed. "Seris learn it's best to keep to themselves," he said. "Best to stay at Tiburón or on land no one else wants. Hope government forgets about us."

Which was an attitude I could certainly understand.

The land was growing bleaker as we neared the northern part of the coastal mainland. From here we would strike across a desolate waste of sand dunes, lava spills, and ancient volcanoes till we picked up the old road leading to California. We would lose the sea's bounty and for at least several days would have to live on water and food we carried.

So we gathered pitahayas to store in pouches, enough for the *burros* to have both food and moisture from them, and filled our water bags at the last sweet water from which both we and the animals drank deeply before we took a last look at the sea and started inland, north and west.

Sand so fine it was almost dust stretching in wavelike patterns to eroded black peaks in the distance, exhausted volcanoes more or less buried by the sand, depending on the direction of the wind. One day of this and a day when black lava spills ridged here and there above the dunes with an occasional blanched ocotillo, cholla, or creosote bush.

Closer up, the mountains resembled vast eroded cones of iron rusted to various hues of dull or shiny lava—chocolate brown, reddish, black. Among the twisted wreckage of lava spills, we found bleached bird droppings and glimpsed eagles, the first creatures we'd seen since entering this waste, which made the sea desert seem a Garden of Eden teeming with life.

Sun glared off sand, reflected from lava, and there was no place to escape it from the time it rose in the morning till it dropped abruptly below the endless dunes at night. During our daytime halts, we rigged our blankets for shade, draping them from improvised frames of rifle, saddles, and packs. Though the moon was gone, we still traveled at night, for the sand hid no secrets worse than its own substance.

Fortunately we had plenty of water to last us to a verdant stretch along an old river that still secreted enough water to fill vast natural rock tanks. Caguama had never been there. This area had been inhabited, if one could call it that, by a very few roving people called Sand Papagos, or Pinacateños.

On the third day we were among the isolated worn-down craters. Sheltered from the devastating sea wind that scoured the region with sand for miles from the coast, there was more vegetation. I rejoiced to see the dusty-green curiously delicate foliage of ironwood, and as the day wore on, we encountered mesquite and paloverde.

Between two craters worn completely level with the ground on their windward side, jutting up in toothed semicircles, Caguama hunted till he found a rock-enclosed hollow that looked dry as a small fox skull tumbled near it. He dug with his machete till moist sand appeared and the *burros* crowded up snuffling, for they hadn't watered in three parching days and the last pitahayas had gone at noon.

More digging and the hole began to fill. Caguama laughed and patted the *burros* as they lowered their heads, straining up the water.

"They could have dug it out themselves," Caguama said. "*Burros* are sagacious and can smell wetness. Also, they will not drink poisonous water, so you will not die from drinking after them, though we will wait for better water at the old stone tanks."

We camped there that night, for the country was too rough now for traveling blind and the sweet slim crescent moon set before it was fully dark. When coyotes set up their yipping, it was like hearing old friends, returning to a place of the living.

Next morning we were up by faintest light. Caguama hoped we could reach the big tanks and shady trees before we had to stop, and so did I. Another bath, another shampoo! And big trees to rest beneath. It sounded like heaven.

Jon kept wanting to ascend a crater and look down inside; so, when we approached one that was not too formidable in steepness, we worked up it at a gradual angle. The rim was perhaps twenty feet wide, circling a vast hollow hundreds of feet wide and at least that deep. Sandy earth had long ago begun to fill in the huge hollow mountain and there were washes in that small world, a few trees, cholla, even some tall yellow grass here and there. The inner sides were jumbled lava rocks and smooth sandy walls where it would have been impossible to get a foothold.

"What a prison that would make!" I breathed. "Do you think a person could get out of there, Caguama?"

He shrugged. "Maybe. Very hard."

"I wouldn't want to live there," Jon decided. From this vantage point we could gaze in all directions. South to the dunes and sand-hidden mountains, east to larger mountain ranges, west and north to other craters dotting the stark landscape.

A ribbon of green showed in the distance with smaller veins branching out. In the Pinacates, as these mountains were called, one could tell where rains collected or ran off because, even though such washes and pools were dry, ironwood, mesquite, paloduro, acacia, and smaller shrubs grew along these intermittently refreshing places. By some of them were large stones hollowed by ancient grinders, stones piled high enough to break the wind.

"That must be the old river where the tanks are," said Caguama, squinting till his skin wrinkled like leather. "*Ay*, that will be our best stop between here and California."

My heart sank at the thought of weeks more of this. I started to suggest we spend some days resting ourselves and the *burros* where there was shade and water, but so long as we were in Mexico, there was a chance Court might find us. We had to push on. But the rest of this day and the night would be a blessing.

"Real water, Lindos!" Jon crooned to his beast, who batted her ears and rolled a yellowish eye back at us. She clearly had an opinion about people who took innocent *burros* through such infernos.

Distances played tricks in that country. That tantalizing fringe of green seemed no nearer than when first glimpsed while we plodded on. For a while it vanished behind hills. Then we skirted these and were in the beginning of a stretch of small trees that verged into large ones. There was grass, coarse brown and spiky, but grass, and many small fragile wild flowers nestled in shade or swayed in the slight breeze. Bees and hummingbirds grew more delirious as the flowers increased.

"The Pinacateños said that in spring the paloverde are showers of gold," said Caguama. "There are miles of yellow flowers and big white thistle blooms, purple nightshade—many colors, lady."

"Those big trees look wonderful," I said, too glad to be near water and rest to regret the missed beauties overmuch. "But there's no water in the river, though you can see where the torrents rush through these low places and leave debris everywhere. Which way do you think the tanks are?"

We stood in the river course and looked both ways. To our left were gnarled big trees bending along either side of the water's track, but on the right we could see the beginning of a rugged broad channel the river had carved through rock; it rose, buffed and smoothed, to rugged pinnacles that the water had not been able to chastise.

If there had been any question, the *burros* would have settled it. They jogged toward the defile. Silt became paved with rock, which surfaced more and more, rising in uneven hollowed layers. Jon and I slipped off the *burros* and they hurried on, found the first stone trough and began to drink.

Not far behind, we clambered to the next level, where a broad pool was surrounded by rounded boulders and fed by water trickling from a crevice.

There we drank, splashed water over our hot dusty faces and arms, luxuriated in the cool sweetness, looked at one another, and laughed. Tomorrow we'd face the desert again, but for now we could be at ease in this green shaded place with its wealth of water.

"You're the best guide in the world, Caguama," I praised. "I doubt if anyone else could have brought us here without getting lost in those dunes."

"Probably not," said a voice above us. "Now let's see if he can find his way through hell."

20

Court's rifle was pointed at Caguama, whose laughter changed to utter calm. Materializing from the rocks, several gaunt figures cut us off from the *burros* and rifle. Caguama had his machete, but he didn't reach for it, only watched Court as the rifle barked. Caguama spun with the impact, fell as a second bullet ripped through his throat. Jon screamed shrilly, threw himself upon his friend.

"Caguama, Caguama!" he wailed, trying to lift the Seri as blood pumped from his wounds.

I knelt down, frantic to stop the flow, trying to stanch the torn throat with my hands, but bloody foam ran from Caguama's mouth and the harsh rattling breath ceased abruptly, though his eyes were open, staring fixedly into Jon's.

It didn't seem possible. The shy misfit young soldier at the back of the school whom I'd taught to read and write; Jon's companion and teacher, the faithful friend who'd brought us through the sea desert and the lava sands—to end like this, in one instant, one little minute of time. Because he had helped us.

I held him, dazed. Jon sprang up, ran at Court, beat at him with doubled fists. "You killed him. You—you made holes in him! I hate you, I'll kill you—"

Court sent the child sprawling with an open palm, scarcely

looking at him, as if he were a troublesome mosquito. I was astounded even in that terrible moment. Court had never disciplined Jon, though he hadn't spent much time with him, either, as if he could best maintain his avowed relationship by not really knowing the boy.

Jon was amazed, but he scrambled up and attacked again, setting his teeth in Court's wrist and hanging on like a terrier. Halting on his way to me, Court set finger and thumb of his free hand against Jon's cheeks and forced his jaws apart, brushed him carelessly away. At a signal, one of the skinny ragged men with headcloths got hold of Jon.

Kicking Caguama from my arms, Court dragged me to my feet. I was covered with blood, felt more covered in my soul. Caguama, Caguama . . . His eyes golden as an eagle's sheen, Court stared down at me.

"I thought you must come this way."

He slapped me hard across the face, so hard my brain whirled; I would have fallen except for the steel clasp of his arms. And then he kissed me.

At least he didn't slaughter the *burros* that had carried us, though he examined our packs with a curled lip and gave everything but our clothing to the Papagos, even the jewelry and twisted gold. I was wearing my mother's crucifix, of course. He left me that, and our wedding ring.

When the packs had been closed up again, Court was ready to start in spite of the heat. I knew from the way his mouth had seared mine that he burned to possess and humiliate me, inflict the kind of punishment a man can visit only on a woman.

I had gathered Jon to me, full of baffled foreboding at the way Court ignored him. Momentary anger at the boy's attack, that I could understand, but not this cold dismissing attitude, as if the child didn't exist. No move had been made to bury Caguama. He lay sprawled and bloody where Court had kicked him away from me.

The Indians brought mounts. I hung back, glancing at our dead companion. "Let us bury him," I said through stiff lips.

"That carrion?" Court started to refuse, then smiled. "By all means, love. Bury him. You and the brat. Dig the grave yourself and see what this latest folly of yours has accomplished."

At a word from him, a man brought a shovel from one of their pack mules, looked at Court as if thinking he'd misunderstood, and gave it to me.

"I'll help you, Mama," Jon whispered. His face was tear-streaked, but his blue-green eyes had an expression that was suddenly all too adult.

He pushed rocks aside farther down the riverbed where I hoped the sand would go deep enough to make a burial if we heaped it up with stones. The shovel was clumsy in my hands, but the silt was easy enough to dig, though my hands blistered long before I struck rock three feet down. Jon dug with a stick, doggedly, and I thought it good, not horrible, that he should be able to do at least this for his friend.

Sweat and tears mingled on my face. Exertion in the heat made my lungs a furnace and my heart labored, but Court was watching and hatred drove me on.

How I hated him! To kill a man whose only fault was serving me. I should have let Ruiz kill him, but I'd been fuddled by his solicitous care of me and relief that he'd accepted Jon. How could I have let those years of enforced marriage blot out my essential knowledge of Court? A man who had exacted my obedience by threatening to betray Sewa and the Yaquis, who'd tried to buy Trace's death after the battle.

What did he intend? If it hadn't been for Jon, I could have wished in my grief and terrible frustration that Court would kill me and make an end of our tortured life together. But there was Jon. And that was what turned the pit of my stomach icily sick as we dug Caguama's grave.

Court had changed toward Jon. It wasn't temporary spite or preoccupation. No, it was as if he had never seen the child before and didn't want to look at him now.

What did it mean? What would happen? Had my determination not to be parted from my son brought on us some vengeance that would be more crushing than anything separation could have caused?

Somehow the two of us dragged Caguama to his grave. When one of the Papagos would have helped, Court stopped him with a gesture. Jon dug into his pocket and put his amulet of painted turtle bone in Caguama's relaxed brown hand. I slipped off my mother's crucifix and slipped it inside his shirt. We filled in the grave, first with our hands till the body was covered, and then I used the shovel.

"I wish we could have put him in the sea," muttered Jon between sobs. "He could swim with the whales and seals and sing to them."

"Maybe he'll go back," I said. "Maybe he'll be where all the creatures come up at night to tell stories around the fire."

We rolled down the biggest rocks we could handle, for a grave that shallow would have quickly been dug out by scavengers, but we hadn't heaped the cairn as high as I would have liked when Court tossed away his cigarette and came along the river course, followed by his party. He put me on a gelding, mounted his own. Jon rode Cascos Lindos, whose packs were shifted to another *burro*. The Papagos walked, lean silent wraiths.

"I hired them at Sonoita," Court said. "I left a couple of men there to watch for you; they'll escort us home." He laughed mirthlessly, answering the questions that were only now forming in my mind, though I was too spent to care much about how he'd caught us.

He had. And that was final: all too final for Caguama. "There are also men or police watching for you in Nogales, Hermosillo, Yuma, Tucson, Phoenix, and Mexico City. I hunted first in Hermosillo, of course, but when no trace was found, I began to reflect. You're not timid, Miranda, one who fears hardship. The Seri was missing. And so I thought he might lead you through his homeland toward California. It seems that in all this wilderness the single lush spot travelers would visit was the stone tanks, Tinaja de los Papagos. So, with a few hired *pistoleros,* I've ridden from Hermosillo, trading horses to keep a fresh one. We've waited at the tanks since yesterday."

I said nothing. I'd never have dreamed a man's pride could make him take such measures to recover a woman who wished to be free of him, but plainly Court's pride was of another sort.

"Do you expect me to thank you for arranging my release?" he went on. "I would, except that I suspect you had something to do with my arrest in the first place." Head cocked, he contemplated me mockingly. "I don't understand why you do what you do, Miranda, but I have begun to guess what it'll be. Shall I tell you how it happened?"

It took all my energy to hold my head up. I wasn't going to waste strength in amusing him. If only I could blank out his handsome, hateful face and voice, never see or hear him again. . . .

"You hoped the amorous colonel might use his authority to stop our journey, and once you set him to thinking of his power, he began to see glowing possibilities, especially if I were dead." The drawling voice grew even silkier. "Now, why you didn't let him remove me permanently from your life, which I'm sure you now wish you had, I won't pretend to fathom. But you got Ruiz to write an order for my release. And next morning he's found with a smashed neck and a bottle in his hand. Officially he took a tumble in the dark. But what really happened?"

When I didn't answer, Court rode closer. "My dear wife, you'll speak when spoken to or don't doubt I'll spread a blanket and take you right now. In spite of their impassive faces, I'm sure the Papago would find it entertaining."

That reached even through my numbed indifference. I stared at him in outrage and Court gave a purring laugh. "Ah, that brought you back among us. What about it, love? Who killed Ruiz?"

"Caguama."

Court nodded reflectively. "That's what I thought. Even though you shot me once, it's really not your style." His yellow eyes burned over me and I felt as if the heat in them dried my blood, shriveled the depleted veins. "The heart of the matter now, my sweet: how did you get that release signed?"

"Ruiz would be no richer for your death if I didn't marry him, and I made it clear I wouldn't. I promised him money and—"

"And?"

"Some hours with me."

Court gripped my wrist so hard that I could have screamed. The pupils of his eyes swelled till they almost covered the gold. "Did he have you?"

"No. Caguama thought he was raping me and clubbed him down."

"If I'd known that, I wouldn't have killed your cannibal," said Court. "Though, of course, it was not my honor he was defending." After a few minutes he resumed briskly, "I think I see it pretty well, Miranda. Having landed me under arrest, you soothed your peculiar conscience by making sure I'd go free, and set off for California in a glow of self-righteousness. Did you really think I'd follow your advice and divorce you?"

"I offered you the mine."

He watched me till I didn't know whether it was the shimmering heat or his eyes that made me weak and light-headed, as if I were going to faint. "Get this through that lovely stubborn head, Miranda. You're *my* woman. You will be till one of us is dead."

It was like a sentence to which there was no appeal.

When we camped that night, Jon stayed close to me. Court ignored him as we ate, but when the meal was finished, Court raised me from the rock where we were sitting and Jon, too, scrambled up.

"Stay here, boy," Court said. "I want some time with your mother." He could have been speaking to some beggar urchin.

Jon clutched my skirt. He was after all a very little boy. "Mama—"

"Don't hang to your mother like a baby." Court's tone was cold. "The Indians won't hurt you. Get your blanket and go to sleep."

Trying to ward off the impact of Court's strange new attitude toward Jon, I bent and kissed him. "I'll be back soon, dear. Find a nice sandy spot and curl up."

Jon let go of me, planted his legs wide apart, and glared up at Court. "I hate you," he challenged in his child's voice that briefly echoed the timbre of his real father's. "You killed Caguama. I wish you weren't my father."

After an astounded moment, Court rocked back and laughed. Laughed till, scarcely breathing, I took Jon's hand. "Well, you little bastard, you have your wish." Court's acid tone contained a certain grudging respect. "You aren't mine. A riffraff *tejano* got you on your mother before our marriage. So now that I've killed that damn Seri you preferred to me, now that you've shown how much value you placed on my treating you as my son, let's have it all straight and clear. Your mother is my wife. You're her son, but you're *nothing* to me. Learn your place and it will be comfortable. Provoke me and you'll get some lessons you badly need."

Large-eyed, uncomprehending, Jon stared from Court to me. From his friends he knew that bastards were pitied and laughed at, their mothers disgraced. But relief mingled with the shock on his face and I felt a curious lightening, too. At last I could tell him about Trace. Court started to draw me away.

I swept Jon close and whispered, "Your father was wonderful. I'll tell you all about him, but for now you must go to sleep."

As soon as Court had taken me out of earshot, I said in a voice that shook, "How could you be that cruel?"

"Truthful." Court shrugged. "When the boy trotted happily off with you and that cannibal, he showed his blood. After all I'd done for him, he clearly felt not a shred of allegiance. Much better, don't you think, that since he wished I weren't his sire I could say I wasn't?"

"You were brutal."

"Cry quits, Miranda. It was brutal to find you gone along with the child I'd raised as my own."

A horrible fear swelled in me. "Court, you can't intend to publicly repudiate him, treat him badly."

"He's your cub and you may keep him by you in peace provided he finds a civil tongue. Of course, I don't intend to stain my own name with the facts." His tone roughened and he spread the blanket he'd been carrying, brought me down in his arms. "What I mean to do is get you with child. That will give you someone else to think about except that bastard of your dead *pistolero*."

His mouth found my throat, his hard hands stripped away my clothing, trembling as they found my breasts. He entered me with such sudden ferocity that I bit my lips to keep from screaming. He orgasmed in violent spasms, rested, and took me twice more, as if he couldn't be sure he truly had me, before we came back to the sleeping camp.

A week later we were at Mina Rara. Within another week, Jon's sunburn and mine had faded and our journey, the brief heady freedom, seemed a dream. Except Caguama was gone. Captain Ortego commanded the garrison instead of Ruiz. And Court and Jon managed to almost completely avoid each other.

I ached for my son. It hadn't helped him much to know about Trace, though it had given me bittersweet joy to tell Jon how strong and brave his father had been, how much we'd loved each other. Though Jon listened, this unknown, abruptly introduced dead man couldn't assuage his grief for Caguama, the way he constantly missed the friend who'd been with him all his life. Jon wouldn't talk about Court but decisively gave away his presents, including the silver-handled whip.

It was an untenable situation, but I lacked the strength to grapple with it. If Jon continued to mope about the house and avoid his playmates, perhaps Court would let me take him to Las Coronas for a while. He could play with the ranch youngsters and Lázaro and Enrique would take him riding and teach him to rope. There he was Jonathan Greenleaf's namesake and grandson; his paternity was comparatively unimportant.

So, fearing to worsen matters for Jon, I had to submit to Court, who now spent every night in my bed.

"You'll breed for me," he panted one night when we were both exhausted. "If it doesn't happen soon, I'll take you to some doctors who can do more than say you have a tilted womb."

Though there must have been some gossip about my flight, the facts were not known. Court had paid off his *pistoleros* some miles from Mina Rara, so no one knew, except for Jon, Court, and me, what had really happened. Dr. Trent guessed, I think, and stopped to see me every day, bringing me books and periodicals, chatting about outside affairs as if determined not to let me brood.

Revolt was simmering throughout Mexico, held in check only by the hope that Díaz could be moved to name someone to replace the detested Corral. That decision was expected late this month, in September. Madero had been released from prison on bond, but wasn't allowed to travel.

"And it seems Captain Ortega is sniffing after a promotion," Dr. Trent said one wretchedly hot afternoon in mid-September. "He plans to go Yaqui-hunting next week."

My heart skipped a beat. Yaqui to me would always mean Sewa. "Why?" I asked. "It's been quiet on the whole since Bule made peace."

"If a revolution breaks, the Yaqui rebels who are still in the sierra could be a real problem to the *federales*. Of course, I think there's another reason. Miranda, Court's behind Ortega's sudden enthusiasm. Why?"

I shook my head, groping for some explanation.

"I can't think what would set him off, Doctor. Unless—Sewa, the little girl who came here with me, do you know if she's the one they now call La Grulla, the Crane?"

"There aren't many Yaqui girls with one foot," he said dryly.

"Maybe Court thinks I'd try to join her sometime," I guessed. "I can't think of anything else that would make him care about Yaquis. But that seems so farfetched."

"That's as may be," said the doctor crisply. "Ortega told me himself, when he was getting drunk with me last night, that Court has promised him a small fortune to wipe out La Grulla's band." He reached over and closed his hand around mine. "I'm sorry to distress you, Miranda, but I know you loved Sewa and I can't see much justice in this hounding of a wronged people. I thought you might know of some way to warn them. Wasn't Sewa friends with Chepa?"

"Yes, but Chepa never heard from her after Sewa and the women and children got away."

"Strange that she never got in touch with you."

"I was sad about that, but what could she do with me married to Court and a detachment of soldiers at the mine?" I sighed. "She may wonder why I never tried to get messages to her, but I couldn't go myself without Court trailing and I didn't like to involve anyone else." Shutting my eyes, I tried to think.

The Yaquis would cut down or elude a strange messenger. Dr. Trent was too old for such a trip, even if I could give precise directions, which I couldn't. I'd come that way over six years ago with my love, with Trace; he had laid me down on the trail in the mountains and given me pain, joy, and our son. But if I reached the general area, lookouts should pick me up, and I should be remembered by the Yaquis, both for hiding them in the mine and buying out the survivors in Yucatán.

So I must go.

Once that was clear, my mind flew. Court left early for the mine and didn't always return at noon. If I had horses ready in the morning, Jon and I could be a long way into the mountains before we were missed. Court might even think we'd gone off to Las Coronas or made a dash for Hermosillo. At worst, it would bring the soldiers some days earlier than they would otherwise have come, and this seemed the only way the Yaquis could be warned.

I didn't consider leaving Jon. Wherever I went, I'd take him. If Court or the soldiers didn't take us, I hoped to escape to Las Coronas and perhaps hide out there, possibly in Cruz's old canyon or one of the outposts. That could all come later. The important thing was to warn La Grulla, whoever she was. In my heart I hoped she was Sewa.

"What are you planning?" asked Dr. Trent, white brows knitted. "If I can help you in this, Miranda, I should be glad."

"Thank you." I kissed his cheek. "It might help if you'd remember that I've talked a good deal about Las Coronas, said that I'd like to take Jon there."

The doctor nodded. "I can remember that." He held my hands to his whiskered face and I knew he was thinking of his daughter who was dead. "*Vaya con Dios,* Miranda."

21

Jon had been brought up on Yaqui stories Sewa had told me and he knew about her and Ku and Ratoncita. When I told him we were going to try to find her and warn the band about Ortega's hunt, his eyes lit like the deep sea with sun on it and he squirmed in an effort not to show his excitement in an unmanly way before he quieted and frowned.

"But *he* won't let us, Mama." *He* was how Jon now referred to Court when it was absolutely necessary. They rarely spoke face-to-face. When they did, it was "boy" from Court, "sir" from Jon.

"We can't tell him," I said. "And this is where you must do something important. We should leave as early as we can in the morning. After you get your breakfast, can you coax a horse and Cascos Lindos out back of the stables? Give them oats and dried peaches and don't let them wander off. I'd like the chestnut mare, but the dun will do. Fill two water bags." I smiled at him, ruffling his unruly black hair. "I'll be out as soon as I can, we'll saddle and be off."

"What if Roberto sees us?"

Roberto was nominally in charge of the stable, though in

practice even Court usually found and saddled his mount. "If we see Roberto, we'll tell him we're going for a ride," I said. "But he's not likely to be about."

Jon laughed, really laughed, for the first time since Caguama was killed. "It's an ad-adventure!" he brought out triumphantly. "Isn't it, Mama?"

I nodded and hugged him. "Yes, Jon. It is that."

My plans worked without a hitch. Court obligingly dropped the remark that he was going to look at some interesting ore formations an hour's ride from the mine and wouldn't be home till evening. Wonderful! With any luck, by the time he missed us, we'd be talking to Sewa.

Even if Court guessed where we'd gone, he didn't know the way. And it would take time to get soldiers on the march. Ortega might refuse to bring them against alerted Yaquis, at least by night. Chances were good that there'd be no pursuit till morning, and by then La Grulla's band could have melted into the deeper mountains. I had a growing hope that I didn't dare voice to Jon as we rode up the spiraling mountain trail.

If Sewa was La Grulla, perhaps she could be persuaded to come down to Las Coronas with me, especially if Domingo favored the idea. I wondered if she still had Ku and what she and Jon would think of each other. I hadn't known how much I longed to see her till now, when I could permit myself to imagine the joy. Sewa was dear to me not only as a person but as a link with Trace, who had saved her life by taking her to Cruz.

We passed the place where I'd wounded Court a few days before Reina and the soldiers descended on the mine, but it was farther up among heaps of gleaming quartz-studded rock that I reined in the chestnut mare, turned to gaze at Mina Rara, glistening like a mountain of gold.

Women always look back, even when fleeing Sodom. The settlement in the valley looked much as it had when I first saw it six years ago, except for the garrison sprawled above the village.

"Will we be coming back, Mama?" asked Jon restlessly. Boys don't look behind them. Or much ahead either. This was the first question he'd asked about the future.

"I hope we can live somewhere at Las Coronas, Jon."

"Where *he* can't find us?"

Oh, most especially where he can't find us.

I nodded and we rode on. I wanted to say to Jon, Away from the trail is a shallow cave where powdery sand is blue and gold and crimson. That's where your father made me a woman, where you were conceived by my dear love whose eyes and mouth and hair you have, whom you will never know.

This high stony road I'd traveled with Trace brought him strongly back. His arms and mouth, memories I usually forced away, haunted me now. For a time I again tasted his loss, lived it in flesh that stirred at the thought of him and smoldered when my mind tried to quench its unreasoning need.

I must stop that. He had given me a son, something of him to breathe and laugh and live; he hadn't perished utterly, and for that I must be glad. Bringing my attention back to the trail, I realized that we couldn't be far from where we should descend to the small hills stretching between these mountains and the palisaded ranges to the southeast where the Yaquis hid. As I stared, I seemed to recognize the distant silhouette of peaks by the gorge that led tortuously into the basin.

With that for a guide, I studied the jagged hills between, the maze of arroyos, and tried to plan the best route. I knew all too well that once down where the small hills towered above us, where one arroyo branched into several or ended abruptly, finding our way would be vastly different from spying it at this eagle's height. But it also seemed that if we kept to the right of the most continuous sawtooth of hills, we couldn't fetch up far from the narrow pass leading into the Yaqui fastness.

I pointed this out to Jon, who squinted his eyes and nodded gravely. He had smuggled a melon from the kitchen. Dismounting, I took this from the bag holding it behind my saddle and cut it open. Jon and I had a few juicy bites and he fed the rest to his *burra* and the mare while I got out cheese and tortillas. After a drink of water we left the high trail and started down the mountain.

The only thing wrong with my plan was that ridges and arroyos that had looked unimpressive from above frequently became impassable and we had to loop out from the landmark hills. In spite of this we made good time. The sun was still above the crags when we approached the rearing granite cliffs. But where along this serried mass was the defile?

As we rode along the escarpment and every fissure ended in solid rock, I began to worry. Had I been wrong about the guardian silhouette? Was the passage in the opposite direction? Suppose we couldn't find it by nightfall and had to stay along the cliffs till morning, losing much of our time advantage?

"Mama," worried Jon dramatically, "do you think someone exploded up the pass and it's not there?"

"You're a comfort," I said tersely.

"Cascos Lindos might remember," he ventured.

I smiled in spite of my growing concern. "She's a fantastic beast, Jon, but that's expecting rather much."

As if to refute my words, the *burra* slanted her ears and speeded its pace, passing the mare to round a spill of boulders and disappear.

"She did remember, Mama!" Jon's voice trailed back. "She found the way through the cliffs!"

Heart lifting, I sent the chestnut after the little donkey. We passed by what seemed to be an impenetrable barrier till a sudden jog revealed a narrow way. Not far from that was a spring—what the *burra* must have scented—where our animals drank and we rested for a bit, lying back on smooth broad stones warmed by sun but not unpleasantly so since it only reached them a few hours in the middle of the day. A breeze whispered.

So good to rest. But we must move along. If we approached the retreat after dark, we might be killed before we could make ourselves known.

"Let's go, Jon," I said, stretching and sitting up.

I blinked and looked again. Into the barrel of a pointed rifle.

After the first shocked moment in which I instinctively drew Jon to me, I stared into the brown face with a hope for recognition while I tried to remember.

Had I seen this man before? I thought I had but could not be certain. Slowly, I greeted him in Yaqui.

He frowned, glancing about. The rifle never wavered. "You are alone? You and this child?" When I didn't understand all the Yaqui, he repeated in Spanish.

"We are alone. I seek La Grulla or Domingo or anyone of Lío's band."

"Lío?" questioned the guard sharply. "What do you know of him?"

"That he is dead," I answered. "Dead in Yucatán. But I believe he was my friend. When I was here six years ago, my name was Miranda Greenleaf."

The man nodded and uncocked the rifle, swinging it over his back. His eyes lit with excitement his tone tried to suppress. "I remember you now. You were to die at dawn in place of your sister, and you were kind to La Grulla when she was a girl. You are the one Yaquis call the Lady Bought with Rifles."

He made a whistling trill like a bird, was answered, and gave a satisfied nod. "Rosalio will watch the pass."

"I have come to say that soldiers will be hunting you. I think they cannot start before tomorrow from Mina Rara, so there should be a day but—"

"Rosalio will guard." The sentinel handed me the chestnut's reins. "Let us go quickly to La Grulla."

As we followed the labyrinthine way into the stronghold, our guide asked no questions and answered mine with monosyllables or "La Grulla can tell you better than I," till I fell silent and watched how the highest peaks were tipped with gold though the rest were in shadow. It took me back to that morning when I waited for the sunrise and thought it my last.

But Cruz had come. And Lío had traded my life for the

rifles Trace had brought from Arizona. The day I went to what I thought was freedom was the last time I'd seen Trace, except for that one brief glimpse in the battle.

We were entering a wider part of the canyon and were suddenly in the basin. Maize, beans, melons, and squash grew in fields protected from goats and horses by ocotillo fences. The makeshift shelters of six years ago were replaced with stone and adobe houses.

At sight of us, children stopped playing and ran to their homes or the ramadas, where people stopped cooking or talking to turn toward us.

I strained to make out faces, but none were distinct. Then a young woman came forward, moving with a certain uneveness, using a staff, a raven on her shoulder. It had to be Sewa. I swung down from my horse.

The man behind her—tall, familiar in a way that wrenched my heart even as my dazed eyes refused to believe that black hair, long mouth, blue-green gaze.

My knees went weak. I held to the saddle horn for support, trying to get my breath.

Trace. He wasn't dead. I started to call his name, then realized the shattering truth. He had escaped from Yucatán, been alive these years, and hadn't tried to see me, hadn't sent a message. While I mourned him for dead, felt the vital secret core of my own life had ended with him, he'd been here.

I looked at Sewa, the strong but delicate flower face, the lithe graceful body that was very much a woman's. The maiming of her foot only added a charming hesitation to her walk.

Shocked with pain as if a broad curved sword had ripped me from belly to breast, I watched them come, knew they were lovers, but couldn't hate them, though I ached with jealousy and hurt. They were both my loves; that didn't change, though for pride's sake Trace mustn't know how I felt.

Commanding all my strength and will, I managed to let go of the saddle and clasp Sewa in my arms as Ku flapped down, squawking at being displaced.

"Miranda!" she cried, and we both wept.

But not for long. There was the sound of running feet. Jon's voice shrilled, "I know you. You're my real father. Mama thought you were dead."

"Jon!" I gasped.

He plunged on, heedless. "Why didn't you come get us?" Then, more slowly, as if the terrible incomprehensible adult world was about to deal him another blow he couldn't understand, "Don't you want us?"

Trace picked up his son, holding him close. "I didn't know about you, *niño*." He stared at me in bafflement. "What's all this, Miranda?"

Sewa looked from Trace to Jon and back to me. "There have been mistakes," she said painfully. "We must find the truth."

My head was in a spin. Tears came to my eyes at seeing Jon where he belonged, in Trace's arms. There could be no argument that they were flesh of each other's flesh. But if Trace no longer loved me—I put away that jumble and turned to Sewa.

"I've come to tell you soldiers from Mina Rara are hunting you. Court has bribed their commander to make a thorough job of it."

She was at once the leader. "How many? When?"

I told all I knew and her brows knit together. "I must find Domingo, Rosalio, and Tomás," she said. "You also, Trace. But first you and Miranda—and your son—must talk."

She moved away, collecting her bird. The limp seemed more pronounced, but perhaps that was a trick of my bewildered senses. Trace took a deep sighing breath and put Jon down, gripped me by the shoulders. His touch sent liquid fire coursing through me, burning out the welter of confusion.

"Whatever, whyever, however!" he said huskily. "I'm going to do one thing if I die for it."

His mouth took mine, his hard strong body pressed achingly close, and I was the cup from which he drank, his sustenance, while my starved self received like physical nourishment his passion and need and tenderness.

"You thought I was dead?" he whispered at last. "Oh, Miranda. Couldn't you feel me wanting you?"

I had believed him dead because he didn't come for me. The reasons he hadn't were simple enough, once explained, with Jon between us, his arms around this miraculously discovered father, who kept smiling at him, touching his hair as if he couldn't believe he existed.

Sewa hadn't known under what compulsion I married Court, only that I had. Even then, when Trace returned from Yucatán, he'd longed for me and resolved after many struggles with his pride to find some way to speak with me, but the messenger he'd sent to arrange a tryst learned I had a baby and reported to Trace. Never dreaming the child was his, Trace concluded bitterly that I'd succumbed to Court's charm and was content.

Besides, vowed to aid Lío's band, he couldn't promise me even safety. So he'd tried to put me out of his heart.

"It didn't work," he said, tracing my face with his hand.

All these years . . . A wave of tumultuous sorrow for the lost time swept through me but subsided in the ocean-deep joy and peace of being with him. Then I remembered Sewa. It was a question I had to ask.

"Trace, it—it's been a long time. Are you free?"

He gathered me to him, bringing Jon into our embrace, though his mouth told me it couldn't be long till we merged in a way that excluded all the rest of the world.

"There has never been any doubt that I loved you. If we come through this alive, you'll be mine."

"Sewa—"

"Sewa is a wonderful person. And she loves you." He glanced toward the group by the nearest ramada. "Come along. We'd better join the council."

22

"Eighty soldiers," pondered Domingo.

Like Sewa, he was easily recognizable, though he had grown to man's height and was muscled like a puma. He had bent his face to my hands, greeted Jon warmly, and now everyone was intent on Ortega's invasion.

I had expected them to melt away into the ravines and higher mountains, but no one suggested this, except as a luring tactic.

"Court will suspect I've come here," I said hopefully. "It may be that Ortega won't attack if he thinks you're warned."

"In that case, good," said wizened, monkeylike Rosalio, who, with Tomás, had thanked me for buying his freedom from the henequen plantation. "But if he comes, that can be better. We are twenty-four rifles. We can pick them off once they are in the canyon. Not a one will live."

Tomás spat. "We can deal with eighty, maybe twice that. But then what? Ortega's superiors would have to make reprisals for such a defeat. Our mountains would swarm with soldiers. Even if we survived by some wonder, the government would punish any Yaquis they could seize."

It was a forceful argument. No one spoke for a while. The germ of an idea worked in my mind, suddenly took form. "But if Ortega attacked a peaceful ranch," I said, "if the ranch people, armed and vigilant because of frequent bandit raids, fought the soldiers, thinking them bandits, for surely the Army would not battle law-abiding citizens—"

"What ranch?" Rosalio demanded. "What citizens?"

Trace nodded slowly. "It might work. We could leave a trail even the Army could follow. Probably the best place to draw them would be to the horse camp. Most of us could take cover in the buildings, but enough could hide in the arroyo leading to Cruz's canyon to make sure that no one escaped. For this plan to work, there must be no soldier left to say they followed Yaquis." His mouth thinned. "Miranda, of course, must send a most indignant message to the general-in-chief of the First Military Zone, demanding to know why her ranch was set upon. What is it to her that this Ortega was reportedly planning to rebel, get a jump on other revolutionaries? Why should he decide to start his lawless career on her ranch?"

Domingo said admiringly, "The general will most humbly beg her pardon. And if he wonders why a small ranch force could overcome trained soldiers, no doubt he will be too furious at their treachery to care much."

It was decided that the women and children would take the animals and refuge in a smaller, even less accessible valley till word came that the danger was past. If that word didn't come, Yaqui women had raised children alone before, and when the young ones were grown, well, there would be warriors among them.

So two parties left the basin that night, going opposite directions, though the family group wouldn't travel far in the dark, just to the next valley, from which they'd move on at dawn. I tried to send Jon with them, but he begged so hard to stay with us that at last Trace struck a bargain. Jon could ride with him to the ranch but then must let me take him to the women at the big house for safety.

Jon, from the glory of his perch behind his father's saddle, generously told Sewa she could ride Cascos Lindos, who did seem to remember her onetime mistress, though she heaved her flanks in a *burra* sigh at being mounted again after such a short rest.

Cascos Lindos, like my mare, had been unsaddled, watered, rubbed, and given precious maize. Domingo strode ahead by Sewa, who had left Ku with friends. Rosalio had a raw-boned gelding as did two other men. The foot warriors went in front. Trace and I, with Jon, rode at the end of the column. Where there was room for us to ride abreast, we often touched hands; where we couldn't, our hearts touched anyway.

We reached the horse camp in the middle of the night. Dogs ran out barking, horses whinnied from the corrals, and someone shouted from the house that had been Trace's, "*Quién es?*"

"Miranda Greenleaf and her son," I called, never thinking of styling myself Sanders. "I am here with friends. We require the camp for a few days."

"Forgive me, señora." I recognized Enrique's voice. "Can you and the small *dueño* come forward alone to assure us you are not captive or speaking under threat?"

"Good thinking, Enrique," said Trace. "I will escort them."

There was silence. "Can it be?" marveled Enrique. "Don Trace?"

"No other."

We rode forward. Enrique stepped out of the door and Jon slipped from behind Trace and ran to the vaquero. "See, Enrique? It's me, with my mother and *real* father."

Briefly, Trace explained how we hoped to draw the soldiers to the horse camp. "You had better move the horses till this is over," he counseled. "And if anything goes wrong, if the soldiers take us, the people of Las Coronas are in the clear. You heard shooting but thought it was gangs of bandits."

"With permission," said Enrique, "I will stand with you, Don Trace. My *compañeros* can move the horses."

Trace had dismounted and now he dropped his hand on the vaquero's shoulder. "Thanks, my friend. But *la señora* must take Jon to the main house. Perhaps you will ride with them?"

"I am at your orders," Enrique promised.

Three other men had come out of the houses. They all remembered Trace, greeted him with delighted awe, nor did they argue the situation. As soon as they could saddle, they began moving the horses from the corrals, the task simplified by the fact that it didn't much matter where the horses went so long as they did.

Enrique caught me a fresh horse and roped out a gray gelding he said he'd been gentling for Jon's next visit.

"Can you sit a saddle?" I asked the child, for we had been riding most of the day and night and I myself was exhausted and sore.

" 'Course I can," he said proudly.

After we had a drink and stretched a bit, Trace lifted him up and we made for the headquarters of Las Coronas, twenty miles away, with Enrique leading.

It was after sunup when we got there. Consuelo and Catalina were already in the kitchen and recovered quickly from their astonishment to give us chocolate and *pan dulce* and bear Jon off to bed when he fell asleep with the sweet flaky bread in his mouth.

"You must sleep, too, señora," said Consuelo. "I will see your bed is fresh."

I rose, yawning. "Call me in an hour, *por favor*. I must go back to the horse camp."

Consuelo and Catalina cried out in protest. "Oh, no, señora," Catalina scolded. "Let them do their fighting. I tell you plainly it is all one to me who dies, Yaquis or soldiers. But you must stay here with Juanito!"

"I must go to Trace Winslade. He is the man I have always loved, and until today I thought he was dead. Sewa, too, is there, whom as a child I took for my sister."

Catalina scowled but bit off the numerous remarks she clearly longed to make and hurried me to bed. Consuelo helped me out of my clothes, washed my face and hands and feet with tepid water.

"I rejoice that Don Trace lives," she said.

I clasped her warm hand gratefully and fell into slumber.

An hour later she helped me dress again. There was fragrant coffee and eggs cooked with chilis that Catalina insisted I eat. I tried to persuade Enrique to avoid the horse camp, but he said he'd have no manhood if he let me go that way alone. A staunch man always, back to the day he'd buried the massacred Yaquis for me because I'd prevented Court's rape of Consuelo.

It was midmorning when we started, carrying all the fresh-baked bread and tortillas available, along with cheese and barbecued meat. We were an hour's ride from the camp when we heard distant firing.

Enrique and I exchanged glances. I bent forward to urge my horse, but Enrique caught the reins. "Señora, you can't ride into that." As I set my jaw and tried to strike aside his hand, he held on and pleaded. "Will it help Don Trace for you to be shot? You cannot get through to him now till the fight is over, one way or the other."

In spite of my frantic need to be with Trace during the battle, I knew Enrique was right. There was no way to reach the houses without being a target. But as I made an assenting gesture and let my horse drop back to a steady pace, I was tormented.

What was happening?

The soldiers had come earlier, much earlier than I'd expected. Was Court with them? Would the advantage of the buildings' thick adobe walls compensate for numbers? But I hated the thought of all the soldiers dying, too, the young ones forced into the Army like Caguama, like the young men I'd taught to read and write who'd been homesick and lonely. I didn't want them to die, but the alternative was worse.

A lull in the battle sounds held, with only an occasional shot. Over so quickly? Then there was a burst of rapid fire which dwindling to a few isolated firecrackerlike pops followed by silence.

That time Enrique put his horse into a gallop alongside mine. "It sounded like the fight," he shouted. "And then the *degüello*, the throat cutting."

That had been my thought. The long exchange, then the

shorter fusillade and scattered shots. Surely the soldiers couldn't have overwhelmed the buildings that soon? But we hadn't heard any firing for some minutes now. The battle must be over.

Who had won?

We sped through a stretch of hills, following a sandy wash that slowed our horses, and we came in sight of the camp. Vision blurred by motion and wind, I saw men moving prostrate forms, dragging them to a central place while down by Cruz's canyon mouth, others seemed engaged in the same task. It was too far to distinguish clothing, but the location of the fallen had to mean they were soldiers. At the same time that my heart swelled with relief for Sewa, for her people, and most of all, for Trace, I felt sick to my soul for the young men in uniform spilling out their blood and strength at the bidding of corrupt men.

Caguama might have been dead out there; others like him were. I began to suspect there was no way to ever be wholeheartedly glad about a victory; there would always be the waste of young men who had no real choice of whether or for what to fight. But what drove me now was fear for Trace, and then for Sewa, then Domingo.

Did they live?

The wash narrowed into a gorge walled by rock and brush. We had to go slower here. Enrique took the lead. As my horse maneuvered between thorny acacia on one side and jutting rocks on the other, something like steel clamped around my waist, dragged me from my horse, held me against the rocks.

Enrique turned at my gasping cry, reaching for his rifle. "Hold it!" Court snapped, leveling his revolver at my head.

He spoke with difficulty. Sweat stood out on him and he was pallid beneath his skin's weathering. "Listen well, vaquero. I am dying. I can take this woman with me or I can let her live—but she shall not live to be Trace Winslade's." He paused, breath wheezing. His face contorted with pain, but the ugly black barrel didn't waver. "Go tell Winslade that if he wants your mistress to live, he must come alone to this place and let me kill him. When he is dead, she can go."

"But, señor! If he is dead already—"

"Bring me his head. But use no tricks. If I suspect any, I will kill her at once."

"Don't do it, Enrique," I cried, struggling, trying to provoke a bullet. "Don't. I would rather die."

Grunting, Court thrust me under his knee, pinned me with sheer weight. Blood dripped sluggishly from his side and groin. "Ride," he said panting. "And don't think to wait till I've bled to death. When I feel that coming, I'll kill her."

Enrique whirled and was off.

"Court," I choked, half-suffocated by his bulk, rocks grinding into my arms and back. "Court, let me bandage your wounds. They may not be as bad as you think."

"What's the matter, you don't like having my blood on you?" He shifted enough to drag me up, though I was still trapped between his body and the rocks. "No, my dear, I've seen enough men die to know when I've had it, or I'd have let you pass just then and healed, grown strong, and when I came for you again, I'd kill Winslade myself, not leave it to be bungled."

"You—you knew he was alive," I accused in sudden understanding. "That's why you got Ortega to organize that expedition."

"Exactly. I had thought he was dead, but when I went hunting for you, my sweet, I glimpsed him in Hermosillo with that young thug, Domingo. I couldn't guess why he'd never come for you, but I was damned sure if you ever learned he was breathing, you'd be after him like a bitch in heat." He gave a short ugly laugh, eyes smoldering. "And I was right."

"I didn't know he was alive," I returned dully. "I just went to warn Sewa and the others. I hoped if Ortega knew they were alerted, he'd call off his attack."

"He wanted to," Court said contemptuously. "But I happen to know that he's been flirting with Obregón's revolutionaries. Since I had proof enough to land him in front of a firing squad, he decided to take his chances. I didn't dream you knew my little plan, but when I had to go home at noon yesterday for some equipment I'd forgotten, I found you gone and Roberto had noticed you riding up the mountain. I got Ortega on the move as quickly as possible, wouldn't let him wait till morning."

"You found the passage into the stronghold?"

"Yes, but we were using lanterns, picked up all those tracks coming out, heading south. We camped till first light. As soon as we could follow your trail, we did."

"Didn't Ortega suspect a trap?"

"Eighty soldiers should be able to beat a score of Yaquis." Court's mouth twisted in self-mockery. "Funny. Those men you bought out of Yucatán made the difference. Without them, we'd have had Winslade and your precious Sewa."

His voice was weary.

"It—it's inhuman," I burst out. "Awful that in this time you cling to hatred."

"And my love, too," he reminded inexorably. "If my love has seemed your doom, Miranda, remember it has been mine, too."

He bent his head and kissed me. The taste of his mouth was blood salt. The sound of hooves came faint, then louder. Court raised to peer over me. I writhed my head about, saw Trace at the mouth of the arroyo.

"Sanders, I'm here."

"Get off your horse. Walk this way. One shot will be better for us all."

Trace came forward, weaponless, arms loose at his sides. Court's revolver pressed against my ear, his body clamped mine down till I couldn't stir.

It was too wretched. I heard myself moaning, pleading. "Kill me," I begged. "Oh, please, kill me." My head was the only part of me that could move. I thrashed it back and forth, tried to sink my teeth into Court but was frustrated by his clothing.

"That's good, Winslade."

I heard the words, muffled by Court's body, a rising frenzy that blotted out reason. It wasn't reason or any conscious process that told me Court was lifting himself slightly, readying his aim, but instinct triggered me into a sudden upward paroxysm, a violent wrenching of head and arms, upper body just slightly freer with Court's changed position.

The shot exploded. I felt terrific impact, desperate force spasming above me, and there was another shot. Trace must have turned Court's own revolver on him. The hard-muscled body that had so often collapsed on me after love now sagged with finality, drained of all that power and will, hate and desire, soaking me with its blood. But Trace pulled me free, carried me into the sunlight, and lay with me there.

The Yaquis returned to their mountain refuge, though Sewa and Domingo promised to visit Las Coronas. "And we shall invite you to our wedding," Domingo said, standing tall and proud by Sewa as they said good-bye.

"We will have a feast and *pascolas* dancing," she added and I knew we were all remembering what Cruz had foretold back in those miserable days while she recovered from the loss of her foot.

"Remember," I said, holding her slim brown hand, admiring the way she had let Trace go, though her heart still showed in her eyes when she looked toward him, "if any Yaquis wish to settle at Las Coronas or Mina Rara, it can be managed."

"Thank you. Some of the widows may." She shrugged and her face matched Domingo's. They were Yaqui warriors, able now to replace Lío, lead without tutelage. Sewa was still a flower, but one armed with thorns. "I think it will be a long time before there is peace for the rest of us."

"Send if you need me," said Trace. He gave me a troubled look. "I may have to fight, Miranda. If a revolution comes—"

My heart contracted with dread, but I managed to smile. "We will all do what we must, but that needn't ruin the time between. Come to us, Sewa, as soon as you can."

We embraced. She mounted her horse, our gift, and led away her fighters.

The soldiers, dead from Ortega to the newest conscript, had been rolled by the Yaquis into a ravine. Rocks and earth had been tumbled over them and the place was known from then on as Soldados Muertos, Dead Soldiers.

With Trace's help, I composed an outraged letter to the general-in-chief. Since it proved, indeed, that Ortega had been negotiating with revolutionaries, the general believed my story and, as Trace had predicted, sent apologies.

My solicitor, fussy, old, bearded Señor Otero, found a manager for Mina Rara. Trace and I settled with Jon at Las Coronas and were married quietly in the chapel, with Dr. Trent watching in vast content. Enemies who had known of Trace's sentence to Yucatán were dead and the government had a great deal more to worry about than one escaped gringo.

On October 4, 1910, Díaz became president for the eighth time, with Corral, nicknamed Death, as his vice-president. A few days later, Francisco Madero escaped into Texas and began organizing support.

Mexico seethed; Obregón and Maytorena in Sonora, Zapata in Morelos, Villa in Chihuahua.

"The whirlwind is coming," I whispered to Trace one night as I lay in his arms. "I'm afraid, darling, so afraid. Afraid it'll whirl us apart again."

"What can I say, love?"

He kissed my eyes and mouth and throat till need for him, delight in his strength, glory in our closeness, swept away everything else.

"We have now," he said.